£1.00

A SMELL OF BURNING

A Smell of Burning

A novel by Margaret Lane

THE BOOK CLUB

121 CHARING CROSS ROAD, LONDON, WC2

Printed in Great Britain
By Ebenezer Baylis and Son, Ltd.
The Trinity Press, Worcester, and London

'IT's getting chilly,' said Miss Townsend from the doorway, 'and I think you should come in.' She considered the long narrow concentrated back of her brother-in-law, who neither moved nor replied. Sighing, she stooped under the low lintel and came out on the roof, already losing the last of the sun and turning blue with shadow. Here she joined Lytton in silence and laid her arms like his on the whitewashed parapet, still warm from the day and velvety to the touch. Beneath them, out of sight, the wall dropped sheer to a roof forty feet below, where a handful of washed rags hung out on a line and fowls apathetically picked among crumbs of rubble.

They both gazed down at the town and the distant harbour, from this point often difficult to distinguish. It was a view demanding patience and even skill, for the open honeycomb of walls and roofs, intricately descending the rock in a maze of angles, was complex and very baffling to the eye. One had to direct it by landmarks, the blue roof, the spire of the mosque, the solitary television aerial, before one could be sure of the slip of water down which the fishing boats at this hour puttered from the inner basin. Once in the main harbour they were easily seen, and beyond that made ribbons of disturbance far out into the bay, tiny as flies but still audible even at that distance, where they described a series of arcs on the silken surface, heading away to the straits and the profitable fishing-grounds.

Lytton sighed and shifted his position, letting his right hand slip a few inches down the outer surface of the wall to the point where the plaster was rough and the whitewash ended. Here the warmth of the sun could still be felt, and he had a sense of being in touch with something living, some essence of the past residing in the stones, a secretion of all the years before he came there.

'It never fails, does it?' he said, moving his fingers gently to and fro, so that some crumbs of plaster detached themselves and made a soundless fall to the roof below. The hens ran avidly to inspect them, then turned away with an air of cynicism and went on with their routine checking of dust and droppings. 'The light, I mean,' said Lytton, 'it's never the same.' He waved his hand at the complex of town and bay. 'Look at those hills, the colour. And the change in the water. It's all taking place in the sky, everything reflects it.' Miss Townsend looked obediently as he directed, lifting her eyes to the veils of cloud, mere wisps of vapour, unravelling like gauze in the upper atmosphere and turning to dazzling gold in the slanting light.

'How Sarah would have revelled in it,' he said, as she didn't answer. 'What a marvellous subject for a painter. What a fascinating problem.'

'She would have liked it, certainly,' said Miss Townsend after a pause; 'she could hardly fail to. But I'm not sure . . .' Her gaze wandered over the roofs below, unable to help noticing how shabby and unpainted, how sordid to be perfectly frank, most of them were, and she could not imagine Sarah making a success of it. Besides, it was too difficult. A certain skill with flowers and watercolours would be no match for this alien scene with its welter of planes and angles, its terrible foreignness.

Her eye sought, and found, a narrow chasm some distance below which she had originally noticed and identified with surprise, since it was in fact a street, the only point in the whole prospect where one could actually see human beings coming and going. One had command of only a few yards to be sure, and that at a steep angle, for the alley was dark and narrow and the houses tall; but on the further side of the street (if one could really call it such, which Miss Townsend doubted) there was a doorway, and in it there was nearly always a woman standing, plainly to be seen even at night under the naked electric bulb hanging between the buildings in a tangle of wires. The figure, muffled to the eyes, was plainly female, and the men who seemed to frequent the house at all hours (or who perhaps lived there?) pushed past her without ceremony. But what was she there for,

6

apparently speaking to no-one and doing nothing? Miss Townsend had several times very narrowly observed her, and uneasily wondered. Lytton, if asked, would jump to salacious conclusions, and she particularly did not wish, right at the beginning of their life here, to know more than she need about circumstances likely to worry her.

'Come on then, Phoebe,' said Lytton, 'let's move if we're going to,' and left off stroking the wall and straightened his back, bracing his shoulders and jutting out his beard at the now apricot-coloured city, like a man long absorbed in a problem who now comes to a decision.

'I've made the tea, Henry,' she said, moving aside to let him pass through the doorway and observing the frown of annoyance which appeared like a protest at the sound of his Christian name. This was an old difficulty, to which she had long been unequal. He did not care for his given names but set store by his initials; friends and admirers addressed him as 'H.B.' This Phoebe Townsend, who had known him from the days when he had come, somewhat gingerly, courting her younger sister, was totally unable to do; and this failure on her part (after all it was a small matter, and it shouldn't, she painfully thought, have been beyond her) was one of the things which made their relationship difficult. She *did* manage it, it is true, when speaking to other people. 'H.B.'s hoping to get started soon on another book,' she would say, or 'I'm not quite sure about lunch, I'll see if H.B. can manage it;' but face to face the initials stuck in her throat, and she blushed if she tried to use them to him in private.

Why this was she could not say, but it had to do with the image of her sister's husband, arriving as Mr. Lytton and remaining as Henry, who had not become H. B. Lytton or achieved even the smallest literary reputation until so very much later. The use of initials had a bearing on reputation; it somehow strengthened it. Again Miss Townsend was unable to say why. It was almost as though men felt safer with initials than under their christened names, especially if there were only two, and the second letter were either B or G. What, she wondered, as she felt her way carefully down the precipitous stairs, had initials got that men should be so attached to them? For it was clear that Lytton not only felt more masculine as H.B. than he did as Henry, but also (the connection eluded her) more literary.

The stairs, tiled in blue and white and inconveniently steep, brought them to an arch leading to an open courtyard, which still, after a fortnight's exhausting residence, presented a scene of discouraging confusion. The paving was piled with sand and rubble which an aged Arab was scraping into a basket with a shovel not much larger than a grocer's scoop and emptying into panniers on the back of a donkey. Each load of rubbish, amounting to perhaps a sackful, would have to go more than a mile before it could be tipped; the donkey and his owner spent the whole of each day on this undertaking, which could have been disposed of in a few minutes if the street had been wide enough to admit a lorry. The old man redoubled his efforts as Lytton and Phoebe appeared, and with gap-toothed grin and much grunting demonstrated the arduous nature of his calling. They smiled and nodded as they passed. No matter what he did it would make no difference; it would all be just as bad the following morning.

Arches and doorways opened from the courtyard into a number of rooms, none of which was finished though most of them by now were basically habitable. The parlour, as Lytton wished the main room to be called, was typically long, narrow and disconcertingly dark. It was proving difficult to furnish; everything he had brought from Gloucestershire looked wrong in it. A sad pair of cretonne-covered armchairs and a leather sofa, a few nondescript tables piled with china and a packing-case full of books were all that it so far contained, and these made a poor show under the single electric bulb which hung on a tangled flex from the high ceiling. Nevertheless he was not discouraged. The things were his and he was used to them; the general appearance would develop later. This, naturally, was Phoebe's responsibility. She had already made a tolerable sitting-place at the far end of the room, with two armchairs and a table with the tea-tray on it; the death-mask of Sarah Lytton, a pallid waxen face in a velvet frame, had already been hung on the wall in a central position. It dominated the room, as Lytton intended it should, and Phoebe always sat where she needn't look at it.

'The lamps should be ready tomorrow,' she said, 'this light is too depressing.'

'On the contrary, the gloom is meant to be restful. Shade is a relief in a country with so much sun.'

'Oh, shade, yes. But the sun never comes in here. One can't see to read or sew or do anything properly. If we could have the windows enlarged it would make all the difference.' Lytton complacently smiled, stirring his tea.

'But if we enlarged the windows the whole character of the room would be altered.'

'For the better, in my opinion.'

'I fancy your opinion may change when you've been here longer. Besides, it's out of the question. Those windows look down on another roof. There are very strict laws for protecting domestic privacy.'

'Yes, but those windows,' she looked up at them as she spoke, 'are a good eight feet from the ground; no normal human being could ever look out of them.' They were, indeed, no more than cubes of daylight high in the wall, square-cut whitewashed passages straight to the sky, open and inaccessible.

'Nevertheless,' said Lytton, closing his eyes, 'if those windows were larger, and one stood on a table, one would look straight down on to next-door's roof, which is a private domain and the special province of the women. One must be prepared to respect the customs of the country.' He was trying not to hear the involuntary sound which she made when she swallowed her tea. She was quite unconscious of making it and he could not tell her. Sarah had always drunk silently, as everyone should, and his sister-in-law's audible swallow annoyed him as much as his habit of dragging his feet when he walked irritated Phoebe. Since they were not married to one another and never likely to be, protest and even comment were out of the question.

'Well, all the same,' said Miss Townsend, sticking to her point and raising her voice above the leisurely scraping noise going on in the courtyard, 'there's a perfectly good window in that end room, at a normal height too, and nobody seems to mind if one looks out of it.' She had often peered out of that window, which had shutters and a grille, and gazed down on a very dirty roof where she had never seen anybody. More than once she had remarked on the unattractiveness of the outlook, for this end room had been chosen as their guest-room, and a guest-room without a view was dull to the point of being inhospitable.

'I fancy,' said Lytton, who was fond of this tentative preface to a firm opinion, 'that the window is considerably older than the house it overlooks. *This* house is built on the foundations of the old ramparts. The structure below, whatever it is, was added, I should judge, much later.' He passed her his empty cup and hunted about in the plate of disappointing biscuits. 'I shall have to find out the exact date of building from somewhere, and what there is beneath us. Our foundations, I suspect, go down to the solid wall.'

Phoebe knew better than to dispute this, for ferreting out the history of any given patch of ground, or at least speculating on it, was Lytton's speciality, one of the favourite nostalgic features of his essays and a source of pleasure to him generally.

'I dare say you're right,' she said with reserve, returning his cup. 'I've never seen anyone yet on that other roof. It's disgracefully neglected.'

'All the more reason for not looking out.' He seemed pleased with himself. 'There's the grille and the sky, which are pretty, and when the sun's on that side one's supposed to make use of the shutters.' The subject, in Lytton's view, was finally disposed of: he glanced up at Sarah's mask as though for approval. It was only quite lately that he had developed this eerie habit, and Phoebe, though she sympathised of course and deplored her sister's loss as much as anyone, considered it affected. She ignored the glance and gently pursued her theme.

'All the same, it isn't a cheerful room for a young person. I wish I could think of a way of brightening it up. I've kept the windows open all day since the rain stopped, but it doesn't seem really *fresh*. In fact yesterday, when the sun was on it, I distinctly noticed something . . . well, a smell.'

'What sort of smell?'

'It's hard to say. Like something gone bad, I thought at first, but yesterday I could almost swear there was a smell of burning.'

'Cooking smell,' said Lytton. 'Rancid frying oil. You know what they're like.'

'But nobody lives in that house. The thing's a ruin.'

'Of course it is. It's been locked up for years. Mackannis made inquiries in the beginning, in case I wanted it. But no one would be fool enough; it's beyond redemption. Luckily for us, don't you think? We get enough noise from the rest of our Arab neighbours.'

'How do you account for the smell, then? I don't get it anywhere else, only that window.'

'Plaster drying out. What else can you expect, after a five days' deluge? My hat turned green in the cupboard after three days. If the rains are really over it'll soon disperse. Trouble is, the fabric's thoroughly sodden.'

'Oh, do you really think so? Ought we to put Tavy in that room at all, if it's going to be damp?' She looked apprehensive. The very idea of her nephew's adopted daughter, for whom everything, or at least a high proportion of things, seemed to have gone wrong, filled her with misgiving. The whole idea of having her out there was to make amends, to give her a second home; and if she were to get ill, worse still if she were not happy, the thing would be a dreadful mistake instead of a blessing.

Phoebe had approved the adoption at the time but that was fifteen years ago; since Eric's wife had run off and was no more heard of she found herself sometimes wishing it had never happened. It was one thing, she privately argued, to adopt a child for the wife's sake, quite another for the husband to be left alone with an unprepossessing adolescent, whom—she didn't wish to be ungenerous but it was sometimes obvious—he hadn't much use for. Phoebe was fond of her nephew and saw his difficulty, but in theory at least her sympathy was with Tavy.

'Oh, she'll be all right,' said Lytton, already bored with the subject. 'She'll settle down, I don't think you have to worry. Youngsters are very adaptable, she ought to be grateful.'

'It's not gratitude I'm looking for, you know. I want her to be happy.'

'Well, well, she will be. Let's not imagine disasters before they happen.' He thrust his hands in his pockets, feeling for his pipe, remembered with a frown that he no longer smoked and got abruptly to his feet, squaring his shoulders and looking keenly about him. 'I'm going to start unpacking these books.' He moved with an air of decision to the tea-chest. 'They've stood about long enough.' He began to lift off layers of dusty newspaper. 'And while we're on the subject, my dear, hadn't we better get used to calling her Octavia? Tavy's such a silly name; a girl of her age, who'll soon be grown-up, can't go through the whole of her life answering to Tavy.'

'Oh, I think it's rather pretty,' said Phoebe musingly. 'Octavia's a bit of a mouthful; not very suitable, either, in her case.'

'Agreed, a damn silly name to choose for an only child. They should have had more sense.' Lytton was deep in the tea-chest, lifting out books with care and stacking them according to size on the crowded table.

'She'd already been christened that when they adopted her. She was an eighth child, you know, in her original family. There wouldn't have been much point, do you think, in changing it?'

'Oh, I don't know,' said Lytton. 'She wouldn't have cared at that age. They could have changed it to Una.' He laughed silently, scratching his little beard.

'I don't think it's safe to assume,' said Phoebe evenly, 'how much children care about things. Too many changes are unsettling; they do harm.' She spoke with an air of authority, partly assumed. Though she had spent many years of her life in a school she had never, she knew, had the gift of establishing an easy relationship with the girls. What she had to do she had done, conscientiously and efficiently, without distinction. She had not been absolutely shattered when the school closed down, her eyes being already fixed on the goal of retirement.

The front door banged on her words with a booming slam,

and there was sudden silence. The old man and his donkey had gone at last, leaving the courtyard empty after the long hours filled with the rhythm of shovelling and scraping. The silence was almost stunning, it was so complete; the noise had become such a part of the background of life that one's ears made a murmur of their own in the sudden absence of it. It was not until a little interval had elapsed, disturbed only by Lytton's stealthy rustling among newspaper, that the remote orchestra of sounds from behind the walls, faint echo of distant clamours which went on all day, flowed in by the open courtyard and the high windows: a full score made up of a thousand alien noises which her unpractised ear was only beginning to distinguish. She sat still and closed her eyes, intently listening. Far away and below, a cock crowed. This call, so rarely heard at home nowadays even in the country, had surprised her at first by its frequency; she identified it now with pleasure as a voice from childhood. Cocks had crowed every morning from farms and cottages when she and Sarah had been girls, but nobody in England seemed to keep them now; or perhaps only reared them indoors for a month or two, in electrically lighted arks, where before they were old enough to crow they were judged ready for the spit. It was a pity. Here at least, in this ancient and crowded and unnerving town they spoke with many voices and at all hours. The one on the roof below was often moved to his shrillest utterance at midnight, and as soon as he spoke there were others, near and far, competitively answering. Did they pass all their lives on roofs, since the houses were pressed too close for yards or gardens? She supposed it must be so. They kept up their tiny clamour all round the clock, from corners fenced in with boxes and tangles of netting, among washing-lines, skeletons of bedsteads, rusting pipes, scraps of wood, plants grown in ancient paraffin tins, bare fragments of discarded plumbing. It was extraordinary what these people threw out on their roofs and left to rot, making a landscape of wreckage which was yet alive, inhabited by prowling cats and imprisoned poultry.

Now, also far below, a dog barked, and the yelling of children, muted by distance and thin as the screaming of swallows, was received by her ear and identified; this too was a constant theme, which only darkness silenced. It puzzled her that such countless hordes of children should be always at large, darting about in the alleys like bats, running, shrieking, yet never, it seemed, colliding with the rest of the throng or with one another—why were they not at school? For schools there were; from the roof in the morning, when she paused at the parapet, she had often heard the sound of monotonous chanting, and in their very street had been moved by breathy voices behind shutters, reciting in droning chorus: learning the Korán, Lytton said, even infants, squatting in a room like a smithy, packed together on the floor behind a curtain of sacking.

She roused herself with an effort, stood up, suppressed a shiver, lifted the tray. It got cold once the sun was down; one perceived the damp. Very soon, Lytton said, all that would be over: there would be months of sun and heat, they would forget the cold. Phoebe devoutly hoped so. In the past week she had suffered more than she was willing to admit, when every day had begun with wind and rain, both with a brutal sting from the whipped Atlantic, and the walls had streamed and the tree in the courtyard dripped, and the mud and cold and discomfort had been past bearing. On some of the days it had deluged with scarcely a break, so that the smallest venture out of doors, even to the *bakal* at the corner for tea or bread, had been a weird experience, like walking under water. She had feared for her rheumatism; even more, with reason, for Lytton's precarious health, for the life of a man with one lung, or to be precise a lung and three-quarters, was supposed to be a ceaseless campaign in which weather was the enemy; indeed the whole object of coming to Morocco had been that his life should be prolonged by warmth and ease. Of course it was early in the year, only March still, and it was sensible to come in spring when the whole summer lay before them; but the beginning had not been auspicious, and Phoebe doubted. One must have faith, she told herself, pushing open the door to the courtyard with a cautious foot; it would all be different soon; everybody said so. All the same, as she steered a course with the tray to the kitchen opposite, avoiding the wet where she could and the sweepings of plaster, she wished that the open space could have been glassed over, even with one of those hideous patched-up domes that she saw on the roofs of so many Arab houses; the loss in appearance would have been such a gain in comfort.

Still, there it was. Glassing in the courtyard would have meant the loss of the fig-tree, and this was something Lytton would not hear of. It had looked miserable enough when they arrived, a leprous bole with swollen wind-scarred branches; but already leaves were breaking on the upper limbs, and in summer, Lytton said, they would be glad of the shade. He for one looked forward to sitting under it.

The kitchen door, as usual, was hard to open; this too, it was predicted, would improve with the dry weather. She pushed it with a solid hip and went inside, glad to return to a place which had already been brought into a semblance of decent order. There was a tiled sink, a geyser fed from a *bidon* of gas and a small second-hand cooker. Rather than switch on the light (electricity was expensive) she opened the shutters on the courtyard and set about washing up.

The geyser roared, the water ran hot; she was reassured. Hardly had she submerged the cups than her heart leapt at a sudden blow on the knocker, followed by two more; that terrible implement of iron, like a ring in a dungeon, which could resound like a presage of doom on the studded door, and too frequently did so. She stood still with her hands in the water, shot through with alarm; absurdly, as well she knew, for the knocker went off like that at least twenty times a day, when carpenter or plumber or mason arrived with their train of underlings, or came back with a can of paint or to fetch tools, demanding a ladder by signs or her private broom, or other requirements in a mixture of Spanish and Arabic, all more or less vaguely menacing and incomprehensible.

'I'll go, don't worry!' called Lytton from the courtyard, and she heard his loose slippers dragging across the tiles, growing fainter as he progressed slipshod down the dark passage. She moved the china softly about in the water, listening for the door.

Two noisy tugs, a clatter, and then voices. The tones were English, pitched high in cordial surprise; she gratefully relaxed.

Lytton's presence darkened the kitchen window. 'My dear Phoebe, we have a visitor, a positive caller—my old friend Askew-Martin. Can you produce some drinks?' Phoebe dried her hands hurriedly and came out into the courtyard. Behind Lytton stood a bulky figure as tall as himself, a ruddy-faced man, not old, say a well-preserved sixty, good easy clothes, expensive-looking pouches under the eyes, quite notably presentable.

'What luck,' said Lytton, wringing his hands with pleasure until he cracked the knuckles, 'I had no idea . . . Gerald Askew-Martin, Miss Townsend, my sister-in-law. This really is delightful.' They shook hands and amicably murmured. 'I'm afraid you find us in very primitive conditions, we're only just moving in, the place is in chaos. Phoebe, my dear, we have glasses somewhere, I fancy, and something to put in them? Come across to the parlour, my dear fellow, let's not stand in the open. You've struck bad weather, I fear. We shall do better presently.'

'Well, you know,' said Askew-Martin, smiling at Phoebe, 'I wasn't at all sure it was you, but I thought, well, there can't be *two*. So I risked it and wandered along, hoping you wouldn't mind. I must say your house is jolly difficult to find. I've been piloted by horrible boys whom I couldn't shake off, and arrived three times running in the Kasbah.'

'Oh, I *know*,' said Phoebe warmly, 'they're a real menace, they think everybody wants the Kasbah square.' She was trying to remember where she had hidden their sole bottle of whisky, bought for possible medical emergencies and at considerable expense. Like most things of value it was probably locked in the trunk at the foot of her bed. With the stories one heard, and the workmen, one had to be careful. Feeling in a pocket for her keys she went off to forage.

When she returned, carrying the tea-tray now laden with glasses and bottles, they were sitting in comfort together under the death-mask and Lytton was off on the familiar theme of why he had decided to give up the house in Gloucestershire. She could not have said why, but she had the impression that in spite of their cordial voices they were not very intimately known to one another. Still, Lytton was obviously delighted to receive a visitor; it made everything at once more real, as though they had been there much longer than they had, and were established residents.

'Yes, I thought when I heard the name,' Askew-Martin interrupted him, 'I thought, well, it *must* be you, but I naturally wondered. It's a number of years since we met—at the Garrick, wasn't it? And I'd heard you'd been ill, though I never knew the details. And then, just to hear in a bar that you'd bought a house here! I couldn't resist it, H.B., I had to investigate.'

'My dear fellow, how right you were. It does me good to see you. Just mineral water for me, Phoebe, thank you. No ice, I suppose, is there? No, I thought not. My dear, er, Gerald, you can't think how glad I am. What are you doing here, for a start? On holiday? Not nursing a shattered physique, I hope, as in my own case? But no, I don't need to ask. You look aggressively healthy.'

'Well, yes, I'm remarkably well.' Gerald extended a hand to arrest the whisky bottle, which had splashed out a good half-tumbler. 'I'm on holiday, yes, in a sense; on my own for the moment. I'm expecting my wife tomorrow.'

'Your wife?' Lytton looked up in surprise, the tilted bottle suspended over the tray. 'But I remember your wife . . . Elizabeth . . .' He set down the bottle and shifted the glasses about, covering his embarrassment.

'I married again,' said Gerald quietly, 'two years ago. An old friend, I don't think you've met her. Much younger than myself; I'm very fortunate.' Having caught the glance cast up at the velvet frame, it was Askew-Martin's turn to look uncomfortable. In the pallid light from the single bulb Sarah's waxen features looked remarkably ghostly.

'Ah, well, so am I,' said Lytton resignedly, glancing at Phoebe. He poured her a modest measure and added soda. There was a stiff little silence, in which Phoebe tried to think of something to say. Below, as though in derisory comment, a cock crowed.

'I hope you intend to stay a good long time,' said Lytton at length. 'I don't like you seeing the house like this, it's a pig-sty. We shall have it all to rights in a week or two; you'll see. My good Phoebe here will work wonders.'

'I think it's tremendous. Great, great possibilities. You've been so right to choose the Medina, or is it the Kasbah? I'm never quite sure where one ends and the other begins.'

'This is the Medina. It's quite simple, the Kasbah's the old citadel at the top, within the wall, where the prison is, and the square and streets all around it; quite a small complex actually. We're just outside it, this is part of the old ramparts. You must have come down through an archway, didn't you, and some cobbled steps? It's merely the Arab town, between here and the sea. Not large in extent, but to a newcomer very confusing. You're staying over in the European town, I expect, at one of the hotels?'

'We've got a furnished flat in the Rue Poincaré. Nothing particularly attractive, but it works. We thought of staying for a month, or perhaps six weeks, rather depending on how Anthea likes it. A flat seemed more practical.'

'Of course, quite right.' Lytton approved of newcomers keeping to the new town and only tentatively visiting the quarter that was to become his province. 'Naturally in our case it was different. I didn't want a modern villa outside the town; we neither of us drive a car, and in any case this area's much cheaper. We're here for good you see, if that isn't the wrong word to apply to a hypothetical twelve months.'

'Twelve months?'

'That's what the doctors give me.' Lytton had made his point, and waited for the reaction.

'They don't say that, do they? How monstrous! I thought they'd quite given up saying that sort of thing, they're so often wrong?' He glanced for support at Phoebe, but she smiled non-committally and looked away.

The doctors, in fact, had said nothing of the sort, whatever views they might have expressed in private. The operation was apparently successful, and all they had done was to give him explicit advice and warn him to be careful. The determining factor, they said, would be Lytton's state of mind: where there was a positive attitude complete recoveries were not unheard of. So on the whole it had been, one would have said, encouraging; but Lytton's mind had always secretly leaned to the side of drama and it clearly gave him a perverse pleasure to see himself as a man with a year to live. It was not right, Phoebe considered: it shocked people. Worse, it was embarrassing. However, it was not for her to contradict. She tasted her whisky, glanced from the corner of her eye at Sarah's death-mask, and said nothing.

'Sarah, Sarah,' she mused, following her own thoughts, 'what is the truth about this Henry you've left me with?' She moved slightly in her chair, impelled for once to look straight at the waxen image, almost as though she expected the eyelids to lift. If one looked long enough one could imagine the eyes were there, not even asleep, only closed in some private mockery, sly and secretive. Sarah had always been pale, and the tint of the moulded lips was not far wrong. Even in wax the mouth was sensual, disturbing. Its curving corners were no more solemn than when Sarah had been alive and unpredictable, conceiving some lazy taunt or ambiguous comment. One never knew where one was with her, not after childhood; there was always so much she might have told, and never chose to. Rightly perhaps, Phoebe had sometimes suspected; there were things that were better kept from a spinster sister. 'But why did you never tell me?' she silently questioned. 'What was wrong between you and Henry? Did you have lovers? Why did I always imagine he was afraid of you?' She felt the strain of staring and closed her eyes, hearing the drone of voices as though from a distance. When she opened them after a pause her focus was blurred and Sarah's features lit up in a way she remembered. She fearfully gazed; the corners of the mouth curled upwards; in a moment, surely, the lips would smile or speak 'But why should I tell you now?' came the familiar voice, a whisper inside her skull, a voice in a shell. 'My life was my own, thank God, and you were always so stupid. I did try to tell you once, have you forgotten? You preferred not to know; it wasn't for you, poor Phoebe. And now you're stuck with him, aren't you?

19

And he won't die. It's all lies, my Phoebe, all lies, and always was. I wish you joy of it.' A shiver passed over her skin, making her hand shake and spilling some whisky over the edge of the glass. Was this why Lytton turned to the mask so often, did he hear this voice, were there often these silent colloquies? But the face, when she looked again, was perfectly still, remote in its frame of glass, embedded in velvet, waxen, incommunicable. What morbid tricks one's imagination got up to! She was startled and ashamed. This was no way to behave in the life she had accepted; accepted willingly, since Lytton was a man in need and her own future empty. She turned her head and stealthily regarded him.

'I don't think they're often wrong in cases of cancer,' he was saying, affecting an off-hand manner but keeping an eye on Gerald to see how he took it. Gerald took it with provoking calm, not wincing at the word as Lytton seemed to expect.

'Wronger in cancer, I'd say, than in most diseases. I've known several cases. There's no positive way of knowing; they simply can't tell. The only thing is to behave as though one were going to live for ever. Miss Townsend, you must tell me frankly: will it worry either of you if I smoke?'

'Not at all, of course not.' Phoebe could see as she spoke that Lytton was disappointed, but he proffered matches and watched without envy as Gerald started a cigar. In spite of his long addiction to a pipe she knew that he had given it up without a struggle and even derived a curious pleasure from the abstention. 'I don't use tobacco any more myself,' he told Gerald, 'though I've been a lifelong pipe-smoker. I miss it, of course, but I don't feel it as a deprivation. When one faces an ultimatum, as I've had to, it does unexpected things to one's values. Tobacco, now, to me, is simply a poison. I should just as soon think of taking prussic acid.'

If the truth were known, it was not so much the tobacco he missed, the taste on the tongue, the haze of smoke, though both were comforting; it was the pipe itself as a personal talisman, almost an occupation in its own right; to be filled, lit, prodded at, excavated with a little instrument bought for the purpose, knocked out on his heel, thoughtfully sucked on when empty, useful as something to gesticulate with and in argument to point with effect at other people. It had been as much a part of his persona as his beard and initials. He had replaced it as best he could by changing to a specially complex kind of spectacles. He now used a steel-rimmed pair which as well as being furnished with hinges in the usual place had a cunning little extra pair at the centre of the shafts, so that they could be folded not once but twice and fitted into a leather case of approximately half the usual dimensions. This arrangement gave unrivalled opportunities for manipulation. They could be taken out, unfolded, then again, put on, taken off, refolded twice, fitted into the case and returned with abstracted care to the waistcoat pocket. It was not a property comparable with a pipe, certainly, but it was something, and could be deployed any number of times while working, reading, at meals, or in the course of conversation.

'My niece, or rather great-niece, arrives tomorrow,' said Phoebe, making an effort to shake off her private thoughts. 'I think you said your wife was coming too? Perhaps they'll come together on the same plane?'

'They must, I think; there's only one. How surprised they'll be to find we know one another! You'll be meeting the plane, of course? Can I take you to the airport? It's not a vast car, but there's a good boot; we ought to be able to manage plenty of luggage. Anyway there's a rack,' he added, remembering that Anthea was supposed to be bringing a friend, and women were capable of arriving in strange bulk.

'Oh, how very kind. I *should* be grateful.' The burden of ordering a taxi and of going by herself had already begun to nag at the edge of her mind. 'I'd been worrying about the Customs, too, when the child arrives. Not that she'll have anything that matters, of course, but it's always so alarming. It would be a great support to go with you if I may. That is, if it's not a trouble.'

'I shall look forward to it,' said Gerald, his face glowing ruddily through the cigar smoke as though he were really pleased. 'Good, that's settled. Could you be ready to start at four, perhaps? I'll come for you here. We can while away the airport tedium together.' He finished his whisky and stood up, a benevolent presence, emanating ease and capability. 'Well, thank you for the reviving drink and for letting me have a first glimpse of your fascinating house. You must both come over and eat with us very soon. I hope you'll drop over, H.B., whenever you feel like it. I want Anthea to meet you both.' They came out into the shadowy courtyard, where empty doorways, patches of damp on the walls and the all but leafless tree were already constructing a pattern of gentle gloom. Phoebe hastened to switch on the passage light, so that the coloured panes of the little gimcrack lantern threw at least some sequins of brightness over the whitewash.

'I'll walk with you a little way,' said Lytton, unwilling to relinquish his audience so soon. 'You don't want to get lost again, it's too easy.' He had already perfected several routes in and out of the Medina and was looking forward to a display of navigation.

The door banged heavily behind them and Phoebe returned to the courtyard. She made a methodical round of several doorways, switching on lights. It would all be much better soon, when the lamps arrived and could be plugged in wherever one chose: at present, if Lytton were out, she did not care for the aspect of the house at night. The rooms got cold if windows were open at this hour but with everything closed they became unnaturally quiet. It was better, both warmer and lighter, in the rooms upstairs, where she and Lytton slept on either side of the roof—almost a second patio, one might call it, or perhaps a terrace, with a rectangular well in the middle looking down into the courtyard between the branches of the fig-tree. Up there one could always hear sounds of life and movement, dogs barking, children screeching in the alleys, cocks crowing, a woman beating a carpet, even at times an unmelodious rhythmic tootling and banging which sounded cheerful and must, she supposed, be a street band, a wedding, a procession, or some other unimaginable festivity.

The place she still liked best at night was the kitchen, for here there was good bright electric light and the room was freshly painted and soon got warm. By the time she had heated the soup and laid the table (they ate little at night, as much from habit as from necessity) she would be feeling quite cheerful and resolute again, more than willing to listen to Lytton's account of their recent visitor, and what Mr. Something-Martin had thought of everything. And after that, there was always the comfort of bed.

Before turning finally to the kitchen she crossed to the far end of the small patio, passed under the imposing archway, moulded and denticulated, the best and indeed the only good feature of the house, and opened the narrow door into what she already thought of as Tavy's room. It felt almost too full of air: she closed the window, standing for a moment to look about her, judging the effect. The crimson bedspread and cushions were very cheerful, she would be sure to like them. There was not much else in the room—a chest of drawers, a chair, a table with a red cloth under the window, a rug which was still rolled up for fear of damp. The old woollen curtains from the spare room in Gloucestershire framed the deep window and looked quite presentable. Phoebe had taken trouble for Tavy's sake, and was pleased with what she saw. Lytton was right after all: the wall was so thick, the window embrasure so deep and the grille so striking, there was really no need to notice the outlook at all. One thing about the room she was sure Tavy would like, since no child could resist it: a narrow tiled staircase leading to a small loft or box-room with a wooden door. This little chamber was fairly full of luggage space and too low to stand up in, but it had a pleasant smell and was an amusing annexe to have to one's own bedroom.

She moved to the darkening window for a last look. She could just see, peering down, the ruined structure covering the top of the stairs. It was roofed with glass and iron, a sorry skeleton of rust and broken panes. The low door, fastened with a padlock, had been crudely patched with scraps of packing-cases, and what looked like the windblown refuse of many winters lay several inches deep against the sill. There was even a clump of weed growing bravely out of it, nourished by heaven knows what in that derelict place. Clearly the door had not been used for a long time. There was no washing-line, no plants in tins, no rags, no cooking-pots, none of the usual signs of habitation. She could just make out the abrupt descent of the stairs, the wall half-tiled like their own in blue and yellow. But the treads were littered with fallen débris, the whitewash stained with the green of many rains. That was it, then; the place was empty. Vaguely relieved, since she hadn't cared for the thought of such squalid neighbours, she locked the door and returned to the bright kitchen.

2

For the third time Anthea got up from her place on the long plastic-covered banquette, one of the endless airport travesties of leather sofas, and wandered to the huge window facing the runways. This whole side of the building was made of glass, giving a sense, in spite of the central heating, of bleak exposure. Rain swept over the tarmac in freakish gusts, and the light (there was little enough still from the leaden clouds) was reflected upwards from surfaces gleaming with water. It really was an extraordinary scene; in the distance were areas of grass, stretching almost to the horizon, which the runways divided and crossed in sweeping patterns; one could almost believe them, after this last deluge, to be swampy islands in the spate of some huge river. But even as she stood and watched the clouds were parting; the sun, first feeble and watery, then hot, came out on the dazzle of water with blinding brilliance. Almost at once the tarmac was steaming, then drying, and from every quarter little vehicles appeared, fussing hither and thither through the puddles and out to the waiting planes with ant-like activity.

Anthea felt in her satchel for dark spectacles and moved closer to the glass. Without them the light was too brilliant to bear, and she was held by the weird commotion going on below. There was nothing human about it; it was a dream, an insect ballet, a scene from science fiction. Several jets had flown in, and were crawling with gleaming wings to their appointed places, submitting to being towed by diminutive tugs, giant lepidoptera in the power of some lesser species. A Caravelle, as she watched, came slowly to rest, and the little vehicles ran busily about, nosing and clustering under the huge wings, pastoral ants tending some monstrous aphid. Finally a weird step-insect top-heavily appeared, running with surprising speed and

centipede smoothness, its legs concealed under the metal carapace. The illusion was so complete, her imagination so repelled
by it that it was a shock when figures appeared and descended
the stairway. The picture slipped into focus and became normal:
Madrid airport on a stormy morning, with herself fretting under
the long delay and the non-appearance of Consuelo.

She turned back to the place where she had left her hand-
luggage, picked up her overnight bag and newspapers and set
off on the tedious walk to the information desk. The stalls and
boutiques she already knew by heart, each with its little group
of bored transients aimlessly brooding over the tempting rubbish.
Spanish leatherwork, Spanish dolls, mantillas faked up with
sequins, purses, handkerchiefs, scarves, Toledo jewellery; she
had looked at them all before, idly in the first hour, then with
exasperation. There must be some news by now; it was becoming
ridiculous. As she came in sight of the Iberia desk she was relieved
to see a little group standing before it. She took her place behind
them and waited her turn.

The man in front of her was standing very much at his ease,
an Air Maroc bag hung slackly from one shoulder. Her eyes
wandered to his neck, where the dark springy hair, not too
recently cut, caught her attention as sharply as though she knew
him. His shoulders too, and the loose hang of his coat, touched
a nerve which had long been unresponsive. She became conscious
of inner trembling, as though something utterly impossible were
about to happen. And then the tremor died, as though switched
off. The man had turned, and was not like James at all. She collected herself: the stranger was speaking to her.

'It seems there's a little strike or something,' he was saying
casually. 'You waiting for the Tangier-Casablanca plane too?'
She found herself looking into a seamed face, battered but not
ill-looking; darkish skin, heavy eyebrows, deep grooves running
from the nostrils to the corners of the mouth. From the way he
spoke he might have been an old acquaintance, which he certainly
was not. It was not a face to be known and then forgotten.

'I . . . yes, I am.' She responded with a faint smile. 'Is that
really the cause of the delay? What are they doing about it?'

26

It was absurd that this man could ever have reminded her of James: almost as tall, he was far more heavily built, and his clothes and breath smelt strongly of tobacco. He looked her in the eye with curious directness, raising his brows as though he had asked her a question.

'I'll try and get some sense out of these dollies,' he said, 'you stay right here,' and had shouldered his way to the counter and plunged at once into a mixture of French and Spanish. The girl at the desk, buttoned up in musical-comedy uniform, smooth as a dummy, answered him in English.

'I am afraid there is a short delay. You will be called as soon as the flight is signalled. Refreshments will be provided in the transit-lounge restaurant.' She handed him a printed ticket.

'Two,' he said, and after a further exchange between the girl and a group of Spanish businessmen, to which he listened attentively, came back to Anthea with the tickets, wearing an expression half-humorous, half-exasperated.

'Well, there it all is,' he said, putting a ticket in her hand. 'What shall we do? Have lunch? We can't just stand here.'

'I don't think I will,' said Anthea evasively, glancing away. 'It's too early. I think I'll just go and sit down, and wait for the announcement.' This sounded prim, she knew, but she was not quite sure how to take this easy tone, which might or might not be civility. He stooped and picked up her bag, as though from habit.

'Anything you say. Where were you sitting? I think, on the whole, food rather passes the time. These tickets they give you are derisory, though. Have you ever tried to eat on them, let alone drink?' He was walking familiarly beside her; there was no feeling of impertinence, no tension. His manner was mildly friendly, not over-eager; he seemed simply concerned, as he said, with passing the time. She began to feel she was making a fuss about nothing.

'I don't know that I ought to leave the transit lounge. I'm supposed to be meeting a friend. She hasn't turned up so far, I don't want to miss her.'

'Coming from where?'

27

'From Paris. The plane she was supposed to be on has been in some time. Mine got in from Rome about an hour after it. I expected to find her here.' She looked about her, over the empty acres of boredom in which other castaways sat or stood or slept or wandered disconsolately. On the seat where Anthea had been sitting was a thin, rather sallow and sandy-haired schoolgirl, crouched with her elbows on her knees and her chin in her hand, staring at nothing, and the middle-aged man in spectacles with two boys in tow (one of them distinctly odd) was still walking them up and down the interminable expanse, as though nothing would answer their case but perpetual motion.

'Did they give you any indication how long we might have to wait?'

'Not likely. They're not committing themselves. Something'll happen presently, we shall hear on the blower. Are you sure you won't join me in some coffee, perhaps a sandwich? Air travel's always composed of a succession of horrid little meals; there's always the dread of missing something, one isn't strong-minded enough to break the habit.' There seemed no point in arguing. They passed into the large, pretentious-looking restaurant and were shown at once to a window table. A number of people, mostly, to judge by appearance, businessmen, were already eating, importantly beckoning the wine waiter or studying the menu. Others, apparently well below expense-account level, provided like themselves with printed tickets, apathetically waited to receive more modest refreshments.

'What'll you drink?' He ignored the tickets, summoning a passing waiter with a brisk gesture. Anthea noticed and was puzzled by something not quite American about his accent; from his looks and clothes she would have sworn he was English. 'I'm going to have a whisky myself, will you do the same?' He noticed her hesitation and suddenly smiled, an unexpectedly pleasant smile, made and marred by irregular tobacco-stained teeth; it did much to redeem the harshness of his features. 'I do rather seem to have taken charge, I'm afraid? I should apologise. The thing is, when I first turned round I thought for a moment I knew you. And then I wasn't sure, and now I begin to see I've

28

been very bold. My name's Robert Quattrell, by the way. I rely on your not being offended.'

'Of course not. I thought I knew you too, until you turned round; your back reminded me of someone. My name's Askew-Martin, Mrs. Askew-Martin.' She saw him take the point, and smiled to conceal her boredom. 'I don't like travelling alone, especially when things go wrong.'

'Good, then we'll have that whisky, shall we? For moral rearmament.' Without waiting he ordered two, and handed her the menu. 'We'll ignore those insulting tickets, they only entitle one, I think, to Coca-Cola and biscuits.'

'A sandwich will do for me.'

'No, no, let's have an omelette. The bread's quite good,' he pinched a crust, 'and there's plenty of butter. We need a little something hot to keep up our strength; we may be here for days.'

As the omelettes were set in front of them Anthea was startled by a sound at her elbow; a sort of moan, though not plaintive; it had a questioning note. She turned to find the spectacled man with the two boys standing at her elbow, waiting to be directed to a table, and for the first time saw that the something odd about the elder one, which she had noticed earlier, was more than an eccentricity of gait and bearing. Though about sixteen he was holding his father's hand, looking about him with hen-like pecking movements of the head, uttering those strange sounds which had surprised her. She quickly turned away and began to eat, raising her eyes only when the trio had been settled at their own table. The father seemed perfectly confident in this public place, holding his son's hand, arranging his napkin, even once, in a gesture unusual and touching in a man of his appearance, giving him a tender encouraging pat on the cheek. The younger boy, who was about fourteen, looked quite normal.

'Sad, isn't it?' said Quattrell, helping himself to bread. 'I admire people who take on a job like that, I must say I wouldn't be equal to it.' He looked at her speculatively. 'Have you any children?'

'No.'

'Nor I, worse luck. A good thing, I dare say, though I like

kids. Mad about them, in fact. But I can't see myself setting up as a model father.'

Anthea smiled, not caring to pursue the subject but not very sanguine either about her chances. It ought to be possible, but usually wasn't, to hold a conversation with a stranger without becoming involved in their whole history.

Passengers whom she had seen at the information desk continued to filter in in ones and twos. Evidently there was no news yet. Though she listened with strained attention each time the loud-speaker, booming like an oracle, broke into gnomic utterance to be interpreted as one pleased, she had heard nothing yet which referred to her own flight. Everyone wore the look of stoic aimlessness peculiar to people marooned in the world's airports. The sandy-haired girl, who had just appeared in the doorway, looked particularly forlorn, bored, embarrassed and irresolute. After a pause she passed within touching distance and sat down with painful self-consciousness at the next table. Touched by some echo from her own lanky and unprepossessing girlhood, Anthea felt sorry for her.

'I never can get used,' she said, 'to the way children travel about the world by themselves. I know the airlines take immense care of them and all that, but it must be rather alarming. I don't think I'd have liked it when I was young.'

'You're still young, and you still don't like it, I gather.' He gave her a teasing glance to which she replied with a deprecating shrug and a smile, avoiding his eye. That kind of compliment fell flat when one was nearly forty. To her relief he did not pursue it; his eyes had wandered to the girl at the next table. 'That's not a child, she's sixteen at the very least.' He studied her critically, the long straight colourless hair held back in a headband, the knee-high socks, the shabby anorak which she still, in the warm restaurant, wore like a clumsy shawl round drooping shoulders. 'She'd look older, and better too, if she wore make-up. That's one of their affectations now, I believe? I'm not over-impressed—are you?—by unadorned nature. Look at those white eyelashes, for instance.'

Anthea stole another look, and saw that her eyebrows and

lashes, thick and shapely, possibly her best feature, were indeed unfashionably neutral and unemphatic.

'I had almost exactly that colouring at her age. I rather like it now, but I didn't then. I don't like a lot of make-up on young faces. She's younger than you imagine.'

Quattrell had finished eating and had brought out a crushed pack of American cigarettes. He tapped it expertly on a finger and held it out to her, his eyes turned in overt appraisal on her face.

'You haven't got white eyelashes, what nonsense. And your hair's not sandy, it's blonde; at least in places.' She laughed, disarmed in spite of herself by his unembarrassed gaze, now frankly focused on her mouth and splendid teeth.

He continued to stare, not impertinently, but with a steadiness under which she felt uneasy. He seemed intent on trying to remember something.

'The name Askew-Martin rings a bell somewhere. I used to know a Gerald Askew-Martin once, when I was working on newspapers. Would he be any connection?'

'Yes, that's my husband's name. How very extraordinary Did you know him well?'

'No, not at all.' He inhaled heavily and blew out a cloud of smoke. His expression had changed to one of reserve; almost, she thought, she detected a look of caution. 'It was a long time ago. I remember him as rather impressive. I didn't know he was married.'

This was not a theme which Anthea cared to pursue. Was there, or was there not, an undertone? She took it steadily.

'Oh yes, he's been married twice. His first wife died some years ago. I'm the second.'

'I see.' He continued to look at her speculatively, as though puzzled. 'And is it a second marriage for you, too?'

'No.' There was a pause, in which she could almost hear him thinking. Defensively, she glanced about for the waiter. 'Shall we have some coffee now? There's bound to be time.' This was an extraordinary conversation to be having with a stranger. Not wishing to give it another chance she said at once, when

31

the coffee had been ordered, 'Are you still in the newspaper world?' She had a feeling that any silence might break into a question. Perhaps the man was after all an American. With them this kind of probing passed for civility.

'Only from time to time. I do this and that. I'm one of those changeable types. Seven trades and the victuals lacking, as they say in Arabic.'

'Oh, do you speak Arabic? How enviable.'

'Up to a point, yes. I wouldn't like to be pressed, I've forgotten most of it. I taught English once in a school in Cairo for a time. Though Egyptian Arabic's rather different, it won't be much use to me in Morocco.'

'Won't it? What a pity. Are you going to stay long?' She was at ease now, accepting a cigarette with a sense of relief: they were on a safe topic.

'That'll depend, as they say. I'm at a bit of a loose end, between jobs; thought I'd scout around a bit, see what happened. I'm working on a script right now and felt I could do with a change. Had to have one, in fact, if I wasn't to go quite crazy. Do you ever get like that?' He gave her an oblique smile. 'No, I suppose not. You're happily married, I can see. You're lucky, you know; long may it continue. Though all my instincts tempt me to wish it wouldn't.'

This was evidently gallantry and Anthea ignored it, smiling only faintly as she looked round again for the waiter. If only one could say, 'Don't bother: it's a waste of time: you don't have to go through this formula. I'm finished with it.' She reached for her satchel and began to search through a muddle of mixed currency.

'You know, something interests me,' he went on, quite undiscouraged; but at that moment the loud-speaker hissed and cleared its throat and the announcement they had been waiting for boomed out in portentous tones from the corners of the restaurant. The waiter appeared by magic; they argued briefly and amicably over the bill.

'Nonsense,' he said finally, pushing away her note with the back of his hand. 'You haven't got any pesetas, and besides, think how bored I'd have been if I hadn't met you. It's cheap at the price.' He settled the bill and picked up her bag with his own. 'We count as acquaintances now, since I know your husband. You're not going to say we can't finish the trip together?' They had joined the stream of passengers moving along a seemingly interminable distance, involving corridors, ramps, stairs, a variety of levels leading to the indicated exit.

'No, no, of course not; I'm grateful.' Her long legs and relaxed pace went easily with his own, and again, by a perversion of memory, she had a feeling that somewhere, as in a dream, all this had happened before, in another place. Though strange he was oddly familiar; their walking together had the reassuring ease of the habitual.

They moved out in straggling procession across the tarmac, eyes dazzled by the sun, hair and clothing snatched at by gusts of wind. The girl in the anorak, dragging two canvas hold-alls, awkwardly struggled ahead in the wake of the stewardess, flat shoes slipping at the heel, hair blown across her face in flying strands. Everyone, after the long delay, was caught up in a futile hurry to get aboard, as though, with the steadily increasing flow of passengers streaming out like ants from a crack in the base of the building, the least show of hesitation might leave them stranded. The queue on the metal steps moved clumsily upwards, filed past the waiting stewardess, sorted itself out down the long hollow shell of the plane and subsided at last into what theory or superstition suggested were the best places. The father with the two boys had taken possession of a trio of seats on the right-hand, the elder boy pressing his forehead against the window. By the time Anthea and her companion, followed by an Indian lady with a muffled child, had squeezed themselves into the seats behind them, the plane was full. The fair-haired girl had gone up the gangway ahead. Search as she might Anthea could see no sign of Consuelo.

'I'm still worried,' she said, fastening her seat belt and turning to scan the rows of faces behind her, 'about that friend of mine, the one I was supposed to meet. I can't think what's happened to her, but I don't know what good I'd have done by staying behind.' After all, Consuelo was not a child; she was far more capable and independent in some ways than herself.

'Oh, she'll be O.K. Something's held her up, I shouldn't worry.' It was clear he preferred the situation as it was, with no addition. The cheerful manner in which he was stuffing his raincoat into the rack and packing his long bulk into the space beside her suggested that he was enjoying himself. He extended a finger to the child beside him and relieved the Indian lady of wraps and baskets. 'Who is she? Do I know her? I'm quite prepared to find that I know not only your friends but your entire family.'

'Her name's Consuelo Carpenter. It's quite possible. She works on a women's magazine, so I suppose you might have encountered her somewhere in Fleet Street.'

'Not my department, I'm afraid. My undistinguished career was mostly in America, nothing to do with cookery or knitting. What's she like, your friend? Good-looking, like you? Married? I'm curious to see her.'

'She's not in the least like me and she isn't married. She's spent years and years looking after an aged father that she was devoted to. He died some while ago. This is the first time she's had the chance, or the money, for a proper holiday.'

'And you're very fond of her, and have planned this trip as a reward in the goodness of your heart?'

'Well, no, it's not like that. I *am* very fond of her, and as we're out here for a while it seemed a good idea. She has some scheme of going on to Algeria, we're only the starting point. She's taking three months off; so marvellous for her to have some freedom at last.'

He was fastening his belt and feeling in his pocket for cigarettes, impatient for the moment of take-off so that he could smoke. He had lost interest in Consuelo, if he had ever had any. The stewardess's voice broke out from the loud speaker, hideous with distortion, offering a speech of welcome and routine instruction, in Spanish first, then in Arabic and English. The plane roared and vibrated, described a jolting course to the main runway, paused, doubled the volume to deafening pitch, so that everything trembled, and set off on a catapult rush between flying prairies. Lifted at last without effort in a steep ascent which pressed their bodies backwards, in a space of seconds they had left the dwindling airfield far below them.

As though at a signal the boy in front of Anthea flung himself suddenly backwards against the seat, so that it lurched on its springs, within an inch of her knees. Involuntarily she put out a hand, but by now he was straining forward, buttocks clear of the seat, held back from a standing position only by the belt, which his father had fastened. The back of the seat regained its normal position, and immediately his weight fell back on it again, rocking the structure so far that it touched her knees. He rose once more, repeating the manœuvre, and it became clear that he was embarked on an indefinite spell of this rocking-horse rhythm.

'This is charming,' said Anthea in a low voice. 'Do you imagine we're going to have this the whole way?' They exchanged ominous glances. The father of the boy remained perfectly unconcerned, jerking each time with the lunge but apparently wholly absorbed in his Spanish newspaper. Experience had presumably developed detachment to the point of coma. The younger boy, on his left, was studying the maps and folders he had found in the seat-pocket, not giving his brother a glance. This sort of performance was evidently normal.

'Jesus God,' said Quattrell, 'we would pick this seat, wouldn't we? What about changing places? I'm tough, I can probably take it.'

'No, no, it can't go on. He's bound to get tired of it.' Even changing places would be a considerable feat, since there was no room to do this without climbing out into the gangway, moving the Indian lady. She by this time had removed some layers of wrappings, and the child was sitting up with shining eyes, captivated by the performance. The mother's face, plump and smooth above layers of cardigan and sari, wore a look of resigned placidity suggesting a long endurance of the vagaries of children. Little support, if any, was likely from that quarter. Anthea leaned back in her seat and closed her eyes. The rhythm of the rocking, smiting back and forth with the precision of a piston, was easier to bear if she could not see the boy, whose appearance, like his gestures, was distressing. He was uttering a hooting cry at each backward plunge, when the crown of his head, narrow, ferret-like, topped with a crew-cut thatch of sun-bleached hair, came momentarily into view. From time to time he threw up slender arms and clasped his hands, or paused for a moment to press his face to the window, always at once resuming the frenetic rocking. None of the other passengers was visibly suffering; the thing was past cure; the only conceivable course was stoic endurance. Even the stewardesses, making their way down the plane with a drinks trolley, after an experienced glance decided to ignore it. The father continued to read with placid indifference.

Quattrell paid for two whiskies and passed one to Anthea. 'If we drink ourselves into a stupor it'll be easier. Only another hour to go, unless he breaks up the plane.' She opened her eyes, feeling the touch of a glass on the back of her hand, 'Only thing is, I wanted to talk to you, I need to know more. We've got an hour in hand, and this isn't exactly an aid to conversation.'

'It isn't, indeed. I think we'd better postpone it.' She drank, holding the glass with care against the repeated blows of the seat in front of her. A wave of fatigue and exasperation engulfed her. This wasn't the time or the place for remorseless questioning, however friendly, nor was she, now or ever, in the mood. Yet with these imbecile antics going on, shaking the frame of the seats every three or four seconds, it was futile to close one's eyes or to feign sleep. She moved back the curtain of her porthole and looked out. They were flying over a dead and forbidding landscape, folded and ridged sierras veined with snow; impossible to believe that in an hour or less, if the moving continents of cloud continued to disperse, they would be making a smooth descent to the Mediterranean.

'You being met?' said Quattrell suddenly in her ear. 'Can I give you a lift from the airport, or anything?'

'Oh, that's very kind, Gerald's sure to be there. You must meet him again; see if you really remember him.'

'Oh, sure, I'll remember him all right.' He sounded put off and faintly mocking, as though conscious at last that her motive was simply discouragement. He relapsed into silence, dragging with a sucking sound on his cigarette, blowing out clouds of smoke with his eyes closed, to the discomfiture of the Indian lady. Anthea noticed that two fingers of either hand were stained to the second knuckle. Something warned her that Gerald, if he remembered him at all, would almost certainly dislike him.

The sea, after a long interval in which neither of them spoke, appeared with dramatic suddenness. Gibraltar itself was wrapped in cloud, but almost at once they found themselves tilting down towards a silken surface which quickly revealed a wrinkling, a ribbing of waves, through which a speck-like steamer ploughed without visible progress. And then, in a space of time quite absurd for the traverse of any sea, they had crossed the neck of the straits, had glimpsed a fringe of white on the dark Atlantic, and at an improbable angle were sweeping over a toy harbour with a bleached and ancient honeycomb above it. Fields green as rice-paddies, hills dotted with chalky villas, the sea again, a beach, a ribbon of road, and they were sailing in like a kite on the empty airport.

Even before her luggage had been chalked Anthea caught a glimpse of Gerald's head, looking through the panes of a door beyond the point where an official was slowly scrutinizing passports. She had known he would be there, but the sight brought disproportionate relief. Everything would be easy now, there was no problem. She had not much liked the idea of a prolonged drive and more probing and parrying conversation with Quattrell.

'Hello, my darling, I'm glad to see you. The plane's disgracefully late.' Gerald was all smiles, looking pink and pleased. 'Is this all your luggage? Have you got a porter?' He took the satchel from her shoulder and slung it on his own, turning her by the elbow to face the quiet-eyed woman standing beside him. 'My wife,' he said, 'Miss Townsend. We came to the airport together. She's meeting a young niece; have you seen anything of her?'

37

'She's there, I can see her,' said Phoebe, and raised a hand. The girl in the anorak was emerging from the passport struggle, dragged down by luggage. Having no free hand she answered Phoebe's signal by shrugging her shoulders. She did not smile; her face remained curiously impassive.

'This is my young niece, Octavia Williams.'

'Hello,' said Anthea, with one of her dazzling smiles, 'I saw you in Madrid, and on the plane.' She had become aware of Quattrell at her shoulder, holding her overnight bag, and turned to include him in the introduction. 'Mr. Quattrell's been awfully kind. There was a long wait in Madrid, we had lunch together.' He and Gerald shook hands, a trifle awkwardly, with the alacrity of men not normally hand-shakers who fear that omission of the ceremony may give offence. There was just the faintest suspicion of constraint. Glancing from one to the other she was struck by a ludicrous contrast in their appearance. Both tall, both potentially bulky, they could hardly have been less alike in bearing and feature. Gerald was carefully dressed, Quattrell was untidy; Gerald's face was smooth, Quattrell's craggy; even Gerald's hat, a shade too small and young for a man of his age, rakishly tilted to hide diminishing hair, might have been chosen as a rueful comment on Quattrell's mop, a thick growth with a strong curl in it which seemed to boast that he normally went uncovered.

'We met, I think, years ago,' said Quattrell, 'I daresay you don't remember.'

'We did?' Gerald looked surprised. 'I'm getting deaf. I don't think I quite got your name.'

'Quattrell, Rob Quattrell. Something to do with financing a film, wasn't it? I remember we met in a bar once, with Dave Iremonger.'

'Was that it, how stupid of me. Nice to see you again.' Anthea could not be sure from his expression whether Gerald in fact remembered him or not. 'Have you got transport? I'm afraid we're a full load, or I'd offer you a lift. Maybe we could all squeeze in.'

'Thanks, that's all right. I'm taking the bus to the terminal.'

He turned to Anthea with a privately amused look which she could not interpret. 'Be seeing you,' he said, and with a nod to the four of them was gone through the glass doors into the wind and sunlight.

*

In the car Anthea said, 'Did you really remember him, that man, Quattrell?'

'I'm not sure. I may have met him somewhere. One can't remember everybody.'

'He knew your name, anyway. He was quite a comfort on the journey; paid for my lunch, and bought me several drinks.'

'That was civil of him.'

'There was this long boring wait in Madrid, where I completely failed, as you see, to find Consuelo.'

'Ah, I forgot.' One hand on the wheel, smoothly taking a curve on the road, Gerald produced a telegram from his pocket. 'She's altered her plans, coming on Thursday. I made a note of the flight.'

'Oh good, so I needn't have worried.' She turned round to Phoebe and the girl; she had almost forgotten them, sitting there in the back of the car in polite silence. 'How nice to find that we know each other already. Your brother's bought a house here, Gerald tells me.'

'My brother-in-law,' Phoebe carefully corrected her. 'Yes, it's really a question of health, he's far from well. When the house is finished, and he can rest, we rather hope he'll benefit from the climate.'

'Oh, he will, surely. Have you been here long? Has the weather been good so far?'

'No,' said Phoebe truthfully, 'I can't say it has. It's improving now, but in the last two weeks the cold and the wind and the wet have been past bearing.' Her voice shook unexpectedly on the last word, conveying an impression of indignation and suffering. She smiled quickly, glancing with a look of apology at her niece. 'But it'll all be better now, so everyone tells me.

39

I want Tavy to have a good holiday, with sunshine and bathing. We must get to know some young people. But we've been so busy with the house, we've hardly been out at all. And so,' she concluded lamely, 'I'm afraid we don't know any.'

'There were two boys on the plane who live here,' said Tavy, speaking for the first time. 'I talked to the younger one at Madrid; he was at the bookstall. They're English, he's called Nick Parsons. Their father's in some business here, to do with machinery.'

'Do you mean those boys,' said Anthea, 'travelling with their father? They sat in front of me. I must say the elder one seemed rather odd.'

'Oh, he's a looney. His name's Pete. He can't even talk properly.' A hint of a smile, the first, crossed Tavy's face. 'But the younger one's all right, I didn't mind him. He goes to school here, he says he can speak Spanish and a bit of Arabic.'

'Well, that's nice,' said Phoebe doubtfully. 'Perhaps, when you know him better, you could ask him to tea.' She could not for the life of her imagine the house ever reaching a state fit for so normal an entertainment, but the idea of Tavy, now that the girl was here, was beginning to disturb her, and she clutched timidly at a straw.

'Oh, I already have. I gave him the address.' Tavy turned her face to the window. Presently she said, looking without enthusiasm at the admittedly unsightly streets through which they were passing, the windblown dusty outskirts of the town, 'This isn't a bit like what I imagined.'

'Well, no; this isn't really the interesting part, dear.'

'I didn't suppose it was.'

This reply was succeeded by an uncompromising silence which neither Phoebe, who felt snubbed, nor the Askew-Martins, busy with their own thoughts, felt it advisable to break, and they sat through the rest of the drive without speaking.

*

Waiting for the lift when they were finally alone, Gerald lightly kissed his wife on the cheek.

'I'm glad to see you, darling girl. How was everything? Did you enjoy Rome?'

'It was all right. Very nice, in fact. Extraordinary to see it again, after so long. It hasn't changed as much as I imagined.'

'None of your art-school pals still there, I suppose?'

'Only one old professor who said he remembered me. I'm not convinced he did.' They packed themselves into the lift, which was extremely small, seemingly designed before the invention of luggage. On the way up, her chin almost touching his shoulder, she said, 'How's Enrico behaving himself? Is it a success?'

'Yes and no. He's made rather too many friends. It becomes tiresome, we seem to frequent all the same bars and restaurants.'

'I thought it wouldn't work.'

'No, but it won't last long. He's already been offered another job, and seems to be toying with it.' They reached the fourth floor. Gerald moved the luggage and rang the bell. 'I do this on principle, I must explain, on the very remote chance that he may be at home. There are occasions when he hasn't an engagement.'

The door, however, was opened at once, and Enrico, his Italian good looks enhanced by a pale tan, received them in his best manner, as though the sight of them, and especially of Anthea, were all he needed to complete his pleasure. He carried her luggage through the flat with the pride of a proprietor.

'You're looking very brown and well, Enrico.'

'Thank you, madame. I can say the same.' He gave her an ardent glance. 'Roma was O.K., yes?'

'Very O.K. As always. Are you liking it here?' Enrico jutted his lip and raised his shoulders, making a see-sawing motion with his right hand.

'Like this, like that. The weather is not so good.' His eyes flicked momentarily to Gerald and his face assumed a passive, correct expression. 'I have put the drinks and the ice already in the salon.' He withdrew discreetly, shutting the door very slowly, without sound.

'His English has improved, at any rate,' said Anthea, subsiding on the bed with a groan, kicking off her shoes.

'He's had plenty of practice this past fortnight, believe me. His social life's terrific.'

'And yours, my darling? How have you found it, by yourself? Rather nice discovering the Lyttons, wasn't it? How well d'you know him?'

'Not awfully well, but he's an interesting man. Might be a great asset.' Anthea lay back on the bed and closed her eyes. 'Look, I'm going to bring the drinks in here. You look exhausted.'

'A bit.' She did not open her eyes. When he had fetched the tray and poured out two whiskies she made an effort and propped herself on an elbow. 'I thought his sister-in-law rather appealing, didn't you? Dull, I dare say, but quite sweet? But that girl! What will she do by herself, with just two of them? She can't be more than fifteen; and they're both quite old. I felt sorry for her.'

'On the contrary, I feel sorry for *them*. Imagine being stuck with such an incubus! Here, of all places. I thought I hadn't seen such a *farouche* specimen of English girlhood for a long time.' He sat on the end of the bed and laid his disengaged hand lightly on her ankle. 'I wouldn't have thought Lytton a child-lover, not by a long stretch. Miss Thingummy I dare say's different. I gather it's *her* niece, not his. But what a horror!'

'Oh, Gerald, don't exaggerate. I was just as pasty and unappetising at that age.'

'My dear, that is just *not* possible. That fishy-looking skin and depressing hair! At her age I'm sure you were glorious.'

'All that'll change very soon; you'll see. She'll be better at sixteen. And Miss Townsend'll probably do something about her manners.' She looked round the bedroom, taking in its decorative enormities for the first time. 'Good heavens, look at those iron goldfish! Whoever would have thought of that?' Wrought-iron goldfish (in outline only, mercifully) with metal rings representing graduated bubbles, had been screwed to the distempered wall in several places. Density was greatest over the dressing-table, where they swam and bubbled in diminishing sizes. The furniture, to which her eyes now turned in fascination, was all apparently made out of iron braid, a material lending itself to exuberant arabesques and tendril curling. Thin little cushions had been tied to the seats of the chairs, the dressing-table was skirted in draped cotton.

'Oh, that's nothing. Wait till you see the sitting-room. The tables are all equipped with plastic hyacinths.'

'Good heavens,' said Anthea faintly, and lay back on the pillow. She closed her eyes once more, holding her glass at an angle on the edge of the bed. Gerald considered her attentively.

'Enrico *has* prepared some cold food, but I thought you might prefer to go out to a restaurant? They're not very famous, though, and you look so tired. Which would you rather, my sweet? Perhaps it's rather an effort; one always meets people.'

'Oh, don't let's do that. Are there people here that you know, besides the Lyttons?' She looked drowsily comfortable now, murmuring with eyes closed, as though half asleep.

'Well, yes, a few; I've been here a fortnight, you know.' He looked at her doubtfully. 'The other day, at a cocktail party actually . . .' He broke off, undecided; she did not stir. 'The fact is, my dear, I ran into Molly Brockhurst, or at least saw her. I thought I'd better tell you, because when we go out. . . . You can imagine what it's like here; in this place one's continually running into people.'

Anthea opened her eyes, gave Gerald a dazed glance and shut them again. It struck him that her face had lost every vestige of colour. But she was plainly exhausted; it might have been his fancy.

'Oh *no*,' she said after a minute, then abruptly sat up and swallowed the last of her whisky. 'Is that really true? Dear God in heaven! Is she staying here or something?'

'She's bought a house, I'm afraid. She looks a most frightful wreck. I hardly knew her. I was told the whole story before I'd begun to realise who she was. When they said she'd been the sole survivor from a yacht disaster, and never quite recovered,

43

I still didn't think of James until this chap said, didn't I remember, it had been in all the papers, the husband was a famous Q.C., and there'd been several other people lost as well. So then I said, "*What* was the name?" But I had an awful feeling, and then he said, "Brockhurst," and I took another look, and I saw that this woman on the sofa was our friend Molly.'

'Good God. What does she look like now?'

'Much thinner. Rather shaky. There was some kind of companion with her, who I suppose looks after her. James was heavily insured, I suppose? He must have been, I imagine she's perfectly O.K. financially.'

'But what are we going to do?' She looked stricken, sitting on the edge of the bed, clasping her hands.

'Do? Why nothing. I don't think she goes out much, we probably won't meet. I told you just in case, to avoid a shock.' He reached for her hand and took it. 'Besides, what does it matter? She always knew about you and James. She's the last person to want to spread the story.'

'Oh, I know. It's not that. It's just . . . oh, I don't know what I feel. It's shaken me.' She rubbed her eyes with a fierce, distracted gesture. Gerald got up and poured her another drink.

'Have this one, and then we'll go out. This isn't the night for eating cold stuff at home. It was a mistake. We'll let Enrico have it and go out to a place I know, and get happily plastered.'

'I'm trying not to drink.'

'My dear girl, what you drink wouldn't hurt a fly.'

'Oh yes, it could. It does. I've had a lot of whisky already with that Quattrell person.'

'Well, now you can have some with me. I'm a safer type.' He put the glass in her hand. She looked at it abstractedly, then drank it off at a draught, with reckless suddenness. 'And then we'll go to that place, shall we, and Enrico can do as he likes? Come on, my girl, I'm not going to have you brooding.'

But three hours later they were still there, and Enrico, his cold collation disregarded, had changed into lilac jeans and skipped out into the night.

3

THE first days of Tavy's company were less of an ordeal than Phoebe had feared, since she spent much of her time in her room with the door closed, emerging only at long intervals or when summoned to meals, rubbing her eyes as though recovering from sleep. This in itself, however, was a worry, for the whole point of having her there was to do her good, and no one in their senses would have said the child looked happy. When she appeared it was in silence, and when spoken to she had a way of holding one's eye for an uncomfortably long moment before replying, as though deliberating several annihilating answers. Talking to her at all made Phoebe nervous, and this nervousness was the more exasperating because it was absurd. The girl was only fifteen and had everything to learn. Phoebe became increasingly apprehensive that the visit would prove a failure and that Tavy would do herself harm by antagonising Lytton.

Her arrival at the house had been inauspicious. Lytton's was the last door at the end of a long gully (technically a street, but Phoebe still could not think of it as one), several hundred yards from the last point accessible to a taxi. Gerald's car was not large, but as they started on the precipitous descent from the Kasbah, surrounded by a horde of running and shouting boys, he had lost his nerve, seeing it as probable that he might not be able to turn. Phoebe, who could not drive, had not dared to reassure him. So she and Tavy and Tavy's luggage had been set down there and then, with apologies, in the midst of the crowd, and had proceeded laboriously on foot while Gerald gingerly backed the car away. Tavy had spoken only once, when she had set down her bag at the head of a flight of steps, the first of several to be climbed to their own quarter.

'But why are we coming up here? This can't be the way.'

'Oh yes, it is, dear.' Phoebe was out of breath. 'It's only a little bit further; you'll soon see.'

Tavy had looked at the walls with a blank face. Ahead lay a shadowy tunnel where the houses met together in a ceiling of beams; doors were darkly ajar on either side and the street so narrow that with outstretched arms she could have touched them. Small children sitting on doorsteps stared back at her with astonishment. Grimly she picked up her luggage and went on.

Phoebe breathlessly followed, wishing, as they emerged from the tunnel and continued the slow ascent to their own cul-de-sac, that on this occasion the paving had been somewhat cleaner. It was nothing to complain of really when one was used to it—fragments of orange peel, some vegetable refuse, scraps of paper, a corner strewn with herring bones and ashes—but on Tavy, who could not know that it would all be leisurely swept by hand in the morning, it must, she feared, create a poor impression. She smiled encouragingly when at last the bags were set down at their own door.

'The children make rather a litter, I'm afraid, but it all gets swept up twice a day.'

Tavy said nothing. Failing in the poor light to find her key Phoebe knocked loudly, twice, and presently Lytton's dragging step was heard, a bolt was drawn, the heavy door creaked inwards and they found themselves together in the quiet courtyard.

'Well!' said Lytton at length, rubbing his hands, when greetings and explanations had been got over, 'what do you think of it eh? Are you going to like it?' He smiled expectantly at Tavy, waiting for appreciation, even astonishment. The courtyard had been swept clean, the upper branches of the fig-tree were in tender leaf, he had switched on lights for effect in several places. Above, in the open rectangle of sky, swallows were darting and screaming in the last sunlight.

'It's quite pretty,' said Tavy, not looking at anything in particular. Lytton cracked his knuckles, waiting for more. 'But the street's a slum,' she said in a flat voice, unsmilingly meeting his eye for the first time.

'A slum?' Lytton tilted up his beard to look about him. 'Is

46

that really how it strikes you? Well, that's original. It's different from Ipswich, that we must expect. But a slum, my dear Tavy? Could you not, on second thoughts, have chosen another word?' Phoebe could see from his eye that he was annoyed.

'The street was a little untidy,' she put in mildly; 'the children, you know.' She slipped her arm through Tavy's. 'Come and see your room now, dear. Nothing's very finished, you know. You must make allowances.'

'Oh yes, of course,' said Tavy, 'I don't really mind.' And with a sidelong glance at Lytton, who was gazing over her head with his hands in his pockets, she turned and followed her aunt down the bare courtyard.

Perhaps she was aware of having given offence, or perhaps her own room, when she saw it, really delighted her; Phoebe could not tell. She stood for a moment in the doorway, her expression come to life with a flash of surprise.

'But this is quite something,' she said, and went at once to open the casement window. 'Are all the bedrooms downstairs? Do they all have bars?' She laid a hand on the grille. 'Which way is the sea from here? I can't see it.'

'You can see the sea from the terrace. I'll show you presently. I'm afraid there's not much view from here; it's the only one with an outside window, though. Rooms in Arab houses generally open inwards, you know, into the courtyard.'

'Does yours do that?'

'No, your uncle's and mine are upstairs, looking on to the terrace. It's a small house, there are only the three bedrooms.'

Tavy hooked her fingers into the grille and pulled herself forward into the window recess, looking down. The walls at this end of the house were formidably thick.

'Who lives in all these other houses?'

'Arab families.'

'Nobody like us at all?'

'So far as I know, nobody.'

'This roof below looks pretty slummy, doesn't it?'

'That's an empty house, nobody lives there. It's been empty for years, I believe.'

'It stinks rather,' said Tavy, and drew back from the window. After this first burst of communication she seemed to have lost interest; turning her back she lugged her bags on to the bed and began loosening the straps.

'That's right, dear, you unpack. I should have a rest too, if you feel like it. I'll call you when supper's ready.' Tavy seemed to think this not worth an answer, for she went on with what she was doing without looking up. Her manners, Phoebe reflected, left room for improvement. No doubt her mother's defection had done much damage. First it would be necessary to establish confidence; understanding, perhaps affection, would come later. If Lytton would only be patient she could do much. Warmed by a sense of mission and by no means discouraged Phoebe discreetly withdrew and went off to the kitchen.

*

As soon as the door was closed Tavy abandoned her luggage and began a methodical inspection of her room. There was not much in it; she took in the meagre furniture at a glance. Her serious concern was with the door, which had no lock. There was, however, a bolt, which like almost everything else of the kind in the house was stuck fast with paint. She worked at it patiently, easing it little by little with long fingers. It yielded at last; the heavy bolt moved gradually into the slot. Next she turned her attention to the stairway, kicking off her shoes and going up the narrow steps on stockinged feet. The tiles were cold, the handrail smooth and warm; the wooden door at the top had a pleasant smell. The iron bolt was new and opened easily. She pushed the door with caution and looked in.

What mystery she had expected she hardly knew. It was only a small loft, too low for standing up in, the further half stacked up with boxes and luggage. But to Tavy it had a private, extraordinary look; she could almost imagine that no one knew of it but herself. She bent her head and stepped cautiously inside. At once in this stooping position, her eyes came level with a narrow slit of window. It was a casement, opening inwards,

48

looking through a tunnel of wall to the open air. She put her head in the opening and found herself looking down on a lower roof where a woman was hanging out washing and an old man in a djellábah was rubbing some whitish substance about in a basket. They were so close, so absorbed, so unconscious of her presence that she felt a dreamlike thrill: she was invisible. Seen from this point, herself unseen, every movement of the two below became significant, actions deliberately mimed in a strange play. The old man sat cross-legged, rubbing and rubbing the white stuff round in the basket, while the woman, her skirts tucked up above long and gaudy bloomers, moved leisurely along the washing-line, straightening a threadbare blanket, pegging out odds and ends of clothing, prepared, apparently, to leave them there all night. The domed skylight of their roof was already faintly luminous from below; pressing her forehead against the bars (even this dwarfish window had a vestigial grille) Tavy could just make out, as at the bottom of a well, an area of black-and-white paving and the frame of a doorway, through which, as she watched, a girl passed with a lamp. It was extraordinary: not only was she invisible, she had powers to see into the very heart of the house. She watched for a long time, lips parted, breathing all but stopped. When the old man gathered his skirts and went below, and the woman, after a little perfunctory sweeping of the roof, followed him through a door and disappeared, she still remained without moving in her cramped position, watching the glass of the skylight, waiting for a sign. When nothing further happened she still stayed, gazing at the jumble of roofs like a city in ruins, at the square green minaret of the mosque, at the flutter of washing like signals all over the town, at the darkening outline of the hills, the curve of the bay. When finally she stirred it was almost dark; she could hear a gentle knocking on the door below.

'Are you ready for supper, Tavy?' Phoebe knocked again and tried the handle. Tavy came noiselessly down and sat on the bed. At the third knock she said, 'Yes?'—speaking in a muffled voice, as though just awake.

'Supper's ready, dear. I can't open your door.'

49

'Coming.' She put on her shoes without hurry and slid back the bolt.

'Why, you're all in the dark. Were you sleeping?'

'Yes.'

'You haven't unpacked, I see. Shall I help you later?'

'No, thanks.'

'Well, just as you like. I expect you have your own method. You'd like a wash, I expect. The bathroom's just up there, at the head of the stairs.'

'I had a wash in Madrid.' Tavy held out her hands, which were large and pale. 'They're quite clean still.'

'Just as you like.' Phoebe turned and led the way across the dark courtyard. The table had been laid in the parlour, a new departure, since she and Lytton had so far fed in the kitchen. Candlesticks had been found and candles lighted. Lytton had arranged his books. It all looked inviting.

'So now,' said Lytton, bent upon bonhomie, but with an element of caution since he had already been bitten, 'we find ourselves, for the first time, Tavy, in Africa. How, on a first impression, does it strike you?'

Tavy looked up from her soup with a slight frown, as though considering how to deal with a stupid question.

'Does this count as Africa?'

'Of course. Have you looked at the map?' He warmed to his subject. 'What do they teach you at school? Some Roman history? This is the furthest north-west point of Africa to be colonised by the Romans. Tingis, they called it. An important stronghold. Under this house, the foundations, if one could only be sure . . .' He waved his spoon, unconscious of the bead of soup descending his beard. 'And then, in later times of course, Catherine of Braganza. You know I assume, that this was part of her dowry? Here, on this very spot, I believe—at least, I must make certain—there was a garden on the ramparts. The Arabic name translates as the Captain's Garden. It can't have been more than a walk on the parapet, perhaps, with a few hardy flowers. That didn't last long, however. You remember Pepys? Writing his report to the Admiralty, sitting up there in

50

a courtyard, in the Kasbah? And afterwards, you know, the raids of the Barbary pirates. All those red-haired people one sees in the lower town. Descendants of Scottish prisoners from merchant ships, taken in the straits yonder and sold as slaves. Have you noticed their colouring, Tavy? Or haven't you had time?'

She gave him a wary look, crumbling bread in her soup.

'The light wasn't very good. I saw some children.'

'And were they red-haired, any of them?'

'I wouldn't know. It was dark.'

'We'll go for a walk tomorrow,' said Phoebe soothingly, aware that Lytton was off on his hobby-horse and would be difficult to stop. 'There hasn't been time to show her anything yet. I'm sure she's tired.'

Lytton took no notice. Tavy was a poor audience, but she was at least new. The meal continued as a surreptitious accompaniment to his monologue, Phoebe changing the plates and passing the butter, Tavy eating with melancholy concentration, occasionally raising her eyes to Lytton's face. She was not, Phoebe suspected, paying attention. The indigenous Berbers, the Arab invasions, the spread of Islam, the Romans, the Moors in Spain, relentlessly and indifferently passed her by. When her head drooped over her coffee Phoebe took action.

'The child's listened long enough, Henry. She must go to bed. Drink up your coffee, Tavy. Or don't you want it?'

'I don't like coffee. I always have cocoa at home.'

'We'll get some tomorrow, then. Leave it, it doesn't matter.' She got up with decision and swept Tavy off to her room.

*

Later, when all was quiet, she found Lytton sitting in the dusk on the top roof. The breeze had dropped; the air was cool and still. He was wearing his white djellábah, the hood drawn over his head. In the delusive light, his hands hidden in the sleeves and his beard jutting out from the cowl as a dark triangle, he had the rapt, remote air of a contemplative. Stirring a little in

51

his basket chair, however, he spoke at once as Phoebe sank creakingly beside him.

'I'm afraid we've made a mistake, Phoebe. A bad mistake.'

'You mean Tavy? You must give it a little time.'

'Of course. But she makes a discouraging impression. It was uphill work at supper, even you must admit. It's given me indigestion.'

'Oh, you can't judge by first impressions,' said Phoebe dreamily, soothed by the peace and beauty of the hour. Seen from the low parapet the town was seamed with crevices of light. There was a smell of cooking in the air and a hum of voices, diffused and continuous as the sound of a distant sea. Nothing moved at all but a narrow shadow, a cat flat-bellying its way across a neighbouring roof. Somewhere below, quite near, a lamb bleated. In spite of the quiet and the stillness the town internally murmured and seethed like a hive; it vibrated with hidden life.

'Well, the burden will fall more on you than on me, but I don't feel too sanguine. I wonder if she's even intelligent? And her manners! Whatever can her parents have been thinking of? Sarah was always doubtful about that adoption.'

'It was a risk, of course, but it worked well enough until Eric's wife disappeared. He's had enough to worry about since then, quite apart from Tavy. That's why I was anxious to have her here, as you know. Anyone can see what's the matter. She lacks security.'

'So do we all. It's part of the human condition.'

'Yes, but Henry, at her age! And she was always a fanciful child. Eric once told me, years ago, long before she knew she was adopted, that she had this idea, this obsession, that he and Martha weren't her real father and mother.'

'Not so fanciful, surely, as it turned out?'

'Well, yes, it was at the time. She was only about seven. They came home from the theatre one night to find her at the door of the flat in a state of hysteria. She'd got this idea in her head, and was quite heartbroken. They had a most awful job to reassure her.'

'Why didn't they tell her the truth?'

'My dear Henry, at seven years old? You can't be as rational as that with small children.'

'But they told her eventually?'

'No, someone else did. There's always that risk. Some busy-body.'

'Charming.'

'Eric always said it was that that made her so secretive.'

'So she's secretive as well, our Tavy? What about?'

'Well, uncommunicative, then. You saw for yourself. That's what I hope to break down in time, when she knows us better.'

'You'll have your work cut out.'

Phoebe sighed. There was another bleat from below, tremulously near.

'I do want to ask you,' she said, after a conciliatory pause, 'not to be quite so . . . in short, Henry my dear, be very patient. I'm responsible, of course, but I do appreciate . . . It's your house, after all, and you've been wonderfully kind. I don't want it to spoil things for you in any way. I know how much . . .' She broke off uncertainly, at a loss for words.

'Nonsense, rubbish.' Lytton creaked about testily in his chair. 'I'm delighted, on second thoughts. Entirely with you. Tavy's a part of my plan, as you well know. What is the use of all this' —he drew out a hand from his sleeve and gestured at the distance—'in my situation, with no future, though we won't discuss that, if I can't turn it to good account in the end? If I can't make it memorable?'

'I know,' said Phoebe gently. 'I admire you for that.'

'Nothing to admire, it's simply a romantic notion. I should like to feel, before I go, that my being here, that my having as it were a haven or asylum to offer, had made some difference to the lives of a few people. Tavy's a beginning. We shall progress to others. A pair of illicit lovers, perhaps, who can't meet elsewhere. *That* would be a kindly action. Or a starving poet or political refugee. Perhaps someone on the run?' He glanced at Phoebe, and his long teeth showed white in a sudden grin. 'Who knows what wrecks and rescues you may find yourself harbouring here, before I'm through? How many people may be saying, in a year's time, "If it hadn't been for old H.B., none of this would have happened"?'

'None of what?' said Phoebe, suddenly irritated. 'I hardly think Tavy quite comes into that category.' She shivered and clasped her arms. 'It's getting cold. I think we should go to bed.'

'Why don't you wear a djellábah, like me? I could stay here all night.'

'You're more adaptable than I am. I was never one for dressing up.'

'You mean you're conservative and insular. If one lives in a country one must be willing, to some degree, to be absorbed. The djellábah's one of the most practical inventions of the human race. One must accept such alien benefits as come one's way.'

'I wouldn't be accepted here, no matter what I wore,' said Phoebe, getting up with an effort and pulling her cardigan closer. 'I should only look a fool. People would laugh. They laugh at us as it is, I shouldn't wonder.' She moved to the edge of the parapet, looking down with a shiver in which the feeling of cold was sharpened by a touch of distaste. All the misgivings, all the strangeness and petty ordeals of the last weeks returned with a sense of foreboding which dismayed her. 'I sometimes think they hate us,' she said in a low voice.

Lytton gave a snort of laughter.

'My dear Phoebe, you're hysterical. Go to bed, there's a good creature, do. You've had a tiring day. I'll follow soon.'

Phoebe did as she was told, going down the steps to the lower level in silence, shutting herself with relief in her own room. Here at least, in this whitewashed cell, with curtains drawn and among her own possessions, she felt secure. She switched on the bedside lamp and folded the bedspread, aware, as she pottered about, unpinning her hair and slowly beginning to undress, that he had thought her a fool. Almost everything here, in Lytton's eyes, was perfect. He was the last person to perceive that things which to him were romantic, his chosen material, could also be a source of alarm, even of suffering. He would never guess that the briefest sortie from the house, even to buy the bread or to go to market, was frequently an ordeal; that she often stood for minutes before opening the door, listening with apprehension to sounds and voices. Sometimes the street was quiet, and she would give thanks. More often, as she descended to the tunnel, she would find herself in a yelling throng of children whose rending voices almost physically hurt her and to whom her presence was simply a riotous diversion. It was acutely painful to her to be conspicuous, and here there was no help for it. She was a freak, an alien, a circus, a figure of fun. Cries of '*Allo*', and '*Bonjour, madame!*' assailed her from all sides; a forest of hands shot out, all urgent to be shaken; small fry rushed off to fetch others to share the treat. It was all very harmless, no doubt, nothing but high spirits; but the turmoil, the numbers, the uproar were all unnerving: it was like being obliged to pass through a human explosion. But this was only the beginning. Once out of the shelter of their own street and threading the complex maze with purse and basket, she became at once an even more vulnerable target. No disguise was possible; she was seen by every eye for what she was—a stranger, a castaway, legitimate prey, a tourist whose very existence spelt possible profit. The boys were bigger here and knew their business. '*Allo, Engleesh!*' they cried, and 'This way Kasbah!' running beside her, trying to deflect her from her route (so painfully learned, so very easily lost), fighting to carry her basket, to guide her to a shop, and all at the top of their voices, crowding and pushing with a vehemence and persistence quite unmanageable. It was outside Phoebe's comprehension how these demon children, who seemed totally beyond control and whom she had come to regard with something very like hatred, could ever grow into the dignified Arabs who passed her closely by with such decorum. Veiled women, bulky in thin white wrappings or elegantly all but invisible in dark djellábahs, slipped by with scarcely more than a curious glance. Beautiful old men, bearded and reverend, with robe and stick like so many prophets and apostles, gave her not even that. She could have blessed them. But boys and even young men were a different matter: in jeans

55

and singlets, with mocking stare and grins which were surely impertinent, they stampeded roughly past without pause or ceremony.

She was obsessed by a haunting fear of losing her way. She had learned her route to the market by trial and error; each time she missed a turning or paused to consider the boys she dreaded were about her at once like hornets, clamouring and pushing. Once, turning the corner of some nameless gully, indistinguishable from the rest as any of the winding passages of a formicarium, she found herself walking into a quiet cul-de-sac, where a blind man crouched on a doorstep and little girls were intent on a game of hopscotch. It all looked anciently peaceful, but she had missed her way. She stood still, frowning with concentration. And in a flash, as though by radar, the hornets had found her. First one, then two, then several running boys appeared, and before she had gathered her wits there were at least a dozen, all shouting and jostling and pointing in different directions. The dreaded word 'Kasbah!' as usual the burden of their theme, with cries of '*Allo!* This way closed! Spik Engleesh? Parles Français? Deutsch?' they surrounded and physically swept her back to the corner. Here the din and confusion increased as they whirled about her, so that her courage failed completely and she began to tremble.

'It doesn't *matter*,' Lytton had more than once insisted, when she had sometimes bemoaned the hazards of finding her way. 'Just keep walking steadily, you'll soon find it. And if they think you know where you're going they'll leave you alone.' But this time she had lost her head, and they all knew it. She set off at random down a blind alley, was checked as before, surrounded, felt herself jostled. A hand was laid on her arm, another on her basket. It was almost as though they intended to carry her off bodily, a flustered captive held to petty ransom. A spasm of rage went through her; her face flushed. 'No!' she cried with fury, 'go away!' She raised her empty basket and waved her arms. But at this, as though seeing her frightened provided additional stimulus, their frenzy increased. They danced shrieking and laughing in front of her, uttering shrill cries, so that at last, with the despair of the hunted, she dived in panic into an open doorway.

As ill-luck would have it this was the entrance to a mosque. Through a fretted screen she saw a man at his ablutions, and beyond, squatting or kneeling on the matted floor, motionless figures at prayer in the quiet interior. She stopped, appalled; and as though the extremity of her anguish had conjured him from nothing, there was suddenly a grave and white-clad figure before her, one of those bearded patriarchs of the streets, austere and medieval, who struck his stick on the ground and uttered a command, at which the shrieking demons instantly melted, dissolved as it were into air by an exorcism. Without trying to thank him, beyond words, she turned and fled; and at once, at the next corner, there was the tailor's booth which was her landmark, the fruit-stall she knew, the women with charcoal and cheeses, the shop hung with blankets and kaftans which she passed each day, all the leisurely sounds and movement of a known area.

It had been a walking nightmare, and she was ashamed of it. What had happened to her, at sixty, that children should terrify her? What harm could they do? Lytton would laugh at her cowardice and he would be right. Alone in her room the recollection distressed her; she would make an effort to forget it. Other people were not intimidated; they came and went with classic calm; even tourists, trailing in droves and conspicuous in horror, hung about with the trophies of their calling. Lytton had been in the place no longer than she had and dawdled for hours by himself in the crowded *souks*, stopping when he chose, throwing up his head to scrutinise an arch or gateway, searching his pockets for tiny weightless coins suitable for beggars, impervious to importunity or impertinence. If only she could achieve his lofty calm! She knew she could not. With Tavy at her side it might be different. But at present, dreading the daily encounters and humiliations, she secretly suffered.

57

4

THE following morning began with a burst of activity. The carpenter arrived with an underling and was followed by the plumber. Both proceeded purposefully upstairs, where several new door-handles had fallen off and a cistern was jammed; the house soon rang with the blows and clangs of hammers. Mackannis, the dry little house-agent from whom Lytton had bought the property, appeared with plastic brief-case and went up to the top roof on a tour of inspection. He was reputed to be a Greek, though his name was a puzzle. Neat and meagre as a grasshopper, he had a finger in every pie and was full of resource. Lytton enjoyed his visits; he spoke excellent English and specialised in answering questions and solving problems.

Tavy slept late and did not appear at breakfast. This in a way was a relief, for the Arab woman who arrived each morning to clean, and whom Phoebe was learning to speak of as the *fátima*, was a sociable creature who enjoyed conversation and hand-shaking. Knowing no word of Spanish and alarmed by Arabic, Phoebe had been dreading the dumb-show of introduction.

Hadíjah arrived each morning swathed in white, cocooned from head to foot, only the eyes visible. Hands must be shaken all round and greetings exchanged; after which she removed her shoes and unwound herself, appearing at last as a lean and handsome grandmother. Communication was minimal, but she was energetic. Everything that she could be shown to do, she did, often with cries of surprise and spasms of laughter, to say nothing of a number of things which Phoebe could have dispensed with, but on which her mind was set. Thus, although it had been done each day since the parlour was settled, she took up the carpet entire and conveyed it to the roof, where she dragged it over the parapet and beat it with a stick. The aged covers were then removed from the chairs and subjected to the same treatment, and each moveable article of furniture dragged out into the patio, where it got in the way of the workmen and was a hazard. The purpose of this upheaval was to wash the floor, which she did not on hands and knees as one might have expected, but proceeding slowly backwards, doubled like a hairpin, swinging a sodden cloth across the tiles with a practised agility which was certainly enviable. Phoebe could no more have bent herself into that croquet-hoop than she could have levitated; still less have receded, without once straightening herself, through the entire length of the parlour and across the patio. Even the mason's labourer and his donkey did not dismay Hadíjah; as soon as they appeared she rhythmically swept and washed their boundaries like a tide, drowning their causeway to the door, reducing their rubble continent to an island, a force of nature indifferent to man's convenience.

All things considered, she was a comfort. Once the house was finished, once everything was in order, the donkey seen no more and the last workman banished, a routine, Phoebe hoped, would be established. Hadíjah did not cook, and was not required to; she could do, and did, a number of things of which Phoebe was incapable, and which proved essential to the comfortable running of the household. The bed-linen, for example, whole armfuls of it, she carried up to the roof and washed in a cauldron, scrubbing and slapping on a wooden board until half the terrace was awash, the lines cracking and billowing with wet linen. She ironed it all, moreover, the following day, a task which Phoebe, brought up on laundries, would have thought impossible. Padding backwards and forwards in the tiled kitchen, bare feet making no sound, she shook and folded and thumped with her heavy iron and hung it all to air in improbable places. Though apparently middle-aged—or was she? one couldn't tell—she was astonishingly strong. She shouldered not only carpets but even mattresses, and would often be met in narrow doorways, wedged with some bulky object on her way to the roof. 'It *can't* be good for her,' Phoebe protested, but Lytton was enchanted. 'Let her alone, she knows her business. These are a fanatically

59

clean people. They believe in the sun, my dear, they know its worth. An hour on the roof does more than your vacuum cleaner.' So Phoebe let well alone and continued to marvel, stepping warily about over acres of washed tiles, cautiously ascending stairs which dripped and glistened, groping across the terrace through groves of sheets. The woman had her own routine and was not to be deflected. As Lytton said, one must accept such alien benefits as came one's way, and as far as Hadíjah went Phoebe agreed with him.

She could have wished, however, that on this particular morning the roof had not been full of Lytton's underwear. The mid-morning coffee had barely been cleared away and the carpenter's shavings swept into a corner when Gerald and Quattrell appeared, heralded by knocker blows within a moment of one another.

'We call on you like a deputation,' said Gerald, stooping his head in the doorway. 'We met only yesterday, and here we are, arriving like old friends. I hope we don't interrupt the morning's work?'

'It isn't begun,' said Lytton, delighted, cracking his fingers. 'The working routine's not established yet, I fear. I'm embroiled, as you see, in domestic reorganisation.' There was not much evidence of this, the last hour having been spent in drinking coffee and setting up a portable record-player in the parlour.

'My mission,' said Gerald, 'is to apologise, abjectly, for having abandoned Miss Townsend and her niece so abruptly yesterday. The narrow street unnerved me, and when I'd backed myself out of it they were gone. It must have seemed extraordinarily rude.'

'Not at all, my dear fellow. They were very grateful.' Lytton's eyes were fixed interrogatively on Quattrell. 'I'm delighted to see you both.' He held out a hand.

'Quattrell's my name. Have you got any rule against strangers? I heard you were here, and decided to make contact. I'm a great fan of yours, I need hardly say. I hope you'll allow that to pass as an introduction.'

'Good heavens, how stupid of me.' Gerald looked mildly surprised. 'We arrived together at the same moment, I took it you knew one another.' It seemed no apology was needed. Lytton was shaking Quattrell warmly by the hand, his jaws working with pleasure.

'Well, that's excellent! Are you a neighbour? A fellow writer? Nothing could please me more.'

'Both, on a humble scale.' The heavy face lit up with a sudden smile. 'Not in your class, I fear, either as writer or householder. I've been lent a shack on the coast for a month or two. Nothing to compare with this, but it'll do.' He looked round the court-yard with interest. 'This is impressive, I must say. How did you find it?'

'Oh, through an agent fellow. He's somewhere about the place, or was just now. It's a freak of a house, you know, I bought it cheap. However, it has its points. The view's good. Come up on the terrace and look at it.'

'The roof's full of washing,' said Phoebe, speaking like an oracle from behind the shutter. She came out into the courtyard and looked up. Above the branches of the fig-tree, straining at their lines, sheets were cracking and bellying like sails. On wash-ing mornings the roof was more or less impassable.

'Never mind, we'll go up to the top.' Lytton was already shambling across the patio. 'It's really a remarkable view, I'd like you to see it. One gets a sense, which one can't do from the ground . . . layer upon layer, the gradual accretion of centuries . . .' His voice receded upwards as the others followed.

On the second roof, their heads emerging from canyons of sheets, they came upon Tavy. She was lying on a rug in shorts and a heavy sweater, and scrambled to her feet with an exclam-ation.

'Ha! Sunbathing,' said Lytton. 'Beware of the wind, my dear, it's not all that warm.' He turned with a wave of the hand to Gerald and Quattrell, slowly ascending the narrow steps behind him. 'You met our young niece yesterday, I think? Yes, yes, of course you did; you brought her home. Tavy, my dear, will you bring us an extra chair? That basket one below.' But Tavy, as soon as the steps were clear, had sidled past in silence and bolted down them. Lytton waited a moment and then went on.

'A nymph surprised and unwilling, an unusual combination. Well, well, never mind; there are some at the top.' He went on up the last few steps to the highest roof, where the two old wicker chairs from the Gloucestershire summer-house leaned drunkenly against the parapet.

'We startled your niece, I'm afraid,' said Gerald. 'We must have looked rather fearful, rising like apparitions out of the sheets.'

'Yes, well, it's an awkward age. She has no manners.' Lytton dismissed the subject and confronted the view, breathing deeply and squaring his shoulders, waiting for their comments.

'She looks a nice kid,' said Quattrell, sitting down on the edge of the parapet and staring at the swaying sheets through which Tavy had vanished. 'It's a serious business, you know being a teenager. They're expected to be unco-operative.'

'No doubt. We shall see.' Lytton was anxious to proceed. He shaded his eyes with his hand; the light was dazzling. 'Now you'll agree, I hope, that this prospect is really extraordinary? One can see the coast of Spain on a clear day, but that isn't what interests me. It's this, *this* . . .' He outlined the scene below with a sweep of the hand. 'Isn't it staggering? The light, the shadow, the planes, the geometric complexity? Can you see that outcrop of wall, on the left hand? It takes some time, of course, to accustom the eye. That's a part, I believe, of the Portuguese fortifications. This house is built on a buttress, and also on rock. If one could take a section, what layer upon layer of history would be uncovered! What hidden testimonies! What deposits of human experience!'

'I certainly see why you chose to live here,' said Gerald, gingerly drawing to the edge and looking down. He had a poor head for heights. 'The interest must far outweigh the inconvenience.' He felt in his pocket for spectacles and put them on. 'What is the thing I see moving on that lower roof? The one with the broken door. Could it be a sheep?'

'Certainly it is,' cried Lytton, delighted. 'In less than a week we shall have the Feast of the Lamb. I am looking forward to it. Every family slaughtering its own beast. Listen, you can hear bleating; the town's full of them.' He held up an admonitory hand, and indeed, in the far-off diffused din of a fine mid-morning the cries of sheep and perhaps of goats could be heard, now near, now far, mingled with the crowing of cocks and the hum of voices.

'You're not squeamish then,' said Quattrell. 'The streets'll be running with blood. I remember it in Egypt.'

'My dear man, I'm passionately interested. Life and death are still real in this ancient place. I can't bear to miss any of it.'

'Right. I'm not criticising you, I feel the same. But not everybody shares that view.' He glanced at Gerald, who had removed his spectacles and was sitting down, apparently content to take the scene from a distance.

'If you ever find yourself in my situation,' said Lytton soberly, lowering himself into a chair, 'and I hope you never will . . . I have cancer, I ought to explain, they give me twelve months . . . you'll find that it alters your response to the smallest experience. Things which were trivial before, become significant. One comes to everything, even one's breakfast, as though it were unique. Unique, and at the same time universal. As Dr. Johnson said, it concentrates a man's mind wonderfully.' There was a constrained pause; Quattrell eased it by comfortably hugging one knee, apparently considering.

'To a writer this must appear as a specific challenge. From your work I would expect you to take it as precisely that.'

'You are absolutely right.' Lytton bowed his head in grave acknowledgement. 'I am not yet sure what form it ought to take. I am still at the planning stage, arranging my notes. A journal, possibly; a day-to-day record of reflection and experience. I can see it in my mind's eye. A summing-up in a sense; something final. I think it will probably be that.'

'It's certainly the sort of thing you do supremely well. I particularly liked that fragment of autobiography—what was it called?—about childhood and youth in the country.'

'Ah, *Fosbury Beacon*. I'm fond of that myself. A self-indulgent book to have written perhaps, but it seems to have been liked. Still in print, by the way. I still get occasional letters from people who found it stimulating.'

Gerald, who remembered the book and had thought it over-written, a poetical-imaginative chronicle which he suspected Lytton had made up as he went along, creaked anxiously in his chair. It was becoming necessary to say something.

'You've never continued the theme,' he said. 'The later years, surely, would have been just as interesting?'

'In a sense, that is my task now. My life has been unusually rich. What I lack is time. And every day there is something new, fresh layers of experience added. Others, as one looks back, gradually uncovered. The difficulty is to keep a just perspective. One must see it whole.'

'You're right,' said Quattrell. 'And you won't find it easy to work here, I imagine.'

'Why not? I have everything I need.'

'The social life, for one.' He struck a match on the wall and began to smoke. 'Too many trivial temptations. This is a bizarre place, as of course you know. Not to say *louche*.'

'I have nothing to do with that,' said Lytton with dignity. 'Would you mind not throwing your matches over the wall? There's quite a code to be observed about other people's roofs.'

'Sorry.' Quattrell looked down from the parapet with sudden interest; there seemed to be something below which had caught his attention. 'Well, we don't have to hang around the bars, though most of us do. Or go in for cocktail life, or luncheon parties. There's quite a choice, however, of other distractions.'

'I am not concerned with them,' said Lytton. 'The life of the English colony is not for me. I have other interests.'

'Such as?' Quattrell was still intent on something below. The sound of voices, followed by the heavy thud of a beaten carpet, made Lytton aware that he was watching a woman.

'My dear fellow, if you don't mind, don't sit on the wall like that and stare. It's rather *mal vu*.'

'Sorry,' said Quattrell again, and came off the parapet. He slid down easily to the floor and sat with his back against the wall, his knees up. From the other side of the roof, from the hidden street, they heard the monotonous dirge of a beggar chanting.

'Now what is he saying?' said Lytton, raising a hand. '*That* is what interests me. The immemorial traditions of these people. The life of the streets. You may think me foolish, perhaps . . . at my age, in my predicament . . . but I spend my evenings struggling with the rudiments of Arabic.'

'Excellent idea,' said Gerald, 'but it's a long-term process, isn't it? I mean,' he checked himself, 'it's said to be very difficult.'

'And does it help you with the life of the streets?' said Quattrell, slyly amused. 'Of course it must. What d'you reply, for instance, when accosted?'

'One isn't accosted at my age.'

Quattrell caught Gerald's eye and all but winked.

'Oh no? That's something to look forward to, then. I'm propositioned every time I walk out in these streets at night, by both sexes. The ladies are the more discreet, being in the minority.'

'Oh, come now,' Lytton grimaced with enjoyment and scratched his beard. 'The boys are professional beggars. Or if not exactly that, hoping to sell something.'

'Sure they are. The commodity's not in doubt. I'm not in the market as it happens, but you come for a walk some night if you don't believe me.' His eye turned merrily to Gerald for confirmation, but Gerald was looking at the sky, which was full of swallows. They were sweeping and skimming the air at a great height, diving from time to time almost to the roof-tops, the rush of their wings in passage fleetingly audible.

'Well, of course.' Lytton assumed a worldly, knowing air. 'One isn't blind. The reputation of this place is fully deserved. There's a long tradition of tolerance, remember. Some cultures permit one variant, some another. I take a neutral position, a mere observer. One deplores, if anything, the almost total absence of discretion, but for that, alas, the fault is with ourselves rather than the Arabs.'

'You don't mind then,' said Quattrell, looking up attentively under his thick eyebrows, 'its being assumed, as it will be, that your settling here has to do with these cultural advantages?' He turned to throw his cigarette butt over the parapet, remembered it in time and crushed it under his shoe.

'Not the least bit in the world, my dear man. My life is an open book. I am not quite unknown. If I possess such a thing as a private reputation, which I doubt, apart from a hypothetical literary one, that reputation is founded on a unique marriage. That has been the great thing in my life, as everyone knows. If it had not been for Sarah,' he lifted his eyes, as though searching from force of habit for the wax image, 'I might well have been an indiscriminate lover of women. As things fell out, however, I have been more fortunate. A wide experience is rarely the most intense.' He rubbed his beard and frowned: there was another pause.

'You may be right. I wouldn't know.' Quattrell took a frayed cigarette from his shirt pocket. 'In your case, I suppose, well obviously, yes. One can't generalise . I'm not myself an advertisement for marriage.'

'Few people are,' said Gerald, still watching the swallows. 'The remarkable thing perhaps, is that it sometimes works.' The rush of wings overhead was almost startling as a flock of pigeons exploded into the sunlight.

'You've been married, however, I take it.' Lytton's voice expressed a polite, perfunctory interest. He looked inquiringly at Quattrell.

'Still am, technically. The whole thing's a bit of a mess. I'm glad to get out of it for a while, if you want to know. These things have a way of settling themselves, given time.' He seemed quite cheerful about it, leaning his head against the wall and looking from Lytton to Gerald with a glint of amusement.

'Ah well, one mustn't probe.' Clearly Lytton had no intention of doing so. 'The thing I miss, I confess, is the shared experience. Phoebe, my sister-in-law, such a dear good soul . . . but how two such different women could ever have been born sisters . . .' He lifted a long hand and eloquently dropped it. 'Whereas Sarah . . . I must show you some of her work, also the remarkable portrait mask in the parlour. Though the eyes, naturally, are closed, it has a quality . . . Such passionate response to life, she would have loved all this.' He lifted his hand again with an expressive gesture. 'That's what I regret so much, being unable to share it. I compensate, you know, as well as I can, but her presence here would have given the whole thing meaning.' There was, except for the swallows, a melancholy little silence, Quattrell smoking with his eyes closed and Gerald stealthily tilting his hat forward. The brim was extremely small, the sun hot; his face, already pink, was beginning to worry him.

'After twenty years of companionship,' Lytton went on, 'it's not easy to adjust. However, I have my plan. I've cast off my old life and embarked on a new one. The only point is to make this latter end memorable.'

He paused for encouragement, but as neither of the others spoke pursued his theme.

'If I were a rich man, which I am not, I should like to make this house more than a mere working-place. I should like to make it a refuge for my friends.'

'You've done that already,' said Gerald, shifting his chair. 'We've begun to frequent it.' The breeze was freshening; he thought with longing of the fig-tree and the shaded patio.

'Ah yes, an auspicious beginning. But I mean something different. I was thinking of people less fortunate than yourselves. Well, Tavy's a start in a way, though she's really Phoebe's. My theory, you see, is that a situation like mine . . . after all I am not penniless . . . imposes, humanly speaking, an obligation. And this place, at least this is how I see it, has a certain quality. Put it like this: it has therapeutic properties. It has already done something for me. I begin to feel spiritually well. I am groping, shall we say, for a technique of extending the experience.'

'How unfortunate does one have to get?' said Quattrell, opening one eye. 'Don't I qualify? I could give you a list of disasters if you want them.'

'Possibly, possibly.' Lytton gave him an oblique glance. 'I would say you were very well able to take care of yourself. You don't, I must positively say, make a helpless impression.'

'Oh, if it's helpless candidates you want,' said Quattrell, blowing down a stream of smoke from his large nostrils, 'I'd say this town could provide them as well as another.'

'Quite. There's a great deal of poverty. But I wasn't actually thinking of organised charity.'

'Me neither. I was thinking of someone I met last night in a bar. What she was doing there I couldn't quite figure, certainly not drinking; just propping the bar with a rather prissy young gentleman.' His eyes searched Lytton's face. 'D'you remember the story of a yacht which was lost somewhere hereabouts, maybe two years ago? The husband, a top barrister, was drowned; most of the party as well, if I remember. I'd say she was just up your street. Poor lady gone round the bend after a front-page disaster.'

Gerald creaked forward, his hands on the arms of his chair.

'Do you know, I'm most awfully sorry, I can't stand much more of this sun. I have one of those unfortunate skins, I shall be scarlet tomorrow.'

'My dear man, of course. We'll descend to the parlour for a drink.' They stood up and moved to the stairway, where Hadíjah came suddenly in view, dragging a shallow basket and unpegging the sheets. Lytton's nightshirt and pants had discreetly disappeared. 'You mean Molly Brockhurst, I take it. Ah yes, I know her. A very sweet woman, poor thing; I remember the whole thing too well. One doesn't get over a tragedy like that in a hurry. But you're rather astray in your judgment; she's perfectly rational.' He fumbled his way between the sheets, pausing to fend off an aggressive pillow-case. 'A bit neurasthenic, perhaps. But people are kind to her; here she'll eventually recover. She's made quite a nice little life one way and another. I must make a point of inviting her to our house-warming. You'll both come too, I hope? So glad you reminded me.'

They came down the inner stair to the cool house, groping through patches of darkness, blind from the dazzle. Mackannis and his men had disappeared, leaving a wrack of débris to mark their passage. Tavy's door was shut and Phoebe was peacefully laying the table in the kitchen.

'I won't stay for a drink this time, thank you so much.' Gerald had removed his hat and was fingering his brow. 'Anthea's expecting me for lunch, I'd better not be late.'

'Another time, perhaps.' Lytton concealed relief. 'Though we have some whisky somewhere, depend upon it.' He looked about him vaguely, cracking his fingers, as though on the chance of surprising a bottle in the patio.

'No, really. It's been delightful. You must let me bring Anthea soon to see your house. She has quite an eye for these things, she would appreciate it.'

'Well, since you positively won't . . .' He avoided Quattrell's eye. 'We must fix a date for our gathering. Not a crowd, of course; I prefer impromptu occasions. But I want to make sure of you both: can we say Sunday week? That'll give us a chance to be rid of these barbarous workmen.' He tripped over a pile of shavings and recovered. 'Phoebe, my dear, our guests are leaving. Are we not going to have a glimpse of you?'

She appeared from the kitchen and they went through the usual civilities.

'You must return our call,' said Quattrell, clasping her hand so powerfully that she winced. 'Bring that niece of yours to my sea-house, we'll have a picnic.'

'Oh, that would be delightful. But isn't it a long way off? We have no car.'

'That's no problem. I have a battered wreck on wheels, it goes with the house. I'll come and fetch you.'

'That would be lovely. We've been cooped up here for weeks. I long for the country.'

'Not *cooped*, my dear, surely?' said Lytton. 'You should go out more.' He opened the heavy door and looked out into the street. There was a delicious smell of new-baked bread, and as usual from the opposite doorstep, almost within touching distance, a trio of very small children looked up from their concerns, agog for the least crumb of entertainment. They had been patiently teasing a cockroach in an old sardine-tin, a large and active specimen, offering excellent sport. As they stared open-mouthed it intelligently made the most of the opportunity, clambering out of the tin and strolling back into the house, as though glad to go home and get on with its ordinary business.

'On no account,' said Lytton, shuffling after his guests on loose slippers, 'omit to look in at the bakehouse a few doors down. Just pause and take it in. It's really extraordinary. A scene straight out of Chaucer.'

'We'll do that very thing,' said Quattrell. Presently he said, when they had traced the delicious baking smell to its source, an earth-floored cavern where trays of loaves were emerging from a brick oven, 'Well, what d'you make of it all? I'm sorry you said no to that drink. I could have done with it.'

'I thought we'd stayed long enough.'

'You think so? Our friend showed no sign of running down, I noticed. He certainly hates himself, h'm? What d'you make of the set-up? Have you known him long?'

'A number of years. Not well. He's an unusual man. I don't much care for his work, but he has a following.'

'Isn't it mysterious? I'm not keen on that sensitive childhood-in-Puddlecombe stuff. I wonder how it sells.'

'I gathered from what you said that you were an admirer.'

'Oh, one can't say what one really thinks to writers. Why should he take criticism from me? He's found a saleable line and he's sticking to it.'

They passed into the gloom of the tunnel, where earthen crocks of charcoal flickered on doorsteps, set out in the draught to kindle for the midday meal. There was a smell of frying oil, a whiff of fennel. At the bottom of the street, at the steps, they were hailed with glee and surrounded by a swarm of children.

'I can see the aesthetic attractions of the Arab town,' said Gerald, raising his voice above the clamour, 'but living in it, I should think, is an abrasive experience. I should dislike the noise, the smells, these hellish brats. What surprises me is the way Lytton seems to thrive on it.'

'It's not for the thin-skinned,' said Quattrell, pausing to light a cigarette and making a feint of throwing the match at the shaven ring-wormed head of the boy beside him. The child ducked and grimaced, and Quattrell made a sudden pounce and caught him by the shoulder, giving him a playful shove and a word of Arabic. The group followed a little further, skirmishing and shrieking, and at the next corner melted suddenly away, as though observing some known law of tribal territory. Another turn brought them to a wider passage, between shops little bigger than closets. Here women like bundles of washing crouched on the paving, presiding over neat arrangements of bread and vegetables.

'There's quite a story there, though,' said Quattrell, pursuing his own thoughts. 'I wonder if Lytton's made use of it? Publicity-wise, that is.'

'I'm not sure I follow you.'

'Well, it's a gift, isn't it? Writer with twelve months to live, packs up and settles in Morocco, writing his last journal and all that, dreaming up these schemes about his friends. I'd say it was a natural.'

'He may not want publicity, however. He strikes me as the kind of man who might dislike it.'

'I've yet to meet a writer who did. He'll need it for his next book. I could probably help him there; I should have asked him.'

'Perhaps, if you think he'd be interested. Are you connected with publicity?' The question was over-casual; it sounded wary.

'Lord, no. I occasionally wring an honest penny out of the newspapers.'

'Ah yes, I remember. But I still think, if I may say so, that Lytton's a man who likes to be left alone.'

'Could be. I wouldn't know. None of it's true, of course.'

'What makes you say that?'

'Just a feeling. The whole thing struck me as sententious. Makes it up as he goes along, I shouldn't wonder. Let's cut through here.'

Quattrell made a sudden dive to the right, into a passage so close that they were obliged to thread its length in single file. When they emerged it was into a busy street that Gerald remembered.

'You seem to know your way very well.' They were once more abreast, in a strolling crowd among clothing and camera shops, bazaars hung with rugs and brassware, jewellery stalls, all crammed with meretricious merchandise.

'I remember this town pretty well, I've been here before.'

'Very easy to lose one's way, I find. I do so constantly.'

71

'The thing is to walk at night, when there isn't such a mob. One can take it slowly then and concentrate. It's not without interest.'

The street abruptly widened into a small square, dominated by a singularly bleak and unattractive café which Gerald had seen before and decided to avoid, not caring for the looks of the bearded disciples, most of them long-haired and all elaborately unkempt, who usually frequented it. They occupied the pavement tables at all hours, watchful and silent, as though there were a biblical epic being filmed in the neighbourhood, and they were out-of-work extras.

'Care for that drink now?' said Quattrell, coming to a standstill.

'I don't think I will, if you don't mind. I must keep an eye on the time, I'm already late.'

'Not even a quick snort? To see the freaks?'

'Another time. I've really got to get back.'

'Pity. This place can be boring, you know, if one doesn't experiment.'

'Forgive me. I think I told you before, I'm lunching with Anthea.'

'Ah well, give her my love. Persuade her to come on that picnic.'

'I will, yes. Perhaps you'd better ask her yourself.'

'I might, at that.' Quattrell considered the idea. 'I don't know where you're staying, do I? What's the phone number?'

'Dear me, how stupid. I never can remember it myself.'

'Don't worry, I'll get it from Lytton.'

'Lytton doesn't know it, I'm afraid.'

'Well, well, we reach stalemate, don't we? Not to worry, however, I'll find it somehow. One can usually find what one wants here, if one takes the trouble. You must have found that?' He put his head on one side with a smile that was perfectly friendly, but at the same time provoking. 'You leave the whole thing to me. I wouldn't like you to worry.'

Gerald met his eye quite sharply, but the heavy face had resumed its lazy expression. The walk, Gerald noticed with distaste, had made him sweat. It was obvious he did not intend to pass that café.

'I'll try not to worry,' said Gerald drily, 'I think I can promise you that. Good-bye,' and walked off in the direction of the port from which he could find his way without further difficulty.

He was tempted to look back and did not, on an odd suspicion that he was being watched. He was therefore unaware that at a distance, hands in pockets and moving at a relaxed pace, Quattrell followed him all the way to the Rue Poincaré.

5

AT THE end of a week Phoebe persuaded Lytton to get in touch with the Parsons family and ask the younger boy to tea.

'We've positively got to do something. We don't know any young people at all and the child's bored. She spends half the day in her room and the rest of it on the roof, sprawling about in the hot sun and reading a lot of rubbish. I'm not making any headway.'

'You should take her out with you more. Explore the town a bit, go about together. You're being rather inadequate, my dear. Naturally she's bored.'

'That's all very well, but I haven't unlimited time. I take her to the market in the morning, which is a penance, and after that I've enough to see to in the kitchen, to say nothing of a thousand and one things to be done in the house. You must help me, Henry, really. If Tavy had some friends it would be easy. At fifteen she doesn't want to spend her time with a woman of my age. You must make an effort, I'm afraid, instead of just sitting there and saying I'm inadequate.'

So Lytton strolled down to Mackannis's office, which had not only a telephone but an English-speaking typist who found the number for him, and spoke to Mrs. Parsons in cultivated tones, explaining himself, his niece, the invitation. It was just as Tavy had said: the boys' father represented an engineering firm and travelled far and wide in the cause of refrigeration. His wife sounded pleased to have Nick asked out anywhere.

'He's not going to school this term, he had a touch of rheumatic fever when he was staying with his auntie in England and he's not quite strong yet. I should have gone with them really, but you know how it is, I've got my old mother with us now, I felt I couldn't leave her. Usually they're perfectly all right with my sister-in-law, she's marvellous with the older boy, he's handicapped you know, takes a lot of patience and understanding, I have my work cut out I can tell you. But this time Nick got this rheumatic fever and was in bed for a fortnight and I thought well, he won't miss much if he stays at home for a bit but I don't like him hanging around with the local boys, it'll do him good to have an outing.'

'Quite,' said Lytton, consulting his watch. 'I'll send a taxi tomorrow at four o'clock. The house isn't easy to find. I'll see he gets home all right.'

'Oh, he'll soon pick it up, don't worry, he knows his way about pretty well, after all we live here, I don't believe in coddling children, but perhaps after the rheumatic fever . . .'

So at a quarter past four the following day Lytton and Tavy walked down to the end of the tunnel and met the taxi, and there was Nick Parsons, looking smaller than Tavy remembered but still perfectly presentable, not bothered at all by the children who trailed behind them all the way to the door. One of the boys had a sheep in tow which had to be alternately pushed and pulled and which at one moment butted Lytton's legs in confusion, but Nick took this quite as a matter of course and ignored both boys and sheep with steady composure.

'There's an Arab family in our flats,' he told Tavy. 'They don't kill the sheep at home, they take it to the butcher.' He offered this information in a sociable manner, making conversation while the children pressed around them and Lytton searched for his key. 'They wouldn't be allowed to do it on the roof, you see. My father and the rest of the tenants would complain.'

Phoebe met them in the courtyard with an eager look which suggested that she had been looking forward to the occasion, which was true. By her standards it was the first really normal function the house had seen, and she had taken time and trouble over it. Brown bread and butter, a glass dish of apricot jam and another of wild honey, tomato sandwiches, a glistening flan from a Spanish *patisserie* and a plateful of almond cakes from the Arab baker had been set out on a wooden table under the fig-tree. The wind had dropped for once and the air was warm.

75

Hadíjah had left the courtyard as clean as a beach after a spring tide, carpenter and plumber alike had been driven from the scene. The place was beginning to look habitable.

'You're the only English people I know who live in the Medina,' said Nick, taking his place at the table. He looked smaller than ever sitting down, his legs being long in proportion to the rest of his body, which was short from shoulder to hip. He seemed neither shy nor awkward, in fact perfectly at his ease and quite prepared to be communicative.

'So you know this part,' said Phoebe encouragingly. 'You've been here before.'

'Oh yes. One of my father's clerks lives in a street between here and the Petit Socco. I've been to their house several times. Abd-es-salaam's got a son of sixteen and one of twelve and a little boy of seven.'

'What's the house like?' said Tavy. She rested her elbows on the table and her chin in her hand, raptly watching, as though there were something new and extraordinary about the way he helped himself to bread and butter.

'It's all right. Nothing special. Hamid, that's the big one, he's keen on electronics. He's got a shed on the roof with tools and all sorts of things. He's building his own radio.'

Phoebe considered this and glanced at Lytton.

'And your parents, they're quite happy, are they, for you to visit an Arab family?'

'My dear Phoebe, of course. What an extraordinary question.' Lytton signalled displeasure with his eyebrows and passed the sandwiches.

'Well, I don't go there often, but I do sometimes. My father's away a lot, you see, and my mother looks after Pete, so I go about mostly by myself. I like it, actually.'

'I should like it too,' said Tavy, staring at Nick and absently spreading honey over a sandwich. She seemed quite fascinated by the boy, and Phoebe noted this development with approval. He was young, to be sure, but this was a promising beginning. She had been right in thinking it bad for Tavy to be cooped up with old people.

'My brother's a defective, you see,' said Nick in a tranquil voice. 'He was like that as a baby, it wasn't anything that happened to him.'

'You saw him at the airport, remember?' Tavy's eyes flickered momentarily towards Phoebe. 'He was awful in the aeroplane, walloping about all the way. They didn't do anything to stop him.'

'Well, you can't really.' Nick's gaze, which had been wandering rather abstractedly over the table, focused on the glutinous pastry, already cut into triangles and well within reach. His hand rose and hovered over the plate, but he recollected himself in time and offered it first to Lytton. 'He's quite good actually. We don't have a lot of trouble. Of course he can't be left alone, that's the only snag. My mother gives him a sedative if he's naughty.'

'How sad . . .' Phoebe began, but Lytton cut her short.

'How wise. I can see your parents are very sensible people. We can't all be exactly alike, can we? And it's better to be at home than in a hospital. Here, I would say, a boy like your brother, mentally handicapped though you say he is, could have quite a happy life. There's none of that feeling of separateness. That's one of the life-giving things about an ancient culture, something we've lost. I see people every day in the streets here who in another country, in Russia say, or for that matter anywhere in Europe, would be made to drag out their lives in institutions. Here, as in the Middle Ages, the halt, the maimed and the blind are a part of life. The beggar is not despised, he has his profession. A place, even if humble and wretched, in the community. I don't know what they do about lepers here.' He put on his complex spectacles and looked at Nick. 'What are the figures, do you know? Is there any leprosy?'

'I couldn't say. Father might be able to tell you.'

'Do ask him, I should be interested. And holy fools, you know; your brother might possibly be considered in that category. In the past people didn't just put up with them, they were venerated. Even if they begged their bread in the streets they had a part to play.'

'A wretched one,' Phoebe put in quietly.

'It was more humane, in my view, than the modern system.'

He elaborated in this vein for some time while Nick got on with his tea in a well-behaved manner, occasionally glancing speculatively at Lytton.

'There's a man who eats glass here,' he said. 'I saw him one day. He'd taken off his shirt and was bleeding all over the place. The police were afraid of him, so were the ambulance men. In the end they had to get the fire brigade.'

'Gosh,' said Tavy, fascinated, 'what did they do?'

'They crept up behind him with a net when he wasn't looking. He was eating glass, real bloody bites, I saw him. He was so busy chewing and bleeding he didn't notice the net. So that was how they caught him.'

'Good gracious, how horrible,' said Phoebe, putting down her cup. 'I'm not sure that's quite a subject for the tea-table.'

'Oh yes, it is, Aunt Phoebe, let him go on!' Tavy put her hands to her cheeks and pressed them with excitement. Lytton, too, enthralled by this evidence of archaic modes of behaviour— a net! so primitive, so practical!—was rocking gently backwards and forwards in his chair, hardly waiting for a pause before resuming control of the conversation.

'And the crowd, Nick? Were there lots of people watching?'

'You bet. They were laughing their heads off. The police couldn't do anything.'

'You see?' Lytton cried. 'This is much more real, more healthy. We are all members one of another, and here it's *true*. How much better for that poor man, how much more satisfying, to work out his frenzy in a crowd, to the plaudits of the multitude! Relief, catharsis—good heavens, the ancients were right! Whereas nowadays, the clinical approach . . . but I won't go into that, it's too depressing. And the same thing, Nick, you'll find, applies to the criminal. Justice must be *seen* to be done or emotions are crippled; primitive, necessary emotions are left to curdle. It's an unfashionable view nowadays but I assure you there's something to be said for public executions.'

'Then I would prefer you not to say it,' said Phoebe, getting

78

up from the table. 'Have you quite finished your tea? What would you two young people like to do now? Go up on the terrace, perhaps, and look at the view? Or show Nick the house?"

'I'll show him my room,' said Tavy, beckoning to Nick with a movement of the head, anxious to be gone.

'No, no, the terrace first. He mustn't miss that.' Lytton laid a hand on the boy's shoulder and propelled him gently in the direction of the staircase. 'It's a remarkable view, Nick; no doubt you'll be able to confirm some of the landmarks. There's a mosque I haven't quite been able to identify. From the street, that is. Have you got a good sense of direction?'

'No, Henry, let them go alone.' It was Phoebe's turn to signal and cut him off. 'Let them do as they like for a bit, I'm sure they'd rather.' She handed Lytton the teapot and hot-water jug, which he took with abstracted docility like a sleep-walker, and with meaning glance drew him after her to the kitchen. When he returned from this forced errand Tavy and Nick had disappeared, presumably to the terrace. He looked up through the branches of the fig-tree, but there were no voices. He stood for a little while, going very slowly through the business of folding up his spectacles, polishing the lenses with a handkerchief and breathing on them; but nothing happened; the house was unusually quiet. Presently Phoebe heard the drag of his slippers and looking through the shutter saw that he had given up and retired to the parlour.

*

'This door hasn't got a lock,' said Tavy, 'but there's a bolt. It was stiff at first, I oiled it with a piece of soap.' She slid the bolt to and fro and then Nick tried it.

'Good idea. I wouldn't have thought of that.' He looked round the room with interest. 'Where does the stair go to?'

'That's what I'm going to show you. That's my private place, nobody goes there but me. It's got a bolt too. Be careful, don't make a noise.'

79

She went up the stair with exaggerated caution and Nick followed, creeping close at her heels through the low doorway. It was impossible to stand upright when they were once inside, but it occurred to neither that this was an inconvenience. The luggage and boxes had been rearranged so that they could be sat upon, and the little sweet-smelling loft seemed quite spacious.

'Look,' said Tavy, kneeling on a leather trunk that belonged to Lytton. She opened the tiny window and looked out. The old man was there on the lower roof as usual, sitting on a sack, mending a broken shoe with needle and thread. He was wearing a very old faded stay-at-home sort of garment with a piece of towelling round his head as a turban. In a corner beside him, in the shade, was a heap of greenstuff; it might have been grass or clover.

'I can't see,' said Nick in a whisper. Tavy gave way an inch, hunching her shoulder. They watched for a space in silence, their heads together.

'They've got their sheep already,' said Nick, speaking close to her ear.

'How d'you know?'

'That's its fodder, in the corner. They've nearly all got them by now.'

'I haven't seen it.'

'I expect they keep it downstairs. Don't you ever hear it?'

'I hear bleating quite a lot in the morning sometimes. I can hear one now, I think, but it's a long way off.'

They listened, and sure enough among the many remote but identifiable noises of the late afternoon they could hear the cries of sheep, though there were none to be seen.

'Is it true what Uncle Henry said, that they kill them on the roofs?'

'Yes. It happens tomorrow or the day after, I think; I'm not sure. You'll get a good view from here.'

'Oh, I shan't watch,' said Tavy off-handedly, drawing back from the window. Almost immediately afterwards in the same tone she said, 'How d'you know when they're actually going to do it?'

'It starts quite early in the morning. They fire a gun, a big one, you know, a cannon, and then everybody cuts their sheep's throat and hangs it up to bleed. There's masses and masses of blood, they have to wash it down with buckets.'

Tavy thought about this for a while, repelled and at the same time fascinated, her eyes returning to the old man at his cobbling, thinking how different and how terrible it would be when the roof ran with blood. With one part of her mind she made a resolve that she would certainly not watch it, and at the same time was aware of a furtive something which had stored up the probable date and time of day, and that other clue, the firing of the cannon, which Nick had mentioned. She would not watch it, of course; she was quite positive. But there was still this sensation of trembling in the pit of the stomach, and each time her thoughts returned to it the trembling increased, so that she knew and admitted to herself that she was excited.

Presently she said, remembering that her room had other advantages and that the loft with its spy-hole was not the only one, 'There's an empty house next door. Would you like to look at it?'

'You mean we can go in?'

'No, but you can see the roof and into one of the doors and a bit of the stairs.'

'Come on, then. Let's go.'

They drew back stiffly from their kneeling position, taking a last look at the old man before Tavy surreptitiously closed the window. He seemed to have finished with his shoe repairs and had taken off his djellábah, sitting in a clean and modest white undergarment rather like a pinafore while he examined the seams of the woollen robe, holding them close to his nose and with horny thumbnail raking the likely places.

'I keep this one shut most of the time,' said Tavy, when they had come down again to the level of the casement window, 'because when the sun's on this side, like now, there's rather a smell.' She opened the window and they both leaned out; the embrasure was very deep. This wall of the house was even thicker than the rest and the window not easy to see out of because of the grille, which spread stout rusty arabesques from side to side and from top to bottom of the aperture. There was just room, if one stepped on a chair, to perch on the sill and take hold of the flaking ironwork; from here there was a view of the far side of the roof, the broken panes of glass and derelict stairs, but most of the near side remained invisible. The level of the roof was about five feet lower than the floor of Tavy's room.

'Can you smell it?' said Tavy. 'Stand on the chair, you can see further.'

Nick did so and knelt in the window, his face pressed to the grille.

'Pooh, what a stink.'

It was not in fact very bad, for the wind which had dropped so pleasantly during the afternoon was beginning to rise again, sending dust across the roof in little flurries and shaking the tuft of weed growing out from the door. The air was fairly fresh and smelt of the sea. All the same there was an undercurrent, a warm rank sweetish disturbing odour which Nick found readily enough and sniffed critically.

'It's something dead,' he said. 'I know that smell all right. Probably a cat.'

He leaned hard against the ironwork, holding the bars with both hands, squinting down.

'I often see cats,' said Tavy. 'They're always about down there, I often watch them.' The cats of the neighbourhood, a lean wild population which hunted the roofs at night and lay out in sunny corners during the day, stretched on disintegrating rags or fragments of old wood or any dry surface where they could warm their fur and watch the swallows, were one of Tavy's unfailing private interests. They were an unattractive breed, threadbare and spiky, bearing little resemblance to the cats she had known before. There was only one she had seen that had anything to recommend it, a thin-flanked creature the colour of coffee-grounds, which had once scaled the broken wall carrying a kitten, holding the inert mouthful like a dead rat or some gobbet it had found in the street and would devour at leisure. But the prize as Tavy watched had proved to be its own, and the two had settled down in a corner of the roof for a quiet domestic interlude of washing and sucking. They reminded her of something she had once seen years before, in that other life before her mother had gone away, when her parents, reconciled after one of their inexplicable quarrels, had taken her with them on a ten days' visit to Paris. Tavy remembered little of this uncomfortable holiday, when they had gone about in sight-seeing buses and spent many weary hours in museums and galleries; but there had been one place, it might have been the Louvre, where she had found herself staring into a glass case, and the shelves of the case had been filled with the figures of cats. These too had been lean and spare, made of bronze or stone, and had gazed from their pedestals with an air of ineffable remoteness and tranquillity. They had been Egyptian, her father had told her, and very ancient, and the one she remembered best had been lying very much at her ease, suckling her litter, thin flanks relaxed in a shallow curve and small head erect, an image of feline serenity preserved for ever. This was the one, the perfect one, of which the wild self-sufficient roof-cats dimly reminded her. *La déesse chatte* the label had said, and this too she remembered; it encouraged a belief she had long held that cats, unlike other creatures, were somewhat magical.

'I can't see anything,' said Nick, shifting his weight with a jerk and disturbing her trance. She stirred and took hold of his leg with quick impatience.

'I know, I've often tried. Come down, let me have a go.' But Nick stayed wedged in the window, exploring the grille.

'This bit's loose, did you know? It's rusted through at the top, I think I can move it.'

'It can't be. Where? Come down, let me have a look.'

'Here, at the top. If I push it out, like that, it comes loose at the bottom.' He worked away with both hands, pushing and scraping. 'It *does*,' he said at last, on a note of triumph. 'Leave me alone, will you? I bet I can move it.'

It was perfectly true. The grille was made in two parts, and the topmost spike of the right-hand section was rotten, no more than precariously in touch with the crumbling plaster. As Tavy watched he pressed his whole weight outward, tugging the thing from its base, and after some hard breathing leaned back with a section of ironwork clear in his hands.

'Take it,' he said, 'it's heavy.'

He handed it down to Tavy and hung out at a reckless angle from the window.

'Oh, *please* come down!' She looked round in an agony of impatience, and finally dropped the piece of iron on the bed. Since Nick did not move, or only shifted to project himself still further, she stood on the seat of the chair and pinched him sharply.

'It's a cat all right,' said Nick, resisting her. 'Been dead some time, I should say. Looks like a tom.' He withdrew his head reluctantly and Tavy scrambled on to the sill beside him. Her pushing and his sense of justice finally prevailed, so that for the first time she was able to lean out from her own window.

What she saw was nothing extraordinary; the first glance was disappointing. A drop to the roof below, some fallen plaster, a brick and the remains of a basket were all that up to now had been hidden from view. But to the right, in the angle of the wall, there was indeed a cat, a cat flattened and beaten upon by wind and rain, its fur no longer fur, its teeth exposed, sharp like the teeth of a fish, its ribs gaping.

'Oh gosh,' said Tavy, 'oh gosh.' Now she could really smell it, the full warm charnel breath rising from below, an odour so richly rotten that she sickened at it. She came down abruptly from the window and sat on the bed, beads of sweat breaking out on her upper lip. 'What'll we do? It's nauseating.'

'Tell your aunt, I suppose. Someone could go down and shovel it up.' He climbed to the window again and leaned out. 'I could go down if you like,' he said over his shoulder. 'If I had a rope or something. It's not far.'

'No, no, I don't want them in here.' She picked up the piece of grille and thrust it at him. 'Put it back, Nick. I'd rather they didn't know.'

'All right. What about the smell? It'll only get worse.'

'That's not the point, stupid, I meant the window. Put it

84

back, Nick, *please*, like it was before.' She pushed him quite hard with the end of it. 'There'll only be a fuss if they know, and they'll have it mended. Let's not tell anyone at all, let's keep it to ourselves. We could go down there some time, we could explore the house.'

'That's not a bad idea.' Nick took the grille in both hands and set to work, fitting the bottom spike into its socket and tilting the whole thing upwards to the old position. It fitted quite well enough, the points of the ironwork resting in worn grooves. No-one could tell without shaking it that it had ever been disturbed.

He came down and sat on the bed. They stared at one another.

'I'm not going down there alone,' said Tavy. 'You must come back another day.'

'All right. Any time you like. Won't they suspect something?'

'Why should they? We'll bolt the door. I can say we're doing things in the loft. I stay here for hours and hours by myself with the door bolted.' They were both beginning to feel a little light-headed, gazing at one another as it all sank in.

'That's an idea. I could come tomorrow if you like. Or any day in fact; I'm not busy.' He spoke in a coolly practical voice, as though used to dealing with just this sort of emergency. 'I dare say we'll need a rope.'

'There's a piece of rope in the loft, on one of the trunks. It's not much of a drop, is it? It'll probably do.'

Speaking in low voices and without haste they made their plans, like old campaigners who perfectly understood one another. Finally they went up to the roof top, calling out cheerfully to Phoebe as they did so, and admired the view, working their way round gradually to the point where Hadíjah's washing-line ended and the derelict roof could be seen if one leaned over. There in the corner, perfectly obvious if one had known where to look, was the horrid grotesque oblong of sodden fur, a target for all the bluebottles in the neighbourhood. They came down the steps again in a series of leaps.

'Aunt Phoebe, there's a cat on the roof next door, a dead one. That's what's making that funny smell. Come and look!'

The announcement was met with gratifying consternation. Both Phoebe and Lytton went up on the roof to inspect.

'Oh dear, how very tiresome! What on earth can we do, Henry? I must say I'm glad it's been discovered, that smell was really getting bad.'

'I'll get Mackannis in the morning. He'll send a man down, or up, whichever is the easier.'

'It's a terribly long way down from here. Would he have a long enough ladder? What a pity he can't get out through Tavy's room! If it weren't for the grille it would be simple.'

'Oh, it's not worth taking out grilles and making an operation of it. He might get permission to come up through that empty house, if he knows whose it is.'

But Mackannis when he came measured the distance with his eye and decided that a ladder from the top roof was the simplest method.

'It is of course possible,' he said, rubbing a dry hand over his grasshopper face, 'to get in touch with the owner, but these things take time. The entrance to that house I know—two or three streets below this, the distance would surprise you. And always these falling-down places have several owners, brothers and uncles and cousins of the same family. All would have to be consulted before I am allowed the key. I am able to do this naturally, but it will be tedious. I recommend we have here a man with a long ladder, and he goes down from the top with a basket and disposes of the trouble.'

So the following day this was done, critically observed from the roof by Lytton and Tavy. The old man with the donkey arrived with some sand and a spade, as though summoned for a burial. A sectional ladder had been found and precariously lashed, and the old man, groaning at the personal hazard and the responsibility, removed his djellábah and shoes and went down barefoot, the basket and spade being lowered on a rope after him. He inspected the cat carefully and covered it with sand, scraping it over the body and making a tidy shape like a child's sand castle. He seemed to think that this was all that was required, for he began to climb back up the ladder, muttering and groaning.

'Put it in the basket, you fool,' called Lytton, leaning out from the parapet. '*Le panier, la canasta,* idiot!' He racked his brains for the Arabic. '*El khetta,*' he tentatively shouted, '*el Khetta* you fool, *el koffah!*'

Slowly the old man went down again, rung by rung, and the carcase was laboriously basketed and hauled to the roof, bumping the wall as it came and occasionally swinging perilously under the ladder. From the roof it was carried below and dropped in an empty pannier on the back of the donkey.

'Well, *that's* a blessing,' said Phoebe, when the old man was paid and gone, followed by a string of children in ribald procession. 'I'm very much relieved. You must open your window, Tavy, the room will be nice and fresh now. I'm sure you'll sleep better.'

It was hardly, perhaps, an ideal night for sleeping, for this was the eve of the feast and the town was noisy; alive in a peculiar way, as though the very walls conducted currents of excitement. Tavy went to bed early to brood on the possibilities of Nick's discovery, but when she bolted her door and stood at the window she was uneasy at the sound of bleating from every quarter, a diffused clamour which might almost have been the prelude to a country market. There was also a sound, quite near, of religious chanting, as though one of the neighbouring houses were having a prayer-meeting. A man's voice powerfully declaimed a series of phrases, and others, women's among them, intoned responses. It went on for a long time, monotonous and solemn, strophe and anti-strophe in grave rhythm. There was something else, too, which had gone on all day, a heavy thumping noise, insistent and unpleasant, which came from one of the nearby houses and vibrated through unknown channels to the very floor. Lytton might have guessed if she had asked him that it was women, somewhere, pounding the festive spices. He had peered into open doorways and seen them at it, drubbing through endless hours with pestle and mortar. But Tavy had never asked him and the noise was ominous, thudding and thudding away like a muffled warning.

The beggars too, who cried every morning and evening in the narrow street, were more numerous and vociferous than usual, as though hoping for greater liberality at this season. She knew them all by voice, though she rarely saw them; nothing could be seen of the street from her bedroom window. There was one she liked because his voice was beautiful. There would be a tapping stick, a pause, then a musical utterance, melancholy but assured, the voice of a priest repeating his evening office. Others were less agreeable; some were frightening. There was a woman who came every night and could be heard from afar, starting her cry on a sobbing note and rising to a banshee wail before she had done. She never varied the performance, which exacerbated the ear; Tavy wondered how anyone could be moved to charity by that witch's clamour. Another, a sing-song voice, belonged to an ancient blind woman whom Tavy had seen, a pitiful bundle of rags draped in a towel with nothing visible of the face but the sunk eye-sockets; she shuffled slowly, uttering her ritual wail, guided by a barefoot child who held out a grubby paw and whined for pesetas. And there were men who came in twos and threes, in ragged djellábahs with hoods pulled over their heads in sinister fashion, who paused at each door in turn and shouted a string of prayers that might have been curses. Lytton had opened the door to them once and sent her for money, but Tavy had been much too frightened to give them anything.

Tonight she listened to all these sounds uneasily, wandering about the room as she undressed. Now and then she stood at the window and looked out. The stars were very bright and the wind was rising, but nothing could be seen below. The house next door was silent, the stairway dark. She kept her thoughts away from it as well as she could, for at this hour, with this throb and mysterious tumult all about her, the idea of exploring it with Nick was inconceivable. At length, having frightened herself more than she liked by staring at the grille, she fastened the window with care and drew the curtains, blotting out the stars and the darkness, the roof where the cat had lain, the crumbling wall, the wind, the empty house. She lay awake for an hour or more in the dark and slept at last with the sheet drawn over her head.

Phoebe too was conscious of a pervading excitement, in two minds as to whether she should try to ignore the ferment or in a sense share it. Tavy was in bed, Lytton was off on one of his evening prowls, and she felt free to use the darkness in her own fashion. Wrapping herself in a shawl against the night wind she went up to the top roof and sat for a while in one of the basket chairs, gazing down at the town and its mystifying roof-top activities with feelings of half-pleasurable apprehension. There were things going on which had never happened before: small fires flickered brightly on several roofs and there were moving shadows everywhere, coming and going. She did not remember seeing men on the roof-tops before, or only occasion-ally; tonight they were much in evidence, occupied with ladders and trestles and talking in low voices, busy with preparations at which she fearfully guessed, but could not interpret. They were concerned with tomorrow's slaughter, which lay on her mind as though she herself were approaching some personal ordeal. This was the chosen scene and she the spectator, looking down on the place of atonement as into an arena.

She had heard various things from Lytton about the feast and knew that it had to do with the lamb in the thicket, with God's demand for a sacrifice from Abraham. This had never been a story she had cared for, since everyone, even God, ap-peared in such a bad light. It was outrageous to cut the throat of one's son because one fancied God required it; outrageous of God if He had; and the fact that a sheep was provided at the last minute was a matter of luck and nothing to Abraham's credit. But the feeling of mounting excitement had little to do, she suspected, with the old myth. It was something far deeper and older; it was primitive. She knew this, or dimly guessed it, from the stealthy responsive stir in her own blood. A year ago, perhaps, she would have been shocked, but now she felt it as natural and inevitable and herself as having, in a way, a passive part in it.

This was not to say that she was unmoved by the tremulous

89

bleating from every quarter, or had seen sheep and lambs dragged through the streets without a spasm of pity. Such scenes in the last few days had given her walks to the market a touch of nightmare. In every street she would encounter sheep being dragged or pushed, driven and prodded with sticks, or even, with roped legs and gentle heads erect, riding as passengers on the backs of donkeys. Sometimes it would be a great ram, planting his feet with fine obstinacy, and giving the maximum trouble to his purchaser, who dragged him by the horns and whacked his rump in a general uproar of shouting and noisy laughter. Sometimes the captive was a half-grown lamb, and these, to her distress, seemed always to have been handed over to the children of the family, who dragged it hither and thither, made it a party to their games and treated it as a sort of persecuted pet. In their own street there was a curly black one which she often passed, meekly tethered and chewing clover on the doorstep; the children of the house were small and evidently loved it, for one morning it had been wearing a necklace of buttercups. Yet these same children, she was sure, knew precisely what the lamb was for, and for that very reason were the more excited by it. They would watch it die, Lytton said, as a matter of course. This was right and proper; any other approach to the matter was sentimental. How much better, said Lytton, how much more realistic than our own system, by which a lamb in a field was a pretty plaything and bore no relation at all to a frozen cutlet. The lamb was symbolic, a chosen and God-given victim; it could be loved and played with and eaten, and everybody, children included, would be the better for it.

Phoebe was not sure how far she agreed with this in theory, but there was no denying that the children of the neighbourhood were having the time of their lives. Perhaps, as Lytton said, this was a more robust approach to the subject than her own. She was glad at least to think there would be no tears, no screams, no psychological complications when the plaything of many days was publicly slaughtered.

Before going down to the lower roof to see if Lytton had returned (no light was showing through his shutter though it was nearly midnight) Phoebe stood up and moved to the edge of the parapet, drawn by a flicker of flames reflected from below. From here she looked down on the roof that Tavy so constantly observed from the loft window, and the sight that she saw, though not startling, was unusual. A fire of wood and charcoal was crackling in a pot and a woman was busily fanning it and feeding it with splinters. All round her, on sheets of blackened metal, were rounds of dough, something like thick pancakes, and as Phoebe watched she lifted one on to a griddle and began baking it. It seemed to cook quickly, for she turned it often by hand and felt it with her fingers, fanning and blowing the flames and lifting each flapjack aside as it was done. So this too, Phoebe saw, was preparation for the feast, the women's midnight share in the coming ritual. She watched for a while, counting the scones or cakes as they came off the fire, but when half a dozen had been cooked there was double that number still waiting to be done, and she silently left the roof, since it looked as though the woman would be at it until the morning.

Lytton, as she had guessed, had not come home. He was rambling the streets of the Medina at his shambling pace, unmolested as always even by the giddily running and darting boys, who possibly detected something minatory in his bearing. If accosted he never answered and if jostled he failed to notice. Hands in pockets, beard pointing inquisitively this way and that, he made his accustomed progress through the teeming alleys.

The current of excitement which Phoebe had sensed from the roof and Tavy (though she could see nothing) at her bedroom window ran with an almost audible crackle in the streets. Everyone seemed to have some business to attend to instead of going to bed; shops were open at midnight, flares and torches flickered at busy corners, the doors of the mosques were thronged with men coming and going, knife-grinders with their wheels kept up an almost continuous screeching and whirring. Pedlars and vendors not normally seen there were squatting on the littered pavement with their stock-in-trade. They offered two things only for sale: black twisted iron skewers and businesslike broad-bladed knives. Both were selling briskly at this late hour, and Lytton paused several times to pick up a knife and test it against his thumb. He did not buy one and had no intention of doing so. The action was symbolic, a participation; to exchange a glance and a word of Arabic with the knife-seller gave him a satisfaction so peculiar that more than once he found himself faintly trembling. At one corner he narrowly avoided colliding with a man bent double under the weight of the sheep he was carrying on his shoulders. The animal's legs were tied fore and aft and the man had them gripped round his neck like the corners of a shawl, the horned head on a level with his own and the heavy dark-fleeced body sagging behind him. Lytton jerked to one side, so close that the yellow eye of the sheep met his own in the passing. He went on further, keeping to the crowded streets which by this time smelt sweetly of dung and trodden grass. The soles of his shoes, he could feel, were caked with droppings. When finally he turned for home it was with sudden exhaustion, as though the fever he had determined to share had passed its crisis. The crowds, he noticed now, were beginning to dwindle, though the knife-grinders still had their clients and were pedalling busily, making the wet stones sizzle in a shower of sparks. There was nothing to do, he told himself, but wait. The moment of truth (he put it to himself in those words, quite without irony) was something he must be ready for in the morning.

*

Later in the night, after a spell of that haunted and uneasy sleep which often follows emotional titillation, Lytton woke to a stealthy tickling in the small of his back and knew that he had a flea. He lay perfectly still, hoping he was mistaken, but the purposeful creeping sensation could be nothing else, and groaning with annoyance he put his hand to the light and prepared for action. For this emergency as for most others he had his system; even in so humble a matter the self-esteem of the Old Hand soon asserted itself and he methodically reminded himself of what he must do. First he pressed a cautious hand over that portion of his nightshirt, lifting the mosquito net (he had slept under this from the beginning though it was early in the season) and got gingerly out of bed. Next he put on his spectacles and collected ammunition, an aerosol spray and a piece of soap from the wash-basin, and gave himself a couple of shots down the back of the neck. He waited, keeping the left hand in position, and then warily, an inch at a time, drew off his nightshirt and laid it in a heap on the bed. The curtains were blowing quite briskly and he began to shiver, his long thin legs and washboard ribs shrinking to goose-flesh under the night breeze, but he knew what he had to do and was too intent on his quarry to take much notice. Bending over the bed, moistened soap at the ready in his right hand, he opened the folds of the nightshirt with his left. The manœuvre was successful; the second fold when lifted exposed the enemy. It made a jump, but the spray had had effect, not paralysing the creature, that was too much to hope for, but causing a certain confusion in its reactions. The leap fell short and Lytton got him with the soap, pressing him in with a thumb until he was thoroughly embedded. He straightened himself, breathing hard, and went to the basin and cracked the flea with a thumbnail, drowning it under the tap with feelings of triumph.

This done, he examined his face for a moment in the mirror, scratching his beard and baring his front teeth, and went back yawning and shivering to his nightgown. With it over his head he paused, debating whether to change it for a clean one; but this he decided was unnecessary; fleas do not hunt in couples and nothing in his nature had ever disposed him to extravagance. He buttoned the collar, looked at his clock (it was nearly half-past three) and went to the window. The stars were thick and the moon must have set already, the fugitive crescent moon that had heralded the feast. It would be five hours at least, even six, before the guns sounded. He listened for a long moment, and the idea of death (in the daylight hours so resolutely kept at bay) fell on his heart like the touch of a cold finger. He yawned and shivered, fretfully scratching his ribs. He must wake early, he told himself, he must not miss it. But his face betrayed no

93

eagerness and at the thought of what was to come his bowels flinched. He crept back stiffly under the mosquito net and after sitting for a while with his knees up, plucking at the sheet, reached for his travelling alarm-clock and turned off the alarm.

*

Phoebe awoke at sunrise and looked at her watch. It was early yet, but already there were sounds unusual at this hour, which the crowing cocks and the swallows had normally to themselves. Nothing had happened yet, she judged; sheep were bleating still and she could hear voices. She lay for a while considering, then got up and dressed; taking her time, since although her senses were alert and her mind made up it would not have been true to say that she was eager. She had decided with some misgiving that she would see it through. Tavy must not watch, of course; that was out of the question; but Lytton would be there from the start and far from blaming her curiosity would approve of it. She put a shawl over her head and went out on the roof.

It was a glorious morning, not a cloud in the sky. Swallows were sailing and darting in the clear air, there was a sound of crowing all over town and for once in that wind-scoured place not a breath stirred. She rested her arms on the parapet and looked over. Already, as she expected, people were about. On the roof below someone had erected a trestle, and a counterpane, as though for shade, had been stretched and tied with string across one corner. Could this be, she wondered, a sign of delicacy, an improvisation to spare her an unwelcome sight? It seemed unlikely. The families below, men and boys mostly and a few children, were intent on their own affairs with no thought, she was sure, either of her presence or of any freakish notion of consideration. She made herself inconspicuous and they did not look up. On several roofs, where she had not seen one before, there was a sheep tethered.

By half-past eight Lytton had still not appeared, and she became uneasy. Had he overslept, was he unwell, or had he just forgotten? She moved across to his window and looked in. The shutters were partly open and the curtains drawn; nothing stirred; she did not like to disturb him. After an interval, however, when she had wandered down into the house, listened at Tavy's door and softly set out teacups and put on the kettle, she was startled by the heavy boom of the first gun and made her way hastily back to Lytton's window. He *must* be awake, those guns would be heard a mile off. She pushed back the wing of the shutter and looked in. But the ghostly net was motionless and Lytton invisible, only a hump of bedclothes, tightly drawn, betraying the fact that there was anyone in it.

'Henry!' she whispered urgently. He did not move. 'Henry, the guns are firing!' The heap of bedclothes stirred but nothing emerged. Puzzled, she came in from the terrace and opened his door. 'Henry, it's half-past eight, are you going to get up?' But he flinched away when she touched him and only reluctantly, when she persisted, partly uncovered his head, which was turned away from her.

'What's the matter? Aren't you going to get up?'

'Go away. I'm not well.' He buried his face in the pillow.

'Henry, what is it? Tell me.' He certainly looked very odd, though he showed no more than an ear and a tuft of whisker.

'I'm not well, I tell you. Go away. I've got a stomach-ache.' Phoebe was taken aback. She had never known him have stomach-ache before.

'Let me get you something, then. Some bi-carbonate of soda?'

'I don't want a damn thing,' said Lytton, speaking thickly and with venom into the blankets. 'Not a thing, not a damn thing. Only to be left alone.'

So Phoebe prudently left him, feeling puzzled. A cup of tea might help, or if that were refused, slowly sipping a glass of very hot water. She went down to the kitchen and assembled a little tray while she waited for the kettle. The guns had finished firing and the house was quiet. It would be best to wait a little before calling Tavy.

Tavy as it happened, dead to the world for the past nine hours and submerged to a depth which not even guns could penetrate, slept like a log until ten o'clock, when she came out into the court-yard in her dressing-gown, stretching herself and yawning and looking for breakfast. Phoebe had gone back to the roof some time ago, having failed with both tea and hot water, and was peacefully standing at the parapet, observing the practical after-math of the excitement.

It was not at all as she had feared; it was not horrific. There were carcases here and there hung up by the heels and the whitewashed roofs were being soused with water. Flaying had begun already; the old man on the roof below was gravely at work, loosening the skin with his knife, drawing down the matted fleece, ex-posing a peeled and pearly under-surface. A boy was scraping entrails into a bucket and the woman whom Phoebe had seen baking was sweeping a mess of ordure into the drain. All over the town, on roofs and walls and even on washing-lines, caked and blood-sodden fleeces were spread in the hot sun to harden and dry. It was not offensive to watch, and Phoebe stayed. She felt almost proud of herself, though with some surprise that the ordeal was so soon over. Lytton had behaved very oddly, that was the puzzle. But then he was an odd man; how odd, only she and Sarah perhaps knew. He was not ill; of that she was fairly sure. 'No more ill than I am,' she whispered scornfully.

What none of them guessed, since they did not go out until later, was that their own alley for a time had been running with blood. A ram had been slaughtered almost on Lytton's doorstep and the blood had flowed down the central gutter and mapped out its own tributaries among the stones. It smelt warm and strong as it gushed from the slit throat, and the creature's bowels had emptied in the death struggle, making the children squeal and skip, crowding into the doorways to watch it die. The smallest threw scraps of grass into the bright stream and followed them down to the drain with solemn interest.

By the time Phoebe and Tavy emerged with their shopping baskets the alley had been sluiced with water and was shiningly clean, though it still smelt strongly, something between a butcher's shop and a stable. Everyone had disappeared; the street was empty. Only two little boys were sitting on a doorstep, playing with a bloody ram's horn and an old tin. They banged the tin on the stones and made noises in the hollow horn, engrossed in the lovely din and as merry as crickets.

6

CONSUELO, after a second telegram of postponement, arrived early in the morning on the day of Quattrell's picnic. Anthea drove alone to the airport to meet her, and was cheered (so far as her numb spirits could be cheered by anything) by the sight of that faintly absurd little figure, tight, compact and brisk on sparrow legs, purposefully making its way across the tarmac. Consuelo took great trouble with her appearance and always, by a narrow margin, got it wrong: skirts too short, sun-glasses too large, reddish-tinted hair too elaborately dressed; but the whole effect, though bizarre, had its own integrity, expressing an innocent confidence and good humour.

'My darling! At last! I couldn't get away Thursday. Are you furious?'

'Of course not. It's marvellous to see you, Consie.' Anthea kissed her. 'You've arrived in the nick of time, we're going for a picnic.'

'Oh boy, am I tired! Never mind, I'll soon recover. I never say no to an outing, do I? After all these years.'

She had brought, to Anthea's surprise, a minimum of luggage, and this was soon flung in the back of the car and they were on their way.

'My God, look at the colours of this country! I've never seen anything like it.' Consuelo wound down the window and drew several ecstatic breaths before turning to Anthea. 'What goes on here? Is it fun? Are you liking it?'

'I think we will. It's all right. Gerald's enjoying himself.'

They were driving fast through a stretch of country which to tell the truth was anything but beautiful, flat for the most part, tilth and cornfields rising to shallow slopes of stony pasture, where gullies of erosion marked out vanished streams. But the colours, as Consuelo said, were a revelation, the young corn green as new-sown grass, pastures blazing with blue and marigold yellow, wild flowers crowding the ditches in starry profusion. Everything had burst into flower these last few days, the very air was sweet with honey and pollen. The earth was full of moisture, the sun hot. Soon it would all be over, scorched by the sun and raked by the salt wind, but the brief spring while it lasted was bursting with life, flooding the barren landscape with tender colour.

Anthea glanced at it briefly, without interest. She was beginning to feel accustomed to this feeling of indifference, hateful and unfamiliar though it had been in the beginning. Given time, one could get used to anything, and this state of half-being had persisted, more or less, for close on two years. What saddened her most was the change that had taken place in her powers of vision, difficult to describe because quite unrelated to any normal experience. It seemed as though it were not in herself but in the world as she saw it, which appeared (it was impossible to define) as a meretricious imitation of nature. She knew that the colours Consuelo remarked on were beautiful; could see that the bugloss was blue and the marigolds yellow; but in some distasteful way they were not quite real; the landscape was bright to the eye, but artificial. The corn, if she looked at it steadily, had no life; it might just as well have been made of coloured raffia. Even the leaves of the eucalyptus, tossing like silvery plumage in the light breeze, had an unaccountably false and tinny glint, as though they were not leaves at all but painted metal. The illusion was insidious, and on Anthea, who had always extravagantly depended on visual pleasures, the effect was one of numbing melancholy. It was related, she knew, to that general deadness of feeling which had crept on her unawares after James had died. It had been a relief at first, like finding oneself in a dream, out of reach of misery; but for a long time now she had cared very little about anything. Gerald knew, and was kind; with him she could always rely on delicate perception. Consuelo too was aware that something was amiss, but thought of it simply as James's aftermath, from which it was reasonable to suppose she would recover. And in a sense she had recovered: she felt nothing. The surface of life was smooth, she went through the motions of living as though nothing had changed. Anyone but Gerald would have said she was perfectly happy.

'And you, my love,' said Consuelo presently, 'how are you doing? You look all the better for your trip. You're looking fine.'

'Oh yes, indeed. I'm feeling better and better. Gerald's found one or two friends here, you'll meet them presently. A writer called H. B. Lytton; have you come across him? And his sister-in-law, rather a pet; and a young great-niece. And another man, called Quattrell. I picked him up on the plane, coming from Madrid. He's the one who's taking us all on this so-called picnic.'

'Aha!' said Consuelo archly, 'so you *are* better! I must tell you, I had rather a curious encounter in Paris. A friend of Dave's turned up whom I hardly knew, and we suddenly found we were getting on together madly. That's why I stayed on a bit, there were a few parties. It's so extraordinary, being on my own; I can't get used to it. I keep remembering it's Pa's mealtime or something, it gives me quite a turn. I don't know what he'd say, seeing me cantering all over the map like this.'

'I expect he'd be glad you were having a holiday at last.' Anthea remembered Mr. Carpenter without enthusiasm, a querulous invalid, gone beyond reach of ordinary communication but with enough wit left to see the advantage of keeping Consuelo captive. It was creditable of course, that she had been wholly willing, but here again the thing had a morbid touch; she had been too fond of the old man, almost slavish, and Anthea could not regret that he was safely buried.

'I miss him though,' said Consuelo wistfully. 'I can't get used to racketing around on my own. Not that it isn't fun; it's bloody marvellous. But I haven't quite reached the point where it feels normal.'

'Don't worry, you'll feel normal here. There's plenty to amuse you. Wait till you see the flat we've got, it's rich in horror.'

'Really? What sort?'

'Oh, decoration mostly. It's been furnished for letting, you know the sort of fantasy. Wrought-iron goldfish on the walls and trails of plastic foliage in the bathroom. Oh, it's all right; just funny. Gerald found it and seems pleased with it, so I don't criticise. It serves its purpose. I can't say I care particularly.'

When they arrived, however, Consuelo saw nothing funny about the flat. In fact it was much to her taste, and in this as in other respects she thought Anthea lucky. Gerald wasn't James, admitted, but one couldn't have everything. He was amiable, presentable, even conveniently rich, and remembering the basement flat and all the shifts and predicaments of the old days she considered that Anthea was doing very comfortably.

'I think Gerald's marvellous,' she said presently, *à propos* of nothing, scattering her belongings at random over the bedroom. 'It's all turned out so well, I'm really glad for you.' She stooped to the dressing-table, examining her face. 'Good God, what a mess. Can I go like this, or is there time to do something?' She began to beat her cheeks with a powder-puff, carefully lifting the frame of her gilt spectacles.

'No, come as you are. We're supposed to start at eleven. There's nobody you need impress, it's only a picnic.'

'What about your glamorous friend? The one from Madrid?'

'He impresses easily, I suspect. And he isn't glamorous.'

'Oho, I shall judge for myself. I'm on my own, remember. I'm not going to let you collar everybody.'

'He's yours for the asking,' said Anthea with a faint smile. She rested her hands on the dressing-table, watching Consuelo. 'There's something I want to tell you, though. Not that it matters.'

'Ah, now we're coming to it.' Consuelo was concentrating on her hair, pulling up loose strands and back-combing vigorously.

'No, we're not; but Molly Brockhurst's here. She lives here now—would you credit it? Gerald's seen her.'

Consuelo was not as impressed as Anthea expected. She went on teasing her hair, her eyes bulging intently at the mirror.

'Well, what of it? She can't do anything to you now, I don't imagine. Or is she coming on the picnic?'

'Heavens, no. I haven't even seen her. I mentioned it only in case you happened to hear, or we ran into her.'

Consuelo threw down the comb and looked up curiously. 'It's all of two years now, isn't it? Are you still feeling badly?'

'I don't feel anything at all.'

'Really?'

'Really.'

'That's my girl! That's what I like to hear. You did the right thing, you know. I think you've been *simply* marvellous.'

'I haven't been anything,' said Anthea, and moved away. 'I just exist, that's all.' The conversation struck her with sudden boredom. 'Come on, I think Gerald's waiting. We'd better start.'

'No, I really mean it,' said Consuelo, preparing to follow. 'Not everyone would have snapped out of it the way you have, with a minimum of fuss. I call that very respectable. I admire you for it.'

Gerald was standing in the hall watching Enrico fasten the picnic basket. The lunch, it had been decided, would be a joint affair, since there were so many of them. Quattrell was doing the drink and providing the transport, Phoebe had promised a cake and plenty of sandwiches. Gerald, who at first had been noticeably cool about the whole thing, had finally suspected that Anthea was hankering to go and had ruined Enrico's morning with orders for a lavish salad and roast chickens. Quattrell was to bring his car, Gerald had his; the weather was all that one could wish for a successful picnic.

Lytton's group was already assembled on the pavement and Quattrell busy with his car, his head under the bonnet. It was an old Mercedes, large and conspicuously scarred; the wings and fenders in particular seemed to have suffered. There was plenty of room in it, however, which was just as well, since Gerald's car was small and he disliked crowding. They were nine people altogether, Nick having been included for Tavy's benefit, and a young man whom Quattrell carelessly introduced as Ozzie.

Ozzie was slight and dark and wore a fringe, carefully combed to disguise a narrow forehead.

'I didn't quite catch your name,' said Lytton, observing him with interest. He had worn a fringe himself in his younger days and the style pleased him; though commonplace now in certain quarters it had been daringly intellectual in his own youth.

'Everyone just calls me Ozzie.'

'Ozzie, just like that? Short for Oswald?'

'I'm afraid so. No one remembers my surname, it's too silly.'

'He answers to Hi! or any loud cry,' said Quattrell, wiping his hands on a rag. 'Come on, let's get going.'

Anthea, Consuelo and Lytton went in Gerald's car, the rest with the baskets and bottles packed into the Mercedes, which was strewn with tools and sand and old newspapers, the debris of unfastidious expeditions. In a few minutes they had left the town behind, speeding through the groves of eucalyptus and plantations of mimosa, and were running through a flat country of dunes and grass between opalescent hills and the blue sea. Soon on the right hand there were splendid beaches, empty and endless, a landscape of rolling breakers and dazzling sand. It was all marvellously uninhabited, reminding them, as Lytton said, of those happy days when motoring had been a pleasure; no traffic at all to speak of, only market-women bent under huge loads or strings of men and boys on jogging donkeys. Occasionally they caught a gleam of whitewashed walls, vestigial farms half-hidden in barricades of prickly-pear, primitive and solitary dwellings glimpsed at a distance, as though mistrusting any nearer approach to the road. On the points of their thatched roofs there were storks' nests, and on the apex of each a solitary stork stood sentinel. Everywhere as they drove there were drifts of colour, bugloss purple and blue, marigolds blazing the fields with orange and yellow, rose-pink convolvulus starring the grassy verges. More than once Phoebe exclaimed in amazement, long-ing to stop, to wade in the knee-high meadows for armfuls of flowers, to smell them, touch them, cover her hands and arms with sap and pollen; but Quattrell drove at speed and Gerald was not to be outdone, so they went on steadily into a grey-green region of saltings and sandy country, where fences of wattle were almost buried in sand and the flowers were brittle and sparse and no longer a tapestry.

At last Quattrell gave a laconic signal and turned off on a gravelly track in the direction of the beach, following the shallow bank of a small estuary. They bumped their way to the crown of a dune, among scrub and thorn-bushes sculptured by the wind, and there in a hollow, facing the beach and defended by fortifications of prickly-pear, came suddenly on the house. It was hardly a house, it was a cottage, a remnant of what had once been a peasant holding; it had an interfered-with and uninhabited look, the look of a place that has lost touch with its old life.

'Why, it might be English,' said Phoebe, getting out from the car and surveying the cottage with pleasure. 'Not the cactus, of course, that's very African; but the general appearance. It might almost be Devon or Cornwall, mightn't it? And so near the beach! What a wonderful place for holidays, especially for children!'

'If you wanted to get rid of them,' said Quattrell, lounging across to the door with the key in his hand. 'There's a splendid undertow here, they'd be drowned in no time.'

He turned the key in the lock and the party followed, crowding the dark doorway while he opened the shutters. There were only two rooms to be seen, with a door to a passage or annexe out at the back, but both were well proportioned and modestly spacious. The owner of the cottage, or perhaps Quattrell himself, had arranged them for rough convenience, the larger for sleeping and working, the smaller for cooking and eating, a habitable kitchen. The living-room had low divans against two walls, covered with old rugs and sea-stained cushions. There was only one chair, a wooden one, and a solid table on which a good many odds and ends had been thrown together—binoculars, a typewriter, books, papers, a shell filled with sand and cigarette-ends, an empty bottle, some glasses, a bathing towel, a comb, a pair of plimsolls. This slight squalor, such as it was, was confined to the table; an effort had clearly been made and the rest of the room was in order. The floor had been tiled at some time and was covered with matting, the walls were white-washed and not too badly stained. Though Quattrell had left his traces the place had an oddly sterile and lonely look, as though it had never been lived in by more than one person. Obviously it had been, once, but it must have been years since it had known the daily stir and warmth of a family.

'Well, this is quite wonderful,' said Lytton, stooping his head in the doorway and rubbing his hands approvingly at the room. 'An anchorite's cell, no less! What a wonderful place to work in. However did you find it?'

'I didn't. It belongs to an American I know, he lent it me for nothing. He never comes here hardly. He won't sell, or I might be tempted to take it off him. Waiting for the day when they develop this coast, most likely.'

'Oh no! That would be unthinkable. Develop this endless solitude? I won't envisage it.' Lytton flinched and slapped the back of his neck. 'Mosquitoes! And I've been bitten!' He examined his hand, found nothing, and stared at Quattrell.

'They're around, I know. That's marshy ground where the stream runs out on the beach. They don't bother me. Maybe I taste bad.'

'People always say that,' said Tavy to Nick in a whisper.

'Good gracious,' cried Phoebe, 'I thought one never got mosquitoes so near the sea? And we couldn't be much nearer.'

'That's a fallacy.' Ozzie was quietly unpacking a carton of beer. 'I've been bitten to the bone, often, right here on the beach.'

'They're only bad at night,' said Quattrell, 'and only then if there's no wind, which practically never happens. However, if they've really got you,' he turned to Lytton, 'I think I can meet the situation. I've got some stuff.' He disappeared into the kitchen and came back with a tube of ointment which Ozzie solicitously applied to Lytton's neck. There was no doubt about his having been bitten; a white disc had appeared, as big as a shilling. Gerald watched the treatment with deep sympathy; thin-skinned himself, he was always a potential victim.

'We must sit in the sun,' said Lytton firmly, fingering his neck, 'they won't bother us there.' So the food, which Phoebe and Anthea were already unpacking in the kitchen, was carried out and spread on a sandy slope under the prickly-pear, overlooking the beach. The sea was so marvellously blue, the distant rollers so magnificent, each flying a smoking crest in a wind which was not from the Atlantic but from the east, a land wind, dry and steady, that to eat indoors, as Phoebe said, would have been a pity. They made themselves fairly comfortable with cushions and rugs, stripping the divans, and settled down to the meal with all the cheerful makeshifts and mishaps incidental to a picnic. Quattrell did little beyond smoke and talk but Ozzie was invaluable, pouring out the drinks, dealing round salad and butter and plates of chicken, seeing that the young ones had enough to eat, looking after everyone. He had evidently been invited with this function in mind, being one of those agreeable young men who combine domestic gifts with general efficiency. Phoebe took a great liking to him.

'Are you here on holiday?' she asked him presently, with kindness, when the last jug of coffee had been passed round and he had brought his mug beside her, sitting back on his heels in the warm sand.

'No, gracious, I live here. You passed the end of our road on the way out. We have rather a special garden; do come and see it some time.'

'Thank you, I should like to. But who is "we"?'

'Ah, I should have said. I'm sort of secretary-what-have-you to Mrs. Brockhurst. You haven't met her?'

'I don't think so, no. I haven't met many people, we've been too busy.'

'You've heard of her, though, I expect. Poor darling, she doesn't go out much either, she's too frail. She had a terrible experience, you know; you probably heard about it? She was married to this marvellous man, a madly serious and fascinating barrister, and their yacht was run down in a fog and everyone was drowned. Everyone but her, that is, poor sweet. She was dreadfully ill for a time. It's nearly two years now, and of course she's marvellous; but I know, and I can tell, and she still hasn't recovered.'

'Good gracious, I'm not surprised. What a terrible tragedy!' Phoebe was no great reader of newspapers and this was the first time she had heard the story.

'Miss Townsend, you have *no* idea. When I first met her, I *promise* you, she was a wreck. Her nerves! Well, you can imagine. *Living* on sleeping pills and in and out of nursing homes, it was *frightening*. So I said to myself, you know how you do, I said, Is it possible to help this person? And one thing led to another and in the end I took it on, because you can't see someone *quite* at a loss when you know you can do something about it, can you?'

Phoebe considered the question, not sure whether to take it rhetorically or not, and whole-heartedly agreed. Whatever unhappy state one found oneself in she was sure this gentle young man would be a comfort.

'Mrs. Brockhurst's fortunate, in that respect at least. Are you related?'

'My dear, I'd never set eyes on her before that day. Isn't life *amazing*? Since then, of course, we've simply never looked back. We did the house together, it was quite fabulous, and now I'm trying to get her keen on the garden.' He regarded Phoebe gently with his head on one side. 'I'd love you to meet her, Miss Townsend. I make her go out when I can, but it's a teeny bit difficult. Psychologically, she's starving; she's got to that tricky stage when she *needs* people.'

'Ah, we all do that,' sighed Phoebe, settling down happily to what promised to develop into a comfortable talk. But at that moment Tavy and Nick decided to bathe, and when towels had been found and promises made about depth and not going out of sight, and Quattrell had been consulted about undertow and currents and Phoebe begged them to be careful about waves ('Such big ones, dear, they look quite dangerous') Ozzie gave a little cry on his own account: he had been bitten inside the ear by a mosquito. The tube of ointment was searched for and found on Gerald, who, unobserved, had been furtively anointing his wrists and the back of his neck. He produced it with some embarrassment and offered it to Ozzie.

'Oh dear, what a beastly thing. Can you actually see it?' Ozzie pushed back his hair from the ear and Gerald put on his spectacles.

'I can indeed. The brute's still there, or the remains of him. Let me do it for you.'

Phoebe watched sympathetically while Gerald peered, dislodging the dead mosquito with the tip of a finger. Consuelo, stretched on a rug and half asleep, opened one eye and observed them with lazy interest. Lytton and Quattrell were deep in talk, at least Lytton was talking and Quattrell listening with his eyes shut, shirt unbuttoned and knees up, sifting a handful of fine sand through his fingers. Tavy and Nick were splashing at the water's edge and Anthea, who had followed them half-way down and removed her sandals, was strolling along the beach in the direction of the estuary.

'Shall I put it in for you?' said Gerald. 'It's a nasty bite.'

'Oh dear, yes *please*. How *vile*. I swell so monstrously. I keep telling and telling Rob he must *do* something, but he doesn't take a blind bit of notice.'

'Hold still, then.' Gerald took a blob of ointment on his little finger and very delicately introduced it corkscrew-wise into Ozzie's ear.

'Is that far enough? Can you feel it? Have I reached the spot?'

Ozzie shook his ears like a dog and then stood still, consulting his sensations.

'A little more, do you think? I'm making a shaming fuss, I know, but you *are* such a Samaritan.'

The operation was repeated, and it struck Phoebe that they both made a little more of it than was quite necessary. Consuelo, too, she suspected, thought the same; she had raised herself on an elbow for a better view, and when she caught Phoebe's eye made a sly grimace. Still, it was better to be careful; a bite could turn very nasty and Lytton on these occasions was just as bad. She was slightly disappointed, however, for she had been enjoying her talk with Ozzie and now that the treatment was over they had taken the stuff to the kitchen and not come back. She waited a little, feeling increasingly drowsy, and presently saw them walking together, a long way off already, on the crown of the dune. Ozzie's hair was blowing and his shirt fluttering, and as their figures dwindled she could see him earnestly gesticulating, deep in talk. Where she and Consuelo were camped there was no wind, though lower on the beach it was combing up wisps of sand. Consuelo had gone to sleep, it seemed; her eyes were closed, and Phoebe turned her attention to Nick and Tavy. If everyone else were walking or talking or asleep, she had better keep watch. But the children looked safe enough and her eyes were heavy. Presently she eased her legs, reached for a cushion, sighed, and settled down. Quattrell and Lytton were growling away at a distance; nothing could be more soothing than their murmuring voices.

*

When Anthea came to the estuary she found it shallow; the tide was low and the stream spreading out like a fan on the firm sand. It had carved itself into innumerable channels but even these were no more than a foot deep, and she found she could wade across with little difficulty. At this time of the year, with the stream shrunken, tide and wind together had swept away all trace of a permanent channel.

Much further along the beach she could see rocks, low masses thrusting out from the dune to the sea, making a little headland. Since it was no more than half a mile away she decided to make it her object, walking slowly in the last petering-out fringes of the ebb-tide breakers, watching the sea run over her feet and back again, hearing the suck and roar, feeling the wind and the sand and thinking of nothing. The beach and the dunes were so aridly, splendidly empty that it might have been a stretch of desert, a view of the moon; nothing at first sight moved but a film of sand blowing thinly along the surface, and always on her right hand, the distant smoking breakers and the loud sea. The sound of the sea was hypnotic and at the same time ominous, as though, if one listened closely, echoes or voices could be heard which it was better not to hear. *The melancholy long withdrawing roar*, she thought, and turned her head quickly from the sea and towards the dunes, since to think of James on this alien beach, in this rising wind, filled with the waves' noise and the suck of the tide, was too dangerous a test for trying the heart's apathy. It was better that every pulse and nerve should be still; she had got used to that; and coming out of shallow water on to the wet sand she turned her back on the sea and began to follow a churned-up track of footprints.

This had been made by donkeys, as she soon discovered, for they came down through a gap in the scrub at the head of the beach, walking delicately and with discipline in single file, each small back bulky with old and sodden panniers. She caught their spicy smell as they passed, not looking to left or right or varying their pace but returning without interest or protest to that part of the beach that had seen them already a dozen times that day, to stand in the sun and be loaded to the last spadeful. 'I am like them,' she thought, standing still to watch; without great pity, with acceptance rather, as though seeing the inevitability of their condition. The old man walking behind them, his ragged djellábah blowing about his legs, passed her without a glance, uttering the admonitory cries without which it was not God's will that one should drive donkeys. He strode on through the sand, barefoot and patriarchal, and as his flapping figure receded she saw Quattrell.

She stood still and waited, watching his approach.

'Brilliant!' he said admiringly, when he came up with her. 'I thought we were never going to get away. That was quite brilliant.' With a mute glance she fell into step beside him and they went on slowly together in the direction of the rocks.

'I can't claim any great brilliance, I'm afraid. I just came for a walk by myself.'

'No! Is that true? You disappoint me. Let's cut all that out, don't you think? I thought we were going to go on where we left off.'

'Were we? I'm not sure I remember where that was.'

'Don't you? *I* do. We were starting to talk about you and me, remember? When can I see you alone?' He looked at her seriously. 'Can you come tomorrow, by yourself? I could pick you up anywhere you say.'

'Well, no, I don't think I could.' Anthea's thoughts sheered off to an evasive distance. She felt neither pleasure nor surprise at this approach, in fact nothing at all, and this nothingness made it seem very simple to deal with.

'We've got to talk to one another,' said Quattrell meaningly, and she was struck, not for the first time, by his simple assumption that whatever his feeling might be she would naturally share it; and again it seemed hardly worth while to disabuse him. Her thought for a moment veered to Consuelo, and the zest with which she would have entered the arena with this adversary. She gave him a sidelong glance and said nothing.

'I've never even called you by your name,' he said, stopping to light a cigarette, cupping his hands round the match because of the wind. 'Have I, Anthea?'

'I can't think of your Christian name. I suppose I've forgotten it.

'It's Robert. Rob. You might use it occasionally, if it's not too much trouble.'

They came to the first of the rocks and he held out a hand. They were slippery and dark with seaweed and they crossed them slowly, Anthea's hand in his, steadying him quite as often as herself, since he was wearing plimsolls and she was barefoot. The rocks extended further than at first appeared, and when they were half-way across they came to an island of weedy sand and climbed down to it. At the bottom he put his free arm round her and kissed her.

'Relax,' he said. 'You're tied up in knots, aren't you?'

'Not that I know of.'

He held her close for a moment and she breathed in the smell of tobacco, beer and sweat.

'You're a funny girl, I must say. I'm going to talk to you.'

Still holding her by the hand he drew her after him, moving up the channel between shoulders of rock until they came to a dry place where the sand, out of reach of the tide, was soft and warm. Here, as though they had reached a place they knew, they both sat down, facing the sea but out of the troublesome wind, sheltered by grassy dune and sloping rock. He made no further attempt to touch her but took out his cigarettes and passed them over. They leaned their backs to the rock and smoked in silence.

'How long have you been married to that man?' he asked her presently.

'I thought you said you knew him. His name's Gerald.'

'Sorry. How long have you been married to Gerald Askew-Martin?'

'Nearly two years.'

'And before that?'

'Before that I wasn't married.'

'Who was it, then?'

'I've told you, I wasn't married.'

'You don't have to tell me if you don't want to.'

'Of course I don't. Besides, there's nothing to tell.'

Quattrell frowned, burying the end of his cigarette in the sand. He glanced at her under his eyebrows as he lit another.

'All right, we'll come back to that later. Would it bore you, or shall I tell you my own history?'

'If you wish.'

'I do wish. As you'll see, it has a bearing. I've been married twice. The first time wasn't much; it was soon over. The second one still goes on, but it's breaking up.'

'I see. Are you sorry?' She hardly wished to know, but it was something to say.

'Yes and no. Constance has money, I haven't. I'm an unreliable husband, she's exacting. It's a bad mixture. I don't want to annoy her more than I can help, but I suspect it'll be better for both if I don't go back. Would that be your advice?'

'How can I possibly give any? Besides, you don't want it. You're telling me this for some other reason, not for my opinion.'

'Quite right. I should be more direct. I will be, now that you begin to know me better. I don't care for the oblique approach, but this foxy manner of yours, this trick of being somewhere else and a long way off, makes me feel I have to be circumspect and careful.'

'Oh, that's what you're being; I see. I hadn't guessed.'

Quattrell smiled, and after a moment laid his hand on her arm. 'I like you, you know. You're miles and miles away, but I like you a lot. I want you to come back from wherever it is, but I'm not going to hurry you. Can you get away tomorrow, d'you think? Come to the cottage.'

'Of course not.'

'There's no of course not about it. It would be marvellous. You know it would be marvellous.' His fingers had closed round her wrist and it was apparent from the change in his breathing that the contact excited him. 'I shall be there all day,' he said. 'I shall be waiting for you.'

He leaned abruptly across her and began kissing her. His manner was unexpectedly tender, but at the same time there was no ambiguity about it. This couldn't go on, she knew, but it was difficult to stop. His tongue had surprised her at the first kiss, her head against the rock; now his weight was across her and as she caught her breath she felt his muscles harden. She observed these things with a sort of dreamlike detachment, as though they were happening at a distance, to someone else. But the thing was absurd and she made a murmur of protest. When he lifted his head she made a perfunctory effort and pushed him off.

'I'm sorry. I must have misled you.' She scrambled to her feet, brushing at her skirt and legs which were covered with sand. 'I'm rather preoccupied, that's all. Don't be offended.' Quattrell still sat where he was, breathing through flared nostrils, as though uncertain whether to be angry or not. After a moment he got to his feet, feeling in the pocket of his shirt for a cigarette.

'I offended? You're a strange one, all right. What's it all about? Tell me. Loyalty to Gerald?'

'We'll go back now, if you don't mind. Come along, Robert, Rob, come too. We needn't quarrel.'

'Why not? I should rather like to. I know all about it, you know. Let's stop pretending.'

'You don't know anything,' said Anthea. 'You're kind, and I rather like you, but you're quite mistaken.' She turned away

113

and began without haste to climb up the shallow rock. The surface was dry and Quattrell easily followed.

'Tell me why you did it,' he said, as they came down into a smooth gully. 'I know about Gerald, he's a queer, a well disguised one. Why did you marry him?'

'It's none of your business. I don't have to answer your questions.' She was gone again, up the next slope, stooping to steady herself on the sharp ridges. The rock was broken here and painful to walk on, but she could see the beach. The wind was blowing strongly where there was no shelter, and the sea was streaked with white and had changed colour. She slipped, recovered herself, and jumped from the final ledge into deep sand. Quattrell heard her gasp and slithered after her. She had come down almost on her knees, as though she were hurt, but as he reached the sand himself he saw what had happened: she had landed within a yard of a man's body.

He lay in the lee of the rock, face down, one arm flung out on the sand and partly covered. A tattered garment was over his head and shoulders and against his legs the wind had built up the sand in shallow ridges. He had been there for hours, for days; he was dead, he was drowned. Anthea crouched where she was, her face contorted, and when Quattrell touched her shoulder he found she was trembling.

'He's dead,' she whispered, hiding her face in his arm.

'He's no more dead than I am. My darling, what is it?'

'He's dead,' she said again, on a sobbing breath.

'I promise you he's not. Look here.' He pulled her to her feet and went close to the sleeping man.

'Don't *touch* him, Rob. He's dead.' But Quattrell had stooped to shake him and the man turned over, an old man, startled and affronted, who sat up with a croak of alarm and stared up at them out of one dark, one milky eye. Anthea suddenly saw him for what he was, a beggar, partially blind, aroused from his private sleep by outrageous strangers. She turned away, struggling with absurd tears, but the shock had gone like a blow to her very centre and she could neither control her breath nor the foolish crying. She heard Quattrell speaking to the old man and watched through her fingers as he stooped and gave him money. The gnarled hand shot out from habit in the moment of waking, and now though he still looked angry, he was intoning his ritual phrases, the beggars' blessing.

Quattrell was quickly beside her, his arm round her shoulders, and this time she was glad of his touch and leaned against him. They walked slowly along the beach, their heads together.

'My dear girl, why did that frighten you so much?'

'I don't know. Wasn't it stupid?' Her breath still shook. 'I thought for a moment he was drowned.'

'Up there on that dry sand, in the sun? You must have been dreaming.'

'But it wasn't a dream, it was real. I knew someone once who was drowned, a long time ago.' She wiped her tears with her hand, shaken by a hiccuping breath.

'Very long ago? Recently?'

'Two years ago. I don't want to talk about it.'

'So that was it,' said Quattrell, and pressed her arm. They went on through the windblown sand for a while in silence.

'Look,' he said presently, coming to a stop and taking her by the elbows, 'I don't want to know anything, at least not until you want to tell me, but it's important we should understand one another. We'll be back with the others in a minute, there's not much time.' He stooped and looked her in the eyes, screwing up his own against the wind and sand. 'Pull yourself together, Anthea. Use my handkerchief.' She wiped her face and blew her nose; they smiled at one another. 'That's my girl. That's better. Now listen to me. You and I are not strangers; we're going to be very important to one another.' He gave her a little shake. 'Are you paying attention?'

'Yes. But it isn't true.'

'It *is* true, and you damn well know it. Speak the truth.'

'How can it be?' But she felt a stir of the nerves even as she spoke, an echo of something lost which had once been precious. She gave him a puzzled glance. Looking at him now she saw the unhandsome face as full of concern, the blue eyes under their heavy brows searching her own with a look both doubtful and tender; and again the illusion came over her that this was nothing new, that she had been through it all before, that his face, his touch, his very ugliness was familiar. 'How can it be?' she said again, but with a changed inflection.

'You can get away tomorrow, surely? Even for an hour?'

She shook her head. 'I really can't, you know. There's Gerald and Consuelo.'

'You can't be together all day. And I noticed Gerald went off for a walk with Ozzie.'

'You needn't draw conclusions from that. I know Gerald too well. In any case it's just impossible.'

He dropped his hands and they resumed their strolling walk, their arms as though by habit linked together.

'Nothing is impossible,' he said, 'if you really want it.'

'Ah, that's the point. I'm not at all sure I do.'

'Don't be afraid of love, my dear. That's a bad mistake.'

'Oh, love.' She shielded her eyes from the sand. 'I couldn't start that again. It's over, finished.' But as she said this she felt a curious flicker of response, for the sand weaving a thin veil along the beach was suddenly alive, and the sea, indigo dark and whipping up frothy crests, pierced her senses with movement and stormy colour. Whatever might happen with Quattrell she was no longer dead. She knew, it was absurd to doubt, that this was the beginning of recovery.

They came in sight of the dune where the house was hidden, the hedge of prickly pear, the house itself. The rugs had been gathered up and there was no one to be seen; the wind had evidently driven them all indoors. They casually loosed hands and Anthea searched for the spot where she had left her sandals.

'I'm not going in until we've decided something,' said Quattrell, watching her put them on. 'How are we going to meet? Can I telephone tomorrow?'

'Of course you can. Any time.' She stood up and swept the hair from her eyes, standing with her back to the wind. Her colour had returned and she had a sense of lightness and well-being, as though she could walk for miles on that waving sand.

'Yes, but when will you be alone? I don't want a public talk.'

'Ah, that I can never be sure of. How can I be?' She was too privately intent on her own sensations to care about his anxiety or how he would solve these problems of his own making. But his look of impatience, shot almost threateningly from under the heavy brows and tangle of hair, touched her with faint compunction, and she smiled.

'I shall ring you in any case,' he warned her. 'You must manage it somehow.'

They turned away from the sea, ploughing through the moving sand in the direction of the house. As they did so Tavy and Nick came over the crest of the dune and ran down the sandy slope with birdlike cries. They were abandoned to the wind and their own speed, waving their arms and leaping, landing on their heels, and it struck Anthea that Tavy had mysteriously changed into another creature. She had pulled on an old jersey over her bathing-suit and her long honey-coloured legs and flying hair made her seem wild and childish, suddenly desirable. Nick's skinny arms and legs came flailing after her and they raced together down the slope, pursuing their flying antics to the door of the cottage.

'How different she looks!' said Anthea. 'That boy's good for her, isn't he? Do you remember how dismal she looked, that day at the airport?'

'I remember how *you* looked,' said Quattrell. 'You're different too.' He slowed his pace, as though about to say something else, but at that moment Phoebe and Lytton appeared in the doorway and they saw that everyone had returned and that Consuelo and Ozzie were packing for departure.

'Isn't it a shame about the wind?' said Phoebe. 'We're packing up, the sand was getting into everything.'

'That's the curse of this place.' Ozzie was busy with the bottles. 'It practically never stops blowing.'

'Oh, I've enjoyed it,' said Anthea lightly, taking in the dishevelled room and everything in it, the flaking walls, the litter, their wind-burned faces, as though she were really seeing them for the first time. 'It feels clean and cold. It's a marvellous wind.' Consuelo looked up from her packing and raised an eyebrow. Her eye had a glint of amusement which Anthea ignored.

'It's more than a wind, it's a gale,' said Lytton fretfully. He had wrapped a scarf round his throat and was well buttoned. 'I wonder you can stand it out here,' he said to Quattrell. 'Look what's blown in on your papers. There's sand in everything.'

But Quattrell had turned gloomy and seemed anxious to be gone. 'I don't notice it,' he said, and picked up the carton of bottles and went out to the car.

They drove back as they had come, except that Consuelo went in the Mercedes and Phoebe got into Gerald's car to be near Lytton. He was coughing a little and fidgeting with his scarf, and her mind was already on whisky and hot-water bottles. It was certainly a freakish change from the glorious morning. The sky had turned to a leaden white and in places the sand blew across the road in a steady relentless flood like a pale river. The colours of the hills were still brilliant but the trees when they came to them were thrashing their heavy plumes in the growing storm and the road was streaked with drifts of torn mimosa. Gerald was intent on his driving and Anthea sat beside him in a trance of vision. Everything, the wind and the flying sand, the moving sky, the clouds, the tossing grasses, ravished her with the joy of recognition.

7

THE following morning Lytton woke with a cold and stayed in bed, nursed by Phoebe with an air of cheerful efficiency which concealed panic. His raucous breathing, the way his eyes watered with self-pity, even the words he used when he spoke in a plaintive whisper—lungs, bronchial tubes, fever, mucus, pulmonary congestion—filled her with alarm and made her breath come short and her hands tremble. If this were it! If Henry were to die! She disguised her fear with an unnatural and excessive briskness, going up to his room more often than was necessary, opening and closing windows, changing hot-water bottles, dosing him with aspirin and glasses of sugared lemon-juice, all with an air of optimistic gaiety. In this she was wiser than she knew; it was the right treatment. Lytton was only slightly unwell but he was frightened, and Phoebe's hospital-nurse composure, which annoyed him, acted as an entirely salutary irritant. He met it at first by pretending to be worse than he was, closing his eyes when she came into the room, fretfully rolling his head as she arranged the pillows, letting his hands wander feverishly over the blankets. Phoebe observed these signs and inwardly trembled, with the result that she redoubled her efforts to appear cheerful. She even hummed as she moved about the room and arranged the medicine bottles, in a way that appeared positively light-hearted.

'You seem to have had good news or something,' said Lytton at one point, opening his eyes and staring at her with hostility. She gave him a rallying look and took a duster from her apron pocket.

'I was thinking what a good thing it is that you should have a few days' rest before the party.'

Lytton replied to this with a fit of coughing.

'There isn't going to be a party,' he said in a hollow voice, letting his head fall backwards on the pillow.

'Of course there will! I'm starting to plan already. Mr. Quattrell came in this morning, he was full of ideas. I told him he couldn't see you, but he's anxious to help. He says the invitations will be a difficulty, unless you write them. He suggests you put in a telephone.'

'A telephone! Great God!' A flush crept up Lytton's neck at this impertinence, but even as he began to wheeze a thought struck him. 'We may need it,' he said faintly, clutching the sheets. 'It's madness not to be able to call a doctor.' He closed his eyes again and lay very still. Phoebe went on humming and dusting and presently he opened one eye and covertly watched her.

'As to that,' she said, pulling out a drawer and beginning to arrange his socks and handkerchiefs to her liking, 'we can get a doctor any time you like, simply by sending a message. Tavy got the name of a good one from Mrs. Parsons, he lives in the same block. If you think he could suggest anything we're not doing already I can easily send for him. Or her, to be exact. It's a woman.'

'Dear God,' said Lytton, disgusted; 'why not a vet?'

'Well, there's a very good vet, too, I believe,' said Phoebe serenely, 'but in my opinion you'll be up and about tomorrow and won't need either of them.'

This encouraging response was followed by a long silence, broken only by a slight increase of stertorous breathing.

'You'll remember this, I hope,' said Lytton at length, 'when I've had to be flown back to England and rushed by ambulance into some third-rate hospital. Sarah would turn in her grave to hear you say a thing like that.' Phoebe gave him a frightened glance, not liking the mention of Sarah and also fearing that perhaps she had gone too far. But his colour was really quite reasonable and the breathing, she was thankful to observe, was already quieter. The wheezing, indeed, if she had only known it, had been rather an exhausting performance to keep up.

'Sarah would be doing exactly what we're doing now,' she

said, 'only, of course, much better. She would be keener than anybody on your throwing off your tiresome cold and enjoying your house-warming.'

Lytton thought this over for a minute, then put out his hand to the clock on the bedside table.

'What time did Quattrell appear? Is he still there?'

'No. He wanted to come up and see you, but I wouldn't let him. You *have* got a cold, after all, we don't want to spread the infection.'

'I never heard that congestion of the lungs was infectious. You talk as though I'd contracted the Black Death.'

Phoebe permitted herself a little laugh.

'Your sense of humour hasn't deserted you, I'm glad to see. That shows you're better already.'

'I'm nothing of the sort. I'm worse.' He followed her round with his eyes. 'I could certainly have talked to Quattrell for a few minutes. It would have done me good. A man like that's indestructible. Strong as an ox.'

'Well, he's coming back tomorrow,' said Phoebe soothingly, 'so that's something to look forward to. Your breathing will be better then, you can discuss the party.'

'There isn't going to be a party,' said Lytton weakly, rolling his head on the pillow like a man in delirium. Phoebe was startled by his expression, which had turned into a dying grimace, showing only the whites of the eyes. She moved softly to the door, thinking that after all she would send for the doctor, but as she glanced back she saw that Lytton had propped himself on an elbow and had reached for his pad and pencil and was making notes.

Downstairs in the patio she encountered Tavy, hunched in a basket chair in a patch of sunlight, writing on her knee.

'How's Uncle Henry?' she asked without looking up, scribbling away in an exercise book with her hair touching the page.

'He's better, dear, I think, but I'm wondering if it wouldn't be wise to let him see the doctor. I could write a note and you could take it, perhaps? You could find it, couldn't you? It's the same block as the Parsons.'

'O.K.' said Tavy, putting her pencil in her ear. 'I was just writing to Nick, telling him to come over. I could take it at the same time, I suppose; it's in that street opposite the main post office.'

'Are you sure you know the way?'

Tavy raised her eyebrows, looking pained.

'I told you, it's opposite the post office. I can ask, can't I?'

'Well, yes, I suppose you could. It would be very kind.' Phoebe hesitated, calculating the hazards. But Tavy knew the way to the market by now and from there to the post office it was easy. No harm would come to her, surely; it was encouraging to find her prepared to do anything on her own initiative.

Phoebe crossed over to the parlour, found writing paper in a drawer and sat down at the table. Immediately and almost furtively, as though this were what she had come for, she raised her eyes and looked doubtfully at Sarah. She was not going to allow herself a direct question, even an unspoken one; that earlier exchange between them had been too uncanny. All the same she longed for a crumb of comfort, and Sarah's calm expression was reassuring. Looking at the closed face, the beautiful straight nose and curving lips, it was difficult to believe that Lytton's illness was serious. Sarah seemed almost to smile at the thought, knowing far more than anyone about his pretences, at which she had laughed rather cruelly in the old days. It was only a cold, surely? He had no temperature. His hands were cool to the touch and his breathing was difficult only when he remembered it. But Sarah's face, though serene, was noncommittal, and Phoebe was touched with fear and began her letter. She wrote rapidly, anxiety growing as she saw the words on the paper. It now seemed extraordinary that she had waited until almost noon before sending for the doctor.

Lytton by this time was sitting up in bed with his notebook, jotting down points of procedure to be discussed with Quattrell. He was exasperated at having been cheated of his visitor, for he had taken a liking to Quattrell and saw him as a man to whom he could talk with confidence. It would be a pleasure to ask his advice and help about the party; indeed his co-operation would be essential, since he already seemed to know a good many people, and though Lytton had no intention of doing anything extravagant he could see that reputation was involved and was not prepared to make himself ridiculous. Besides, Quattrell was obviously a man for parties and might like to share it, which would be a double advantage. Lytton had been impressed by the lavishness of the drinks at yesterday's picnic.

He wrote down the word *champagne*, added a careful question mark, then crossed them both out. They would have Moroccan wine, of course; it was much cheaper. Then there was the question of guests. A dozen people, perhaps? Twenty, thirty? He became engrossed in his plans and happily scribbled on over several pages. The very exertion of writing made him feel better; it was a tonic action, the one that never failed. Putting pen to paper, even with a shawl round his shoulders and wadding on his chest, reminded him that he was H. B. Lytton, and this impressed him. Today it was a tremendous comfort, for he had had a bad morning. The least hint of illness sent his thoughts scurrying in all directions, which was natural enough, since he was far from robust and had gone through the terrors of a disease which would have put the fear of death into any man. But at the same time, on some profound level of consciousness which was the more powerful for being out of reach, there was an enormous sceptical resistance to the whole thing. He knew that he had had a cancerous patch removed from his lung and reason told him that he might well be nurturing another; but on this deepest level, from which on other subjects he so often received cryptic and disquieting messages, there came only a profound unshakeable disbelief. It was as though there were something there which refused the idea of death, either now or later. Whatever it was, on this point it was as immutable as it had ever been, even in childhood. On this foundation he was able, with only a surface distress and that not always, to indulge his imagination with gloomy fantasies, to enjoy the glamour of a doomed man and see his pronouncements received with a weight of respect which the situation conferred on them. He had worked himself into the part with sombre relish, sometimes alarming himself more than he intended and fully as much as he occasionally alarmed Phoebe. But always underneath it all, giving him strength when he was most in need of it, this speechless instinct sent up reassuring signals, calm messages about a future in which he himself had a part and death was inconceivable.

Unconsciously it reassured him now. He had thrown himself into the drama of catching cold with all the alarm and fretfulness of which he was capable, exacerbating his nerves with a continual nagging check of his own symptoms; but as soon as he had made his point and piqued himself with the suspicion that Phoebe was not taking his condition seriously, he fell into acute self-pity as a man who was being cheated of his own party, and indignantly set himself to redress the balance. He saw the house-warming now as something essential and himself as the centre and occasion of it, overcoming all difficulties. He would certainly not see the doctor; or if he did, only to demonstrate his triumph and her discomfiture. He would make the party a large one, regardless of expense. Or if not exactly that (since there was always the possibility of Quattrell's sharing it) he would make it at least an occasion to be remembered. He would get Quattrell to bring a few guests and possibly the Askew-Martins could be made use of as well, so that his first appearance on this chosen scene should be—not lavish or ostentatious, that would be out of character—but reputation-enhancing, impressive, memorable.

When Quattrell turned up next day, as he had promised, Lytton was sitting in the sunny centre of the patio, a rug over his knees, swallowing vitamin-tablets and drinking coffee. The doctor had been and gone, regaled by Lytton with the history of his operation and barely allowed so much as to bring out her stethoscope.

'My dear lady, I haven't reached the advanced age of sixty-four without gaining a certain familiarity with my own symptoms. It's my good sister-in-law here whom you should be treating. It's due to her nervousness, not mine, that you've been brought on this unnecessary errand. A child can deal with a cold;

mine is dealt with already. But for Miss Townsend perhaps you might care to prescribe a mild sedative?' So the poor Frenchwoman, whose English was not fluent and who had been filled with professional zeal when she read Phoebe's letter, had gone away not much wiser than before, except for a sour conviction that the British were hysterical. Lytton had enjoyed the interview, and Phoebe, who at first had been coldly angry at being made to look foolish, comforted herself with relief at his recovery.

'The difficulty is,' said Lytton, when Quattrell had arrived and they were all three settling down to some fresh coffee, 'the difficulty is, frankly, that we haven't been here long enough to know a party-full of people.'

'Keep it small, then,' said Quattrell, 'you're three, I'm four, the Askew-Martins six, no, seven with the girl in spectacles, Ozzie if you like and Mrs. Brockhurst nine, maybe Tavy would like the Parsons kid, the parents too for good measure—that's twelve already.'

'I don't want to come,' said a voice high up in the fig-tree.

They looked up to see Tavy's long legs, and above them a silhouette of dangling hair, balanced on the low parapet bordering the well of the roof.

'Tavy! That's not at all safe. Come down at once, or at least get back on the terrace.'

'It's quite all right, Aunt Phoebe, I'm holding on.'

'Do as you're told for once,' said Phoebe, her voice sharpened by alarm.

The legs drew up slowly out of sight and even at that distance they heard an exasperated sigh.

'Well, but d'you really want the kids to come?' said Quattrell in a low voice. 'It won't be their notion of fun, that sort of party.'

'Of course she must come,' said Phoebe, slightly nettled, 'and Nick too, if she wants him. It'll do her good.'

But when Tavy appeared downstairs and came slowly across the courtyard on dragging sandals it was clear that she had already made up her mind on the point. She stood at some distance from the table, twisting her hair behind her head with both hands, as though she had suddenly decided to put it up.

'I don't like parties, honestly,' she said. 'I'm always let off them at home, I never go.' She kept her eyes on Phoebe with only a momentary glance in Lytton's direction. She did not look at Quattrell.

'But this is our house-warming, Tavy. It's for you as much as for us. Besides, I shall need your help.'

'I'll help you beforehand, then. I used to do that at home.' She had pulled her hair round in a thick handful on one shoulder and was laboriously plaiting it. Quattrell and Lytton were both watching her and Quattrell's gaze had a touch of fascination. This irritated Phoebe.

'You can certainly help me, and come to the party as well. You can ask Nick too if you like. You can hand round the drinks and things, and be useful together.'

'No, thank you,' said Tavy gently, squinting sideways and with concentration as her fingers plaited and separated the thick hair. She seemed quite remote from the conversation and unembarrassed, as though it were a foregone conclusion that she would not come. 'I'll ask Nick, and we'll help you beforehand, like I said, but we'd really much rather not stay, if you don't mind.'

'How do you know what Nick would like?' Lytton asked, struck for the first time by the surprising thought that this alien creature had already imposed a pattern of conduct on the household, and had a life of her own. He looked at her with astonishment, taking in the long lines of arms and neck and the way the plaiting movement was lifting her cotton jersey and hinting at the shallow outline of both breasts.

'I do know. He's like me. He'd be bored.'

'Oh well, if that's how you feel about it.' Phoebe recognised defeat and turned back to her coffee with a prim expression, unwilling to waste more time. 'You must do as you like, of course. But I shall expect you to give me some help in the afternoon.'

'Of course I will, Aunt Phoebe.' Tavy still spoke gently, but

126

her face as she tossed back her plait showed a faint triumph. 'We'll both of us help you beforehand, like I said,' she added, and went off without hurry or excuse to her own room.

'Well!' said Phoebe, looking affrontedly at Lytton as the door closed. But Lytton was not at all sorry that his party need no longer be complicated by the presence of children, and turned to Quattrell for approval.

'A good thing. I never care for children at a party, they're nothing but a nuisance. Passing plates round every other minute and getting in the way. Absolute death to conversation.'

'You know, the kid's right,' said Quattrell, mechanically offering his cigarettes to Phoebe and appearing not to notice when she recoiled. 'I hated grown-up parties at her age. She's probably seen enough of them.'

'I doubt it,' said Lytton, glancing at Phoebe with a smile not quite free from malice. 'Her father's an insurance agent in Ipswich, with little margin, I fancy, for entertaining, and as for her mother . . .' But at this point he caught Phoebe's eye and prudently desisted. 'Well, let's get on with our list, and work out the number of bottles and all the details.'

'What I *can't* understand,' said Phoebe, unable for the moment to shake off her annoyance, 'is why, when everybody's doing their best to be kind to her, she has to be so *hostile*.'

'Oh, it's not that,' said Quattrell seriously, shaking his head, 'I know kids, you must too, you can't have forgotten what it's like? They feel up against it with all of us, it makes them prickly.' He gave her an easygoing smile from under his thick eyebrows, putting himself on her side, as though they were in this together, members of a tolerant and experienced generation. She returned his look and felt the beginnings of liking. How fortunate for Lytton, she thought, how unusual for herself, to have fallen into such easy friendship with this stranger.

'You're right, of course. And Tavy's been rather unlucky. Her parents are separated, it's all been most unfortunate. My nephew's not good with children, he hasn't the time.'

'He hasn't?' said Quattrell. He looked incredulous. 'And her mother?'

'Not really a very nice woman, though I shouldn't say it. She ran off with some other man, we don't even know where.'

'Too bad,' he said, shaking his head and frowning. 'Poor kid, poor kid. Too bad.' He crushed out his cigarette in a thoughtful manner, as though brooding on the unlucky aspects of Tavy's history, so that although she guessed from the creaking of his chair that Lytton was growing impatient Phoebe felt no more than a twinge of guilt over her indiscretion. By the time Quattrell got up to go, however, it occurred to her that she had given a wrong impression, and in a contrite spirit she accompanied him to the door.

'Mr Quattrell, I do hope you don't mind my saying this, but what I told you just now about Tavy's parents . . . I begin to feel I shouldn't have said it, but you'll treat it, I know, as having been said in confidence.'

'Why, of course. I took it as that.' He laid a hand on her arm and gently pressed it. 'I'm famous for keeping secrets. I don't talk.'

'Thank you,' said Phoebe gratefully. 'I was annoyed for the moment, I'm not usually so indiscreet.' They looked at one another in the gloomy passage and it seemed to Phoebe that a current of warmth and sympathy passed between them. 'And there's another thing,' she went on, 'since I've already said so much. I wouldn't like you to think, from what I said about Tavy's mother, that there was any bad heredity, or anything like that. My nephew and his wife are not in fact her real parents. They adopted her.'

'You don't say!' Quattrell looked genuinely surprised. 'That kind of complicates it, doesn't it? Is that another secret?'

'Tavy knows, but we don't talk about it. It's one of the things, I'm afraid, that's rather unsettled her. I don't think she feels she belongs to anyone. That's why one must try and remember, and make allowances.'

'Well, I think she's a swell kid, anyway,' said Quattrell, laying his hand on the latch. 'And she's damn lucky to have such a good aunt. You know what? I think that's the thing that's going to make all the difference.'

They smiled at one another again and Phoebe's anxiety dissolved in a feeling of pleasure.

'You're very understanding,' she said, 'and I'm glad I told you. It'll help you understand a few of our difficulties.'

She opened the door and Quattrell stooped under the lintel, turning as he went with a final friendly nod and wave of the hand. She stood for a moment, watching him descend to the tunnel, and as his bulky form receded it struck her that the street, for all its claustrophobic narrowness and traces of squalor, was suddenly much less alien than before. 'I am beginning to feel at home here,' she thought, and was pleasantly surprised. It was no use pretending that in a foreign place one wasn't enormously dependent on one's own people. 'Things will be different now that we're beginning to have friends.' She smiled a little to herself as she closed the door. It was a long time since the exchange of a few words with anyone had given her such pleasure.

*

Several days flew by in preparations for the party. Quattrell came and went, conferring with Lytton on the guests and telephoning invitations from some private haunt, since Lytton was still in two minds about installing a telephone. There was hardly time, he pointed out, and this was true, though his chief objection was on the score of expense. Phoebe made several trips to the European town, where there were good delicatessens, and to the nearby *souks*, from which she and Tavy returned with armfuls of flowers. The variety and cheapness of these intoxicated her; for the equivalent of a few shillings she was able to transform the patio with arrangements of arum lilies which would have done credit to a wedding.

'Good God, have you been robbing a church?' said Lytton, when he came upon them cutting the grassy binding from the stalks. 'The place looks like an undertaker's. Is this supposed to be funny, doing it like a funeral?' But he said it with quite a smile, so that she was taken aback only momentarily.

'They're so wonderfully beautiful,' she said, 'and so cheap, I couldn't resist them. But if you'd rather I got something else, perhaps carnations. . . .'

'No, no, I was only joking. They're very handsome,' and Lytton went back with a chuckle to the meticulous arrangement of his writing-table in the parlour. In these last few days he had been in his best form; symptoms were no more heard of.

'It's wonderful,' said Phoebe to Tavy in an undertone, 'how much Uncle Henry's cheered up at the prospect of a party.'

The drinks, as Lytton had hoped, were to be mainly Quattrell's affair. He had sent in some cases of wine from a wholesale depôt and was arranging for supplies of hard liquor from his favourite bar. This was to be on a sale or return basis, which was a relief, since, as Lytton pointed out, a great many people might prefer fruit-juice now that the weather was warmer. Two large baskets of oranges and one of lemons were brought to the house by boys and carried to the kitchen, where Phoebe and Tavy spent sticky hours slicing the dripping fruit and pumping the squeezer.

The weather promised well, though it was still incalculable. Two days before the party there had been a storm of rain, which alarmed everyone, since if the patio were cold and wet everything would have to be crowded into the parlour. But the following day the rain-clouds began to disperse, unravelled and blown to sea by a wind from the south, and the sun came out and licked up the moisture from the fig-tree, and the out-riders of two unsuspected invading armies, ants and centipedes, appeared from nowhere and opened their spring campaign round the walls of the courtyard.

The ants were numerous but small, not difficult to deal with; Tavy was set to trace them to their holes and sprinkle the cracks in the masonry with powder. They were easily defeated, or so at first it seemed, but no sooner was an advancing column wiped out than sapping and mining would start in another crevice, and the first scouts of a different platoon would suddenly appear and begin reconnoitring the tiles. The centipedes being more conspicuous were more vulnerable, but within twenty-four hours it became clear that they, too, had inexhaustible reserves. They travelled hither and thither about the patio, moving smoothly and on regular lines, like trains. They seemed to prefer the cool and the shade, dying as though sunstruck if they strayed too long on the hot tiles at midday, creeping to the edges of the walls or roots of the fig-tree and there giving up the ghost without further struggle, tightly curled on themselves like ammonites. Tavy swept them up into a dust-pan with feelings of disgust, but once, finding one travelling steadily on the wall of the parlour, she had picked up Lytton's magnifying glass and looked at the creature, and this close encounter, seeing it as it were on equal terms, on her own scale, had neutralised the horror and even brought her to a sort of remote sympathy. Making its way up the wall under the magnifying glass the centipede ceased to be black and was seen to have a carapace of tortoiseshell, mottled, highly polished, an exquisite sequence of smoothly fitting segments. His legs, rowing and rippling under the edges of his armour, appeared as a delicate thick pinkish fringe, the rhythmically stirring tentacles of a sea-anemone. And as though he were aware of the close approach of the glass he paused and raised his head, presenting a round, mild, puglike face which no one in their senses could object to. His tail, carried at a jaunty angle, tapered bluntly like the petiole of a cucumber. Tavy, following him again as he resumed his journey, found herself smiling. It was funny, almost comforting, to find the house had these secret and subterraneous populations, not only indifferent to human presences but unconscious of them, pursuing their ancient lives and multiplying their generations as though the foundations and the very rock had been theirs from the beginning. As indeed, she thought with surprise, they probably had. She put down the glass on Lytton's table and left the centipede where he was, continuing his mysterious ascension to the ceiling.

Tavy's provisioning for herself and Nick, which was to keep them going during the hours of the party, occupied a good deal of her attention.

'Can we have swordfish steaks,' she asked Phoebe, 'cold, with some of that mayonnaise, and garlic potatoes?'

'You can have anything you like, provided you get it yourself and don't get in my way. There's lots of nice little bits and pieces without bothering with swordfish.'

'I'm mad about it, though,' said Tavy, who had a capricious appetite, 'and Nick's wild about garlic potatoes, so I think I'll do them. And could we have a tart from the *patisserie*, and perhaps half of that Arab cheese?'

'You sound as though you're preparing to withstand a siege. Where are you going to have your picnic? On the roof?'

'No fear. You'll be bringing people up, and anyway it's too windy. We're going to have it in my room.'

'Oh, Tavy, I was going to put people's coats in there; Hadíjah must have somewhere.'

'Well, you can't have my room, I'm sorry. I shall bolt the door. There isn't anywhere else the least bit private.'

Phoebe saw the point, and reluctantly gave in.

'But the party may last for a couple of hours, you won't want to spend all that time just lurking in your bedroom.'

'Oh, we won't. We'll probably sit in the loft. I use it quite a lot, didn't you know? It's fun looking out of the window, you can see all sorts of things. I thought it would be nice to eat our picnic up there.'

'Well, if that really strikes you as more amusing than coming to the party,' said Phoebe, with the beginnings of a smile. 'After all, if you find it dull you can always come out.'

'Not till they've all gone, we shan't. Nick's got a pack of cards, he knows some tricks. You needn't worry about us, Aunt Phoebe, honestly.'

So Phoebe gave up worrying on that point at least, since Tavy was obviously more childish and less complicated than she had supposed; the mistake she had made all along was in treating her more or less as a grown-up person. She argued no further, but gave her money and sent her off by herself to the fish market.

And it was here, in a din so outrageous that her senses flinched, that Tavy for the first time forgot the impossibility of being loved and picked up the faint scent of her old happiness. The clamour and pressure of the crowd were beyond belief. Every huckster behind the slabs yelled as she passed, pointing to heaps of glistening octopus, to creels of rainbow-coloured fishes and transparent prawns, gesturing with scaly hands and blood-streaked knife to the shining bodies of fish she had never seen before, pink as coral, speckled, spiny, still faintly stirring when eagerly held out for her inspection, and all with the heady brine-and-seaweed smell which had come with them out of the sea and into the net. She pressed on slowly, ignoring the boys who followed her with plastic bags, with lemons, with garlic, with bunches of mint and parsley, threading her way between heavy-armed Spanish women arguing over their purchases and more than holding their own with the noisy Arabs, until she found the thing she wanted, the dark blue lustrous body of a great swordfish, beheaded and dismembered on the slab, the noble centre-piece of the day's massacre. She pointed to two thick slices of pinkish flesh and stared at the head as they were weighed, at the marvellous sword now useless and severed from the muzzle, at the broad brow, the huge dark deep-sea eye still shining in the mutilated head like a diver's lamp, and took her parcel and paid for it in silence. It was a sobering spectacle, both hideous and beautiful, and she breathed more easily when she had pushed her way through the crowd and left the market.

Her thoughts were not in the streets at all, but in her own room, with Nick, secure from the hateful party going on out-side. In imagination she went up the narrow stair to the door of the loft. Inside, on the floor, or perhaps on Lytton's trunk on a table-cloth, the picnic would be spread for the two of them, a feast in a cave. The loft had become a stronghold to which her spirit often withdrew while she indifferently moved elsewhere. Nobody went there but herself and Nick; it was inviolate. Warm, close, sweet-smelling, comfortably dark, it was the place where she was at once invisible and safe, with a secret eye through which she could watch the alien world, and therefore, in the magic sense, control it. All it had lacked before had been food and drink, and this at last, with the picnic, she would provide. To be hidden, to be safe, to be also deliciously fed, seemed to her so desirable that she swallowed her saliva and unconsciously quickened her pace as she considered it.

But the loft, on which her thoughts so lovingly dwelt, was a stage on the way to somewhere else, and to this her mind was more uneasily drawn. For the magic of the loft to work there were rules to be obeyed, the first and most important being that one had to set foot at least once in that other place. This other house was not safe; the hairs of her skin rose slightly as she thought of it; but the power had been put in her hand like a key and she betrayed both the magic and herself if she didn't use it. The thought which most frightened and at the same time quite peculiarly excited her was that the empty house was four or five stories deep. She had heard Lytton say so; he had had it on Mackannis's authority. The front door, he had positively said, was several streets lower down, almost one might say in a different part of the Medina. There was something singularly dream-like in the very idea, and when she allowed her imagination to dwell on it it was always with a *frisson* of terror, a shiver of doubt. There was something down below, of that she was sure. She was equally certain that everything depended on her going there, with Nick of course, like Theseus threading the labyrinth to the Minotaur. So, poised in a trembling balance between danger and security and weaving her own myths, Tavy was hardly aware of the streets she passed through and wandered unscathed through crowds and noise as though it were she who was awake and the figures she brushed in passing were only dreams. When she came to Lytton's door she stood still for a moment, staring with vacant eyes at the knocker, unable to remember what it was that she had to do. The pupils of her eyes were dilated and her skin had a curious, almost transparent pallor, as though some part of her mind were withdrawn, in sleep or trance.

'Heavens, child, you do look pale,' said Phoebe, when at last the knocker had sounded and she opened the door. 'Is everything all right?'

'Perfectly, thank you,' said Tavy in a cool voice. She collected herself with an effort and stepped inside, her colour beginning to return. 'I've got the fish, that's all,' she said over her shoulder, making her way to the kitchen with that deliberately uncommunicative look which Phoebe knew so well, and no longer minded. It was infinitely more comfortable, now that she had convinced herself of Tavy's childishness, to get on with what she was doing in tranquil silence.

8

DURING the night there was more rain, but only enough to wash the wind-blown sand from the terrace and the dust from the tender foliage of the fig-tree, which was now in brilliant leaf and very beautiful, throwing a pattern of shade over the courtyard at midday and echoing at all hours with the chirping of sparrows. The sun for the first time had a sting of heat, and as it shone down vertically through the branches Phoebe's lilies gave off a sappy smell.

Quattrell had procured a buffet table from somewhere, draped to the ground and furnished with quantities of glasses; cases of wine were concealed under the tablecloth. He had also borrowed armfuls of velvet cushions which proved to have been brought by Ozzie from Molly Brockhurst's. They were fringed and old and expensive-looking, and scattered on several improvised divans introduced a voluptuous note into the patio. Chairs, on the other hand, had not been thought necessary. People would stand, Quattrell said, whatever one provided; they were afraid of sitting down in case they missed something, and if the party went well enough there were always the divans. A professional barman had been briefly considered, but Lytton had been doubtful of the cost; he and Quattrell and Ozzie, he argued, could look after the drinks, and when Gerald Askew-Martin offered Enrico he accepted with relief, since a white-coated man-servant was just the thing and would leave him free to concentrate on his guests. For the rest, Hadíjah was to return in the late afternoon, wearing full dress, and had engaged to bring a female relation to help her. Lytton at first had questioned this arrangement, fearing that they might create too humble an impression, but when they arrived after tea and removed their wrappings he saw at once that they were the finishing touch.

They were robed in voluminous kaftans of flowered brocade, shining through transparent overdresses of muslin, and had bound up their hair with gauzy scarves and decked themselves out with earrings and gilt necklaces. The younger woman was almost as handsome as Hadíjah, in the same lean dark-eyed high-featured Berber style, with a smile full of gold teeth and hands which a lifetime of scrubbing had hardly coarsened: they were strong and shapely, and the palms, like the soles of her feet, were stained with henna. 'Absolutely superb!' said Lytton in a whisper, watching as they carried dishes of nuts and *canapés* to the table; 'you see what they've made of it Phoebe—a Delacroix interior!' They had indeed simply by their presence transformed the look of the place beyond recognition, so that even Phoebe, normally prone to anxiety before any such occasion, saw it suddenly as mysterious and suggestive, full of eloquent shadows and unforeseen possibilities, as though revealed in a different dimension, slightly hallucinated. She lit the lantern in the fig-tree and went up to dress in a tingling mood of almost girlish excitement.

*

'Good lord,' said Tavy, pausing in the act of lighting a candle and throwing up her head, 'don't say they're here already?' The knocker had sounded twice, but the walls of the loft were too thick to be sure of voices. She put the flame to the wick and they both listened; the candle threw dwarfish shadows up the walls of the room.

'I'll go down and look, shall I?' said Nick, peering at his wrist-watch. 'It's seven already, it might be the first arrivals.' He scrambled from his cross-legged position and prepared to step over the trunk, which was covered with a clean cloth and laid like a table. The cold fish and potatoes and an apricot pastry had been arranged as well as the small place allowed on a number of picnic plates and plastic dishes.

'I'm coming too,' said Tavy at once, 'you'll make a noise with the bolt.' They went down the stairs together and after listening for a moment at the door of the bedroom she cautiously slid the bolt and turned the handle. The door opened a fraction, enough for her to put an eye to the crack. It was, as she had guessed, only Quattrell and Consuelo and the Askew-Martins, come early to support Lytton and Phoebe and to save them the despondency of that first half-hour when everything silently waits and nobody arrives. Lytton, she saw, was wearing his velvet jacket and Quattrell for once was quite respectably turned out. They were all talking together under the fig-tree, the amber panes of the lantern as it faintly swung throwing sequins of golden light over Anthea's dress. She was wearing something sleeveless, very straight and cool, but Consuelo had been more ambitious and Tavy widened the crack for a better view. The hinges creaked and Quattrell looked over his shoulder, as though he were on the alert for some private signal.

'Hi, kids! he called cheerfully, raising a hand. 'Come out of there, we know you!' and broke away from the group and came strolling in their direction across the patio.

'Damn and blast,' said Tavy under her breath, hastily bolting the door. They fled silently up to the loft and sank down at the table, both of them suddenly hysterical and out of breath. They looked at one another and were convulsed with laughter, covering their mouths with their hands. Tavy was the first to recover.

'That was a grotty thing to do,' she said, taking up a spoon and helping Nick to fish. 'Another second and that oaf would have been in on us. I can't stand him, can you? Of all of them he makes me the most sick.' This was not quite true, but the effect of Quattrell's presence was always disturbing; it contained an element difficult to interpret.

'Oh, I don't mind him,' said Nick. 'I rather like him in fact. I passed him yesterday in the Petit Socco ,and he turned back and we went into that big café and had ices. He speaks Arabic, more or less. I told him I knew a few words that I'd got from Hamid.'

'How simply terrific for you,' said Tavy, losing interest. They ate for a while in silence. 'I wish it wasn't getting so dark,' she said presently, filling her mouth with the skin of a baked potato. 'If only we could've done it this afternoon. It's maddening.' Her eyes shifted to the tiny square of window; the sky looked almost black by candlelight.

'It won't make any difference,' said Nick calmly. 'The moon's in the third quarter, it'll be quite bright. And I've got the torch and a candle and a box of matches. We couldn't possibly want more.'

'No, I know. It's just the idea. I'm quite good in the dark, actually. I was scared to death as a kid, but I'm all right now. I just wish we could have done it in daylight, that's all I meant. Just this first time.'

'It might have been easier, perhaps, but you needn't be scared. I know what Arab houses are like; I've been in them at night, often.'

'I'm not a bit scared, if you must know. I see very well in the dark as a matter of fact.'

'You won't even have to, this torch is terrific.' He picked up the torch from the floor and moved the switch, flashing a sudden beam into Tavy's face. It was certainly very bright, and she winced painfully.

'All right, you clot, no need to show off.' He obediently switched off the torch and went on eating. 'That's a dangerous thing to do, as a matter of fact. You could damage a person's eyes; my father said so.'

'What rot, he was pulling your leg. Pete and I do it all the time, it's quite harmless.' He cut himself a wedge of pastry and licked his fingers. 'And you can tell him so from me, when you go home.'

'He wouldn't be interested in what little boys believe,' said Tavy loftily. 'My father's a scientist. He works in a lab all day, doing experiments.'

'Well, tell him to experiment on you with a torch, then, and if you go blind he can buy you a pair of black spectacles.'

Tavy thought this over, shifting a crust of pastry from cheek to cheek.

'None of us wear spectacles in our family. We all have perfect sight, we're famous for it.'

'Everyone wears dark glasses out here, specially on the beach. Even my mother does, and so does Pete.'

'Mine doesn't. She says they're an affectation. She travels all over the world and she never needs them.'

'Really?' Nick was unwillingly impressed, but a little sceptical. 'Why does she travel so much? Where is she now?'

Tavy stared for a moment; her eyes widened.

'She's in Persia as a matter of fact,' she said in an offhand voice. 'She's going on to India next week. I just had a letter.'

'From Persia? Have you got the stamp?'

'I don't collect silly stamps. I throw them away.'

'Stamps can be valuable,' said Nick seriously. 'You can save the next one for me, when she writes again.'

'Oh, I really couldn't be bothered.' Tavy fastidiously lifted a strand of hair and placed it behind her ear. 'She writes to me every week, and I throw them away. At least,' she amended, warily meeting his eye and looking away again, 'if I save any at all I send them straight back to my father in London. He has a big collection.'

'I thought you said you lived in Ipswich.'

'Well, so we do, part of the time. We have houses in both places.'

'Pity. I could have done with the Persian one.' He brushed some pastry crumbs from his shirt reflectively. 'I've brought something for you, at any rate,' he said presently, sounding politely reproachful. 'Though perhaps not, after all. You mightn't like it.'

'What is it?'

'Wait and see. We'll have it when we're down in the house.' He looked at his watch again, flexing his wrist and frowning, as he had seen people do in films. 'We'd better take off if we're going. It's nearly half-past.'

They crept down the stairs in silence. The noise of the party had swelled to a steady roar, and as they listened a woman laughed, quite close to the door, and cried, 'I can't wait! Are you coming?' There were sounds of feet on the stairs: evidently a group was on its way to the terrace.

140

'Come on,' said Nick, and opened the casement window. Tavy groped under the bed for the rope and when Nick had lifted the movable half of the grille he tied the rope with knots to the solid ironwork. He knelt on the sill and Tavy climbed closely after him. It was not at all dark outside; the moon was up already and the sky fading from pearl to a deeper dusk, a delusive dark which would soon be clear and luminous. They could hear the voices of children a long way off, and near at hand, like a pulse, the throb of a drum.

'They've been making that noise all day, off and on,' said Tavy in a whisper.

Nick grunted and worked his way to the edge of the window-sill, sat for a moment with his legs dangling, grasped the rope with both hands and dropped out of sight. Tavy heard him land and leaned anxiously out. It was not very far after all; he was within reach.

'Come on!' he said again irritably, 'don't hang about.' He took hold of her legs as she clung to the sill and she came down in a rush and fell heavily against him. 'Easier than I thought. We could have done it without the rope.'

'I don't call it easy. Leave it there all the same.'

'Well, of course. I'm not bar ny.'

They looked round the silent roof, which was deep in shadow. The moon was quite bright on the upper levels but the broken panes of the stair-head were very dark. Tavy had second thoughts.

'We can't get in after all. The door's locked.'

'I know. It always was.' He tiptoed across the roof and examined the padlock; after a cowardly moment Tavy followed. He had turned from the door and was picking at the broken panes. There were several sizeable gaps and the frames were rotten. 'This is the thing,' he said, and knocked in a piece of glass with the point of his elbow.

It fell with a splintering crash on the bare tiles, and Tavy covered her ears and shut her eyes. But when she could bring herself to open them Nick was already edging his way through the gap and had suddenly switched on the torch and was standing inside, sweeping the beam over the stained walls and down the well of the stairs into that part of the house they had never seen.

'Wait!' she cried, shaken with a new fear, and gripped the twisted frame and thrust in a leg, grazing the back of her knee, though in the panic of being abandoned she felt nothing.

'Don't make such a row,' said Nick crossly, gripping her ankle. 'Put your foot *here*. That's right. Look out for your hands, stupid.' And suddenly they were both there, standing at the head of a dirty staircase which went down and turned at an angle into smelly darkness. 'It's easy, you see,' he told her, 'there's no need to get excited.' But he stood for a moment longer, fidgeting at the switch of the torch before swinging the beam round the stairs and beginning, a step at a time, to go slowly down.

*

'The great difficulty, as you will readily understand,' said Lytton, 'was in striking the right note, the happy mean as it were, between what we found and what we wished to achieve.' He leaned forward from the divan for a better view, then turned to Molly Brockhurst on a suspicion that she was not attending.

'Yes, yes,' she said, bringing her gaze into focus with a slight effort, 'it's very pretty.' Her hand crept out to Ozzie sitting beside her; he unobtrusively clasped it.

'Pretty, perhaps? I hope not; that's not quite what one was aiming at. A Moorish house is bare, it has a certain austerity. The Arabs are fundamentally a people without furniture: their nomad blood is indifferent to tables and chairs. So the problem, you see, was to preserve that quality and at the same time, without overdoing it, to make oneself comfortable. I think one can say without affectation that it's a moderate success. Fortunately,' with a deprecating shrug, 'I had little to spend. A richer man, I believe, could have easily spoiled it.' He gave his companion a sharper, more questioning glance. Her lips were slightly parted but she said nothing, only felt vaguely with her free hand for her walking-stick, an ebony cane with an ivory handle which was lying an inch or two away from her knee. She gave the impression of not being entirely present in the conversation, as though she were trying to elucidate something of her own and heard Lytton's voice intermittently, as from a distance.

'I think you've done *absolute* wonders,' said Ozzie, coming to the rescue. 'Of course the fig-tree's a stupendous feature, and with that lantern! I can't take my eyes off it.' He did, however, turn them in anxious inquiry to Molly's face and secretly brought her back with a pressure of the hand.

'Oh yes,' she said, coming to, 'I think it's remarkably pretty. You've done very well.'

They were sitting together in the parlour, gazing through the archway into the patio, which was satisfactorily crowded with standing people. Hadíjah was slowly threading her way with a tray of glasses and the confusion of voices was so great that Lytton was no longer in doubt as to the success of his party. He began to feel that he had unsuitably marooned himself, and saw with relief that Molly's glass was empty.

'You must let me get you a little wine,' he said, getting to his feet and ignoring her murmur of protest, 'I'm a neglectful host when I start talking,' and disappeared a shade too quickly into the crowd, where he was soon seen again, head and shoulders above most of the company, deep in converse with a stylish-looking elderly clergyman.

'Who was that?' said Molly, following him with her undifferentiating stare.

'Darling, I told you, that's H. B. Lytton. *This is his party*. He's a writer.' He gave her hand a couple of affectionate pats.

'Oh, I see. Of course. And who are these other people?'

'I don't know all of them, darling. Rob's imported a lot of strangers. That handsome dark man's a Moroccan, I think he's a lawyer, and that Scandinavian-looking lady in the white dress is Mrs. Askew-Martin.'

'Askew-Martin?' Molly looked vaguely at Anthea; she seemed non-plussed. 'I used to know someone of that name, didn't I, years ago? But the wife was older than that. He was a friend of James.' She peered at Anthea short-sightedly. 'It can't be the same one,' she said, and closed her eyes, trying to imagine why the name should have awakened echoes of the old trouble.

'Well, this is quite a new wife,' said Ozzie cheerfully, 'he's been married twice, so I dare say it isn't the same.' He patted her hand and released it, having caught sight of Phoebe. 'Ah, there's the one I want you to talk to, darling—Miss Townsend. I'll go and get her.' He was on his feet before Molly had grasped his intention.

'Ozzie! Don't leave me!' Her hand flew at once to her stick, as though she would follow him.

'Only a second, my pet. Be back in a minute.' But as soon as he had breached the crowd he encountered Gerald, and as both had empty glasses it was obviously necessary to move to the bar together, so that by the time Ozzie remembered Phoebe she had disappeared and Molly had been companionably joined by Consuelo and Quattrell.

'Rob thinks you don't like him,' said Ozzie tentatively, giving Gerald an arch look over the rim of his glass.

'Really, what makes him think that?'

'Oh, I don't know. He's a peculiar customer. He gets these notions.'

Gerald found Anthea at his shoulder and moved to make room for her. Her eyes were very bright; from habit he looked to see what she had in her glass.

'Do you want another, darling girl, or have you had enough?'

'A small one, perhaps. I haven't had very much. I can't say I'm deeply impressed by our dear Enrico.'

Gerald looked sharply round with a suspicious frown. Enrico was behaving badly, but there was nothing to be done. He had turned up in a frilled shirt, without his coat, and after a token appearance at the bar had plunged gaily into the throng with the other guests.

'*Not* a success. It was Quattrell's idea, not mine. What is it you're drinking?'

'I'm not quite sure; something nasty. I'd rather have whisky.' Whisky was economically absent from the ranks of bottles, but Ozzie knew where it was and went under the table. Anthea waited, not looking at Gerald but idly running a finger round the rim of her glass. They were hemmed in on every side and the noise of a dozen conversations was extraordinary.

'You don't like Rob Quattrell, do you?' she said, close to his ear. 'I wish I knew why.'

'I haven't any good reason. Just a feeling.'

'You can't pin it down? I'm curious.'

'I can if I make an effort, I suppose. It all goes back to a highly disreputable incident. I met him in the company of someone who caused me a lot of trouble. The sort that you had once. I prefer to forget it.'

Anthea looked incredulous and glanced over her shoulder. Quattrell was nowhere to be seen and she felt a moment's uneasiness, having arrived without precisely knowing how at the point where she was constantly aware of him. But not in this connection; the thing was grotesque. She thought with a spasm of recoil of the day two years ago (that buried day of the night when James was drowned) when she had received a clumsy threat from an unknown blackmailer and had flown to Gerald in distress, learning in the course of a long night's drinking and bewilderment that he too, much longer ago and for very different reasons, had had a similar experience. Now almost for the first time since that nightmare incident she could look back on it with detachment, as something that had happened to her old self, in her old life, having neither power nor meaning in her new one. But to think of Rob in the same breath as the thief who had rifled James's love-letters was absurd. Gerald was being unreasonable.

'I remember now,' she said. 'You met him in a bar. But people can be drinking together in the same bar without being in league together.'

'Of course. I wouldn't dream of attaching importance to it. He just gives me an uncomfortable feeling, that's all there is to it.'

'You don't have to worry,' said Anthea, smiling and touching his sleeve with a playful finger.

'Indeed, no. Worry is far from my thoughts.' There was a

slight commotion under the tablecloth and Ozzie emerged, somewhat tousled, with a bottle of whisky.

'My dear! I've been all the way to the kitchen and back by this spelaeologist's route. Isn't it incredible? *Why* do people stand in such solid masses when the other end and the parlour's practically empty?' He opened the bottle. 'But oh, was it worth it, not only for the Scotch but also for a revealing glimpse of your Enrico! He's holding court in the kitchen—to an all-male audience I *couldn't* help but observe—all quelling glances and hand on hip, like a bull-fighter.' He said this to Gerald with an air of innocence, but Anthea saw that he lay in wait for the effect and that his eye had the expert watchfulness of jealousy.

'He won't be our Enrico much longer,' she said, steadying her glass while he filled it with ice and whisky. Gerald's face was impassive, and again she looked over her shoulder in search of Quattrell. This time her glance met his; he was standing in a knot of people at the far end, listening to the frocked priest but with heavy head erect, gazing in her direction. She caught his eye over the distance with a shock of pleasure, and was aware that he felt it too; they had exchanged signals. Both at the same time began to edge unobtrusively away from their group, and when they met in the middle of the crowd it was with a sense of secret advance since they had last spoken.

'I've been wanting to show you the view,' he said conversationally, as though she were a new acquaintance. 'You haven't been up on the roof yet? It's rather fine.' He took her glass and touched her elbow with his fingers, steering her past Lytton's shoulder in the direction of the stairs. There were two young men and a girl sitting on the lower steps, shrilly arguing; they neither looked up nor moved and Quattrell and Anthea stepped over them without apology.

The terrace was in clear moonlight and the air still. From the central well rose a hum of confused voices, filtered and diffused by the fig-tree's heavy foliage. They paused for a moment and looked down, but except for a greenish glow through the leaves there was little to be seen. They turned and leaned their arms on the outer parapet.

'I telephoned three times,' said Quattrell in a low voice. 'D'you have some rule, that you're never the one to answer?'

'No. It's answered by whoever's there. Enrico told me you'd called.'

'I made up my mind you were avoiding me.' He gave her her glass without looking at her and lifted his own. They both drank in silence. Below them the town was sharpening its pattern of contrasts, deep shadow and clear moonlight broken by cubes and canyons of electric brightness. Drums were beating irregularly somewhere below and beyond the arm of the harbour a ship lay at anchor, a glittering ghost pricked out in fairground lights.

'I'm not avoiding you, as you see, but there's nothing I can do.' Her tone was final and regretful, but in the pause that followed something far from final hovered between them.

'I can't do it all,' he said. 'I've done what I can. I can meet you anywhere, any time, and I've got the car. For God's sake don't be afraid of it, Anthea. It shouldn't be impossible.' He moved his hand on the parapet so that their fingers touched, and she had a moment of longing, an exhilarating stir of response so sudden that it startled her. If she had dared in that moment, if she had been prepared for it, she would have turned to him there and then for whatever embracing warmth his maleness offered her. But as the impulse trembled and passed there was the sound of someone stirring and clearing a throat, and a cigarette glowed and faded on the edge of darkness.

'No, no,' said Quattrell conversationally, without turning, 'it's one of those Union Castle boats. There was a mob of tourists out of her this morning.'

'She looks very pretty, anyhow, with all those lights.' They both continued to gaze and sip their whisky, as though they were in love with the hour and had the night before them.

Presently Quattrell said, keeping his voice low, 'It isn't Gerald that's the difficulty, is it? That would be too unreasonable.'

'Partly it is. He's been so good to me.'

'And you to him, I imagine. I know the form: he has to have

window-dressing. But he's not a monster, surely? He'd think it fair?'

'I suppose he would. I'm not sure. It would depend.' Impossible to admit that that had been the basis of Gerald's proposal of marriage, in the days when she was torn in pieces by her long love affair with James, when she had known she must lose him in the end, slowly and with misery, because of his bleak refusal to abandon Molly. Married to Gerald, she knew, she could still have had James. But James was dead, and for two years they had lived together in mutual security and found much comfort in it. And beyond that, nothing. 'I'm afraid he doesn't much like you,' she said at length. 'I don't know why.'

'Well, I do. A., he's perfectly aware that I'm in a state of love about you, and whatever the situation it doesn't exclude jealousy. B., and I'm sure this is it, I knew about a blackmailing incident years ago, even knew the bastard who was responsible, but I'd be angry if either of you believed I was involved in it.'

'I don't, Rob. I don't think even Gerald believes that.'

'Of course he doesn't. But I know about it, and he knows I know, and he'd rather I was dead or some place else. That's all there is to it.'

'I'll think about it.' But her thoughts refused to stir, summoning instead, like the echo of a bad dream, the altogether horrifying glimpse she had had of Molly.

'You think about it hard, there's a good girl. We haven't got for ever.' He looked moodily over his shoulder into the darkness. There was still somebody sitting on the terrace in deep shadow.

'Then there's Consuelo,' said Anthea defensively, with a faint shiver. She clasped her arms: the air felt suddenly cold.

'You must tell her, that's obvious. She'll be on our side.'

'I wouldn't be sure of that. But I *will* think about it.' She had heard a movement, and turned away from the parapet. Mackannis had come down from the upper steps and emerged into the moonlight.

'Like myself, you are enjoying the view,' he said, approaching them. 'Our friend Mr. Lytton has done well with his house, I find. It is an arresting situation, yes? Almost too romantic.'

'Ah, you old devil,' said Quattrell, putting an arm round his shoulder. 'It was you, was it, lurking in that corner? You old spy.'

'You looked so nice,' said Mackannis with dry politeness, making a little bow to Anthea. 'You were grouped like a pair of lovers, you completed the scene.'

They laughed and the three of them went down to the patio together.

*

The party had begun to thin out but a hard core remained; several groups had settled down to talk on divans, on the few chairs, on cushions on the floor, as though they intended to stay for the rest of the night. Enrico and his friends had disappeared. Lytton and the cassocked clergyman were accompanying Molly on a slow-motion tour of inspection and were moving into the parlour to view the death mask, Molly going rather shakily, leaning on her stick. The buffet table was littered with crumbs and ash-trays and used glasses, and Phoebe, with Hadijah in attendance, was making furtive efforts to clear up.

'My *dear* Miss Townsend.' Ozzie appeared at her elbow. 'You're not supposed to be working! I've been trying for the last half-hour to get you to come and talk to Molly Brockhurst.'

'I should like to, very much, but this table's in such a mess. If people are going on drinking we shall need fresh glasses.' It struck her that a great deal of wine had been consumed already and rather excessive inroads made on the whisky. She paused and appeared to listen. The sound of drumming, which at first had been soft and occasional, a muffled pulse, had swelled in the last half-hour until it seemed to creep and vibrate through the very structure.

'But of *course* people are going on drinking. It's a *lovely* party. It's only the odd-bods that have left: good riddance, don't you think? That tiresome boy-friend of Gerald's and his train of harpies, and that odious American who can't stop talking about crossing the Sahara in a jeep.'

'*Whose* boy-friend? Whoever can you mean?' Phoebe looked

startled. But as she said it she remembered a peculiar remark of Quattrell's and could, as she put it to herself, have bitten her tongue out. She wondered if Ozzie were possibly a little in drink.

'That Italian manikin in the frilled shirt, the one who minces about with Gerald Askew-Martin.'

'Oh!' Phoebe was immensely relieved; her face relaxed. 'My dear Ozzie, that's Enrico, their house-parlourman.'

'Oh, is *that* what he is?' Ozzie was deftly lifting and examining glasses. 'Well, I never. How crass of me. I never guessed.'

'I rather share your disapproval, I must say. He was supposed to help, and he hasn't lifted a finger.'

'Never mind, he's gone now.' He gave her a little smile, seemingly satisfied. 'Well, come and talk to my poor Molly for a bit, she's dying to meet you.'

Molly was still in the parlour with Lytton and the clergyman, grouped before Sarah's mask. The sound of drumming was softer but still perceptible, subterraneously punctuating the conversation.

'It's very beautiful,' Molly was saying in a forlorn voice, 'but don't you find it . . . just the least, the tiniest bit . . . melancholy?'

'Why, no, the very reverse,' said Lytton. 'I don't find it melancholy at all. What do *you* say, Father?' He turned to the priest, whose face was not wholly unlike a mask itself, moulded on Gothic lines, grooved and formal.

'Not melancholy, no, no. No, not at all.' His voice was deep and fruity, faintly theatrical. 'So much is in the eye of the beholder, one's response is subjective. What strikes me at once is the peaceful, one is almost tempted to say, the *merciful* expression.'

'But she looks so *dead*,' said Molly in a wailing voice.

Phoebe glanced over their shoulders at Sarah's mask and wondered if Mrs. Brockhurst realised she was talking to the widower. To Phoebe, as always, the face was capable of subtle changes; it was ambiguous. From what she remembered of Sarah's estimable qualities she would not have said that mercy had been one of them.

Ozzie touched Molly's arm in discreet warning. 'Here's Miss Townsend waiting to talk to you, dear, when you've finished your tour.'

'We've only just begun,' said Lytton sharply, 'we're on our way to the terrace.' But Molly's eyes were fixed on the priest and Ozzie could see that the man had made an impression.

'I'm not very good at stairs,' she murmured, leaning on her stick, 'I'd rather sit down again, please, and talk to this gentleman.' She focused her gaze to give him a questioning look. 'What did you say your name was?'

'Emery, dear lady. Father Adrian Emery.'

'Are you a priest?'

'Indeed. Of the Anglican persuasion.'

'Oh, Ozzie, do find me a chair. I really must sit down.' So the group broke up, and Ozzie went back to the courtyard with Phoebe and Lytton.

*

'Mrs. Brockhurst seems very frail,' said Phoebe, when they had found chairs. 'And she's lame, I noticed, poor thing. I suppose that was the accident?'

'Not really lame, just shaky. She's up and down, this isn't one of her good days. And you didn't get your talk, did you, after all my scheming? I begin to think she has a thing about handsome clerics.'

'Quite an intelligent man,' said Lytton, 'If a trifle dressy. I gather he's no longer in practice, if that's what they call it. Rather curious to appear in full fig if he's only on holiday.'

'Oh, but it's so beautifully cut!' cried Ozzie. 'And have you seen his cloak? Silver clasps as big as *that*! I'm mad about it.'

'Is Mrs. Brockhurst religious, then?' said Phoebe. She was sympathetic to the idea, especially for others, and could easily believe that the survivor of such a disaster would need spiritual comfort.

'Not really, I don't think.' Ozzie turned his head for a moment, looking for Molly. '*I* think she needs an analyst, but in her state, poor darling, perhaps . . . anyway she won't hear of it.'

'I doubt whether she'd hear a word the analyst was saying,' said Lytton drily. 'She's switched off most of the time. Very difficult to talk to.'

'Well, yes, you see. And her memory's so bad. She can't help it, poor sweet, and sometimes she's as sharp as a needle; then again you can't tell whether she's telling you something that happened, or just one of her delusions.'

'Oh, how sad for her.' Phoebe was impressed. 'What form do they take?'

'Well, she can't remember people; she mixes them up. And on bad days she thinks—you remember I told you about her husband being drowned—she thinks it was all her fault, that she was responsible.'

'But how could she be?'

'Exactly so. She couldn't. But she's never been the same, I'm not surprised, and that happens to be one of the ways the thing takes her.' Ozzie looked round once more, discovered where Gerald was and with whom, reassuring himself that Molly was still engrossed. 'I rather wish she *would* join some church or other. Something *pretty*, with flowers and incense and beautiful soothing services and weekly confession. I'm sure it would do her good.'

'Then why doesn't she?'

'Oh, it's so *difficult*. She says she'd feel bogus, not being a regular believer. *I* say, that doesn't matter. She's a person who ought to have God, if only to talk to.'

'She can talk to *you*,' said Phoebe with a kindly smile.

'Oh goodness, Miss Townsend, I'm not in the same category. She can talk to me, of course; she does; but it doesn't answer. I can't convince her that she's not a sinner, or that Hell doesn't exist, or that her illness hasn't been sent from God because she deserves it.'

'But surely she can't believe that herself,' said Lytton, bored with the conversation and contributing the remark from duty, as a free-thinker.

'Well, yes, in a funny way she does. It's the way it takes her, poor darling, it's no use talking. I've tried and tried, and she brushes me away like a fly.'

'You must have patience, then,' said Phoebe earnestly. 'You must persist, like a good fly. We all need patience.'

*

'Well, what's new?' Consuelo asked, filling her mouth. She had found some overlooked cheese-straws in the kitchen. 'How's it going with your new beau? Mackannis described quite a touching scene, up on the terrace.'

'The scene was touching,' said Anthea, 'because he was too far off to hear what we were saying. We were looking at the view by moonlight and discussing tourists.'

'Was that all?' Consuelo looked pleased but sceptical. 'Didn't he make a pass, the old gorilla? I thought I saw it in his eye.' She tilted her head on one side with a teasing smile.

'I'm afraid not. I'm not the recipient of passes these days, more's the pity.'

'Well, you could be, it's entirely your own fault. He's the only man I've seen around here, judging by the sample.' She picked up another cheese-straw and bit it reflectively. 'Why do I eat these darn things? My appetite's neurotic. All the same,' her eye slid back inquisitively to Anthea, 'what d'you think of him?'

'I haven't thought very much. What do you?'

'Ah, that's asking! Dynamic, wouldn't you say? Rather my type, worse luck. And not to be trusted.'

'What makes you say that?'

'Oh, I don't know. We just had a drink together, he asked me to lunch. Would you mind if I went? Would Gerald? He suggested tomorrow.'

'Of course I wouldn't. You go. It'll be something to do.'

'Yep, that's what I thought. I will, if it's all the same. Might be amusing.' She seemed relieved, as though she had feared some warning or prohibition. 'He's married, of course. Goes without saying. Did you know that?'

'I believe he mentioned it.'

Consuelo shrugged. 'Well, what the hell, that's his funeral. If one started finicking about *that* one might as well take up knitting.'

'Quite,' said Anthea indifferently. The observation called for a smile, but she felt unequal to it. The idea of Consuelo as an ally had become distasteful, receding, as she had known it must, to its proper distance. She felt obscurely angry and impatient, with herself rather than with Quattrell or Consuelo. He was at least trying.

'I do wish they'd stop this drumming,' said Phoebe, carrying a tray of glasses into the kitchen. 'If only one knew what it was *for*. It makes me nervous.'

'It's another feast, I think,' said Anthea. 'So Lytton told me.'

'Oh mercy, not another!'

'I like it,' said Consuelo, clenching her little fists and raising them to her breast. 'It's like something in a corny film. Like being surrounded by cannibals.'

'Oh dear, don't say that! Do you suppose the children are all right?'

'The children?' Consuelo looked astonished.

'Tavy and Nick. They've been locked in her room for ages. I don't know why; they wouldn't come to the party.'

'Oh, *them*. I couldn't think who you meant. Tavy's not a child, not by a long chalk. With that hair, and those legs? The girl's a menace.'

'She's unusually young for her age,' said Phoebe in a tone of remonstrance. 'They must be longing to come out. It's only just struck me, they might want to go to the bathroom.'

'You leave them alone, that's what,' said Consuelo belligerently. She was a little drunk. 'It's what kids like, and who's to blame them? I've always been keen on being left to my own devices.'

'I think I'll just go and knock. You know . . . in case.'

'I bet they won't hear you,' said Consuelo, 'they'll think it's a drum.' She beat an exuberant tattoo with her finger-nails on the table, as though this idea, or another, had raised her spirits.

9

THE first thing Tavy noticed as they began to go down was a faintly feral smell, as though at some time, before the odours of rot and mildew had invaded it, the house had been inhabited by animals. It was an ancient smell which crept into the nostrils and remained there, the acrid breath one encounters in certain caves.

'Nick! Don't go so fast! I can't see where I'm going.' She had touched the walls with her fingers and now stood still, not liking the dark descent or the feel of the tiles.

'It's all right. Nothing to be afraid of.' He swung the beam of the torch in her direction. 'Look out for that broken stair. I'm on the landing.'

She came down cautiously, a step at a time, and they peered about them. They had reached what appeared to be a central well, framed in a square gallery with iron railings. Doorways from which the doors had been removed opened on four sides into empty rooms; another stair led down from the far corner. The floor was caked with some old and dark deposit and at the edge of the well, where this was thickest, a struggling growth of pallid weed had sprouted. The musty smell was perceptibly stronger here, yet there seemed nothing to account for it.

'Nick! Don't go any further. It smells funny.'

'Probably bats. I think I've smelt it before.' He flashed the torch round the broken edges of the ceiling, and when this revealed nothing but crumbling plaster kicked at a clump of weed and dislodged a fragment. The roots were matted in a blackish substance which gave off a pungent odour of old droppings. 'That's what it is. I expect they roost on the railing.' Tavy snatched back the hand which had been resting on it.

'Bats! How horrible! *Please* don't go any further.' But Nick had already moved through the nearest doorway and was making a cautious survey of the empty room. It was not much bigger than a closet, with nothing in it but the remains of a wooden shelf supported on one leg at a height which suggested it might have been used as a table. On this there was certainly a cluster of dark droppings, and above them, a few inches from the ceiling, the end of a wooden joist protruded from the wall.

'Nothing to fuss about,' said Nick, 'they'll be out now, anyway. I suppose this was the kitchen.'

'This poky little hole? How could it, at the top of the house?'

'Well, yes, it usually is. Easy for the roof. Washing and cooking, all that sort of thing.' He turned back to the landing and they examined the rooms in turn. All were empty, and the dust and fragments of plaster on the floors looked as though no one had been in them for a long time. None had windows more than a few inches square and these were too high in the wall to be looked out of. In the last room they could distinctly hear sounds at a distance which came from the street; voices of children a long way below, the scrape of a pail on stone and a drum tapping; and further off still the voice of the beggar that Tavy knew, importunately crying. Nick switched off the torch and listened to their own breathing while the alternating chant and pause came gradually nearer.

'Can you tell what he's saying?' said Tavy uneasily. 'Put the torch on again, Nick, it's much too dark.'

'Oh, they all say the same sort of thing.' He switched on the beam. 'We don't want to use it all the time, it'll exhaust the battery.'

'What sort of thing?' Hearing the familiar cadences Tavy felt braver. She looked round the room more calmly, but the sound puzzled her. It seemed too far off for the street: she had lost her bearings.

'Oh, the blessing of God if you give to the poor, all that sort of thing.' Nick listened abstractedly. 'Funny thing is, I don't think it's coming from your street. It's down below, but too far off. We must be on the other side.'

He went back to the gallery and pointed the torch down the well. The beam touched the railing of a second storey, then a third, and still the shaft sank further. When he leaned out and shone it vertically down it made a halo of light on the distant floor but beyond that the darkness was complete and revealed nothing.

'Good lord, we're four stories up. That's five, if you count the roof. It's a much bigger house than I thought. I wonder which side the door's on?'

'I'm not going any further,' said Tavy in a low voice, but when he moved to the stairs in the corner she hastily followed and they went down in soft-footed silence to the next storey. This level of the house repeated the simple lay-out of the first, and the third when they reached it was identical, except that the rooms were larger and the floors dirtier. In one there was a ruined mattress covered with rags, but the heap was scattered with plaster and eroded with age, as though it had been months or years since anyone slept on it. There was a different smell on this level, unpleasantly identifiable, suggesting that in the not too remote past some part of the ground floor had been used as a lavatory.

'I'm *not* going any further, do you hear?' Tavy retreated to the stairs. 'You can go if you like, but I shan't. What have you done with the matches? Let's go back where we were, and light the candle.'

The space at the bottom of the stairs was small, hardly bigger than the central well, with only one room leading out of it. Unlike any house that Tavy had seen before it was very much smaller at the bottom than anywhere else, as though the foundations had been pinched for space and the house had spread and enlarged itself as it went higher. There was a heavy door to the street, unmistakably locked, and at right angles immediately inside it a smaller door, slightly ajar. The smell of stale urine from this one was overpowering. Nick looked in with his torch and hastily withdrew. It was, as he had guessed, a hole-in-the-floor latrine of the traditional sort, but it had not had water near it for a long time and the squatting-place was caked with copious excrement.

'Pooh,' he said, gathering his saliva and spitting aside into the darkness, 'we'll just have a look in here and then go back.' Tavy was on the stairs once more but she came down when he went into the open room and stood in the doorway behind him, shivering and staring. There was a mattress in this one too, spilling its palm-leaf stuffing at the edges and covered with old newspapers and rags. It was meagre and dirty like the first but something in its appearance and the methodical disposition of the coverings suggested that it had recently been slept in. There was besides a blackened earthen crock containing ashes, and some bits of stick lying near, some of them charred, as though someone had used them for kindling, or poking charcoal.

'I think somebody comes here,' said Nick, staring at the crock of ashes. They exchanged glances and turned at once to the stairs, Tavy stumbling after her long shadow. At the top they paused for breath and looked at one another.

'How on earth do they get in, though?' said Tavy. She was very pale.

'Someone has a key, obviously. Perhaps the owner.'

'But that dirty bed, and that smell! It doesn't seem likely.'

'No,' said Nick, 'it doesn't.' He frowned, fidgeting with the torch. 'It might be a beggar or something. Perhaps we ought to tell somebody.'

'And get into a row for being here ourselves? What a clottish idea.' They went on up the last few stairs to the door of the roof and looked across to Tavy's open window. The roof was in full moonlight; they could see the rope and the open grille quite clearly. Tavy measured the distance with her eye and was reassured. They could be home in a moment, after all; there was no need to rush. A breeze blew sweetly in through the open panes and the stair-head was cool and fresh, washed clean by moonlight.

'Don't let's go back just yet,' she said, sitting on the top stair with a little sigh. 'We haven't been here very long. It's still early.' Now that they were back where they started her fears had subsided and she began to feel a faint stirring of the old magic, the possession of a secret place which nobody knew. She put up a hand to Nick, glad of his presence and the unfamiliar delight of being in league with him, and he switched off his torch and sat down on the stair beside her.

'Shall we light the candle now?' He felt in his pocket and brought out a candle-end and a box of matches. Though the moonlight was all about them and only the lower house was dark the candle was the finishing touch. It established their possession of the house; they were at home in it.

'I've still got that surprise for you,' said Nick, groping in an inner pocket. He brought out a flat tin box, two wooden stems and a pair of small clay objects and laid them on the top step beside the candle.

'What on earth are those?' She picked up a slender pipe and examined it curiously.

'They're pipes. Haven't you ever seen them before? You get them at the *bakál*.' He fitted the little bowl on the end of the stem and held it out impressively for her inspection.

'Well, what are they for? It looks like a doll's pipe.'

'They're for kief,' said Nick, picking up the other stem and fitting the bowl to it. 'I thought we might have a smoke.'

'Heavens, are you allowed to?'

'Of course not, silly. But I've done it before, with Hamid. You're not to tell anybody.'

Tavy had never heard of kief and the idea of smoking these childish pipes was ridiculous. But something in Nick's expression caught her attention; it was grave and careful, and it came to her with a thrill of interest that she was about to be initiated into something wicked.

'What is it?' she whispered, watching him open the box. It contained a greyish substance, dry and granular.

'It's kief, I told you.' He filled the bowl of one pipe with thumb and finger, pressing it down carefully. 'Lots of boys smoke it here. It's against the law.'

'Why? What does it do?'

'I'm not quite sure,' said Nick candidly. 'Trouble is, it's awfully difficult to keep alight. I've had it twice, with Hamid, but I'm not good at it like he is. It's supposed to make you feel happy or something. I expect it takes practice.'

'Oh, do let me try.' She watched in fascination while he struck a match and sucked the flame into the bowl, frowning with concentration. The bowl glowed red for an instant and then faded, and he blew out a little spiral of thin smoke. He passed the pipe to her quickly.

'Draw rather hard, it's difficult to keep going.' She put the pipe to her lips and sucked convulsively. There was a taste of wood and the wetness of Nick's saliva, and then as the bowl glowed a curious grassy flavour that she didn't like, a bit like the smell of weeds on a smouldering bonfire. She coughed and the pipe went out.

'Light it again,' said Nick, now busy with his own. She dutifully sucked and struck matches and the pipe drew fitfully for a moment, then not at all. But Nick was more successful and sat back with his elbow on the window-frame, puffing at his little pipe and watching her critically. She tried again. Soon the stairs were scattered with spent matches.

'It's no good,' she said despondently at last, 'it doesn't work.' But the final match had heated the bowl and the stuff glowed fitfully as she laboriously inhaled, and for a moment or two there was a little nebula of smoke between them. As soon as this was achieved the pipes were finished.

'I still don't see what it's supposed to do,' said Tavy, poking about in the bowl with the stalk of a match. 'I don't feel anything.'

'Neither do I, to tell the truth. I suppose one ought to smoke several, but it's expensive.'

'Is it? What did you pay for it?'

'I didn't. Hamid gave it me. He has a friend who goes in for it as a business. He hangs around the cafés at night and sells it to Americans.'

'Good heavens, do they smoke it too? D'you mean tourists?'

'No, those odd-looking chaps you see around. They live here, in sort of gangs. You must have seen them, they're always about; with dirty-looking girls mostly, and babies in prams. Well, anyway, they smuggle it out into Spain and sell it at a profit, and come back and live on the money.'

'Good heavens,' said Tavy again, 'what an odd system. I wouldn't have thought it was worth the risk and trouble.'

But as she spoke she became aware of a soothing sensation, a gentle warmth which began in the region of the breastbone and spread very slowly outwards in a glow of contentment. The feeling was faint and diffused, only barely noticeable, but as her eyes wandered over the pattern of the tiles her nerves, which were still on edge, became gratefully aware of it. It seemed to her now that the house was no longer frightening, that it was what her imagination had always demanded that it should be, a hidden place where nothing was of importance but herself and Nick. The darkness and odours of the ground floor were a long way off; in the moonlight and the cool night airs of their private eyrie she no longer believed in them. Or if they stirred her at all it was with a sly excitement, as though an element of danger had always been present in her night-thoughts and fantasies about the house. The loft was familiar and secure, and so in a sense was this; but there was something more; it was even the possibility of risk which made that further territory more desirable.

'I suppose we ought to go back,' she said presently, but she went on sitting where she was, hugging her knees. She looked at Nick with a stirring of new affection. He was an odd boy certainly, and very young, but there was an air of authority about him which she found comforting. He had not been afraid to go first into the house and had remained calm when she had been plainly frightened. She wished she had not been afraid, that she had not told him lies about her parents to impress him. She wished very much to know whether Nick liked her.

'I suppose we might as well.' He looked at his watch. 'Nearly nine o'clock, we'd better be moving.' He knocked out the bowls of the pipes and put them in his pocket, carefully shut the tin and blew out the candle. All his movements were deliberate and serious, as though he were in charge of the situation and naturally responsible. They stood up at last and looked out through the broken frame. A cloud was across the moon and the roof in shadow, but there was still a diffused brightness over the sky and they could see quite clearly. Nick paused with his hand on the frame and stood back politely.

'You can go first if you like, only mind the glass.'

'No, you; I'd rather.' He put a leg through the opening and ducked his head. He was half-way through when Tavy plucked at his arm.

'Nick! I heard something. Listen!' They froze in an awkward posture, their heads together, and from the well below came the unmistakable bang of a heavy door.

'Someone's come in downstairs,' said Nick in a whisper, and drew his leg after him. Without quite knowing how she did it Tavy had scrambled through and was close beside him. This time a splinter of glass caught the palm of her hand but she snatched it away and darted across the roof without being aware of it.

'Wait!' said Nick in an urgent whisper, 'I want to listen.' But she was already reaching for the sill, and after a moment, in which he heard nothing more, he crossed the roof like a shadow and was breathing beside her.

'Give me a leg up, for God's sake.'

'Bend your knee, then. I can't do it if you struggle.'

It was really quite easy, though she kicked with unnecessary force as she went up and all but upset the chair when her foot found it. As soon as she recovered her balance she turned back for Nick, and between her hand and the rope he came up lightly. Together they lifted the grille from the bed; though Tavy's hands were shaking it fitted back into place without much difficulty. She switched on the light and drew the curtains, making the rings rattle. It was only then that they became aware that someone was knocking at the door.

*

'Tavy!' said Phoebe for the third time, raising her voice, 'open the door, dear, will you? I want to come in.'

'I don't believe they're there,' said Consuelo, enjoying Phoebe's difficulty. 'They're lying doggo in the loft. They're having you on.'

162

'That would be *too* silly. They're too old for that kind of thing.' She rattled the door-handle briskly. The bolt slid smoothly back and the door opened.

'What is it?' said Tavy, looking blank, 'have you been knocking?'

'Yes, two or three times. You've been shut in such a long time, I began to wonder . . .' She glanced sharply into the room, which was in perfect order.

'We were in the loft, I'm afraid we didn't hear you.' Tavy shook back the hair from her face and gave Nick a sidelong glance. They both seemed a little out of breath, as though Phoebe's knocking had startled them and they had come down in a hurry.

'Well, come out now, both of you. Most of the people have gone, you can slip upstairs if you want.'

Tavy caught a glint of amusement in Consuelo's eye and perceptibly stiffened. 'I don't think we want to, thank you.' She brushed past Phoebe with an aloof air and Nick followed, shutting the door behind him. The back of his jacket was white with dust and plaster.

'Why, whatever have you two been doing?' said Consuelo, slapping at it with her hand. 'You're all over dust.'

'We've been in the loft,' said Tavy primly, 'playing cards,' and noticed for the first time that her hand was bleeding. She put it behind her quickly but Phoebe gave a little cry as she saw the blood.

'My dear child, whatever have you done to yourself?' She reached for Tavy's hand and forcibly inspected it. The cut was not deep but it was bleeding fast; as Phoebe turned up the palm blood ran between two fingers and splashed on the tiles.

'Oh, I've cut it, I suppose.' She looked hastily away. 'I remember, I was playing with Nick's knife.' She had turned a shade paler than usual and Anthea, who had strolled across and was watching her with interest, took her glance as a signal of distress. The girl was plainly frightened, and had something to conceal; Phoebe must somehow be prevented from making a fuss.

'Come into the kitchen quickly,' she said, 'we'll soon stop it,'

163

and put her arm through Tavy's and led her away, feeling the girl's hair on her shoulder and the weight of her body heavy against her arm. Phoebe bustled after them and the others followed, so that by the time the hand had been held under the tap, and a chair found, there was a suffocating number of people in the kitchen. To Tavy, drooping at the sink, her ears full of a roaring sound and her knees trembling, the confusion that hemmed her in was a kind of relief. No explanations would be needed now; that danger was over. Patches of darkness invaded the place and her head swam. Leaning against Anthea she allowed her hand to be washed and dried and bandaged with a handkerchief, and then, as the nightmare sensations subsided, leaned and drooped still more, unwilling to lose the warmth of that comforting arm. When at last she opened her eyes it was on a circle of faces.

'What's this? What's this?' cried Lytton, looking in from the courtyard with a startled air. Quattrell was close behind him.

'Tavy's cut her hand,' said Phoebe, 'but it's all right now. We've rendered first-aid, I think; it's nothing serious.' Anthea looked up and caught Quattrell's eye: she smiled. His face lit up in response and her spirit lifted. So the mysterious process was still at work, and they were both aware of it, and it came to her with surprise that the uneasiness of the last hour had been nothing more nor less than jealousy of Consuelo.

'She must go and lie down, poor thing,' said Phoebe, taking charge of the situation. 'You've gone quite pale, you know, dear. It's been a shock.' She held out a hand and Tavy got slowly to her feet. The kitchen was suffocatingly warm with so many people in it; even Hadíjah and her helpmate were craning for a view, clicking their tongues in sympathy. Tavy was unequal to the thought of her own room.

'I really don't want to, Aunt Phoebe. I'm all right, honestly.' She put her arm through Anthea's. 'I'll just sit down for a minute. We can go in the parlour.'

They wandered across the courtyard and the group dispersed. Tavy's mishap had signalled the end of the party; Lytton was seeing off the last of the strangers at the door. The courtyard was full of the shadows of leaves and almost deserted, extravagantly romantic under the swinging lantern and the softer glow of lamplight from the parlour. At the end of this room, under Sarah's mask, Molly and Father Emery were deep in talk, drawn very close together in two armchairs. They looked up briefly as Anthea and Tavy came in and Molly broke off in the middle of what she was saying, screwing up her eyes with a look of vague annoyance at the intrusion. Anthea inwardly quailed, but the voices went on. It was clear she had looked at them both without recognition.

'Are you really all right?' whispered Anthea, sinking into the cushions of the divan with Tavy and taking her bandaged hand.

'Yes, thank you. Just a bit shaky, I think. Thank you for being so marvellous.'

'Tell me how it all happened.' Anthea was trying not to listen to the earnest rise and fall of Molly's conversation. It was too grotesque after all these years—five, or was it six at least?—to be in the same room with her; stranger still to realise that this was the Molly she only dimly remembered. There was almost nothing to relate to the old memory, to that far-off evening when she and James had met, and that other more confused and magical occasion when she had sat beside him at dinner and it had all started. But the voice was the same, persistent and a little mournful; the temptation to follow its cadences was irresistible.

'I told you, I was playing with Nick's knife,' said Tavy, leaning her head back sleepily against the cushions. 'I'd rather not talk, do you mind? The thought of it gives me the creeps.'

'You talk when you want to, not otherwise. You just keep still.' Their hands were still loosely clasped and Anthea felt the grateful pressure of Tavy's fingers. She returned it gently and sat still, giving up the futile pretence of not listening.

'There's no difficulty, my dear lady,' Father Emery was saying in his rich voice, which carried splendidly though he had pitched it low. 'You don't have to be a member of my flock; indeed I haven't one nowadays. I'm an old and idle man, alas, at anyone's service.'

'You're very good. The difficulty's mine, I see that. If I were a genuine believer I suppose it would be different. Oswald, my companion, keeps saying that perhaps I ought to consult a psychiatrist.'

'It's not that bad, surely? These hallucinations you speak of are not unusual. In my calling one has often to deal with such things. They are troubles of the soul, after all. There's nothing abnormal about them.'

'I didn't call them hallucinations.'

'I know; but it's sometimes helpful to see them in that light. The priest has to be a psychologist nowadays, in his own way. He always was, of course; it's part of his function. The only change—it's rather an absurd one—is that spiritual advice is sometimes more acceptable if it's clothed in so-called scientific terminology. We all have a burden of guilt to bear, as the Freudians agree, and to sensitive souls the burden would be intolerable if it were not for our faith in mercy. Or call it grace; the final possibility of atonement.'

'But how can I believe in mercy?' said Molly, her voice rising. 'Do you call this mercy, to live as I have to live, after what I told you?'

'My dear lady, we must talk this out at leisure. One mustn't prescribe for a sickness before one understands it.'

'What *are* they talking about?' said Tavy, opening her eyes and looking dreamily at Anthea. 'I wish they'd go. I promised Aunt Phoebe I'd help with the clearing up.'

'They will in a minute, and then I'll help you. There's no hurry.'

Anthea stole a glance in Molly's direction. She was twisting the rings on her fingers and gazing at Sarah's mask over Emery's head.

'I don't like that thing. Why does he keep it on show, do you suppose?'

'It's not everybody's taste, perhaps, but one can sympathise. It's more than a portrait, don't you think? A beautiful reminder.'

'But she looks so *dead*,' said Molly with a grimace, twisting and twisting her rings, 'I don't know how he can bear it.' She looked at the mask unwillingly, as though she hated it. 'Do you believe in hell, Father?' she asked abruptly, returning her eyes to his face.

'Not in the old sense, no.' He smiled professionally, feeling in the breast of his cassock for his cigarette-case, a chastely engraved solid silver one, very handsome. 'I think one would prefer to say it was a state of mind.' He looked round for a match and also for some means of escape, and caught Anthea's eye; she instantly averted her gaze.

'That's what one's told to think. I suppose it's true. But if it continues, you know . . . if there's no means of relief. . . .' Her voice trailed off into silence as Ozzie appeared like a shadow and advanced smiling.

'Time to go, dear, don't you think,' he coaxed her, 'though you'll hate me for breaking in on the conversation?'

Father Emery got up at once and found Molly's stick, while Anthea touched Tavy's arm, anxious to be gone. But Lytton was in the doorway now, and behind him Gerald and Phoebe, and they found themselves standing together in a loose group, hovering with smiles for the imminent and appropriate moment of saying goodbye.

Molly was slow but she collected herself finally and came steadily forward to Lytton, extending a thin hand. Her face still showed traces of emotion and was not quite perfectly in control, but it changed into something of its old likeness when she smiled. Anthea noticed that she was carefully made up. The cheeks were discreetly tinted and the mouth coral-coloured; her hair was still thick and soft, though rather grey. She had been remarkably pretty in the old days and was still only in her middle-forties; the effect she made now was touching rather than attractive, but it was not impossible to see why James had loved her.

'A *most* successful house-warming,' she said, 'and the house so romantic, too; quite poetical. I want you to come and visit *me*, quite soon. My house is nothing like yours, of course, just an ordinary villa, but Ozzie has been quite wonderful with the garden.'

They exchanged the usual compliments and promises and began to move as a group across the patio.

'Do walk with us to the car,' said Ozzie to Gerald in an undertone, 'she's afraid of the children and the steps are a little difficult.'

'Of course. I was just going to suggest it.'

Molly paused for a general farewell and her eye fell on Tavy. 'And you too, of course,' she said doubtfully, making a confused effort. 'I've forgotten your name, I'm afraid, but I remember you quite well.'

'It's Octavia,' said Tavy, blushing and putting her bandaged hand behind her.

'Octavia, I see. I thought it was something different, but my memory's so bad. Usedn't you to have another name? I thought it was Pearl.'

'This is Miss Townsend's *niece*,' said Ozzie, putting her coat round her shoulders. 'You haven't seen her before, dear. You weren't at the picnic.'

'Wasn't I? Oh dear, I am stupid. I don't know what I'd do without Ozzie. I'm always getting muddled.'

The door closed finally behind them, shutting off to some extent the noise of drumming, which had swelled to an alarming racket as the three of them with Father Emery came out into the street. A group of children were parading up and down the narrow alley, thumping on vase-shaped drums of clay which they held in one arm and beat with the flat of the hand. They followed the little group like victors at a triumph, drumming and chanting, and as Molly moved slowly it was some minutes before the nerve-racking din met the tunnel and abruptly faded.

'God, what a hell-begotten row!' said Consuelo. 'I don't think I could stand living here. How long does it go on for?'

'About three weeks as a rule,' said Nick, helping himself from a plate of cheese and biscuits. They were standing among scattered chairs under the fig-tree and Consuelo was looking round in search of Quattrell. 'They give the kids drums at this time of year, sort of like toys at Christmas. Trumpets and whistles too. It's the Feast of Aachor.'

'I wouldn't have thought it necessary to give *these* kids anything to make a noise with. My head's splitting.' Quattrell and

Anthea emerged from the parlour and she beckoned to them gaily.

'They drive my brother crazy too,' said Nick. 'My mother won't let him have one.'

'I don't blame her.'

'Anyway they soon get broken.'

'I'm delighted to hear it.'

Quattrell and Anthea, now joined by Lytton, moved over from the buffet, each carrying a final whisky. The clearing up was going on apace, Phoebe collecting trays of plates and glasses with Hadijah and the gold-toothed beauty in attendance. Tavy was moving softly about in the kitchen, sorting and arranging glasses without paying much attention to what she was doing: she had swallowed a tumbler of wine when no one was looking and was in a state of dream. It was a spacious and comfortable moment, the best of the evening. Duty had been done, the party was undoubtedly successful and each had something either to conceal or to communicate.

'I shouldn't be drinking this,' said Lytton, lowering himself into a chair. 'This kind of thing takes it out of one. I need fuel.'

'Oh boy, so do I.' Consuelo looked longingly at his glass.

'I'll get you one,' said Quattrell, 'if I can catch the whisky.' He put down his drink and went back to look under the table.

'So it's all right, then?' Consuelo spoke in an undertone, almost in Anthea's ear. 'The lunch, I mean. Tomorrow. You sure you don't mind?'

'Of course not, Consie; why should I?' She felt a touch of compunction as she spoke, but the sensation of being alive, of being summoned at last to shake off the emotional ashes, was too delicious to be ignored; scruples were out of place at such a moment. The suspicion of jealousy was gone and she felt only exhilaration, for Quattrell had said, as he put ice in her glass, 'I'm taking your friend out to lunch tomorrow. First move in the campaign,' and the sudden lift in her spirits had been quite ludicrous. She might, she told herself cheerfully, feel differently tomorrow, but tonight she was not unwilling that Consuelo should be sacrificed.

'How are you going to get home, Nick?' she asked presently, smiling at the grave and composed little figure sitting with an air of correctness on the edge of his chair.

'I shall walk, thank you very much. I know the way.'

'We're walking together,' said Quattrell, stooping at Consuelo's shoulder and handing her a glass. 'At least, we'll walk to the car, and then we'll drive. I know the Parsons block. It's on my way.'

'Then you can take us too.' Consuelo turned quickly and gave him an eager smile. She was flushed and a little dishevelled, but reasonably sober. 'I can't walk a step in these shoes, it'd be a charity.'

'What about Gerald?' said Lytton, 'is he coming back?' He was suddenly exhausted and finished; he wanted them to go.

'Oh, the hell with him,' said Consuelo gaily. 'He's got a motor-car, hasn't he? He can jolly well follow us.'

So the house-warming party came to its appointed end, and the only surprise in it was Anthea's, when at the last moment Tavy emerged from the kitchen and breathlessly kissed her. But this was in tune with the feeling of the hour, which on all sides was emotionally preoccupied and a little beside itself, so that nobody, not even Phoebe, thought it peculiar. As for Lytton, he was quite worn out, and yawning audibly and piteously for his bed. He even forgot to clear the débris from his writing-table, which was littered with ash-trays and crumbs, an unheard-of oblation to leave in a place normally sacred to the struggles of composition under the serenely blind clairvoyant eyes of Sarah.

*

'Come with us a little way,' said Ozzie when they reached the car, which had been left beside Gerald's in charge of a tattered man with a hungry expression, and Father Emery had gone off with his priestly stride, 'I've hardly spoken a word to you all evening.' Gerald hesitated. If they were likely to run into Molly from time to time it was essential to find out whether, and in what connection, she remembered them. If it were really true, as it seemed, that she had looked at Anthea without the least emotion, then perhaps there was no need to be over-elaborately careful. But Anthea's name, being unusual, might trigger off memory, and if this should happen total avoidance of Molly was the only course. This in itself was no hardship, rather the reverse; but before taking evasive action a quite separate line of communication must be established with Ozzie.

'I'll come with you part of the way, not very far. Don't forget I shall have to walk back.'

'We'll go all the way, and I'll drive you back. How's that?' So Ozzie disposed Molly and her stick and her rug in the back of the car, and while he was paying the car-watcher and scraping off the children clinging like flies to the fenders Gerald got in as well and sat beside her.

'We met years ago, you know,' he said, tackling it at once. 'I used to know your husband slightly, and you dined once or twice at my house when my first wife was alive.'

'Did we? So *that* was it! I was quite sure I knew your name, as a friend of James. I don't remember your wife, though. She's very pretty.'

'It would be Elizabeth you remember, I think. She died a few years ago and I married again.' He waited for some reaction, but her profile was calm. Ozzie was backing the car to a point where he could reasonably turn and she seemed more interested in this manœuvre than in the conversation. A group of boys were playing football under the street lighting, and as they made no attempt to avoid the car but seemed deliberately to hurl themselves and their ball into the way of it there were some hazardous moments. Finally they were facing in the right direction and Ozzie carefully made the descent from the Kasbah. ('It's not that one *minds* killing one or two, but think of the fuss!') The streets beyond were fairly empty, even of children, who in this quarter seemed never required to go to bed before midnight, and they ran out smoothly through the outskirts of the town and along tree-lined roads where nothing was stirring but an occasional muffled figure or a few goats. In a few minutes they were crackling over the gravel of Molly's drive.

'I won't come in,' said Gerald, 'I've got to get back for my passengers,' and took leave of Molly with an unmistakable feeling that she was glad of his refusal. She looked small and exhausted as she went up the steps; it was safe to conclude that although the name meant something to her she was still hazy and in spite of their conversation didn't remember him. All the same, he reflected with habitual caution, it would perhaps be wise for Anthea's sake to drop a hint to Ozzie.

'Poor Mrs. Brockhurst's terribly changed,' he said, when at last they were driving, more slowly this time, down the empty road. 'I used to know her husband in the old days. A very impressive man.'

'Oh, he sounds *wonderful*, and such a marvellous face! There's a picture on her dressing-table, in his *wig*, that I long to *steal*. Though mind *you*,' he applied the brake on a gentle descent, prolonging the little journey as long as possible, 'I hear so much about him from dear Molly, one way and another, that he's ceased to be a human being. He's just unreal.' They went on in silence for a while, Ozzie glancing from time to time at Gerald's profile, as though there were something he wished to say if he could think how to put it. At last he said, 'It's rather nervous work in a way; had you suspected? I'm so *tied*, you see. If you and your beautiful Anthea would come up and see us one day it would make the most lovely break, and Molly would adore it.'

'Well, that's the difficulty,' said Gerald, thinking carefully. 'There was a little embarrassment in the past, before Brockhurst's death . . . she doesn't remember it, I'm almost sure, but she had it against me at the time and it would be happier for everyone, perhaps, if she weren't reminded.'

There was a dubious little silence, through which Gerald cautiously waited for the next question, assuming from old experience that Ozzie was not the type to be uninquisitive. But 'Oh,' said Ozzie in a pleased voice, 'I *know* how those things can happen! Not such a bright idea after all! But this place is so full of *monsters*, you've no idea. I just thought it would be awfully pleasant to see you again.'

'Well, you must come to us instead, whenever you're free.

Anthea's got Consuelo at present, but perhaps, if it wouldn't bore you . . .'

Ozzie waited expectantly; the car lost speed.

'Oh, I *do* hope you're going to suggest we might snatch a little lunch by ourselves, when there's nothing doing! I sometimes nip out with Rob when he's not at the beach, but he's working now, or trying to, and one mustn't *hamper* him. We could go to the Cuz-Cuz Bar, it's deliciously *louche*.'

'Wherever you say. You must let me know when you're free.'

'Tomorrow? Wednesday? Or am I being rather pushing?'

'I'll check with Anthea and give you a ring in the morning.'

'Oh, *good*. I *shall* enjoy it. The one thing I need is a treat.'

Ozzie pressed his foot on the accelerator and they entered the town at a more conventional speed. It occurred to Gerald, as they ran smoothly along the road that skirted the beach and railway and led to the harbour, that he was embarking on the very thing he was at pains to avoid. But Ozzie was a gentle creature and possibly discreet. Nothing was more dispiriting in the long run than the habit of scrutinising everything for seeds of scandal.

He parted from Ozzie on the waterfront, preferring, since it was not really late, to smoke a cigar and walk the rest of the way. The sky and the precipitous walls of the Arab town, pallid with moonlight, were exceptionally fine, and he had fallen into the habit of taking leisurely exercise at night, memorising the alleys when they were quiet and empty, the jostling crowds dispersed and the shops shuttered, so different from the bedlam activity of the day. In a way the difference was confusing, it was so extreme; landmarks committed to memory in the daylight hours—the corner where sellers of bread crouched on the pavement, booths where tailors sat working their skeins like spiders while tiny boys manipulated the thread—all these, or almost all, were gone, and the streets showed a blank face of padlocked shutters. But the names of the alleys could be read and direction studied, and it was possible to hesitate without being at once beckoned into a bazaar and offered rugs or souvenirs of leatherwork or any of the innumerable useless objects displayed, from tarbooshes to imitation camel-saddles.

He began the ascent at a reflective pace, following a direction that he knew. The smells of the town were often delicious at this hour, for there was almost no time of night when the bakers were not at work and there was nearly always a smoking brazier or two with spicy-flavoured meat being roasted on skewers; sweet smells of mint and tea and the smoke of incense greeted one's nostrils from windows and open doors. There were still a few people about but they passed in silence, stepping round the scavengers bending with basket and broom, sweeping up the day's refuse from dark corners.

The street went steeply upwards for a little distance and Gerald turned several corners with reasonable confidence, but presently an archway yawned and he slackened his pace; the street was badly lit and had none of the distinguishing marks that he remembered; he paused for a moment to look about him and consider. At once a shadow stirred in a dark doorway and a boy stepped out and spoke in a cajoling voice.

'Bon soir, m'sieu. Tu veux le Kasbah, m'sieu?'

'No, thank you.' Gerald moved on.

'Anglais, m'sieu? Tu es Anglais?' The child fell companionably into step beside him, lifting an eager face. He was a pretty boy in shabby jeans and singlet with broken plastic sandals which flapped as he walked. His hair and lashes were dark and thick and he skipped nimbly ahead, smiling engagingly at Gerald over his shoulder. He was perhaps ten years old.

'Moi,' said the boy, walking backwards and pointing to his own breast, 'toi, m'sieu,' pointing to Gerald, 'tu m'ammènes avec toi à la maison?'

'No thank you,' said Gerald with a faint smile, starting to walk again, 'je ne veux pas le Kasbah,' and felt in his pocket for a coin and held it out to him. The child dropped back beside him but did not take it. Instead he looked up with a puzzled expression and laid an appealing hand on Gerald's arm.

'Tu ne m'aimes pas?' he asked, looking troubled. 'Je ne te plais pas? Tu ne veux pas m'ammener avec toi à la maison?'

'Pas ce soir, mon petit. Va-t-en.' Gerald offered him the dirham again and this time he took it with a calculating glance but the flapping trot of his sandals went on as before. He was not to be shaken off so easily.

'Suis bon garçon,' he insisted, looking up again with an anxious air, as though fearing to be misunderstood. 'Peux faire tout ce que tu veux. Avec la bouche, m'sieu. Tu comprends?' He made an explicit gesture with one hand.

'No,' said Gerald, 'va-t-en,' and shook his head, blowing out a cloud of smoke like a visible sigh. The boy's persistence touched and at the same time saddened him. He had been accosted at night before, that was nothing new, but never by a child of this age, and the incident disturbed him. Was it so obvious that he was a potential customer, or did the boy work this beat every night, making his accommodating offer to all comers? His fastidiousness shrank from the idea, whichever way he looked at it. At the same time he felt a slight and not unpleasing sensation from the encounter. Harmless vanity responded if commonsense did not: he had not been considered too old for the transaction.

He came to a standstill and felt once more in his pocket, bringing out a crumpled note. Two figures in djellábahs had silently turned into the street and he put the note without haste into the boy's hand, giving him a light dismissive pat on the shoulder, the gesture of a man giving in to a persistent beggar. This time the boy snatched the money and darted to a doorway, and when the two men had passed and Gerald glanced warily after them he saw that the child had gone. They had been bearded, grave-seeming men and one of them, he thought, had looked at him rather sharply. He walked on with an appearance of calm, lifting his cigar to his lips with a hand which trembled. At the next corner he saw where he was and his pace quickened. Two more streets, a final turn, and he would be at the foot of the familiar steps leading to the tunnel. To the right, where the street widened, he could see the old man squatting against the wall, and beyond him, the object of his watch, the locked car. In another minute he would be knocking at Lytton's door, and then he would be driving home with Consuelo and Anthea.

Climbing the steps he threw away his cigar and made a determined effort to arrange his thoughts, blotting out the details of his solitary walk, preparing for the inevitable home-going commentary on the party. They would both be sleepy, perhaps; he need not talk much. A final drink when they got home; then yawns; then bed. The figure of the boy, however, obstinately rose and danced before his mind's eye, bringing in its train images and associations which at the moment he was unwilling to pursue. The odd thing about the voice still echoing in his ear was that it was not the boy's at all, but one full of lilt and emphasis, remarkably like Ozzie's.

10

MOLLY lay on her bed in the late afternoon under the mosquito net, watching the flies which seemed always to cruise interminably in the centre of the room. It was still only April and habitués of the place had assured her that she need never fear mosquitoes until late summer, when they could be troublesome; but Ozzie had already been bitten at Quattrell's and she herself had heard an occasional whine on windless evenings when she sat in the dusk by the open window, listening to the frogs. There was a pool in the courtyard below with a bubbling fountain, which Ozzie had already freed from mud and weeds; she was sure this encouraged mosquitoes though Ozzie said not, and he had worked so hard on the pool that she hadn't the heart or the energy to discourage him. Besides, the garden itself had marshy areas and was much overgrown; the wind from the sea rarely reached it because of the jungle-like tangle of shrubs and trees, and the hollow where lilies had bloomed in profusion and now rotted and drooped in a wilderness of leaves was an obvious and ideal breeding-ground for the creatures. So Molly had insisted on her net and was glad she had done so, for to creep into the filmy tent and lie there, half-way between waking and sleeping through the long afternoons, gave her a dreamlike illusion of security.

Her mind was so still, she might almost have been asleep, but she watched the cruising flies with remote attention, as though their zany antics would bring her sooner or later to the solution of some problem. They kept up a ceaseless weaving in the centre of the room, half-way between the four walls and precisely the same distance between floor and ceiling; if the area had been mathematically defined the limits of their flight could hardly have been more exact. There were perhaps half a dozen:

each fly pursued a straight course to a certain point, turned at a sharp angle and described another, as though endlessly repeating a geometrical pattern. What do they do it *for*, she wondered, how do they keep it up? She lifted the hair from her forehead and let her hand fall limply back on the pillow. If one could follow the lines of the diagram, if one could draw it, it seemed to her sometimes that it would resemble something. Occasionally a pair of flies would collide and shoot angrily apart, whizzing at speed to the furthest points of the design, but not an inch further; they seemed to obey some inexorable discipline, almost as though aware of the limits of their territory, following a chart laid out with compass and rule. At night they behaved very differently; when the bedside light was on they became demoralised, crashing drunkenly about inside the parchment shade or fretfully exploring the surface of the net, where as the sky grew dark they were joined by all the ephemeral apparitions of the night, small speckled or silver- or lemon-coloured moths, lured to the light and clinging to the mesh, often discovered there, motionless and bemused, when the sleeping-pills wore off and Ozzie came in with her orange-juice in the morning.

Yes, it was like a chart; she had identified it. James, or Ben, sitting hunched at the little chart-table under the lamp, moving the parallel rulers and compass and drawing meticulous lines with a sharp pencil. And it would be night, and the cabin would be warm and close under the tilting lantern, and she would brace herself lightly against the bar of the galley, hearing the sigh of the sea along *Manatee*'s sides and the purr of the gas-flame under her evening cooking. Of course it would be James at the chart-table, silent and absorbed, and there would be the smell of his cigarette and of chopped onion, and the curiously comforting odour of yellow oilskins, and she would reach about into lockers and smooth-running drawers, catching a glimpse of Ben alone in the cockpit. There was someone else as well, whom she could not distinguish. She closed her eyes and waited, feeling the lift and fall of the ship's motion. Was it really that girl, Octavia, with the long hair? No, it was someone different, and her name had been Pearl; of that she was quite sure. And she had been Ben's girl-friend, and a nuisance, and had followed James with her eyes in a way that Molly unhappily remembered. As if it were any use! He was hard to impress. Obstinate and out of reach, impervious to argument, incapable of recognising misery when he saw it, determined to have it his way, to behave as he meant to go on, between herself and Anthea.

The old trouble stirred in the region of her breastbone, making breathing difficult. She turned her head on the pillow and sighed deeply. The pain nearly always came when her thoughts began to stray to the old obsession, but once the vision had risen it was hard to dismiss; she was committed to the night and the ship and the gentle motion. It was extraordinary how clearly she saw it now, what details would rise intact to the surface of memory. At first, after she had been ill, there had been nothing, or almost nothing, but the cold sea and the fog and her own exhaustion, and there had been voices shouting and the thrash of a ship's screw, and hands had gripped her painfully under the armpits and her ribs had been dragged over something hard and her head had fallen helplessly against a thwart. After that there was a great and roaring darkness into which she willingly plunged, so great was the relief. She was safe; she was back on board, on *Manatee*'s deck; the roaring darkness engulfed her, and was not death.

For a long time, she did not know how long, she had believed in this, and the strange cabin and the strange faces had been a bewildering part of the delirium. She still did not know how finally she had wakened to the truth: that the freighter had picked her up at the end of a search, and that *Manatee*, her cabin dark and her engine steadily throbbing, with James and Ben asleep and the girl with the long hair, had split in two under the impact and gone to the bottom.

This vision was always too frightful to be looked at steadily. She opened her eyes with a whimper and stared at the net. The room was harshly bright and the flies still cruising; her mind fled back in panic to the place she knew. Here it was safe and warm, the night was calm. Ben was asleep in his bunk with a bandaged hand—how had she remembered that? it had come up suddenly—and James had thrown off his oilskin and was at the chart-table, and she herself . . . she faltered on the brink of something and then went on . . . she herself wrapped against the night air with her hand on the tiller, alone in the cockpit, taking the middle watch. Everything was smooth and calm, it was very dark. No breeze at all; they had been under engine for hours and the mast-head light moved back and forth with a gentle swinging motion, describing a faint parabola against the stars. The stars had been many at first, and then were fewer, and wisps of vapour had crept on the surface of the sea. And then the cabin light had gone out and she had been finally quite alone in the dark cockpit, only the binnacle lamp, dim as phosphorus, spreading its bluish glow on the compass face. And after that . . . long after that . . . But here the old confusion, the voices, her hand no longer on the tiller, her foot slipping, the terror of the cold and the water rushed over her with such violence that she cried out in a cracked voice and sat up in bed, clawing at the net as though she were caught in its meshes and were choking, drowning. It was well tucked in, and resisted, and she began to sob, only dimly aware that the door had opened and that Ozzie had come into the room carrying a tray.

'My darling! Not *again*!' He hastily put down the tray and untucked the net, twisting the folds together and out of the way. 'You haven't been brooding again? You *are* naughty! And here have I been getting you these lovely biscuits, which you don't in the least bit deserve.'

'Oh, Ozzie, Ozzie.' He sat down beside her on the bed and put his arms round her, and she hid her face in his shoulder and cried a little, but with a sound of relief which told him that the daily crisis was almost over.

'There, there,' he said, 'it's all over,' and patted her absently. He had been through it all before and his thoughts were elsewhere.

'But I should have seen it,' she whispered, lifting a piteous face, 'I should have heard it coming. It was a big ship, she must have had lights, Ozzie? There was no question of her not being lit—they said that at the inquiry. And it was *my watch*, Ozzie, the others were all asleep. James was below and asleep, I was responsible.'

'Well, yes, I know, darling,' said Ozzie, who knew this part of the story by heart, 'but it was very dark, wasn't it? And a horrid fog? And you weren't sailing, remember; there was no wind. You wouldn't have heard it above the noise of the engine.' He disengaged himself gently and attended to the tea. She followed his movements with her eyes, like an anxious child; she was not yet comforted.

'But it was such a *big* ship; compared with us, I mean. They weren't even sure they'd hit anything, they said so in evidence. And *Manatee* was only sixteen tons, Ozzie. They went right over us.'

'Well, yes, darling, *too* frightful. But don't *brood* about it. These things happen all the time at sea, they can't always be prevented.' He gave her a cup of tea and offered her the biscuits and she took one without looking and sat with the cup and the biscuit in either hand.

'The mistake was,' she said, fixing him with eyes which seemed to be at last on the track of an explanation, 'the mistake I made, was in not calling James in time, before it happened. That's what's so dreadful, Ozzie. That's where I was wrong.'

'But, darling, how could you, when you neither saw nor heard it?'

'I mean, when the fog came up. It wasn't there to begin with. He was always so careful, always; such a light sleeper. Always awake in a moment if I said a word.'

'There wasn't time, though, was there? I do wish you wouldn't go over and over it, my sweet; it's so bad for you.' Ozzie frowned at the plate and ate another biscuit.

'No, there wasn't time. But I was responsible, you see. If James or Ben had been there it wouldn't have happened. They were all asleep,' she said miserably, 'and never knew.' Her voice trembled. 'And they all had so much to live for, and I had nothing. That's what I can't bear, Ozzie; it's the irony of it.' Her eyes filled with tears again but she caught Ozzie's tender glance and obediently lifted her cup and drank some tea.

'Irony doesn't enter into it,' he said, trying for the hundredth time to discover some plausible argument to convince her. 'A terrible *terrible* thing happened, and it wasn't your fault, and you mustn't go on as though it were, because that only makes it worse and nothing could have prevented it.' He knew as he spoke that words were useless and that Molly's obsessions were not accessible to reason. He fell back on the surer course of playful affection, smiling and stroking her arm.

'You're wrong, it's God's irony,' said Molly, putting down her cup and seeming from her melancholy tone to be a little calmer. 'God's irony is very frightening, Ozzie; very cruel. I should like to talk about it to Father Emery.'

'Well, if you like; but I don't know that I advise it. Though again I suppose you'd better, if you want to have a chat about God. I'm afraid I can't help you there, I'm such a pagan.'

'Does he still hear confession, I wonder? You came in in the middle of our talk, I was going to ask him.'

'Goodness, I wouldn't know. I dare say he might, at a pinch. But what can you want to confess, my darling, that we haven't gone over and over a thousand times?'

Molly met his gaze in silence and looked away. The pupils of her eyes had grown large, as though she no longer saw the room or responded to the yellow dazzle of the evening light. She had come once more, and with dismaying suddenness, to that point which she approached in dreams or in the moment of waking, of which there was no longer either knowledge or memory but only a warning darkness, a protective blank. It followed on her dreams or visions of the lighted cabin, with *Manatee* running sweetly through the night sea, and when she dreamed, as in terror she sometimes did, of swimming alone in the darkness and clinging to something she found there—some wreckage, some floating box—this area of darkness was behind her, it was already past. Somewhere between the two lay the irony of God; the thing to be finally confessed; the deed to be expiated. There were even moments, rare ones it is true, though lately they had come on her more frequently, when she knew what it was and started away from the knowledge in incredulity and horror. How could *she*, Molly, afraid of the cold and the dark and the engulfing sea, take that inconceivable step, clinging to the rail, letting go, crying out in the final moment to James, whom her death was to punish because he was Anthea's lover?

This was not one of those moments, mercifully; her mind closed. She looked at Ozzie with misgiving, focusing his face clearly for the first time. He was so good, so patient, so unfailingly ready with comfort. She ought not to behave like this, it was bad for him too. She felt penitent and even ashamed, seeing his worried frown and the embarrassed way he fidgeted with his teaspoon. He was quite at a loss, defeated; they had reached this point so often. Even as she smiled at him, putting her hand in his and rising from the bed, she knew that the authority she craved was Father Emery's.

*

The house-warming party, which everyone considered such a success, on Lytton had had a peculiarly unsettling effect. Up to the moment of giving it he had been happy; everything, the finishing of the house, the preparations, the conferences with Quattrell about drink and guests, had been absorbing activities all pointing in the same direction. He had been like a man engaged in plotting a campaign; everything had had a bearing on it and every detail had needed his personal attention. Now that the climax was over he found himself unoccupied and beset by that aimless restlessness which so often bedevils a writer when there seems least reason for it. He had done what he wanted, had established his new life and got everything to his liking, and now that the structure was finished was left with nothing to do but to get on with his work. This, of course, was what he had always been aiming at; the last few weeks had been loud with frustrations and complaints. When the house was finished he would be able to work, thank heaven . . . when the workmen had gone . . . when they had got through the nuisance and upheaval of giving a party . . . when Phoebe had established a routine and he could be left in peace. . . .

And now indeed it was all over, and the house was in tolerable order and the workmen gone for good, and the weather was warmer and the parlour given over to him entirely in the daytime, so that he need never be disturbed; and he was at his wits' end to discover a cogent impediment to working. He was not at all conscious of this, but prowled up and down the parlour for the greater part of the morning, cracking his knuckles and staring at the orderly bookcases and well-equipped desk, fixing his sense of discomfort first on one feature of the room and then on another. With the door to the patio closed it was too dark; with it open he would catch sight of Phoebe adjusting the kitchen shutter or sitting with a basket of mending under the fig-tree, or even Hadíjah with cloth and pail, moving peacefully backwards on bare feet as she washed the tiles, and any of these constituted an interruption. The sensible course, as Phoebe too often reminded him, was to close the door and work by electric light, and this after a time he did, but under protest, since sunlight poured into the courtyard from early morning and electricity was expensive. Now he was immured at his desk, going through the sheets of his manuscript and listening for noises. The parlour was normally quiet, since the walls were thick and Phoebe was considerately careful about sounds in the house. Occasionally he would hear her footstep or Tavy's, or the scrape of a basket chair if they were sitting on the roof, but he had long ago given up the pretext that Tavy's presence could be classified as a disturbance. She was not talkative, and continued to spend much time in her own room, seemingly regarding him as a person whom it was safer not to approach. Still, there were occasional noises of one sort or another, and some of these were the more exasperating because unidentifiable, and in any case quite outside his personal control. The drumming was his chief complaint: it had increased in volume since the night of the party and was now in full spate, tapping and rolling and reverberating, now near, now far, always with the same idiotic monotonous rhythm. How long it was likely to continue he had no idea, and this made it difficult to resolve on a determined effort towards getting used to it. Mackannis said that the drumming, like any of the traditional street games and children's amusements, was strictly seasonal, and that the day would come when drums were no longer in fashion and leapfrog or hop-scotch or skipping would take their place. But that happy day had not arrived, and in the intervals of silence, when he scowled at the page and consulted his notes, his ears were alert for the first tap, the first burst of rhythm and rumbling which signalled the beginning of another intolerable session of merry din. Even worse than the drums because more insidious was the pestle-and-mortar pounding from the house next door. This was an ominous heavy beat which sent a perceptible vibration up through the very structure. Again he had appealed to Mackannis, who had shrugged his shoulders. It would be sugar, he said, not spices; the feast was over. Sugar was bought in solid loaves, being cheaper that way, and pounding it was a regular occupa-tion for the females of the family. They had done it this way, he said, remembering Lytton's interests, for hundreds and hundreds of years, as in the Middle Ages; but for once Lytton failed to see any merit in it.

Sometimes the parlour would be silent for long periods, and he would stop walking about and compel himself to sit at his desk, holding his head in his hands and trying to decide why the written page refused to convey what he intended; and at such moments, almost inevitably, someone on a nearby roof would start beating a carpet, or a cock would set off a whole chorus of senseless crowing, or voices would be urgently raised in what sounded like a quarrel. He had more than once been driven to climb on the table to look out of the window, it was so maddening not to know what was going on. It was never easy to see, for the window was a square hole and would have been out of reach to anyone but a tall man, but by standing on the table he could just manage it, and to spy on these irritating activities gave him a kind of angry satisfaction. Once Phoebe had come on him in this position, and the incident had caused him some embarrassment. He had heard the sound of voices and splashing water, and had climbed up to see a young man taking a bath while a woman was hanging out washing and companionably watching him. It had been perfectly decorous and ordinary; the man was wearing his trousers and washing in a bucket, dowsing his head and splashing himself under the arms; but the scene, being so unselfconscious, had a fascination, and Lytton had stayed on the table with his head in the hole, holding his breath for a moment when the man might decide to remove his trousers. He had not done so, or at least the woman had hung out a blanket at the crucial moment so that what went on behind it was hidden from view, but at that precise moment Phoebe had come in with an urgent-looking document from the post office, and after a moment of astonishment had burst out laughing.

'My dear Henry! You look so extraordinary. Whatever is the matter?'

'Nothing is the matter, apart from a great deal of unnecessary noise.' He drew back his head from the hole with dignity and came down by the chair. 'I was just trying to see what the disturbance was. There's always something.'

'Really? It always seems so beautifully quiet in here. You're becoming too sensitive, I think. Really, my dear, I fancy it could hardly be quieter.' He shot her a furious glance and she controlled her merriment.

'You don't happen to be trying to do creative work, so naturally you don't hear it. I dare say I wouldn't either, if I had nothing to do.' He waved away the paper she offered him and began operations on his spectacles, polishing the lenses.

'Well, I'm sorry. I thought this might be important, or I wouldn't have come in. I thought it might be something to do with the books you sent for.'

'Later, Phoebe, *please*. I'll attend to it later.' She lingered at the door, still seeming to be inwardly amused.

'We all do our best not to disturb you, you know. Are you finding it difficult to work here?'

'Very. And as it happens you *are* disturbing me.'

'You must try not to be so touchy, you know,' said Phoebe and closed the door, leaving him in an enclosed silence in which he could hear nothing at all but his own breathing.

The trouble, of course, as sooner or later he knew he must

privately discover, was not in the noises of the house or even from the neighbours, but in himself, in that centre of consciousness with which, if he were to work as he intended, he must establish a fruitful flow of communication. At present it was dumb; it might as well not have been there. The earlier volume of autobiography had been easy; he looked back on the two years he had spent on it with envious amazement. Everything in it had been his own, it had belonged to his youth. No one had been able to contradict or make hostile interpretations; it belonged to that period of his life before he had known Sarah. The strange thing was that this latter half of his life should have been the more significant, and indeed from the moment when Sarah had gone out of it, it offered the very material he most enjoyed— romantic descriptions in which he could do himself justice, his own touch of atmosphere, a congenial blend of philosophy and speculation. Already he could see how the book would end, on a note of strength and calm, noble and stark against a background of Morocco. He had lived through so much, had passed through so many dangers, had defied death; and now, in these last reflective months that were allowed him he would sum it all up in a *tour de force* of humanity and courage. He could see the book as clearly as if it lay on the table, could even imagine the lettering on the jacket. *The Last Oasis*, perhaps, or something like that. It would establish and preserve his name long after he was gone.

But somewhere in it, somewhere between the beginning and the envisaged end, stood the unavoidable, intractable figure of Sarah. However he thought of it he could see no negotiable route round that stumbling-block. She stood in the middle of the path, with her knowing smile, and every word would ring false when she cast her eye on it.

Now for the first time in all his dissatisfied wanderings about the room he furtively lifted his eyes to Sarah's death-mask. It was rather dim; that end of the room was in shadow and his eyes were attuned to the brightness of the reading lamp. He took off his spectacles and sat for a moment with a hand over his eyes, then rose and paced slowly the length of the room, gazing into the frame with curiosity, as though this were the first time he had clearly seen it. He switched on a table-lamp, lighting the mask from below, so that the waxen features came suddenly to life and a shadow sprang upwards from the cheek-bones and another outlined the curve of the strong nostrils. My God, he thought, what a hateful, implacable face. It was the face of an antique empress who could have everything she chose: lovers, and rivals tortured, and the death of captives, whatever her exorbitant appetites demanded. She could pick a man up, and try him, and destroy him with contempt. And her authority was so potent, so indestructible, she could exercise it without mercy from beyond the grave. Hateful Sarah: always, and with all the power of her femaleness, in the right; refusing to understand how lesser beings could fail under her exactions, not caring how a man shrivelled under that mocking, that alarmingly cool and analytical eye. It struck him afresh how strange it was that though the eyes were closed they gave the impression of being tirelessly observant, following each movement from under the drooping lids. And interpreting everything, always, to his disadvantage. She knew quite well why he couldn't work, and the knowledge diverted her. She had never believed he was any good, not after the disastrous beginning when he had failed her as a lover, and her scorn of his impotence had extended to everything he did, laying a withering touch on vanity and ambition, drying up the very juices of creative life. He had been himself before he met her, there had been virtue in him, but the canker of her derision had driven him further and further into pretence. She knew he was pretending now, he could see it in her face; knew that he did not believe in the imminence of death, even in his own reality in this alien place, or in his power to establish touch with a strange people, or learn their tongue, or be absorbed in any life outside his own, or see himself as he was and set down the intractable truth on a sheet of paper. He worked his jaws convulsively as he stared at the mask, like a cat that watches a bird flown out of reach.

But it was not out of reach, he told himself, feeling a stir of anger. He had hung the thing up himself and he could remove it. He would no longer meekly tolerate Sarah's scrutiny.

Carefully, glancing at the closed door and taking elaborate precautions against noise, he lifted a chair and placed it against the wall. Standing on the seat he could reach the frame without difficulty; he grasped it in both hands and lifted it from the nail. It was heavier than he remembered, and the glass when he examined it closely was filmed with dust. Within, on a bed of velvet, Sarah slept, and the face was suddenly unlike her, crude and waxen. He did not look at it again but came down from the chair and carried it to the table. Here he hesitated, surreptitiously glancing about for a hiding-place. One of the bookcases had a cupboard where he kept his Arabic records and other possessions, and hearing a sound from the courtyard he opened it quickly and placed the frame inside, covering the glass as an afterthought with a newspaper. When the cupboard was closed and the key turned he found himself breathing rapidly and returned to his desk, where he sat for a while without moving, his head in his hands. When at length he stirred and put on his spectacles a minute passed before he felt able to look up. He turned a page, shifted the ink-well a fraction, examined his finger-nails, finally raised his eyes to the empty space. It was extraordinary how blank and anonymous it looked; he was quite startled. The whole room looked mysteriously different without it, which was perhaps not surprising, since the mask had been hung as a centre-piece and the furniture arranged with respectful reference to it. It was positively unnerving, the difference that moving it had made. The cupboard too, which before had been quite unnoticeable, was beginning to assert itself, as though calling attention to the fact that there was something unusual inside, and that the door was locked. This, Lytton told himself sharply, was ridiculous; he was certainly not going to indulge in morbid fancies. All the same his train of thought, such as it was, had been thoroughly upset by the business and was beyond recall. He decided to abandon work for the rest of the morning.

The removal of the mask went unnoticed until after supper, when Phoebe came into the parlour with a tray of coffee.

'Good heavens,' she cried, arresting her cup in the moment

of putting it to her lips, 'wherever has the mask gone, Henry? Don't say it's fallen!' She got up and hurried anxiously to the end of the room, dreading to find splinters of glass and fragments of wax.

'Certainly not. It's quite safe. I took it down.' He turned a page of his book without looking up.

'Did you really? Oh, Henry, why? It looks so empty.' She had never cared for the mask, whatever its position, but now it was gone from the wall her eye missed it. Lytton made no reply and she returned to her chair in silence and drank her coffee. 'Won't you miss it very much?' she said at length, trying to imagine what reason he could possibly have had for its removal, but guessing from his face that he was hardly likely to tell her. 'It was very much admired at the party, I thought. It was quite a feature.'

'I found it disturbing,' said Lytton after a pause, turning another page. 'It set off a train of thought. I couldn't concentrate.' He pointedly frowned at his book and she looked at him in astonishment. Had he too, then, had moments of vision or illusion comparable to her own, when the waxen face had quickened as though it would speak? But if he had, why should it so deeply have disturbed him? He had always been so fond of the thing, he repeatedly referred to it. Phoebe gave up the puzzle and finished her coffee, moving her eyes at random about the room. It was odd how different it seemed without Sarah in it; better, in a way; yes, distinctly. She considered the room critically and began to like it. He had hidden the mask of course, she was sure of that; but it was no use asking. Her eye strayed speculatively round to the bookcase cupboard and after a moment she noticed that the key was gone. So that was it! Really, for a man of his age he was very childish, thinking he could get rid of Sarah by locking a door. It even seemed as she looked at it that the door shook slightly, but she dismissed the absurd illusion and closed her eyes. Faintly through the high window came the sounds that she heard every night at this hour and now listened to with pleasure: the far-off crowing of a cock, a strain of something that sounded like radio music, the hum of the town below, even children's voices. She had learned these sounds by heart and their concord soothed her. Only . . . it was very odd . . . as she listened she caught an echo of something she had long forgotten, a queer remark of Sarah's more than twenty years ago, when they had all been so happy. She had been staying in the house in Gloucestershire and there had suddenly been a quarrel, and Sarah had passed her on the stairs looking pale and triumphant and had said, 'You can have him with pleasure. The man's a sham! What's more, he knows I know,' and had swept upstairs and slammed the door of her bedroom, leaving Phoebe to pass an uncommonly uncomfortable evening alone with Lytton.

*

It was one of those evenings when buying and selling went on in the streets until a late hour, and the cafés were crowded. Long before the dawn there had been strings of country people riding in from the hill villages, trotting and singing along the waterfront under the electric lights, each with a load of produce for the day's market. Women in hats as big as cartwheels, who had walked all night, bent under loads of charcoal and wood, now sat by the last of their stock at the corners of streets, hoping for a few more coins, a final meagre transaction before the long trudge home. What many of them offered was pitifully scanty, a dozen lemons, a couple of cheeses embedded in coronets of rushes, bouquets of parsley and mint smelling sweet and strong, loaves of bread in a clean cloth, two or three fish, a crock of milk, a handful of rosy radishes. But the faces under the targe-like hats were remarkably cheerful, even though the bare feet and gaitered legs would soon be off again on their nightlong journey, and the streets were full of the noisy clamour which always went on until late after a country market.

Quattrell and Nick sat at a pavement table under the awning of a café, finishing their mint tea. They had met by chance in a newspaper shop, and being both at a loose end and reluctant to go home had been more than usually pleased to run into one another. The Parsons' flat at the moment was not a place to which Nick was anxious to return, since his brother was having one of his unmanageable spells, all tears and tantrums, and he had reached the point where he was equally sick of Pete and of his mother and grandmother. He looked at his watch, however, feeling vaguely responsible, thanked Quattrell for the drink, scraped in his glass with a spoon for the last of the sugar and said he was really afraid he must be going.

'I'll give you a lift,' said Quattrell, beckoning to the waiter. 'I've left the car at the top, it's on my way.' He paid for the tea and they set off at a slow pace through the crowded quarter, an oddly assorted couple, Quattrell's hand resting lightly on Nick's shoulder. They paused and looked in the window of an Indian shop, where brassières and nylon stockings were displayed among Japanese cameras and tape-recorders. Nick glanced knowledgeably over the stock and pointed to one of the neat machines with his finger.

'My brother's got one of those, they're Japanese. He smashed it up the first day, and Hamid and I put it right for him.'

'Does he use it?' said Quattrell, surprised, remembering the brother's behaviour at the airport.

'Not really. He makes noises with it sometimes, that's all he cares about. His movements aren't properly co-ordinated,' Nick explained, 'when he tries to press a button he breaks something.'

'Not a very good toy to give him, perhaps?'

'Oh, I don't know. It keeps him quiet. He likes mechanical things, though he can't work them. I gave him a toy camera once, and he threw it out of the window. He knew it wasn't a real one.'

'Smart kid,' said Quattrell absently, returning to his own thoughts. They moved on and turned into a street full of tailors' shops, each with a child moored in front of it by a long skein, moving the silk from hand to hand as the tailor braided his buttons.

'Boring job, that,' said Nick, as one man to another.

'It keeps them quiet, too, I suppose.'

'Oh yes, it has that advantage.'

Quattrell looked down at him with a smile and shifted his

hand companionably to the other shoulder. 'You're an old-fashioned specimen,' he said; 'what d'you get up to at the Lyttons', with your friend Tavy? What goes on in that loft?' It seemed to him that Nick was walking with extraordinary slowness, as though to prolong the conversation; he wondered if the boy had a thin time of it at home, and guessed that he was lonely.

'We play cards sometimes. I know a few tricks. Sometimes we just talk.'

'That all? She's older than you, isn't she? What does she like doing?' He looked down at Nick with curiosity, trying to imagine a scene that he could believe in. They had been a long time out of sight on the night of the party.

'I don't really know yet,' said Nick candidly. 'She doesn't know much, I don't think. I'll tell you something, if you like. If you won't repeat it.'

'Cross my heart.' Quattrell crossed himself gravely with his newspaper.

'She'd never smoked a cigarette in her life, though she's nearly sixteen. I showed her how to.'

'My, my, you are a devil.'

Nick looked up suspiciously, but Quattrell's face was friendly, without mockery. 'It wasn't a cigarette, anyway,' he said impressively, 'it was a pipe. Only a little one,' he amended, relieved to find that Quattrell was not shocked, but laughed in an amused way and pressed his shoulder. 'There was kief in it, as a matter of fact,' he added in an undertone, but as he said this they halted on the heels of a crowd where a great noise was going on and it was impossible to be quite sure whether Quattrell heard him.

They had come upon a group of bearded and eccentric-looking men who appeared to be giving some sort of performance in the street. One blew a horn while another thumped on a drum and the rest chanted together in noisy chorus. They had attracted a staring audience of men and boys and it was several minutes before Nick and Quattrell managed to squeeze past.

'What was that rumpus in aid of?' said Quattrell at length, when they made their way round another corner and the noise had momentarily ceased while the group moved on.

'It's something religious; a sect, something of the kind.' Nick was delighted to be asked for information. 'Something like the Salvation Army, I imagine. Collecting money and drumming and praising God. I heard them say *moomin* just now, that means the Faithful.'

'The Beloved, the Merciful, the Compassionate,' said Quattrell, lifting his rolled newspaper like a conductor's baton, 'the Mighty, the One, the Sustainer—do you know all the titles of God?'

'I know a few,' said Nick, impressed, glancing up at him. 'I know a few words of Arabic, not much of course. I learn a bit sometimes from Hamid. We don't get it at school.'

The street had begun to rise in a gentle gradient and was becoming wider. Nick came to a sudden stop and threw back his head, looking at the face of the walls and the abrupt precarious-looking parapets rising above them.

'That's Mr. Lytton's house up there,' he said, pointing. 'You can't see much, only the corner of the wall on the top roof. But I know it's his all right, I've checked it before. This is the only spot you can see it from.' They stood together and Nick pointed and picked out landmarks until Quattrell got it. There was not much to be seen, an angle of weather-stained parapet and a bit of drainpipe, nothing to distinguish it from the rest. But Nick's attention was fixed with unusual intensity, as though he were bent on solving some private puzzle.

'There's an empty house next door,' he said, looking at Quattrell doubtfully, but with a gleam in his eye. 'I've always wanted to know where it came out at.'

They moved on a few paces, pausing to avoid a beggar who advanced chanting. Quattrell felt in his pockets for a coin, found nothing but a note and saw with a certain relief that the man was blind. He tapped his way with a stick, one hand extended, raising his lugubrious cry, and turned into a narrow alley a little ahead of them.

'I bet it's there,' said Nick, 'there's no other turning,' and followed to the corner, looking under a low archway into a narrow cul-de-sac in which there was nothing to be seen but the beggar, a scattering of ash and refuse, and a heavy door.

Quattrell strolled after Nick and laid an arm on his shoulder. The alertness of the boy's curiosity had not been lost on him; he was on the scent of something, though what it was he hadn't the least idea. 'What are you after?' he said in a whisper, his eyes following the beggar's shanks and dragging slippers. The old man had found the steps with his stick and now stood with his face to the door, groping in his clothing.

'That's it all right,' said Nick under his breath, and Quattrell felt the muscles of his shoulder tighten. He gave him an inquiring look: a thought had struck him.

'Have you ever been in that house?' he asked, keeping his voice low.

'I think so, yes. I'm sure that's the door. It's an empty house, but somebody goes there, I'm certain. Just watch him a minute.'

They stood in the darkness of the archway while the beggar explored his clothing and found a key. He felt with his hand over the surface of the door, passing over the scrawled and peeling paintwork and the iron studs until he found the keyhole, and with the sureness of long habit fitted the key. It was a large key and they heard it turn in the lock. Then the door opened heavily on stiff hinges and the old man faded like a ghost into the dark interior. There was the sound of the lock once more and the thud of a bolt, and then the alley was as dark and quiet again as if the door had never been opened and the beggar were a vision. A cat ran past by their feet, keeping close to the wall, and crouched to sniff over the fishbones among the refuse.

'Well, whaddya know?' said Quattrell, taking his hand from Nick's shoulder to search for his cigarettes 'So that's where you go with Miss Tavy, is it?' He offered the pack to Nick, raising his eyebrows when he refused, and lit one for himself.

'I didn't say so,' said Nick, his eyes on the door. His desire to communicate was very plain, also the fact that he knew he ought not to do so. Quattrell threw away the match and they resumed their walk, his arm resting once again round Nick's shoulders.

'How d'you get in, though? From the top? That's what I can't fathom.'

'I'm sorry, I can't talk about it.'

'A secret, h'm? O.K., I shan't say anything.'

'I'd tell you if I could,' said Nick earnestly, 'but you do see I can't, don't you? There might be an awful row if it came out.'

'Sure, sure. Don't give it another thought. I've already forgotten it.'

They came to the top of the ascent, passed by the flight of steps leading to Lytton's street, turned a corner, another, went under an archway and came to the open space between shuttered houses where Quattrell had left his car. There was nobody about, not even a beggar, and the air smelt late. Even the children for once had been herded in, though their voices could still be heard and there was an occasional rattle of drumming and a snatch of singing to suggest that only the youngest had gone to bed. Nick looked at his watch by the dashboard light as he got in.

'You all right for time?'

'Yes, thank you. I've been later than this, often. Mother gets in a flap sometimes, but she doesn't really mind.'

'Good, we must do this again.' Quattrell switched on the engine and sidelights and the car started. 'And you don't have to worry, you know, about anything you said. I've had a lot of practice in keeping secrets. I'm a real clam.'

'Oh, thank you. Yes, I'm sure you are. Though I wasn't really aware,' said Nick, in his precise voice, 'that I'd said very much.' He was almost sure that Quattrell had failed to catch what he said about kief, but if he *had* heard his mind was at ease on this point. The large presence of this odd and easy-going man, so unlike his father, filled him with confidence; the sensation of sharing a secret with him was delightful.

'Well, no, only about the house,' said Quattrell, switching on powerful headlights as they roared up an empty street, scattering a motley handful of startled goats, 'and I've already forgotten about that, as I told you before.'

'Yes, I know. It's quite all right. I'm glad I told you.'

'Good; we must do this again some other night. We'll do the town.'

'Oh yes, I should like that.' He caught his breath on the tobacco smoke and coughed, raising a polite hand. 'Ought we to ask Tavy, do you think?'

'Can if you like. Or not, h'm? We do rather well on our own.'

'Oh yes we do,' said Nick, 'we certainly do,' and wound down the window and gave himself up to the sweetness of the night air and the pleasure of being abroad in the town at this late hour, roaring through the empty streets in Quattrell's company.

11

'You haven't told me yet about your lunch with Quattrell,' said Anthea, pushing an extra cushion under Consuelo's head. They were lying on plastic mattresses, hideously coloured and inconveniently adhesive, on the balcony of the flat, where the sun was now hot in the afternoons and it was sheltered from the wind.

'There hasn't been much chance, has there? And why do you always call him by his surname? It makes him sound like a night-club. Strip-tease at Quattrell's.'

Anthea laughed, though she wondered about the implications of the crack. 'I don't know. It suits him somehow. I don't call him that to his face.' She poured a little oil into the palm of her hand and began smoothing it over her arms, which the sun had already deepened to the colour of burnt almonds. Consuelo watched her enviously.

'Well, we went to this restaurant and had a rather disappointing lunch, which I noticed was expensive, and a lot of that appalling wine that everyone drinks here if they haven't any sense, and afterwards we walked on the beach, and I got a headache.'

'It doesn't sound much fun after all.' Anthea had noticed Consuelo's uncommunicative air when she returned and had been careful not to seem eager for revelations. Besides, as Consuelo said, there had been little opportunity. Gerald had always been there, or Ozzie or Tavy, and in the last two days they had had hardly a moment alone.

'It was interesting, in a morbid way,' said Consuelo, sitting up with an air of decision and reaching for the oil. She poured a little on her thighs and began gingerly smoothing it over the reddened skin, which was becoming painful. 'He wanted to talk about you most of the time, and about Gerald. About whom, if

I may be so crude as to say so, he seems to harbour singularly few illusions.'

'They don't like each other, I'm afraid,' said Anthea quickly, 'that's becoming obvious.'

'Yes, well, why would they? Gerald's no fool, he's quite aware Rob's got his eye on you, and Rob's not exactly dull either, and assured me in so many words that Gerald's a queer.'

'Charming, I must say. Everybody says that about everybody here, hadn't you noticed? It's never later than the second or third remark in any conversation.'

'Oh well,' said Consuelo impatiently, 'what the hell does it matter? It hadn't occurred to me, I admit. But now, I suppose . . . Anyway,' she had started to oil one shoulder and was squinting down at it, 'I still think you were right to marry him. I think he's marvellous. And I respect the front you keep up, though I wouldn't be capable of it.'

Anthea said nothing for a while but sat with her arms round her knees, gazing at the bay. It was dazzlingly bright and ruffled with catspaws of wind, and the few little sailing boats were keeping close to the shore, all tilted at the same angle.

'I wouldn't want him any different,' she said at length. 'The front, as you call it, doesn't conceal anything particularly sensational. I've nothing to complain of.'

'I'll say you haven't. I couldn't agree with you more. I imagine he wouldn't complain, either, if you followed your fancy. With Rob, for instance.'

Anthea lay back on the mattress again and put her arm over her eyes, aware that behind her sun-glasses Consuelo was watching her.

'My fancy's unadventurous these days,' she said, 'it's out of practice. I'm not even sure it operates any more.'

Consuelo began oiling her feet, examining her painted toe-nails with critical attention.

'Well, as I said, he's certainly got you on his mind. Wanted to know your whole history and all about you. Disappointing for me in a way, not to say irritating. He's dying to be taken up. You could have him by lifting a finger.'

'How much of my history did you tell him?' said Anthea, not choosing to follow this suggestion. She was anxious to know the drift of conversation but shrank from the thought that they might have been talking about James.

'Well, darling, not much. You know me. He knew there'd been someone in your life before Gerald, you must have said something. And I told him the chap died years ago, and I got a distinct impression he wasn't shattered.'

'You didn't say who it was?'

'In a pig's eye! What d'you take me for? With Molly around all the time, and this place simply seething and bubbling over with gossip? Don't make me cross.'

'Well, no, of course not. I'm sure you didn't. You're the perfect friend.'

'That's true, you know, in a way,' Consuelo admitted, transferring her attention to her finger nails, which were long and curved and brightly enamelled, a great responsibility. 'That's why I'd like to know . . . if you're thinking of Rob, I mean, I shan't give it a thought. But if you're *not* . . . the point is, I'm not going to stay here for ever and I'd like to make plans. I did think of going on, as you know, while the money lasts, but if he's positively not on your programme one might reconsider. I won't double-cross you, my love, after all these years. The man has something.'

'I haven't a programme, I assure you. I'm aimlessly drifting.'

'But I think he attracts you, doesn't he? I know one has to be discreet and all that, but I wish you wouldn't be evasive. You've been different these last few days, I couldn't help noticing. And I'm not going to start competing because I'm a practical character and I know damn well I shouldn't have the slightest chance.'

'What had you in mind then?' said Anthea, again evading the issue. She would have given a good deal at this moment to know her own mind as clearly as Consuelo knew hers, but all she was sure of was that something was alive again which had once been dead, and the miracle was enough, and she was almost prepared, if not wholly, to be content with it.

'I haven't got it worked out, not what you'd call *planned*.' Consuelo's frown of concentration suggested that she had. 'I've been through with Dave for some time, as you know, and I'm not getting any younger. Rob's my type, in a way. I could see that the minute I set eyes on him. And his life's in a mess, that's obvious as well. He's arrived at the point where any woman not a cripple could have him for the asking.'

'I wonder. And is he worth having? I remember you said the other day you didn't trust him.'

'Well, no more I don't; but that's a lot to ask, isn't it? After all, you've been fortunate—first James, then Gerald. Snags to both, I agree, but both of them cast-iron characters if ever I saw one.' She turned over on her stomach, taking care to arrange a towel between the areas of sunburn and the blistering plastic. 'In a word, my darling, you must see, if it weren't for his obsession with you it'd be worth a try. I'd want to know, naturally, what your real feelings were, but I won't pretend that I wouldn't like to see if my hand's lost its old cunning.'

'And if I haven't any real feelings in the matter,' said Anthea, still hiding her face with her arm from the hot sun, 'how would you go about it, I wonder? What would you propose to do?' It was odd, she reflected, that she felt only a momentary pang at the thought of losing him. But there *was* a pang, and it gave her a curious pleasure. It came to her calmly that she valued him less for what he might offer than for what he had already given her.

'*Well*,' said Consuelo, propping herself on her elbows and beginning to pluck at the fringe on the gaudy pillow, 'the first thing I should like to do is see him again. One'd know how the land lay then; it'd be more conclusive. He did say to leave a message at that bar if ever I was at a loose end. If I wanted to go to the beach or anything. We didn't discuss you *all* the time, sweetheart, there *were* other topics. In fact, if I hadn't drunk too much at lunch and got a headache, and the wind hadn't got up it did sort of strike me he might have been more forthcoming.'

'I should do that then, certainly,' said Anthea, half-welcoming the idea that Consuelo's experiment might at least put a definite answer to an indefinite question. If she succeeded there would be no more problem, no brink to linger on; and Consuelo would be off on exactly the kind of adventure she set most store by. If not . . . but here she was able to be less precise, less perfectly clear and certain about her feelings. If his motive in seeing Consuelo had been truly what he said, if the response between herself and Rob were not merely an illusion, well then, she would think again. There was even a certain luxury, a coward's comfort, in letting a risk decide between herself and Consuelo.

'You really wouldn't mind, my love? Honestly?' Anthea had almost forgotten her presence as she brooded, and came back with surprise to the flushed and sun-scorched visage close beside her.

'Honest. You try it out. Might be interesting.'

'Oh boy,' said Consuelo, sitting up, 'what a goddamn stupid fool I was to get burned like this,' and fished out a little mirror and examined her face, which was not at its best. 'It's not *fair*,' she cried, 'you lie about in the sun all day and turn a delicious colour without lifting a finger and I only have to sit in it for half an hour and I go like a side of bacon.'

'There's some lotion of Gerald's in the bathroom cupboard. It's said to be good, it's what they use in hospitals.'

'But *you* don't have to do a thing, and I need first-aid.'

'I know, I must be thick-skinned. It's a grievance of Gerald's too, but he takes precautions.'

So the following morning, while Anthea and Tavy accompanied Enrico to the market (Tavy came round at all hours now, so that even Nick was neglected) Consuelo put her scheme into operation. She waited until everyone was gone before she telephoned, spending much time in her bedroom attending to her appearance, and when Anthea returned the lift still had traces of her scent but the flat was empty. A note, very nearly illegible, was propped by the telephone. 'Have borrowed car—are you furious? Gerald not in, so couldn't ask. Back around teatime.'

At five o'clock, however, the telephone rang. Anthea left Tavy on the balcony and lifted the receiver.

'Anthea! What the hell *is* this?' It was Quattrell's voice.

'What's what? Is Consuelo with you?'

'She isn't *now*, but I've had her since twelve o'clock. Was that your brilliant invention, may I ask?' The tone of his voice made it clear he was very angry.

'I thought it was your idea. Didn't you suggest it?'

'You know damn well I didn't. I've been phoning the flat at all hours and there's never an answer. Are you playing some kind of game with me, I'd like to know? Because if so, say so.'

'Not that I know of. I'm not always in when the telephone rings. We go out a good deal.'

'Can I talk to you now? Are you surrounded?'

'I'm not alone, if that's what you mean.'

'Oh, for Christ's sake, who's with you?'

'Only Tavy.' She glanced at the open balcony, where Tavy's long legs could be seen, gleaming with sunlight and oil on one of the mattresses.

'Get rid of her, will you? I'm coming round.'

'I can't do that, Rob; don't be dramatic. What's happened to Consuelo?'

'She left in the car; I followed her in. *Please*, Anthea, I'm serious. And be quick about it, because I've got to talk to you. She stopped off at a drugstore in the boulevard, but she won't be long. Will you do what I ask, just this once? I'm speaking from the *tabac* at the corner, you could be there in ten seconds. If you don't I'll come up to the flat and it'll be embarrassing.' There was a pause, in which Anthea said nothing. 'For God's sake, girl, be reasonable. It can't be *that* difficult.'

Anthea glanced at the window again and hesitated, while the telephone set up its usual mechanical noises.

'Very well,' she said through the crackle, 'I'll be right down,' and hung up and went to the balcony, slipping her feet into sandals and buttoning her dress.

'I've got to go out for a minute. I shan't be long.'

'Oh, bother. Shall I come too?'

'No, no. You stay right where you are. I'll be back in a minute.'

'Shall I make some tea while you're gone?' Tavy called after her, but the door had already slammed and there was no answer.

Quattrell was standing at the corner in shirt-sleeves, leaning on the roof of his car. He snatched at the door as she approached and she got in, aware that they were both nervously watching for Consuelo. He started the car with a jerk and they set off without speaking, roared up a one-way street and over a halt-sign, swung round a corner and gathered speed down the main boulevard which ran out at the end of the town.

'I can't stay long,' said Anthea in a small voice, 'where are you taking me?' He reached for her hand and took it in a tight grasp.

'Just somewhere where we can talk. You're behaving very badly.'

'I?' Her voice cracked with astonishment. 'You're not serious. What have I done?'

'You're behaving like a bitch to that poor silly little friend of yours. And even worse to me, which is inexcusable. I'm really angry with you.'

'In that case hadn't we better stop and you tell me what's the matter?'

'We're going to, presently. But at least I've got you now, and that's something.'

He drove very fast, still holding her by the left hand, and as there was next to no traffic on the road they covered a good many miles in the next few minutes. At first Anthea was incredulous, but it soon became apparent that he was heading for the sea-house.

'Rob,' she said, making an effort to free her hand, but without success, 'I won't be kidnapped like this. Where are we going? I've left poor Tavy alone.'

'And you think she'll drop dead with fright, or fall in the fire? Consuelo's there by now, you can relax.'

'I know, but what will they imagine? I said I would only be a minute.'

'I don't care what they imagine, so put it out of your mind.' His tone was no less intransigent than before; her heart began to beat fast with anger and excitement.

'We *can't* go as far as the house, it's out of the question. You can stop the car here, by the road, and tell me what it is you're creating this scene about.'

'I'll tell you when I've calmed down. I can't drive and talk.'

'Stop driving, then.' But he still continued at speed along the coast road, between the empty sun-scorched landscape and the sea, and presently she gave a little laugh, still angry, but with a sharp sense of the absurdity of her predicament.

'It strikes you as funny?'

'It does, you know. You're being unusually dramatic.'

'I'm a dramatic man.' The tension became slightly easier. 'Don't talk,' he said, and pressed and kneaded her hand against his thigh. 'We're going to be here some time, you can expostulate later.' He loosed her hand after a while and gave her a packet of cigarettes from the nearside locker. 'Light me one too, will you?' She did as she was told and the smoke from their cigarettes whipped from the open window into the rushing air. Anthea found that her hands were shaking slightly.

Presently they came to the cart-track leading to the dunes and the old car lurched off the road and bumped over the hard ruts, slackening speed but still going far too fast for safety or comfort. They were flung together over a grassy hump and came to a violent standstill at the back of the cottage.

'Well I hope you feel better after that demonstration?' She got shakily out of the car and faced the wind. It smelt of grass and tide-wrack and the sea.

'I do, since you kindly ask. A demonstration was necessary.' He took her by the arm and they went through the gap in the prickly-pear and round past the shuttered windows to the front of the cottage. The tide was in, long rollers sweeping from far out and breaking along the fringe of the deserted beach, which seemed even more desolate and empty than when she had last seen it. 'I was mad to come,' she thought, 'but how could I have prevented it?' There was no suddenness or shock about the situation; it had been building steadily. The moment had come when evasion was no longer possible.

Quattrell unlocked the door and they went in. 'Sit down,' he said in a more normal tone, and began opening the shutters. The sun was not far from setting and a dazzle of westerly brightness filled the room. It was much as she had seen it before, a little more strewn with sand and dust and the litter of haphazard occupation, but not repulsively untidy. Only the typewriter and brimming ash-tray and a disorganised-looking heap of papers occupied the table; it seemed to be true after all that he had been working. Anthea glanced around her, taking it in. There was always a dangerous interest in any place so solitarily inhabited; she was aware of this treacherous attraction and guarded against it. She thought she detected, but she was not sure, the trace of some scent which might have been Consuelo's.

'Now then,' he said, and took her in his arms and began kissing her. He thrust his fingers in her hair and held it tightly, drawing back her head and gazing with searching intentness at her face. 'At last,' he said, and they kissed again, standing for a long time without moving, their bodies pressed together and their hearts beating. Finally her knees trembled and she broke away.

'Co ne and sit down, my darling.' He touched her breast and drew her down to the divan, holding and stroking her hands. 'You've got a lot to explain, my girl. Suppose you begin.'

'If only I knew what this was all about.' She could no longer resist the compelling warmth that enveloped her and turned her head and rubbed her cheek on his shoulder.

'It's about you and me,' he said, 'and why you've been holding me at arms' length and ruining my sleep, and making promises and breaking them, and sending that idiotic Miss Carpenter of yours to tease me when you know I've been thinking of you night and day and waiting for you to come.'

'I didn't send her. She came of her own accord. Anyway I thought it was your own suggestion.'

'You know better than that. You should have prevented her. You were supposed to tell her about us, to make things easier.' He put his lips to her neck and moved them slowly across her pulsing throat, pressing her into the cushions with his whole weight. She made no resistance but gave herself up to his urgency and warmth and the harsh male smell of his skin and the taste of his kisses, which were pungent with tobacco. She closed her eyes as the warmth of response went through her, but his embrace was a little too sharp and purposeful, too practised and

206

assured, so that she opened them again with a stab of consciousness: it was clear he believed he had only to let her feel his desire and she would melt under it. This was very nearly true, yet not entirely; somewhere in the blind depths there was a nugget of resistance. She hooked her fingers into his hair and wrenched her mouth away.

'Rob! This isn't the time. Get up, you're hurting me.'

'It *is* the time. Be quiet. Just let me love you.'

'Not now. You've *got* to listen.' She pushed him with considerable force and he shifted reluctantly. They were both breathing hard.

'Be quiet,' he said again, drawing her down by the shoulder, 'don't talk. This is what it's all about, my darling, it always has been. Let it come, Anthea.'

But 'No' she said, 'no, not like this,' and made a vigorous effort and broke away from him, sweeping the hair from her eyes and scrambling to her knees. He leaned on one elbow among the cushions and heavily regarded her. Something in his attitude, the poise of his head, the heavy shoulders and eyebrows, even the tangle of hair over the brow, was like a freak of memory, recalling an image fastidiously unlike him. She swung her feet to the floor and stood up, none too steadily.

'What happened with Consuelo? Tell me. And then I'm going.' He lay where he was and watched her, his eyebrows gloomy.

'Why do you ask? Is this jealousy?'

'I ask because I want to know. I feel responsible.'

'Responsible! I'll say you are. Come back and kiss me.' His face had softened and he held out a coaxing hand.

'No, Rob. I mean what I say. Please tell me.' She moved over to a square of mirror screwed to the wall and ran her fingers distractedly through her hair.

'She came out here, in your car, as I don't doubt you know, and I gave her a drink and a corned-beef sandwich, which I fancy wasn't what she came for. Five bees are better than a pannier of flies, however, as they say in these parts.'

'What am I to deduce from that?' She heard him strike a

match and glanced over her shoulder. He was sitting up now, elbows on knees, regarding her through a haze of sunlit smoke.

'You can deduce what you choose. I'm not interested in Miss Carpenter. I did the polite, however, and eventually she went home. You hadn't prepared the ground, I discovered. Why? And as soon as she'd gone I got mad, if not before. Why did you do it, Anthea? Don't tell me it wasn't your idea. Of course you were responsible.'

'Listen,' she said, turning away from the glass and moving across to lean against the littered table, 'can't you understand that I've got to have time? It's not much to ask. I can't rush into things at this pace, I'm not built that way.'

'You're built the way I am, and you know it. What are you waiting for?'

'I'm waiting to be a little bit sure of myself, that's all. I like to know what I want to do before I do it. Does that seem to you so strange?'

'It's strange that you want to make love, and here we are miles from anywhere, with a good hard bed and all the other requirements, and you won't do it.'

'I don't say I never will. But not now, Rob, not today. Not like this. You seem to think it's as simple as taking a drink.'

'It's not difficult, I assure you.' His face relaxed in a smile and he held out his hand again.

'But I am. I'm sorry, Rob. I dare say it's all my fault.'

'It is, you know.' He dropped his hand. 'So what are we going to do about it?'

'You'll take me home, that's what we're going to do. We'll think out something more reasonable on the way.'

'Such as what? And suppose I decide not to take you?'

'Then I shall walk.'

'Just like an old-fashioned movie, you mean? And all those jokes?'

'Like all those corny jokes. I'm a good walker.'

'You'll need to be. It's all of twenty miles.' He sighed and got up from the bed, throwing his half-smoked cigarette on the floor and treading on it. 'You're the most perverse woman I've

208

ever come across, without exception. I can't think why I love you.'

'I'm not sure you do. There are lots of things I'm not sure of. Let's go, Rob.' They faced one another, exchanging a fathoming look, and for the first time a feeling of tenderness passed between them.

'On one condition,' he said, 'That you promise to take this seriously. That you come to me tomorrow.'

'I can't promise anything. I don't know what Gerald's doing.'

'Then we don't go.'

'All right then, tomorrow.' She recognised defeat, but clung to the comforting thought that it was still conditional. 'We could meet in the town, perhaps? I'll think about it.'

'You'll do your thinking here, my darling. Out loud. With me. Is that understood?'

'I promise to come, if I can. That's the extent of it.'

'You've promised. That's all I ask. I trust you, remember.' He put his hands on her shoulders and kissed her gravely. She returned his kiss, but as his breath quickened she twisted lightly away and moved to the door. Neither of them in all this time had noticed that it was wide open.

They went out on to the hard sand and he locked the door. 'It occurs to me to wonder what kind of a fool I am,' he said as he pocketed the key. 'Nothing as unlikely as this has ever happened.'

'All the better. It makes me feel very fond of you.'

'You've promised me, don't forget.'

'I've promised. As far as I can.' They moved to the car like lovers, arms linked together. The sky was a blaze of sunset light and the dunes were the colour of amber. Anthea saw with astonishment from the car clock that it was little more than an hour since she had left the flat. They held hands on the brief drive home and spoke hardly at all, and as the landscape slipped swiftly by it seemed as though time had played her a strange trick, and that she had lived through days and nights since she first set foot in the shuttered sea-house with Quattrell.

*

Voices were raised in the sitting-room as she let herself in. She could hear Gerald, and as she trod softly past the open door she saw him drinking with another man whose back was towards her and who seemed to be strangely dressed: she concluded, rightly, that it was Father Emery. She did not see Consuelo, but as she reached her bedroom door she heard her voice. There was no sign of Tavy. She washed her face and combed her hair, examining her bruised lip in the mirror. She had not been conscious of this before but it felt vulnerable and tender and throbbed with a tiny echo of sensation. It struck her that in spite of its tan her face was pale, but that otherwise she looked normal. She changed her sandals for shoes and went into the sitting-room.

'Ah, there you are, darling,' said Gerald, 'we have a visitor.' She shook hands with Father Emery and smiled at Consuelo. Consuelo looked small and subdued; she raised her eyebrows, and also her glass in greeting, but said nothing. She did not look particularly pleased to see Anthea again, or as though she were bursting to communicate, and this was a relief. Anthea was not yet in a state to bear confidences or reproaches.

'I dropped in,' said Father Emery, his hand in the breast of his cassock, 'really on the chance of finding our young friend Ozzie. So strange not to know his surname, but I confess it escapes me.' He produced a pipe and displayed it tentatively to Anthea. 'Is it possible? Do you allow this? It's considered rather barbarous nowadays, but I fear I'm addicted.'

'Of course. Or would you rather a cigar? There's a box somewhere.'

'No, no; if you really permit it, a pipe is my vice. Can Miss Carpenter bear it?'

'Go ahead,' said Consuelo without looking at him. She got up and went over to the table for more whisky.

'Well, as I was saying, I thought he might be here, whatever his name is. Rather a charming fellow.'

'His name's Dolby,' said Gerald. 'Not that anybody ever uses it.'

'Really? I must make a mental note. I was out at Mrs. Brockhurst's today and he wasn't there. I was surprised; I thought they were inseparable.' Gerald said nothing. 'You know them both, I take it, quite well?' He was filling his pipe as he spoke and glanced up from this occupation at Gerald and Anthea.

'I used to know Mrs. Brockhurst slightly, many years ago,' said Gerald, preparing a whisky for Anthea and busy with the siphon. 'Ozzie we only met here, since we came out. I don't know how long he's been with her.'

'Well, I must talk to him,' said Father Emery. 'He struck me as devoted and intelligent, but I'm not sure he realises . . . to be frank, I formed the impression today that Mrs. Brockhurst was very ill.'

Nobody immediately said anything to this, and as Gerald gave Anthea her glass their fingers touched and they exchanged significant glances. Gerald's, as usual, was reassuring.

'She's not very strong, I believe,' he said, coming back to his chair. 'You know her history, I imagine.'

'Oh dear me, yes, poor lady. A most shattering experience. She told me about it in detail; I was most distressed.' He sucked at his pipe and crossed his knees with the air of settling down comfortably to a post-mortem. Anthea decided that for some reason she disliked him, but there was evidently more to come, and she drank some whisky. It was surely unlikely, after that first vague meeting, that Molly had identified her, or, still more improbable, had chosen to make revelations to this pompous stranger? But the warmth drained out of her face and her mouth was dry. The skirmish with Rob in the sea-house seemed suddenly false and trivial and far away.

'The thing that disturbs me,' Father Emery was saying, 'is that I feel she needs help, serious help I mean, possibly of a psychiatric nature. I did my best, I am not unfamiliar with this kind of thing, but I am bound to say I made very little impression.'

'I imagine only time will do that,' said Gerald. 'Ozzie's very good with her, by the way. But he did say, I remember, that he thought it would be no bad thing if she saw an analyst.'

Father Emery frowned and smiled and shook his head, waving the smoke away with a large hand.

'Not analysis. No, no. She's in no condition to bear it. It could do no good. But I *do* think she ought to return to England and seek experienced help. That is what I want to impress upon our young friend Ozzie. Otherwise I fear they may find themselves in jeopardy.'

'Jeopardy, God sakes,' said Consuelo, and gave a short laugh. 'That's a word I haven't heard in a long while.' Father Emery looked at her with surprise and decided to ignore her. She was now on her third whisky and it was charitable to suppose that she was tipsy.

'What danger are you referring to?' said Gerald, steadily regarding Father Emery over his cigar.

'Why, it might take any form, I suppose, on the impulse of the moment. But certain repetitions that she made, I thought of an obsessional nature, put it into my head that she was in distinct danger of becoming suicidal.' He drew on his pipe for a moment with a slight frown. 'That is why I have this feeling of urgency about consulting our young friend. I know there are servants in the house, but they're only Arabs, and she shouldn't be left alone. She keeps insisting on it in a way that makes me uneasy.'

'Ozzie will be home by now,' said Gerald quietly. 'He was out this afternoon because he knew you were having tea with Mrs. Brockhurst.'

'Ah, you've seen him, have you? I'm glad to hear that. I rather think I shall telephone him this evening.'

'What do you mean, "insisting"?' said Anthea in a low voice. She could not take her eyes from Father Emery. There was a sound of the front door opening and shutting and in the pause that followed Enrico looked in at the door, his expression suggesting a desire to attract her attention. Anthea did not see him and after a moment of staring he withdrew.

'Well, if you had heard our conversation . . . I don't mean she said in so many words that she had any such intention, but her imagination is very much taken up with the idea. The form it takes is obsessive, perhaps understandable in view of the terrible experience she's been through. She suffers from a very extreme form of guilt complex—as it used to be called in my young days and may still be for all I know; I'm out of date. She fancies that the loss of her husband and his friends was somehow her fault, and she has a compulsive desire to tell people this, as though doing so, poor dear lady, were an expiation. I believe she has told our friend Ozzie this many times. She says he refuses to believe her.'

'I think she was alone on the helm at the time it happened,' said Gerald. 'So in a sense, though the running down of the yacht was a complete accident, she probably feels culpable. She shouldn't have been taking a night watch, in my opinion.' He got up on the pretext of finding an ash-tray, and instead of returning to his chair sat down on the arm of the sofa beside Anthea.

'Ah, but this is the curious thing,' said Father Emery. 'The culpable point is not what one naturally supposes. She insisted to me, several times, that a minute or so before the collision she had already left the yacht, and was swimming in the water.'

'*Left* the yacht?' cried Anthea, 'what on earth do you mean?' Gerald casually laid his hand on her shoulder.

'Precisely. It sounds impossible. But according to what the poor lady now believes she had made up her mind that night to do away with herself. Had done so, in fact, believing that the craft would go round in a harmless circle—I'm not a sailing man myself so I can't vouch for its behaviour in the circumstances—and that by the time anyone awoke to the situation her troubles would have been over. Instead of which, according to her story, a vessel appeared in the fog and it was the yacht that foundered. She makes it all sound very convincing; I'm sure she's quite brought herself to the point of believing it, but one naturally discounts that; it's usually a feature, I believe, of obsessive cases.'

'So it *was* her fault, then, and she's got to live with it,' said Consuelo.

Nobody took any notice of this remark. Anthea moistened her lips and almost whispered. But why should she want to do away with herself? It seems unlikely.'

'Quite. These things are not rational, as you know. I made that very point, and she could give me no reason. Why should you want to do such a thing?" I said. "Had you been quarrelling with your husband, were you worried or depressed about some other trouble?" But no, she could give me no reason; she obviously hadn't any. A very successful marriage, I should judge; a devoted husband, plenty of money, everything she could wish for. But the shock of the experience has injured her, that's evident. And her insistence on this mythical suicide attempt, her obsession with guilt, gave me the feeling that it was dangerously present in her mind. In short, that she might repeat it.'

'She hasn't got a boat though, now,' said Consuelo, 'so that's all right.' Father Emery glanced at her quite sharply.

'My dear Miss Carpenter, an unhappy person, a mentally ill person, has a dozen methods at hand if it comes to the point. Mrs. Brockhurst takes sleeping pills, I suspect in large quantities. There's a pond in the garden and no doubt a gas-stove in the kitchen. Her car has an exhaust, presumably. There are always a dozen ways to choose from when the will to live is gone and the mind unbalanced.' He looked at Consuelo severely, as though he would have liked to say more, but she was clearly in no mood to benefit from reproof and he turned his attention to his pipe. 'It all adds up to this,' he said, prodding about in the bowl with a spent match, 'our young friend Ozzie must be made to understand the situation, and persuade her to seek advice. I would be very glad, if you have the opportunity, if you would make it your business to reinforce my suggestion. I shall reproach myself very bitterly if it's left too late.'

'I'll certainly talk to him,' said Gerald. 'I could see him tonight.' Anthea groped for his hand and clasped his fingers. She had become suddenly cold, as though the chill of the night sea had invaded the room. James was drowned, and this was how it had happened. Molly had taken her revenge, and it had destroyed him. Yet what had brought her to this pitch, when he had left with at least a hope of reasonable compromise? He had not wanted to leave Molly, he had refused to consider it, and not out of selfishness only but from an inescapable sense of responsibility. And all that time, in an anguish perhaps even more grievous than her own, Molly had prepared the final thrust, and

214

it had destroyed all of them. James, and Ben, and Pearl, and the self that she had once been. The only survivor in the end had been herself, Anthea.

She leaned her head against the sofa and closed her eyes. Over the whole dark area of memory, so painfully buried, a harsh and atrocious light had suddenly broken. She had not the least doubt that what Molly had confessed to this man was wholly true. If she attempted it again and destroyed herself, what could it matter? It was the best thing she could do. Yet even as she thought this a muscle of her heart contracted and a flinching pain ran down the nerves of her arm. Molly had loved James as much as she had, and had been even more unhappy. For the first time the knowledge touched her with sick pity.

Gerald pressed her fingers and took the empty glass from her other hand. 'All right, are you?' he said in an undertone, and when she nodded without speaking he got up and went to the table for more whisky. Here he was joined by Father Emery, pipe in teeth and hand in the ancient leather belt of his cassock, a tall, spare, sombre and medieval figure, as perfect in aspect for his chosen role as Gerald in his, Evangelist conferring with Mr. Worldly-Wiseman.

'I'll ring you, if I may,' he said, 'in the morning. When we've both had a word with our young friend I think we should consider. Not another drink, thank you, I've had my quotum. Very glad to have had this chance of talking to you.'

He still lingered, jingling the coins in his pocket, and Anthea, seeing Enrico once more in the doorway, beckoning her with his eye, scrambled up from the sofa as though summoned, intent on reaching the security of her own room. She could think of nothing but what she had heard: her ears rang with it, and she was alive to the danger of being caught in an emotional tête-à-tête with Consuelo.

In the passage Enrico purposefully intercepted her.

'I likea speak to you, please, madame.'

'Not now, Enrico. Later.' She caught sight of her face in a mirror and was shocked by the naked woe of its expression.

'Is important, madame. *Un momento.*'

She followed him into the kitchen, which screamed from every wall with bullfight posters, the tributes of virile admirers and Spanish friends. She pressed her hands together; they were cold and trembling. 'I am suffering from shock,' she thought, and made a distracted effort to fix her attention. Enrico was explaining something with his customary dignity, but it was a moment or two before she could follow him clearly.

'Is that all?' she thought with indifference, her eyes wandering away from his face to the bullfight posters. Enrico was giving notice. He had been offered a trip to the Sahara and would be leaving tomorrow. Everything was in order, he pointed out. He had arranged for the cooking to be done by the *cameriera*.

'I see,' said Anthea from a vague distance. 'You'd better explain about this to Mr. Askew-Martin.'

'I prefer speak with you, madame. Is question of money.'

'We needn't discuss that now. He'll give you your wages in the morning.'

'Is not wages,' said Enrico, fixing her with a stern eye. 'Sahara is long way, you know? Treep is expensive.'

'That's nothing to do with us, I'm afraid. You're supposed to give us a month's notice.'

But Enrico was making a long, devious and largely incomprehensible speech in which Gerald's and Ozzie's names sounded gong-like notes, and it came to her like a roll of drums that Enrico was stating his price for dangerous knowledge. She put her hand to her brow and appeared to consider, but her thoughts were deafened. It was not possible. It was simply beyond the bounds of possibility. Not that what Enrico hinted was unbelievable, but that again, for the second time in her life, she was listening to the cold unanswerable voice of blackmail.

'You must speak to Mr. Askew-Martin in the morning,' she said faintly, 'it's for him to deal with,' and turned abruptly away, her head swimming, groping in panic for her own room before the roaring in her ears should overwhelm her.

She closed the door of her room and leaned against it, then made a lurching effort and reached the table. Here, at the back of the drawer, hidden under stockings and handkerchiefs, was a rolled and shabby band of wine-coloured silk, creased and frayed in the middle, fringed at the ends, the last decrepit relic of a man's dressing-gown. She clutched it like a talisman as she fell on the bed, holding the sash to her mouth, drawing her breath through it, pressing it to her cheek, compelling it to yield some of its old essence. Presently the fetish worked and she began to weep, without tears at first and then with noisy gasps, like the paroxysms of childhood. She lay face down on the pillow for a long time, and had reached a shivering calm when Gerald found her.

'Father Emery's gone,' he said, sitting down on the bed and sorrowfully stroking her ankle. 'Consuelo's as tight as a tick. I've sent her to bed.' She turned her face from the pillow and reached for his hand. 'It's all right, darling girl. It's all over.' He held her hand in his and stroked her ankle, and when his eye fell on the fringe of the sash he looked at it for a moment and glanced away. Presently she collected herself and turned over.

'I think what he told us was true,' she said. 'I don't believe it was an illusion. I think she was telling the truth. It explains everything.'

'Possible, I suppose. It's certainly possible.'

She sat up and wiped her tears with her free hand.

'It's more than possible, it's true. She's made a clean breast of it at last. Give me a handkerchief, please. I've gone to pieces.'

He took a meticulously folded one from his breast pocket and she blew her nose and pushed back her tumbled hair.

'Gerald.'

'M'm?'

'I want to get away from here.'

He did not reply at once but got up from the bed with a frown and wandered to the window.

'I can see it was a shock,' he said, 'but it doesn't alter anything. She didn't mention your name, she's suppressed all that. And we don't have to see her again, or even Emery. We've got the flat for another month, remember.'

'But I can't bear it, Gerald. I want to be alone with you again.

This place has done something to me. I want to get right away from it, and from all these people.'

'I thought you were enjoying it here? You've seemed so much better. Let's think it over, dear girl, there's no need to rush. There's Consuelo to consider, remember. It'll all seem more normal and manageable in the morning.'

'Listen, Gerald. Please.' He came back to the bed and sat down again, gravely regarding her. His face, normally so smooth and confident, had fallen into harassed lines: it struck her for the first time that Gerald looked old. 'Consuelo can have the flat, she'd jump at the chance. And Enrico's just given notice. He's leaving tomorrow.'

'I don't class that as bad news, my dear. I call it a bonus. I shed no crocodile tears over Master Enrico.'

'But he's on to something,' she said, 'about you and Ozzie. He's been offered a trip to the Sahara. He's demanding money.' Gerald met her eye for a long moment and his expression hardened.

'So that's it,' he said. 'The little sod. I might have guessed.'

'What does he know? Have you any clue? I don't want to probe, but I got an ugly impression he means business. Not that it matters here so much, but when he goes back to London. I think we must be careful.'

'Damn. Of course we must. I must get hold of Ozzie.' He pinched his lip and frowned, and Anthea felt suddenly protective and deeply sorry for him.

'Well, see him quickly and get it over, and then let's go back to London. Please, darling, I can't stay here any more. There's a plane tomorrow, isn't there, being Friday? And you can see him in London after all. If he gets Molly to the specialist.'

'Oh, that's not priority, especially. There's no drama. Nothing that won't fizzle out of its own accord.' He passed a hand over his eyes and sighed deeply. 'And what about you, my love?' He looked at her ruefully. 'You've seemed much more your old self lately. I thought you were getting involved emotionally as well? At least that was my impression.'

'I'm involved with you,' said Anthea. 'We're involved with

one another. And it's true what you say, I am better. I thought it was going on for ever, but it's just taken time.'

'I thought it was what's-his-name, Quattrell, who was making the difference?'

'So he was, in a sense, but time would have done it without him, I'm sure of that. I only needed to be patient.'

'I can't do without you, you know.'

'I know it. Neither can I.'

'Shall I go and see Enrico first, or get hold of Ozzie?'

'You'd better do both, while I pack. And ring up the airport in the morning.'

'I can probably get them tonight. There'll be someone in the office.'

They rose together from the bed, exchanged a conspirator's smile and embraced one another.

'United front,' said Anthea, and raised a fist.

'United front, my darling.' He gave her the lightest of kisses and reached for the telephone.

12

WHEN Phoebe came down early to get breakfast she was startled to see a light still burning in the parlour. She opened the door to find Lytton already at his desk, dressed and with a shawl round his shoulders.

'Why, Henry, you *are* up early! Are you feeling all right?'

'Thank you, I never felt better. Now that the weather's so brilliant one doesn't sleep. It's the best time for working.'

'Oh, I *am* glad. It's going better at last, then? Shall I bring your breakfast here, or shall we have it on the terrace?'

'Wherever you say, my dear. It would be nice in the sun.'

Phoebe smiled and went back to the kitchen, taking care to be very quiet so as not to wake Tavy. It was not often that she and Lytton had a meal alone. Tavy was much improved, one couldn't say she was a nuisance, but her presence was strangely inhibiting to conversation.

Without question this was the best time of day for the terrace, the sun already hot but not yet high, so that there was still shade to sit in. In the past week Phoebe had bought flower-pots and filled them with geraniums, obtaining a sack of earth through the resourcefulness of Mackannis, who had once more sent in the old man with his donkey. The plants were already in bloom and seemed sturdy; when they had had time to grow and spread, massing their colours round the central well, the little terrace, she thought, would look quite handsome. She set the table in the shade and drew up two chairs, and as Lytton had not yet appeared wandered to the edge of the roof and leaned on the parapet. It was amazing how different and wonderful it all looked now, since everything at last was settled and she had grown used to it. She could hardly remember her feelings of apprehension, still less her distaste; she had been absurdly nervous, of course, when she first came. Now, shading her eyes against the dazzle, she could not believe that she had ever seen the prospect as anything but beautiful The town was the colour of bone and honey and infinitely various, fluttering with sun-bleached washing on a score of roofs, descending with exquisite complexities of light and shade to the far-off curve of the harbour and the arm of the bay. The beaches of the further shore could be clearly seen, the hills above them were veiled in summer haze. Beyond them again the mountains were just discernible, their tops with a gleam of whiteness which might be snow. It was wonderful to stand there in the hot sun, feeling alert and well and pleasantly hungry, and to know it was all turning out as they originally planned, that Lytton's scheme was a success and she was part of it. Even the nearest roofs, which at first had struck her as ugly and deliberately squalid, now were objects of affection because she knew them. They, like her own, had plants in shady corners, in paraffin tins and jam-jars, some of them whitewashed and all of them carefully tended, oases of green in a desert of dry poverty. The makeshift posts and washing-lines had their own interest and she looked each morning with pleasure at the signals they flew. The wire on the roof below, which since the Feast of the Lamb had been pegged out with strips of meat, no longer disgusted her; the flesh had dried to scraps of parchment which rustled in the wind, and she knew what their purpose was and approved the economy.

Then it was heartening too, and in a sense unexpected, that Lytton's health had improved and that he was really working. He no longer frittered his time away carping and complaining, but was having ideas at last and struggling to express them, as this morning's early rising triumphantly demonstrated. It had done him good, she believed, to remove the mask. It had been a fetish too long; she had never approved of it. Even Phoebe herself, though she could not say why precisely, found the atmosphere happier now that she no longer lived under Sarah's eye. She felt no disloyalty in this; it was simply a fact. What troubles there had been between Lytton and her sister she would never know, but the lie that had persisted for years had been scotched at last and not only Lytton but even the house itself was the better for it.

'Ah,' said Lytton, emerging through the low doorway on to the terrace, 'a glorious morning again! It makes one hungry.' He settled himself at the table and began buttering his toast. Even the bread, Phoebe noticed as she bit into her slice, had won her over at last with its rough flavour. Course, crisp, warm, it had a fragrance of its own, a taste of husk and grain, of wheat or barley. The bread at home had been nothing like this, and at first she had been dubious, but now the fresh-baked loaves from those cavernous ovens, bought naked in the hand and carried home still warm through the evening streets, was one of her simplest and most rewarding pleasures. She ate it at every meal and could have lived on it. She greedily spread her piece with butter and honey.

'I was thinking, Henry,' she said, passing his cup, 'that if you thought there was any point in it, if it isn't too difficult, I should like to listen one night to your Arabic records.'

'Well, that's a new departure, I must say! I thought you hated them?' He looked amused, but Phoebe was not to be put off. She had, it was true, expressed horror at the first sound of them, a man's voice repeating a series of groans and barks in a tone which to English ears was repulsive, guttural, ugly, even menacing. Lytton was fond of playing them at night in his own room, practising the sounds out loud in the brief pauses, and the effect as she heard it across the terrace from her open window was as though he were having a murderous argument with somebody.

'They sound alarming,' she said, 'but I should like to try. It seems silly to spend one's life here and not have the faintest inkling about the language.'

'Agreed! I'm delighted to hear you say it. We might put them on this evening, after supper.'

'It's not as though I knew Spanish, you see, though I'm picking up a few words. I should often dearly like to talk to Hadíjah.' Her sessions in the kitchen with Hadíjah had lately been merry, but they made little progress, being inevitably reduced to dumb-show and helpless laughter. 'She took me to her house one day, and I met her old mother. I liked them so much, you know, Henry; they're splendid people. So jolly and friendly when you know them. If only I could talk to them!'

'Well, this *is* a surprise,' said Lytton, still looking amused. 'You're coming round to my point of view, I believe! Whoever would have thought it? So nervous as you were in the beginning, so very insular! I began to despair of you, my dear Phoebe, I must frankly confess. I'm delighted to hear what you say. Enormously encouraged.'

'You must make allowances for my disposition,' said Phoebe, smiling. 'I'm constitutionally timid, I suppose. It was all so new and frightening, so many alarming things that I couldn't interpret.'

'And now you feel that interpretations are possible, and that it's no longer alarming?'

'Oh yes, I feel that very much. I'm beginning to like it, I think; I really am. I should feel quite at home here, you know, if it weren't for the language. The house feels cosy at last, I've got used to the architecture. It's solidly built; I like that. It makes me feel safe.'

'It's certainly that. They knew how to build in those days. Think of the ramparts below, and those solid rocks!'

'And the people too,' said Phoebe, warming to her subject. 'Now that we begin to know them—I don't mean our English friends, though of course they're a great asset—but the people one sees in the streets, they no longer alarm me. I might even get used to the children in time,' she added, on a pleasant recollection. 'Have you noticed that little boy from the house opposite? The smallest one, who's usually playing on the doorstep? He gives me the most beautiful smile when he sees me come out. He's nicely behaved, too; rather shy. I've taken quite a fancy to him.'

'I can't say I've noticed. They all look alike to me. If their vocal cords were cut I should like them better.' He had noticed, as he did each morning, the tiny sound she made as she swallowed her tea, but his mood was unusually benign and he refrained from frowning.

'Well, yes, they *are* very noisy, I admit.' She raised her head to listen to the obbligato of sound from below the parapet. It was thin and distant yet; their neighbours were not conspicuously early risers. But there was already a clash and hum like a far-off battle, and she found with surprise that the sounds she distinguished with pleasure were children's voices.

'I must go and call Tavy,' she said, suddenly remembering her. 'She and Nick are going to do the shopping for me. He's coming round at ten, they're going to the market.'

'That's another of your successes,' said Lytton handsomely. 'Nobbling that boy, I mean. He's just what the doctor ordered. He fills the bill.'

'Yes, he's a nice boy. She's taken to him tremendously, hasn't she? Though these last two days, I notice, she's rather neglected him. She's got what we used to call a crush on Mrs. Askew-Martin.'

'A good thing too. She's got to grow up sooner or later. She mustn't make a nuisance of herself in that quarter, however. They might find it a bore.'

'That's one of the reasons I'm sending her shopping with Nick. It'll please the boy, and keep them both out of mischief.'

*

The market in the middle of the morning was invariably crowded, but it was roofed and pleasantly cool and Nick and Tavy lingered over their purchases. Everything looked good to buy and nearly everything was interesting; grape-fruit and oranges larger than life, cabbages tight and green and bursting at the seams, every kind of vegetable scrubbed and arranged in pyramids and patterns, bunches of herbs both fresh and dried, butter and cheeses in baskets of rushes, shining tomatoes, grapes from the south, lilies and carnations and early roses all heaped together in splendid and tempting profusion. And besides food there were baskets of every description which Tavy coveted, big ones for marketing, little ones with coloured lids and plaited handles, round ones, square ones, funnel-shaped, even the huge double panniers designed for donkeys. She looked at them all with longing, and the shopkeepers sprang from their stalls and hooked down bunches of baskets for her inspection. She moved away when they did this and passed to the next; it would have been easy to spend all the money she had and buy more than she could carry, and there was the slow walk home, through jostling crowds and most of it uphill, to be considered. Only the poultry stall was distasteful to her, and this she left to the last, not only for the safety of the eggs, which were small and fragile, but because of the living captives she sometimes saw there. The stall would be hung with naked chickens, pallid and thin and stretched to an unappetising length, and there would be hampers of live ones as well, stirring and cheeping, and others in bunches on the flagstones, tethered by the legs, looking up with bright eyes and feathers from under the trestles. There was a meat-safe too at the stall, full of tame rabbits, and she dreaded the moment when the man would reach for his knife and obligingly grasp one. There had been a dreadful morning when she had gone with Phoebe, and the customer before them had chosen a handsome cockerel. The poulterer had released it from the living bunch, smilingly held it to his breast and cut its throat, throwing it immediately away from him almost at her feet, where it squawked and flapped and dragged its feathers in its blood, taking a long time dying. She had burst into horrified tears on that occasion and Phoebe had hurried her away, scarcely less shaken. Tavy had not eaten chicken since that hateful day and dreaded a repetition of the experience.

Today, however, nothing unpleasant happened. She bought her eggs, received them precariously wrapped in a poke of paper and followed Nick out of the market and into the street. They were pursued as usual by boys, grasping at the handles of their baskets and offering to carry them, but this was an extravagance of which Phoebe and indeed Tavy herself disapproved; the baskets were roomy and not inconveniently heavy.

They had plenty to talk about on the way since Nick had decided to tell her about the beggar.

'I'm sure it was the door of our house,' he said, 'it's in the right position, quite a long way below Mr. Lytton's, in a blind street. This character, this beggar with a stick, went in with a key. I saw him as plainly as anything, with Mr. Quattrell.' Tavy came to a standstill and stared at him, changing her loaded basket to the other hand.

'Nick! When was this? You mean that Quattrell went in?'

'No, no; he was with me. We saw it together. I'll show you the door as we go by. I'm positive it's the one.' They began to walk again, finding some difficulty in keeping together since there were plenty of people about and the street was narrow.

'But, Nick, how did he get in? We saw the door, it's locked.'

'I told you, he had a key. He locked it after him too, I heard him. He must sleep there.'

'But it can't belong to him, can it? It's awfully big. Are you sure he was a beggar?'

'Positive. He's blind, with a stick. I've seen him before, I think. He's one of the regulars.'

'How *beastly*,' said Tavy. 'I don't like it. Supposing he's there when we go? Supposing he sees us?'

'He can't, silly, he's blind. It doesn't make any difference. He doesn't come up to the top of the house. We can always listen.'

'I don't like it all the same. The idea's creepy.'

'Oh rubbish. Don't be such a baby. He's about a hundred years old, I shouldn't wonder.' He paused to shift his basket to the other hand. 'As a matter of fact I asked Hamid about it afterwards. I didn't tell him which house it was, I just said it was an empty one and I'd seen this character go into it. And he said people sometimes let beggars and suchlike sleep in derelict property. The owner would know all about it. It's an act of charity.'

Tavy considered this doubtfully. The idea was unpleasing.

'I don't like old Quattrell knowing, either. I hope you didn't tell him we go there? I don't much like him.' Again she felt it was important to be clear about this.

'No fear,' said Nick, 'I'm not such a clot. He didn't think anything about it. It was just an incident.'

They had come to a double turning, not far from the final slope leading up to the steps. The street was fairly empty here but there was a great deal of noise. A sound of footsteps and screaming was coming from the right, and as they turned a gang of children rushed out from the alley and swept yelling across their path and stampeded ahead of them. They were all boys, most of them armed with sticks and all of them shrieking, and the leading pair had the remnants of a basket between them, a shallow ruined object without a bottom, and as they cannoned past her Tavy saw that clinging and spreadeagled inside it was a small kitten. They tore up the alley ahead of her, brandishing their sticks, and as she stared in dismay the kitten lost its hold and fell through the bottom of the basket, and was flying in terror for its life with the boys after it.

'Nick!' she cried, 'stop them! Catch it!' and began to run, the basket knocking her legs, her hair flapping. The kitten dashed at a doorway, fled out in panic and zig-zagged across the paving, black and flattened as a cockroach, its fur staring. The boys fell over one another in their excitement, collided, stumbled, laughing and shrieking, and went after it with sticks. Tavy dropped her basket and rushed after them, beside herself with horror, fearing that in another moment it would be beaten to death. Nick was even quicker than she was. He too abandoned his basket and joined in the chase, swinging his arms and thrusting the children aside, and at last, with more luck than skill, driving the kitten successfully into a corner. He snatched it up in one hand and held it high, kicking at the nearest boy and narrowly missing him. The boy ducked and fell back and they all yelled at him. Tavy, arriving breathless, was relieved to see that they were all much smaller than he was.

'Here,' he said, 'take it,' and gave her the struggling kitten. It clawed its way up to her shoulder and clung with its twenty needles to the stuff of her dress. She held it in a tight grasp and shouted abusively, threatening the astonished children with her free fist. Two elderly Arab women had retrieved the baskets and now approached her, indulgently smiling, and pushed the children gently and reprovingly spoke to them. The group began to disperse, looking somewhat crestfallen, but Tavy was too frightened to wait and see what happened.

'You bring the baskets, Nick!' she called, and fled up the street, not slackening her pace before she had mounted the steps and was half-way up the tunnel. Here in their own street it was unusually quiet. She began to run again, not pausing for breath until she had reached the door and banged on the knocker.

'Good heavens, child,' said Phoebe as she burst in, 'whatever is the matter?'

'Don't shut the door—Nick's coming!' Tavy shot past her into the courtyard and stopped abruptly when she saw Lytton sitting under the fig-tree, going through a pile of papers with Mackannis. She put down the kitten, which was pricking her, and it fled like a scrap of tinder into the kitchen. Tavy burst into tears.

Nick followed more slowly, weighed down by the two baskets. He was out of breath and some of the vegetables had been lost. It was also sadly evident that the eggs were broken.

'How dreadful! You did *quite right*,' said Phoebe, when the emergency had been explained to her. She put her arm round Tavy and patted her encouragingly. 'There, there! It's all right now. We must give it some milk.'

They went into the kitchen together and Lytton followed.

'You're not thinking of keeping it, I trust,' he said anxiously, cracking his fingers. 'Give it some milk by all means, and then Tavy must find out who it belongs to and return it to the owner.'

Phoebe and Tavy paid no attention to this, being engaged in dislodging the kitten from behind the gas-stove. Nick leaned against the sink and watched them, sucking his hand.

'Oh, *poor* little thing,' said Tavy, now on her knees, bringing out the clawing handful and pressing it to her bosom, 'it's so small, Aunt Phoebe, and so frightened! You *will* let me keep it, won't you? It's too young to be out on its own and those beasts would have killed it!'

She scrambled to her feet and the three of them, with varying emotions, inspected the kitten. It was an unattractive specimen and miserably small. It clung spreadeagled on Tavy's shoulder, eyes squinting with fright and tail stiff as a bottle-brush, and opened its pink mouth and spat explosively.

'It's scared to death,' said Phoebe, 'it'll be better presently. Bring it out in the courtyard, dear, let it run about. I dare say we can find a box that it can sleep in.' Tavy plucked the kitten's paws like burrs from her dress and put it tenderly on the floor. It darted away and vanished behind the refrigerator.

'I must advise,' said Mackannis, who had silently followed Lytton into the kitchen, 'against handling this animal, you know. They are wild in this place, not pets. There is much rabies.'

'Rabies?' said Lytton, horrified. 'I thought only dogs got that?'

'No, no. Cats also. It is quite a problem. One little bite, one scratch, and pfft!—hydrophobia.'

'I've been bitten already,' said Nick, looking with interest at his thumb. 'I've sucked it though, I don't suppose it's done any harm.'

'But is this really true?' said Lytton, backing away from the refrigerator as though the kitten might suddenly spring out at him.

'Oh yes. If our young friend here has been bitten he must go to the hospital. They are always giving these injections. It is too bad, you know. These people are never killing unwanted animals. They are putting them out in the streets to fend for themselves. It is a very bad infection.'

'Well, in that case,' said Phoebe doubtfully, 'perhaps we'd better not keep it. I wonder what's the best thing to do?'

'Of course we can't keep it!' said Lytton indignantly. 'It must be caught at once and put in a box and taken away somewhere. There must be a vet in this place, didn't you say so, Phoebe? It can be painlessly destroyed.'

'Oh, *no*!' cried Tavy, and threw herself on her knees again beside the refrigerator, blindly groping behind it with her whole arm.

'I must advise again,' said Mackannis in his apologetic voice, 'that for this you wear gloves. The *vétérinaire* will come, I will telephone to him, but he will definitely not be using his bare hands. He will come with leather gloves, or a pair of tongs. The infection is very serious.'

'You hear?' said Lytton, advancing on Tavy in a manner at once menacing and wary, 'you're not to touch that kitten. Now do as you're told!' But Tavy had got it by the scruff and dodged nimbly past him, and had fled to her own room and slammed the door before he had the presence of mind to intercept her.

'Go after her at once,' he said furiously to Phoebe, 'I *will not* be disobeyed in my own house!' He looked quite pale with annoyance and Phoebe started obediently across the courtyard, but in that moment the knocker sounded and she paused irresolutely.

'I'd better just see who it is,' she said, 'I won't be a minute,' and left Lytton cracking his finger like pistol-shots in an effort to recover his temper.

It was only Consuelo at the door, alone except for the usual children and apparently relieved at finding someone at home.

'The Askew-Martins have gone,' she said, stepping quickly inside and shutting the door herself in the children's faces. 'Isn't it the end? They asked me to say goodbye to you both and all sorts of messages Gerald's had a summons from his office, they'll be at the airport by now Isn't it the limit, though, honestly? I'm absolutely shattered.'

She certainly looked pale and the skin of her neck was blotchy, which Phoebe supposed was a symptom of being upset.

'Oh, I *am* sorry,' she said with sympathy. 'Henry will be *so* disappointed. They're coming back soon, I hope? And what about you, poor thing, left in the middle of your holiday?'

'Well, I'm staying on for a bit, sort of using up the flat. It's paid for to the end of the month, so one might as well.'

'Oh, good; so we'll see something of you. Come and break the news to Henry while I make some coffee.'

Consuelo joined Lytton and Mackannis under the fig-tree

230

and sat down thankfully. She was in rather poor shape for a number of reasons, the chief being a hangover; but the stimulus of drama, her own and others', was a strong tonic, so that by the time she had relayed her news and listened to the morning's adventure, with details of what Tavy had done and how Nick had been bitten, her nerves were a good deal calmer and she began to feel better.

'Well, I suppose the kitten will have to go,' she said, 'but it seems a shame, doesn't it? I mean, Tavy was pretty brave, don't you think? It must have taken some doing.' But Mackannis and Lytton were firm on this point, and there was Nick to be considered. 'I *can't* believe it,' said Consuelo stoutly, 'a bite from a kitten? Whatever next!' She buried her nose in her cup, grateful for the strength of Phoebe's excellent coffee. 'But if you think the kid should go home I can take him if you like. I've got to return Gerald's car some time. At least, it's paid for to the end of the month, like the flat, but I'm such a lousy driver it'll be safer for the population when it's back in the garage.'

'You can take the animal at the same time,' said Lytton, 'or Mackannis can take it, perhaps, as he knows where the vet is. Phoebe must find a box, and be firm with Tavy.'

When Tavy emerged from her bedroom, however, as she presently did, it appeared she had solved the problem in her own way.

'I let it go,' she said. 'I dropped it out of the window on to that smelly roof. Lots of cats go there, I've seen them. Its mother may find it.'

'Now, Tavy, that was very naughty of you. You heard what Uncle Henry said—it should have gone to the vet. It'll only starve out there, you know; you've been rather cruel.' *Really*, Phoebe thought, it was astonishing how callous and thoughtless children could be, even the most emotional.

'Well, it's gone, so what,' said Tavy indifferently, 'and it's got a better chance than if Uncle Henry had done what he wanted and had it put to death.'

'It will die more slowly, certainly,' said Lytton, 'if that's any comfort to you.' He hoped this would strike her conscience with appropriate remorse, but if her face was anything to go by it made little impression.

'I told you it's gone,' she said, avoiding his eye. 'It went over the wall at the corner, where the brick's broken. Somebody'll find it and feed it, which is more than you'd do.' Her tone was not far from rude; it had a note of defiance. It reached its mark, as she meant it to, making Lytton too angry to answer or even look at her.

*

Consuelo was a bad driver but fortunately knew it, and drove through the European town with care, observing one-way notices and no-entry signs and other warnings not always in that locality taken seriously. Nick sat silent beside her, alternately staring through the window and examining his thumb. He seemed to have no desire to talk and Consuelo's head was throbbing with her own thoughts: it was as much as she could do to keep her attention on the traffic. At the main roundabout her eye in an absent moment fell on Nick, and it struck her that he looked forlorn and needed comfort.

'I expect your thumb's all right,' she said, 'isn't it? You won't have to go to that old hospital, it's nonsense.' Nick looked at his thumb again and tenderly felt it.

'It isn't nonsense, exactly,' he said, choosing his words politely, 'it's true what he said about rabies; I've heard it before.'

'But who says the kitten's got it? I bet it hasn't.'

'P'r'aps not, but they usually give an injection, just in case. My mother gets into such fusses, I shall have to tell her.'

'Well, it won't be that bad; cheer up. I'll go with you if you like.'

Consuelo negotiated a zebra crossing, passing under the outstretched arm of a startled pedestrian, and turned with relief into one of the quieter thoroughfares. She remembered this street quite well, having been down it more than once to leave messages at the *discothèque* which Quattrell frequented.

The sight of its neon sign, already lit and winking in broad daylight, put other thoughts out of her head, and she drove as a sleepwalker might, with dreamlike slowness, entirely absorbed in the train of her own reflections.

Too many things had happened too quickly and last night's whisky had left her in poor condition for coping with them. One thing however was certain: Rob was still here and available, and so was she, and strategy and patience (if only her head would clear) must somehow be made to retrieve the situation. Yesterday had been bad, very bad; her confidence had been shaken. But there was still a good deal on her side and propinquity was everything. Moreover since early morning, when Anthea had wakened her, her conscience (which had sometimes to be reckoned with) had suddenly cleared. Anthea was returning to London with Gerald; Anthea cool and collected, mysteriously anxious to be gone; and the flat was Consuelo's if she wanted it, and the hired car, and Rob had been sent a telegram and it was all settled. She had struggled up in bed, under the gong-like strokes of her hangover, and had been kissed and handed coffee, and had seen the flat in a turmoil of packing and departure.

'But what about Rob?' she had managed to say as she struggled to the wash-basin, groaning aloud and swallowing a tumbler of water.

'That's all looked after. I've wired him a handsome apology. I wouldn't lose sleep over that, I fancy he'll get over it.'

'He'll be as mad as hell. Dear God, I can't face it.'

'Then you must console him, my love. If you haven't already,' and Anthea had gone with a cheerful expression into the further room, where Gerald's voice could be plainly heard, heavy with authority, and a burst of staccato Italian from Enrico.

So that was that, and in a sense it was a great relief. She had pulled herself together as well as she could and had parted with some emotion from Gerald and Anthea, and for a time wandered aimlessly about the flat in her dressing-gown under the impression that she had been asked to keep an eye on Enrico's departure. He had wasted no time over this, having triumphed financially, and at last she was alone and could swallow a handful of aspirins and fall on her bed, waiting for the qualms to subside and her thoughts to cohere at last in some sort of order. Anthea's departure was the great thing, though in a way it was a pity: but it put an entirely new complexion on yesterday's dubious interlude with Quattrell. He had not been pleased to see her at the sea-house, and she had felt constrained at first and regretted her enthusiasm. He had just sat smoking and staring while she chattered brightly, with the sinking feeling that she had been mad to suppose the visit would be a success. But after a drink or two he had got the message, and things had gone rather more rapidly than she had bargained for. She made no pretence to herself about her motive, but her gesture had been meant as an experiment, a spirited preliminary. The undignified scuffle in the cushions, though enjoyable in a crude way, had not been part of her programme at all; it had been premature, unseemly. Not that Consuelo minded about that particularly; a romp was a romp and Quattrell a fancied contender; but there had been something angry in the atmosphere, a lack of kindness, an element of contempt, so that afterwards she had been left with that feeling that her pride as well as her person had been tumbled, and that he saw himself less as a lover than as an enemy. She was used to men, however, and made allowances. It was Anthea he wanted; their love-making, if by any stretch it could be called such, had been nothing more than an exhibition of temper. He had even had the grace to look embarrassed afterwards, and had made her a sandwich with his own hands and opened another bottle, so that the last half-hour had been one of comparative amity. But it was only too obvious that he was anxious to see the last of her, and she had put a good face on it for the look of the thing and driven away with a jaunty air which dwindled and vanished before she had reached the road.

The trouble on the edge of her conscience had been simply Anthea, who had insisted more than once on her own indifference; but Consuelo was not too sure of this, and if Anthea made up her mind for Rob that rough and tumble in the sea-house would take some explaining. She had dreaded her inquiring eye and the inevitable questions, and had loitered deliberately on the way home, shopping for sunburn lotion and hairpins, putting off the confrontation as long as possible. Anthea had not been there when she reached the flat, only Gerald and that pompous person, so that the relief had been enormous; but she had still found her knees shaking and her eyes hot, and had been glad to sink on the sofa with a strong Scotch, to recover in silence.

And now, simply overnight, the situation had changed. With Anthea gone Rob was in prospect once more, and nothing in her long experience suggested that a healthy man, however disgruntled for the moment, would puritanically set his face against consolation. Everything was in favour of it; the usual difficulties had melted as though by magic. She had a flat for a month, he had his house. Neither was embarrased by company or pressed for time. Her money would last a while longer, and Rob, though not exactly flush, was certainly not destitute. They might even, when she had brought him round, do a trip together; go south in the Mercedes, following the coast or crossing the High Atlas, venture a little way into the Sahara, make love in the naked sand like characters in a novel, behold the fiery sunrise on the desert, and perhaps camels.

It was a stirring prospect and not, she felt sure, beyond the reasonable bounds of possibility. It would take time, of course, but she was not unskilful; a couple of days and they would be laughing to think that they had ever had reservations about one another. Only one tiny sequence, which memory had tactfully obscured until this moment, was difficult to reconcile with the jolly future. She had been wakened from her second sleep after Anthea had gone and had stumbled fumbling and cursing to the telephone.

'Anthea?' His voice had shocked her. 'What the hell is this?'

'It isn't Anthea, it's Consuelo.' There was an ominous pause.

'She's not gone yet, has she? I've got to speak to her.'

'Yes, they went some time ago. Didn't you get a telegram?'

'God damn and blast, I did. It said hardly anything.'

'Well, I imagine she told you, didn't she? Gerald's been called back to London.'

'When are they coming back?'

'I don't think they are. They've left me the flat for the month. I'm staying on.'

There was a long unpromising silence and she could hear him breathing.

'Why don't you come round for a drink?' she said presently, adopting a sprightly tone. 'We both need cheering up.' She could hear nothing but the crackle of the line but could tell that he was still there. 'I'm going round to the Lyttons' soon, to tell them good-bye. Why don't we meet there?'

'Thanks a lot, I don't feel like it. Got work to do.'

'Well, you can't work *all* the time,' said Consuelo, 'and we might as well soothe our feelings. Specially after yesterday.'

'Later, maybe. I don't soothe that easy.'

'You could try,' said Consuelo archly, 'there are ways and means, you know. A drink can work wonders.'

'I'm not in a wonder-working mood. Give you a ring later.' There had been an uncompromising click followed by dialling tone, and Consuelo had been left staring at the instrument, unable to decide whether to go back to bed until she felt better or make the effort to dress and drive to Lytton's.

'We're here,' said Nick, 'you've passed it. It's the first block.' She came out of her trance with a swerve and drew in to the kerb. She had so totally forgotten where they were going that it was a miracle they had reached the place at all. They went up in the lift in silence and Consuelo braced herself. She had not met Mrs. Parsons and knew nothing about the family beyond a vague impression that Nick had an elder brother. She wished very much she were back in bed and could sleep off the dregs of her hangover through the afternoon.

It was Pete who opened the door, which was a bad start, for he grasped Consuelo by the hand and peered into her face, making his noises, so that she was taken aback and stared at him in alarm.

'My brother's deaf and dumb,' said Nick tranquilly, 'he wants you to smile at him.' She collected herself with an effort and smiled theatrically, showing a great many teeth.

The encounter with Mrs. Parsons was not much better, for she had been having a trying morning and was prepared to be hysterical. As soon as she gathered who Consuelo was, and why she had brought Nick home, she put both hands to her head and sank into a chair, as though this were the final stroke in a day of disasters.

'Rabies?' she said, 'isn't that what dogs get? Oh my word, whatever will his father say? Running all over the town and biting people, there's a lot of it here, I read about it somewhere in the papers, it's the saliva that's dangerous, they do it at the Pasteur Institute, and here am I tied by the leg with this poor boy of mine, not to speak of my old mother who's suffering from gippy tummy, it's the salad, that's what it is, she goes all the time, you have to wash everything three times in running water.' She wrung her hands and looked at Consuelo distractedly, and Pete caught the woe like a contagion and began to whimper, rocking himself backwards and forwards on the sofa.

'Well, I don't think it's as bad as that,' said Consuelo, 'it was only a little bite from a very small kitten, probably as healthy as I am, so if Nick goes and has an injection it's only a precaution.'

Mrs. Parsons was all for the injection, she said so repeatedly, but for complex reasons found herself incapable of doing anything.

'I can go by myself,' said Nick, 'you needn't worry.' But this brought on fresh paroxysms of protest and communication, and Pete twisted his arms behind his head and began to gurgle, and the old lady in the next room called out in quavering tones to know what the matter was, so that in the end it was Consuelo who took Nick to the hospital, feeling by this time (she had had no lunch and nothing but coffee and aspirins to settle her stomach) as if she could very well have done with an injection herself, better still an anaesthetic.

*

When everything was quiet Tavy removed the grille from her window and pocketed the paper of scraps she had collected for the kitten. They had had mackerel for lunch and she had been able to rescue some fragments left in the dish. She had also secreted some milk in an aspirin bottle. She had been in an agony of impatience ever since the morning, but late afternoon was the safest time, while Phoebe rested, and she had bided her time in silence until after tea. Now Lytton was reading in the parlour and the house was quiet; there would still be an hour or more of daylight and no one would expect to see her before supper. They were used to these long absences of hers, when she amused herself in the loft or lay on her bed with a book, with the door bolted.

She climbed on the sill and tested the knot of the rope. It had been frightening the last time, without Nick to help her and only one hand for the rope because of the kitten, but now it seemed simple. It was quite an easy drop and the things she carried were safe in her cardigan pocket. She came down lightly on the floor of the roof, looked round to make sure no one could see her, sped softly across and climbed in through the broken window.

Here in the familiar place she paused to listen. She could hear the murmur of the town a long way off and the thin cries of swallows, but the house was as silent as it always was, and she was reassured. The stair where she had sat with Nick was strewn with matches and the sight of them, still undisturbed, was a kind of comfort. She went down quickly to the top landing, then on to the second level where she had left the kitten. It was half-hidden in the rags of the mattress, curled in sleep, but it heard her at once and stretched its claws on the ticking and arched its back and came mewing across the empty floor to meet her, as though it knew she was bringing food and would be its protector.

Tavy sat down on the mattress and took it in her lap. It seemed no longer afraid and began to purr, clinging to the stuff of her dress and thrusting against her hand with its narrow snout. She stroked its back with the tips of her fingers, feeling the spidery bones under the fur and the electric current of life vibrating through it. It was spiky and thin and small and more

238

intensely alive than anything she had ever handled. It was ugly too, with a pelt that looked cheap and dusty and a patch of white at the muzzle and one pink nostril, and because she was its only friend her heart ached for it.

She took the paper of scraps from her pocket and opened it, and the kitten nudged blindly at the fish, excited by the smell but seeming to have no notion what to do with it. It occurred to her that it might be too young to eat, and she took a tin from her other pocket and filled it from the aspirin bottle, setting it on the floor and tenderly placing the kitten with its nose towards it. But this was no great success either. It dipped its nose in the milk and sneezed, wetted a paw and shook it, and returned to her lap and the fishy paper as though it were hungry and eager but had never had the purpose of food explained to it. She shredded a flake of fish and dipped it in the milk, offering the pulpy mess on the tip of a finger. The kitten smelt it and recoiled, then advanced with electric tremors to the palm of her hand, treading with paws as cold and soft as raspberries. She held her breath and sat very still, her hair hanging over the creature like a curtain. It smelt, then licked, then sucked, and was suddenly eating, gathering its weightless body together in a bristling crouch, eyes half-closed, ears laid back on its head. It purred and sucked, and she felt the rasp of its tongue, its teeth on her finger. She was so absorbed in the tiny miracle that when the air shook slightly from the shutting of a heavy door it was a moment before she remembered clearly where she was, or what the subterranean sound suggested.

She raised her head and listened, but the house was quiet. The sound, which had not been loud, repeated itself like an echo inside her head, and this time she knew very well what it was and lifted the kitten from her lap and got up from the mattress. She moved to the open doorway and stood listening, and at first could hear nothing but the beating of her own heart. The well of the house was already dark and to reach the upper stair she must pass the railing. She was afraid to do this, still more afraid to stay motionless where she was. She pushed back her hair from her ears and strained to listen.

There was no question about it now: the beggar was below. She heard several halting steps and an exclamation. He was a long way beneath her, down at the bottom of the house, and with a shudder of relief she remembered that he was blind. If she crept to the stairs his ears might detect her presence but he could not see her. She cautiously turned her head and looked over her shoulder. The kitten was still on the mattress, gingerly smelling its way round the piece of paper. It would be safe in there till morning; it was unlikely to stray. She took a step towards the railing, holding her breath, and at that moment the beggar said something, and struck a match. The flame glimmered up for a moment in the dark well and she laid her hand on the railing and looked over. Almost as she did so he dropped the match on the floor and it went out, but not before she had seen him. He had been holding it on a level with his eyes, looking directly upwards, and it was not the beggar at all, but only Quattrell.

'Hi, there!' he called at once, and struck another match. 'Anyone at home up there? It's bloody dark.'

She did not answer immediately, but leaned on the railing, speechless with a relief so vast that she was glad to see him.

'Hi, there,' he said again, 'you there, Tavy?'

'Oh, hello,' she said in a flat voice, 'I didn't know it was you.' She glanced hesitantly over her shoulder again and then at the opening to the stairs, but he was coming up from below; she heard him stumble. When he came out on the gallery she turned her back on him and went slowly back into the room where she had left the kitten.

'Well, well,' he said, supporting himself with a long arm in the doorway, 'so this is where we go to hide ourselves, is it? So this is the headquarters of the gang.'

'No, it isn't,' said Tavy, crouching down by the edge of the mattress and dipping her finger in the milk and offering it to the kitten. 'It's an empty house, that's all. How did you know about it, anyway? How did you get in?'

'Aha,' he said, and took a key from his pocket. It was a heavy key and he swung it on his finger. 'I've been in here several times. Does that surprise you? Money's been known to talk, even in small quantities. You're too young to know that. Give to the poor in this world and God'll aid you in the next. Don't you listen to what the beggars tell you? I must teach you some Arabic.'

Tavy said nothing to this, being embarrassed by the equivocal feelings she had always had about him, and presently he came across and sat heavily on the mattress. He took out his cigarettes and lounged on an elbow, striking the match several times and looking first at Tavy and then at the kitten. She caught the smell of his breath, which was strong with whisky.

'What have you got there, for God's sake?' He tossed the match behind him and looked more closely.

'It's a kitten. What did you think it was? Nick and I rescued it this morning, and Nick got bitten, and Uncle Henry said it must go to the vet.' She looked at him doubtfully, caressing the kitten's fur. 'Nobody knows it's here. Would you mind not saying anything? Nobody knows I come here either, except Nick. It's our private secret.'

'Don't worry, I won't say a word.' He put out a hand to the kitten and their fingers touched, and Tavy was moved by this evidence of sympathy. 'What are you going to do with this little monster? You can't keep it here indefinitely.'

'I don't really know. I don't know what to do for the best.' She looked up at him anxiously. 'I thought at first when Uncle Henry was so beastly and I hid it in here, that perhaps I could take it to the flat, to Mrs. Askew-Martin. But now they've gone back to London and I shan't see her again. I don't know what to do, really. It's a problem.' She felt her tears rising at the thought of Anthea and hung her head over the kitten and went on stroking it.

Quattrell frowned and for a minute or two said nothing. He pressed out the half-smoked cigarette in the mattress and lit another, staring at the curtain of softly drooping hair.

'Tell you what we'll do,' he said presently, 'we'll take it out to my cottage. I'll keep it for you.'

'Oh, would you?' She lifted her face and for the first time

looked at him eagerly, her eyes wide and wet, her lips parted.

'Sure I will. But first you must give me a kiss.'

'Oh, don't be such a clot,' said Tavy, deeply embarrassed and stiffening in every limb. 'Oh well, if you like,' for he had reached for her wrist and grasped it and drawn her to him. She lost her breath in the unimaginable kiss and presently struggled, his arms still tightly round her so that they lost their balance together and toppled on the mattress.

'That'll do,' she said in a gasp, and tried to push him, but one of his knees was between her own and her body was pinned to the mattress with Quattrell above her. 'No,' she cried, 'no,' as his mouth stopped her, and her hair fell across her face and he was murmuring into it.

'My darling, my little Tavy, my lovely one, I've always wanted . . . be quiet, just let me kiss you . . . don't be frightened.'

'No,' she cried in a smothered voice, 'no . . . please . . .' hearing his murmur with a terror which was part excitement and part incredulity, blindly aware of something inexorable against which she had no defence and which was wholly unimaginable.

The kitten withdrew somewhat nervously from this commotion, and set out on a voyage of discovery round the edge of the room. The light was beginning to fail, it would soon be dark. It crept round the dusty skirting, sniffing at bat droppings and crumbs of plaster, and presently gathered courage to make several spirited dashes across the floor. It did not go near the mattress again, where the sounds and the movements were arbitrary and not to be trusted. Once Tavy screamed, and it darted in mock panic as far as the landing; but presently as the dusk deepened there was only a murmur, and it played by itself on the stairs and explored the shadows. When at length there was a sound of voices and of feet descending it fled into a dark doorway and hid in a corner, frightened by the one voice weeping and the other consoling, and as remote as Tavy herself from comprehending that the house would at last be deserted and itself forgotten.

*

When Consuelo returned after a short sleep primed with good news about Nick, who had taken his injection well, she found Lytton with his legs on a chair and a rug over them and Phoebe with a little air of muted anxiety.

'Henry isn't very well this evening,' she said in an undertone. 'He'll be glad to know about Nick; I'm afraid it upset him,'

'I'm short of breath, that's all,' said Lytton, whose hearing was acute. 'No need whatever to fuss. I shall be better presently.'

'Well, anyway, the kid's all right,' said Consuelo, settling herself opposite him. 'He took his injection like a trooper, and I saw him home.' She smiled to conceal disappointment, having been buoyed up with an irrational hope of finding Quattrell.

'I'm relieved to hear it,' said Lytton, pressing a hand to his collar-bone as though it hurt him. 'A most upsetting incident. Unlike that half-witted girl of ours he behaved very sensibly.'

'Well, she was kind of upset too, I expect,' said Consuelo. 'You know what kids are about animals.'

'We make allowances for that,' said Phoebe, lifting a fold of the rug and arranging it more comfortably, 'but she's really being quite unreasonably tiresome. Ever since tea she's been locked in her room, sulking. I've knocked several times and told her to come out, and she won't even answer.'

Lytton coughed, moving his legs irritably under the rug. 'Do leave it alone, Phoebe, *please*. And I'm sure you've left something on the stove. I can smell burning.'

'That I'm sure I haven't.' Phoebe lifted her head and expanded her nostrils. 'I can smell something too, I think, but there's nothing in the kitchen. One of our neighbours is probably burning rubbish.'

Consuelo's sense of smell was not particularly acute and today was in no condition to be finely critical. Nevertheless she sniffed sharply and detected something.

'There *is*, you know,' she said, and got up from her chair. She and Phoebe went together into the courtyard. There was no doubt about it: there were creeping wisps of smoke round Tavy's door. They looked at one another in consternation.

'Tavy!' cried Phoebe anxiously, rattling the door handle. 'What are you doing? Come out, do you hear?'

There was no answer.

'Bust open the door,' said Consuelo.

'We can't, it's bolted.' They rattled and shook and knocked, to no effect.

'But this is crazy,' said Consuelo, 'we've *got* to open it.'

Lytton came out into the courtyard trailing his rug and watched in stupefaction while the two women carried the table from under the fig-tree and drove it with legs foremost against the door. The crash was appalling: he opened his mouth to protest but no sound came; he moved his jaws and pressed his hand to his breast. In the distorting shadows cast by the parlour light they looked like Furies bent on grim destruction.

The third blow splintered a panel and Consuelo put through her hand and drew the bolt. The room was empty and in perfect order apart from a section of ironwork lying on the bed and a rising drift of smoke at the open window. Phoebe ascended to the loft, calling, and came down again; Consuelo was standing on a chair at the open window, stretching across the sill with her hand on the rope.

'My God, she's gone,' she said. 'What's that other house? That's where the smoke's coming from. Look, it's on fire or something.'

Phoebe gasped in alarm and rushed back to the patio.

'Henry! Tavy's gone! She's gone into the house next door and that's where the smoke's coming from!' She wrung her hands and stared at him distractedly, and as she did so his face changed colour and he reached for a chair. He caught at the back of it and steadied himself, then very slowly, clutching his rug like a garment, closed his eyes and sank solemnly to his knees. He remained motionless in this posture, like a man praying, and when she rushed to him and tried to lift him he shook his head.

'I can't breathe,' he said in a whisper, and clung to the seat of the chair, his knuckles white and his head bent rigidly over it.

Phoebe ran for Consuelo and between them they half-carried,

half-dragged him into the parlour and lifted him groaning and sighing on to the divan. His eyes were closed and his face was the colour of ashes; by the time they had covered him with the rug his knees were being wrenched upwards in jerking convulsion.

'Jesus, he's having a coronary,' said Consuelo in a whisper, remembering only too well her father's death-struggle.

'Oh, don't say it! It can't be! Whatever shall we do?'

'Give him some brandy if you've got it. I'll go for the doctor.'

'Oh, will you? Do you know where she is? It's the same block as the Parsons. Oh, Consuelo, hurry!'

Consuelo went off unsteadily on her high heels and the door banged. Phoebe remained on her knees beside Lytton, and when his sighing and the contraction of his muscles became more pronounced ran trembling to the kitchen and brought him some whisky and water. He attempted to drink but most of it spilled on his beard.

'I can't,' he whispered, and closed his eyes again, submitting to the authority of the pain which cramped and relaxed his body in griping rhythm. Phoebe felt under the rug and found his hand. It was cold and wet and the clammy feel of it frightened her. She knelt beside him for a long time, holding his hand and shuddering at every spasm. It was not until she coughed with smoke that she remembered Tavy.

*

In a short time Consuelo had accomplished much. By a miracle she had found the doctor at home and prepared to come immediately. She had telephoned a message to Mackannis about the smoke and rung the Parsons' bell to inquire for Tavy. She was not there of course; this she had hardly hoped. She drove back up the hill to the Medina rather recklessly.

The doctor lost no time in giving Lytton an injection. He was to be kept very quiet and warm while she went to the *bakál* and telephoned for an ambulance. In a few minutes she returned and felt his pulse again, then listened to the murmuring heart through her stethoscope. There was nothing to be done now but for Phoebe to collect his toothbrush and pyjamas.

'But what about Tavy?' she cried, wringing her hands.

'I'll stay here, don't worry,' said Consuelo. 'I know where she's hiding, I guess, and the smoke's no worse. Mackannis'll be here before long, we'll soon find her. You pack that bag and be ready to go in the ambulance. She's giving us a fright on purpose, that's what.'

'Oh, I hope you're right! Will you really stay? I must go with Henry to the hospital, I can't leave him.'

'You do that very thing. The situation's under control. I'll cope with Tavy.'

She was not in fact as confident as she appeared, and as soon as Phoebe had gone upstairs decided that she would not wait for the arrival of Mackannis. She took a box of matches from the kitchen and a candle from the brass candlestick in the parlour and switched on the bedside light in Tavy's room. The smell of smoke was strong, but it seemed no worse. She stood on the chair at the window and climbed carefully on the windowsill, hampered by a tight skirt. After a painful moment she removed her shoes. She was not normally agile but she managed the drop to the roof with no more serious damage than a torn stocking. The roof was fairly dark since there was no moon, but she could see the entrance to the stair-head and the broken window. There was no doubt whatever that something was burning in the house; smoke curled from the broken frame, an unpleasant smoke, acrid and unwholesome. It stung her throat and eyes as she climbed in. Yet there was nothing to suggest that the house itself was on fire, no flickering light, no heat, no ominous crackling. Someone was deliberately burning something and she guessed that it was Tavy. 'Silly bloody little fool,' she said aloud, pausing with shaking hands to light the candle. Luckily a house like this would be hard to burn; bare plaster and tiles and ironwork and nothing in it.

She looked briefly into the rooms on the top storey and found nothing. The reek was stronger here, it was coming from below. She went down the second flight, shading the candle with her hand and trying not to cough. 'Tavy?' she called, standing on the second landing. The smoke was much thicker from this point, it was difficult to see anything. It was worst of all in an open doorway and she felt in her pocket for the matches, not liking the idea that a cough or a sudden draught might blow out the candle. The place seemed very airless, however, and the flame was steady. She crept into the room on stockinged feet and at once found the source of the smother and the smell of burning. There was a smouldering mattress on the floor with a charred hole in the middle of it, glowing at the edges, and some rags and scraps of paper already curling to tinder and turning brown, and what looked like a child's garment at the foot of the mattress. Consuelo approached cautiously and touched it with her fingers. It was soft and blue, Tavy's old threadbare cardigan; she recognised it immediately. She picked it up and her eye fell on something else. On the ticking, crushed and flattened, was a cigarette packet. She snatched it up and held it in the light of the candle. It was the cheap Moroccan brand she had smoked with Quattrell.

She got up from her crouching position and went back to the landing. Her heart was beating heavily. 'Rob!' she called, choking on the smoke, 'Tavy! Rob! Where are you?' But there was no reply and something told her it was useless to look further. She continued to call, nevertheless, and went shakily down to the other floors, looking in every room with her candle until she reached the bottom. There was much less smoke on this level and the smell was masked by another which was even worse; the door, as she feared it would be, was firmly locked. There was nothing to do but go back and wait for Mackannis. In sudden rage she threw the empty packet away from her into the darkness and went back to the upper roof with Tavy's cardigan.

By the time she had climbed into the house she was sick and shaking; she helped herself to whisky from the kitchen table. Lytton and Phoebe were gone; only the gaping parlour door and a certain confusion of furniture suggested the passage of the ambulance men with their stretcher. Consuelo wandered in the courtyard, holding her whisky. She knew what she ought to do, but her courage failed her. They had fled to the sea-house, of that she was quite sure; but the shock of her discovery had left her with a curious feeling of physical numbness, so that although her thoughts were racing she could do nothing. She would have liked to lie on the divan and cry, and wait helplessly for Mackannis, but instead she wandered about the courtyard on unsteady heels, sipping her whisky and rubbing her fingers repeatedly across her forehead. Her hands smelt strongly of burning, and this disgusted her. Fire was not clean, as people said it was; the smell of it sickened the nostrils and its aftermath was obscene. She was haunted by the gaping hole in the smouldering mattress.

Presently she washed her hands at the sink and took down a key from the nail which Phoebe had shown her. The thought of driving to the sea-house at night was terrifying; she was not even sure she knew how to switch on the headlights. There was no alternative that she could see, however, and she girded herself for the experiment. The street for once was empty, and for this she was thankful. She locked the door behind her and walked quickly, beating a staccato tattoo on the rough paving.

The difficulty of the lights was solved by trial and error and she drove with exaggerated caution down the arches and cobbled slopes to the modern town. Here the streets were bright and the pavements crowded, a continuous procession ambling in front of the cafés. In one of them, perhaps, Tavy would be sitting with Rob; but she did not think so. They would be at the sea-house already, clenched on the hard divan behind closed shutters. At the thought she gritted her teeth and uttered several obscenities as she pressed the accelerator. What she would say when she confronted them she had no idea, but she drove through the darkness as fast as she dared and only twice ran over the sandy verges.

The cart-track was hard to find and at first she passed it; she turned the car with difficulty and searched with the headlights along the edge of the road. There was nothing to guide her to it but the bank of the estuary, and she changed into bottom gear and bumped over the ruts, staring short-sightedly ahead for a gleam of lights. There was none; the cottage was wholly dark; there was no sign of a car. The moon, a mere shallow remnant, had risen by now and the beach showed a pallid fringe of tumbling breakers. She found the path through the cactus and groped for the door. The shutters of one of the windows had not been closed, or had been prised open; it hung drunkenly on its hinges and she found that one of the window-panes was smashed. She fumbled cursing in her bag and struck a match, trying to see into the room through the broken window. There was no evidence that anyone had been there; the place looked uninhabited. When the match went out it struck her that the table was emptier than she remembered; no papers, no typewriter, none of the usual litter of occupation. As she took out another match she heard a movement and turned to see two boys come out of the hedge. They were not more than ten or twelve years old but their appearance frightened her; she dropped the matches and hastily closed her bag.

'What the hell d'you want?' she said when they spoke to her unintelligibly. The elder boy grinned and said something, pointing to the broken window. 'Did you do that?' she said, pointing too, recovering her courage and beginning to be angry. She could not interpret his answer but there was no mistaking the outstretched hand or the meaning look directed to the bag on her arm. They were both of them standing so close they almost touched her.

'Bugger off, both of you!' she said violently, pushing them aside and setting off up the path to the back of the cottage, stumbling twice in the soft sand in her haste to get out of their reach and back to the car. She did not see if they followed her and if they did so their bare feet made no sound. As she reached the car she was struck by a stone on the shoulder and another followed and caught her painfully in the neck. She got in and slammed the door and started the engine, winding up the window as she did so with her left hand. The headlights swept over the boys as she reversed and the car went off in a hail of well-aimed pebbles.

She drove in consequence badly and much too fast, but there was little traffic abroad at that hour and she had no mishap. She was somewhat calmer by the time she reached the town, and it was a relief when she opened the door and caught sight of Phoebe.

'Where's Tavy?' said Phoebe at once, 'have you not found her?'

'Not yet; she may be anywhere. In a café, or gone to the movies. I tried the Parsons' flat, and one or two other places.'

'Oh dear! Whatever shall I do?' She had been confusedly packing her belongings and her face was colourless. 'How *could* she do this, when I've got to go back to the hospital? She's *never* been as late as this. Something must have happened.'

'Well, yes,' said Consuelo guardedly, 'but it's not ten o'clock. She's gone off into the town, I expect. The cinemas come out late; she'll be back presently.' Her own nerves and Phoebe's exhausted face warned her for the moment at least to say nothing of Quattrell.

'And how could she have got out?' said Phoebe, pressing her temples. 'To go into that empty house like that, without telling anybody! It's the naughtiest thing she's *ever* done and I can't imagine what's happened to her.'

'That's the way she went out, obviously,' said Consuelo. 'I went and had a look myself, but she wasn't there. She must have opened the front door, in the usual manner.' She sniffed the air, but there was hardly a trace of smoke. 'It was only some rubbish burning, you know. Did they put it out?'

'Oh yes, thank heaven Mackannis came. He's been invaluable. I couldn't have managed without him. He's coming back in a taxi shortly, to take me to the hospital.'

'How was Lytton when you left him?' Consuelo's eye had located the whisky bottle. 'Mind if I have a drink? You need one too, I'd say; it's been quite an evening.'

'He's quieter, I'm glad to say. Yes, please help yourself. He's more or less out of pain, the injection was wonderful. They're doing all they can at the hospital to make him comfortable, but he's so *frightened*, you know, poor Henry, and so am I. They're getting us on to a plane tomorrow morning.'

'No kidding!' Consuelo poured out some whisky and drank it neat. 'Can he stand the journey?'

'Oh, it's the *only* thing, and of course he'll go on a stretcher. The specialist's been telephoned in London, it's all arranged. To think that all this time we've been worrying about his lung, and now this has to happen!' She sat down at the table and dropped her face in her hands.

'Have a drink,' said Consuelo, 'you need it,' and poured her a quarter-glassful.

'Oh, do you think I ought? I've got to keep my wits about me and I'm not used to it.'

'Go on, do you good.' They drank for a moment in silence, gazing sombrely at one another.

'The thing that's driving me distracted,' said Phoebe, presently, 'is this business of Tavy. Oh, I dare say it's nothing to be alarmed about, just a heartless prank, but I've *got* to spend the night at the hospital with Henry and I won't have a moment's rest until I know she's home. And then what's to happen, tomorrow? We might get a place on the plane, I dare say, but the thing is, where *is* she?'

'I'll stay here all night, don't worry. I'll phone you at the hospital the minute she's home. Put it out of your mind.'

'Oh, that's so good of you. Are you sure? And you could put her on a later plane, perhaps? Mackannis is looking after everything, if you need money.'

'Sure. It's in the bag. Don't give it another thought.'

Phoebe drank a little more whisky; her lip quivered.

'I wonder,' she said, 'it's improbable, of course, but I was just thinking . . . what would you do in the event of her *not* coming home?'

'Tell the police, I guess. Put Mackannis on to it. People don't just disappear, that's the last thing they do. The kid'll be home before you're half-way to the hospital.'

'I know, but one's imagination can be so frightful. My nerves are all on edge. I do so wish the Askew-Martins hadn't gone away.'

'I can manage all right,' said Consuelo, 'leave it all with me.'

'You might get in touch with Mr. Quattrell, perhaps, if you need advice? He's always so extremely helpful.'

'Sure. I might get in touch with Mr. Quattrell.'

'I've written down the address of the nursing-home, and Mackannis knows everything. Are you sure you can be comfortable here? I haven't had time, I'm afraid, to make up a bed or anything.'

'That's O.K., I won't need one. I'll make free with yours if I feel like it. You get on with packing that bag.'

*

Later, when she had been alone in the house for an hour or more and had finished the whisky, Consuelo discovered she was hungry and helped herself to some scraps from the refrigerator. She had turned on all the lights she could find, going round the patio and parlour and up to the bedrooms, but they did little to reconcile her to the feeling of the house at night. With Phoebe and Lytton there it had been very different; now it asserted an atmosphere, a presence almost, that was quite alien to them, as though they had gone for good and it had forgotten them already. It struck her as unnaturally quiet, but even as she thought this, standing in the courtyard with a cold sausage in her hand, the pounding noise from the next-door house began and the silence immediately became more ominous because of it. Did they never go to bed, she wondered irritably, chewing her snack and wandering about the patio. If only Tavy would come home, if Rob were there, or Mackannis, anyone, she could reasonably bear it. But the long wait alone, while her spirits drooped and fell, made the house seem more like a prison than a place to live in. Mackannis had put back the grille in Tavy's room and had somehow fixed it. The street door was locked and bolted and all was secure. She told herself this repeatedly as she wandered about, but the clack of her heels on the tiles was a desolate sound, and presently she went back to the kitchen and sat on the table. The kitchen at least was bright and felt reasonably normal, but if she had dared to go out to the telephone she would have rung up Ozzie. She did not dare, and besides, what the hell was the use? At this time of night he would hardly consent to leave Molly to keep her company. 'Darling,' she could imagine him saying, '*too* frightful, nothing I should adore more, but I can't leave poor Molly *alone*, can I, she'd go off her tiny rocker.'

'As I'm going off mine,' said Consuelo aloud, but she knew she was only a little tipsy and looked to see if there were still a dreg in the bottle. There was nothing, not even a drop, and she had long ago finished the remnants of Phoebe's glass. She presently slid off the table and returned to the courtyard. moodily wandering, as she had done many times already, around the trunk of the tree into Tavy's room. She had long ago given up hope that she would eventually return. Of course she would not. Already she was miles away, in some bed with Rob, and with envious bitterness she wished them joy of it. Tomorrow she would tell Mackannis, and the fuss would begin. Tonight there was nothing to be done and whatever they did tomorrow would be equally useless.

She opened Tavy's window and leaned on the sill. It was a lovely night as usual; the moon that had risen so late was silvery bright and the walls and the derelict roof shone as white as a bone. The pounding was fainter here, she could hardly hear it. Once, then twice, she caught a feeble sound like a kitten crying, but the roof-tops were lousy with cats, and this was their hour. She leaned on the sill for a while staring at the brightness, then presently shivered and sighed and closed the window.